THE NIGHT I SPENT WITH AUBREY FISHER

CHRISTOPHER M. TANTILLO

The Night I Spent with Aubrey Fisher

Contact Info: christophermtantillo.com
Cover Design by: Nicole Hower
Audiobook Narrated by: Eric Altheide

ISBN: 979-8-9867622-1-0 (hardcover) 979-8-9867622-0-3 (paperback) 979-8-9867622-2-7 (ebook) 979-8-9867622-3-4 (audiobook)

First Edition: May 2023
1 2 3 4 5 6 7 8 9 10

For everyone, like me, who need to get lost to find themselves

AUTHOR'S NOTE

This book contains and implies scenes/themes related to anxiety, depression, drug use, grooming, underage drinking, violence, self-harm, survivor's guilt, sexual assault, and suicide—all involving teens. Please practice self-care before, during, and after reading.

If you or anyone you know is suffering with thoughts of suicide or self-harm, please seek a professional as soon as possible. Or call or text 988, the Suicide and Crisis Lifeline.

A STORM IS COMING, AND BLOOD FROM THE OCEAN WRAPS around my ankles. I'm planted on the beach; my feet stuck in wet sand that glues me in place like cement. There is no one around. No sound. No breeze. No atmosphere. The skies above are overcast and gunmetal gray. Ominous. A half-constructed sandcastle to my right remains unattended.

And he's out there. The boy. Out in the blood-waves as the swell crashes into the rocky shore. I try to reach him, to call out to him, but I can't. My voice won't work, no matter how hard I scream. My legs can't break free of the sand. Blood-water stains the entire beach.

Tears fall down my cheeks, and I'm suffocating. The waves get higher. Blood-mist sprays my face, and the boy keeps getting carried out farther with the tide.

From somewhere beyond, two faint glowing lights race closer, toward me, from out past the boy. Two round lights that force me to squint my eyes.

I scream as loud as I can, but my voice won't work, like the entire world is muted. Only the sounds of the little boy screaming out my name over and over.

I can't reach him, but the sky gets darker, the blood redder, and the waves bigger.

The two round lights closer.

But I just can't reach—

PRE

Sometimes it's hard just to wake up.

I love lying awake in bed, one arm bent underneath the nape of my neck and the other extended as I wave it in and out of the prisms of light that seep in through the cracks of my blinds. Trying to catch the dust. This moment, the quiet signaling the pre-dawn in the mornings before school, is blissful. These are the moments I look forward to. It's the one time when I can hold my breath, stare up at the blank ceiling in the dark, and just sink, hiding from the world. It won't last long. But maybe it will be just long enough.

I roll over in preparation for my alarm clock that's about to blare its ugly trumpet. I'm ready for it; I never give it the satisfaction of getting out more than a squeak before bashing it on the head like a whack-a-mole.

BEEP.

Roll.

BANG.

I swing my legs over the bed and hop down, stand on the balls of my feet until my ankles crack, and then move forward over the carpet. Before I touch the knob, I press my ear to the door and listen to the muffled buzzing of Dad's electric shaver from the bathroom down the hall. I can hear the feathery slap of my mom shuffling a deck of cards in the kitchen downstairs, and I imagine her blue night robe draped around her as the tea boils on the stove.

It's their morning ritual, and it never changes.

It's been like this every morning for six months.

I peer over my shoulder at the last beam of light shining in and extend my hand, bathing in the golden ray. The particles seem to hover, almost trapped. They belong to the pre-dawn—just another thing that unnerves me about opening the door. The beauty will no longer belong to me. I won't be able to control it in the real world.

My hands tremble as I flick on the light, shielding my eyes from the piercing white. I grab my phone from the nearby dresser and see a new text:

UNKNOWN

> i kno a secret about u...

> Liar

Chills.

I've never gotten a text like this before.

But they're right.

After I clear away the screen, confused, the picture on my background comes into focus—me with an arm wrapped around my brother in a headlock. He is wearing the seashell necklace. We are in the tree house we built in the woods. My breath catches in my throat until I cough and throw the phone on my bed.

Goosebumps.

My heart pings and I clutch at my chest. A bead of sweat rolls down my forehead, and I undress for my shower. I suppose, my last shower. And that's when it strikes me for the first time today:

My last shower.

I take off my shirt and stare at the purple bruise below my left rib cage. Run my hand over the bumpy surface and wince at the pain, but push harder to feel the pain deeper. It's the only thing that feels normal. It's exactly what I deserve.

With one last deep breath, inhaling the memory of my room, I place a hand on the brass knob of my bedroom door. It's cool under my sweaty palm. Inside my head, the sirens' wail echo their approach. Even today, months after everything, it tells me this is the only way.

I step into the dim hallway and jiggle the knob to another bedroom door on my left.

Still locked.

Breathe in.

Anybody in there?

Breathe out.

You can come out now.

My name is Grayson Falconi, but most people call me Gray.

I'm seventeen years old.

And today I'm going to die.

24 Hours Until

Breakfast is the worst part of the morning. I make a bowl of off-brand cereal and sit down next to Mom at the kitchen table. It's not that I don't want to spend time with her—I do. But it's hard when it's her love for me that causes the most pain.

Like all mornings, my mother sits at the table and drinks tea, playing solitaire with the same deck she's had since before I was born. She brings the white Mickey Mouse mug to her lips, blows at the steam, takes a sip, and makes her next move. She won't win the game; she never does. One leg crosses over the other; her ankle bounces up and down to an inaudible beat.

I know she called in sick to work. Again. I look below the chair and shuffle my feet rhythmically over the kitchen's white vinyl tiles. Trace a green vein from my wrist to my elbow with a finger until it disappears. Something so fragile yet exposed, just beneath the surface.

"Morning, Mom."

She nods to the cards in response. Mom won't look at me because of the bad memories. Mumbled that once in her sleep when she'd been up waiting for Dad and I went to turn off the

TV. She'd been dazed on Prozac or Xanax or Ativan—her own personal cocktail. She was half out of her mind.

"Want to love you... eyes like his... all I see... never come out... stay away, Gray."

I never forgot it.

We sit opposite each other at the table, and I wonder if this particular cereal will taste different than before. If the empty spot to my left will ever feel less empty.

There used to be a fourth chair at the table.

Dad removed it a while ago.

I pinch the vein in my arm until the tips of my fingers turn white and my eyes water.

"Were you awake when your father got home last night?"

"I don't know," I lie. Look at Mom and want to wrap her in a hug. "Remember when we went on that field trip a few years ago to—"

"Well, he was asleep on the couch when I woke up." She sighs. "He's just going to do what he wants without a thought to anyone else. Isn't he?"

I chew the inside of my cheek. "I don't know, Mom."

She sighs again. I finish my cereal and go to rinse it in the sink—glance over my shoulder and see Mom reach for a crumpled tissue in her pocket. She dabs at the front of her face before re-crumpling it back into her robe. Her hands tremble as she blows at steam from the mug.

I know she's going to talk to me again. About Dad. She never talks about anything else. Like maybe it's the only topic that feels safe. That isn't as painful.

"I'm sure Dad was just swamped with work." A beat. "You look beautiful today."

She swivels around in her chair and looks at me; her eyes glaze over. I look at her face, at the premature crow's feet around her eyes that make her look decades older than she is, and want to tell her everything will be okay. That I love her.

But I don't.

As I walk past the fridge toward the bathroom, I can smell my dad's bitter coffee brewing from the counter as it *plinks* into a black mug. I look at an old Polaroid wedding photo of my parents taken in the church pews. I admire the way my dad leans my mom over, one hand caressing her lower back and the other cupping her chin while he plants a kiss on her lips.

My mom, as she often tells it, had me when she was seventeen and my dad twenty-eight. It was unplanned. A one-night stand. They married almost a year after I was born.

No one in our family likes to talk about it. My grandparents shunned Dad when Mom was pregnant with me, and rumors had been floating around the town for years about their "taboo" relationship. How my father took advantage of my barely legal mother. How he groomed her. People speculated; people gossiped. They still do. It's a small town.

Gray Falconi: Illegitimate Bastard and Destroyer of Futures, Inc.

My dad trudges down the stairs and strolls over to the coffee machine in his pleated black pants and white button-up. The smell of his Old Spice aftershave wafts over to me in the bathroom next to the kitchen. I look out from the bathroom door—foam from my toothpaste still clings to one corner of my mouth—and watch the ritual: unplug coffee pot, take a sip and grimace at the heat, straighten the matching tie, wait by the toaster for bagel to brown just right, tighten black belt, and ignore Mom.

It never fails.

"Gray, I know you have Brian drive you home, but I can't pick up your brother today," she calls to me. "Can you just stop by and bring him home from the elementary school?"

I choke on the toothpaste and spit it out. My father drops his coffee mug onto the counter. When I step out into the kitchen, Mom realizes the error she made. It isn't the first time, and it won't be the last.

"Mom?"

"Oh." She lets her cards fall on the table.

Dad curses out loud and coughs. "Jesus Christ, Marie. What pills are you doped up on now?" He whirls around, not bothering to clean up the spilled coffee. His eyes are like slits; they burn into the back of her head.

"Well, maybe if you came home, *Robert*, you wouldn't have to worry if I was taking anything," she says monotone, not turning around. "Some of us like to face reality."

"Don't start this again," he says under his breath before picking up the dropped mug and taking a napkin to clean the counter. "Corporate is coming down to audit the store in the next few days. I can't babysit you again today, and I can't find my progress reports for inventory on the computer."

"There's a lot in this family we don't need. But do what you want. I won't stop you." She takes a sip. "And if you're referring to those documents on the hard drive, I trashed them Tuesday night. We needed to free up space on the computer. They didn't look important." She hums.

"I backed up the files to the external hard drive." I try to stop what I know is inevitable. At this point, they're on autopilot. Nothing else exists.

Do they remember what tomorrow is?

"Are you kidding me?" he shouts, ignoring my comment. "How am I supposed to take stock for audits?"

"Dad, I can pull up the files on—"

"Should have thought about that the last time you went out with your *boys*, Robert. And you've been cleaning up *junk* around the house, I felt I'd free up some of *your junk* from our computer."

After a pause, he whispers, "Marie, please. I don't want to discuss this anymore."

"And by *this*, you mean our *son*? The one that you refuse to acknowledge anymore?"

Once again, they are talking like I'm not here in the room. Like I can't hear them. Just another regular morning in the Falconi household.

I clear my throat. "Can you guys please st—"

"Jesus Christ, all you do is nag all day." He throws his bagel in the sink. "You're poisoning yourself keeping useless junk that we can't use anymore. I donate things to people who actually need them."

"Dad—"

"You know what?" she sobs. "I really don't care anymore. I really don't. Just go to work. They need you there more than I need you here."

He throws his mug to the ground where it smashes. Mom and I jump on impact. "I should have left this fucking prison a long time ago."

He looks at me, and for just a second, I think he's going to hug me, say he's sorry. There's a flicker in his eyes, but it's gone almost as quickly as it appears. Dad storms out of the kitchen and up the stairs. The bedroom door slams shut, vibrating the floor beneath my feet.

Mom doesn't respond. I push at the pain in my chest and let his words resonate: he wants to leave. I know I should say something, but it isn't anything new. He's been like this for a long time now. After what happened, he just shut down. They both did.

Inside my pocket, my phone vibrates. I pull it out and see a text from Reefer:

REEFER

on way

got a story 4 u, Gray-Gray

luv u :-)

Classic Reefer. Always a goof.

"Are you okay, Mom?" I ask.

"Gray," she says from the table as I bend down to throw out the broken pieces of mug. "I just mopped the floors. Don't get blood on them, please. I'm not in the mood to pick up after you. Okay?"

I wince, wipe up the coffee with a rag, and stare at Mom. At her sandy-blonde hair that she used to dye with my grandmother every few months. She tried to conceal her age, look younger than she already was. But now she lets herself go. Sometimes skipping showers. Wearing the same clothes days in a row before washing them. Eating junk food with pills.

Dad likes to keep thin, running every other morning for a few miles. He took it up a few months ago. My mom and I, however, don't. That's why we have that little roll of pudge in the stomach we can never seem to get rid of.

I never used to be like this. I used to be fit, somewhat athletic, thanks to Kris. But then—

Stop thinking about it.

My phone vibrates again.

REEFER

im here, hurry. we gotta go

im lit-er-a-ly DYING 2 tell u this story!!!!!!!!!!!!

YO. HURRY UP

I slip silently past Mom and leave the sound of cards shuffling behind. My dad walks down the stairs and clears his throat, his eyes bloodshot. He stops in front of me and pats my shoulder before walking into the kitchen. That's his way of apologizing.

It's also the last time he'll be able to do it.

I'll never get to hear him say he loves me one last time.

To see his mouth form the words.

I want to stop and scream at them, want to wrap them both in a hug and tell them I love them and that I'm sorry for my carelessness, for what I took away. I pause as I reach the front hallway to put on my white sneakers. Take another look around the house, at the ocean blue carpets and white walls, the mini-chandelier hanging over the front entrance that casts a golden glow as the sun slowly rises to the full dawn.

At the bedroom door just above the stairs that my parents keep locked. Preserved. No one allowed to enter.

It's going too fast, all of it. I want to slow down and take in all the details. But that kind of stuff only happens in the pre-dawn. Life doesn't let you stop to appreciate the beauty of the small things like those prisms of light. Life doesn't notice the tissue on my father's nick from his morning shave, the red dot in the center of frayed white.

On the wooden hall table, where my parents place their keys and the week's clipped coupons, is my report card still sitting in the white envelope addressed to them. Unopened. It's been sitting in the same spot for over three weeks. But I know its contents:

D, C+, C-, C-, B-, F, C+

Just below the report card is the yellow pamphlet from school:

YOU'RE A SURVIVOR! NOW WHAT? KEEP STAYIN' ALIVE!

Before I open the door, I look over to the living room at a photo of us taken when I was seven, playing and happy at the beach. The only one Dad never took down and stored in a box. The sky is a piercing blue, the edges overexposed from the camera flash. We are laughing as we look past the camera, squinting from the bright sun. I am posing on my knees, my pale, bony body swimming in green trunks. Mom looks young in her polka-dotted bathing suit, pointing at something in the distance while Dad embraces her from behind. The waves are frozen still as they crash against the rocks. If I close my eyes, I can almost hear the seagull cries and smell the salty ocean breeze.

And in my arms, curled up and wearing the seashell necklace, is Bryson.

The honking of the horn brings me back. My heart sinks.

"You can order pizza or something," my mom calls. "I won't be home for dinner. Money will be on your dresser. Your father will be out all night trying to fill that empty void."

"Yeah, I'll be at the store all night, kiddo." My dad sighs. "Your mother will be filling up her prescription bottle to take the edge off."

Did they really forget about tomorrow?

For a moment I think I will say it, just tell them I love them and that I wish we could turn back time to how everything was before.

I pretend the fourth chair is still seated at the table. When I open my mouth and form the words, it's just a whisper:

"I love you guys."

I inhale one more time before opening the door.

Before everything will once again change.

Forever.

～

"Dude. Dude!" Reefer pounds his calloused hands on the wheel of his gray 1997 Buick LeSabre—a hand-me-down he got when he turned sixteen. I never drive, so I always bum a ride for school. "I... I'm in love. Just straight fact. I, the Reef-a-nater, am in *love*."

"Man down, we have a man down," I announce, cupping my hands over my mouth. This I have to force for Reefer. The pretending everything is normal. It's a habit that I'll miss.

"I'm serious. This one fox in particular has me drooling the thirst. Just excreting the thirst from my pores. Ha-ha, I'm such a tool, and I just love it."

"I still have no idea what thirst means," I say and kick at a three-week-old McDonald's bag by my feet. "But tell me about her."

"Mrs. Carmichael. She wants me *so* bad. She was practically asking for it when I was helping her get down a box from her garage. She literally smelled like an angel, Gray."

I look over and laugh. If anyone can make me forget about everything, it's my best friend. We've known each other since the third grade when we played kickball in gym class. I kicked the red ball straight into his face, knocking him out. After I stayed with him in the nurse's office until he woke up, it just clicked. We've been best friends ever since.

Reefer is the class clown, always joking and causing problems in school, which doesn't always sit well with his dad—the principal. He gets detention more than anyone I know, but everyone finds him hilarious—even the teachers. He is stocky and broad-shouldered, an average height for our age. Some people call him overweight, but Reefer is just pleasantly plump—a term he embraced that stuck with our class. If you make fun of his weight, he will give it back in full.

"Isn't she widowed?"

"You bet your sweet cougar-lovin' ass she is. And who best

to help her grieve than this guy?" He points to himself, beaming. "If anything, I'm doing a public service here."

"You're highly disturbed."

"This is true. It's also why I'm currently single. At least we'll always have each other." He winks, his face round and cheeks flushed.

He runs his hands over his buzzed head, scratches an itch, and slams on the brakes, almost ramming into a truck stopped at a red light. He laughs and turns up the volume on the radio to a country station.

I look out the window at the houses whizzing by in a blur as we pick up speed—the morning sky a beautiful orange and red hue. A few people jog past or ride bikes; they appear still as we cruise along. This street, like every other street, is lined with shingled two-story houses, most complete with basketball nets in the driveway—roads that usually have a dead-end. The town is too poor for a cul-de-sac.

An overweight middle-aged man my dad's age lugs a ratty armchair to the end of his blacktop. I look around and think about how I should've said something before I left the house. My parents deserved better.

"You're thinking about her, aren't you?" Reefer screams over some twangy tune.

In truth, I haven't thought about Kris as much as other mornings. Reefer knows what's wrong, knows what this week means for me and my parents. But he's smart enough not to bring it up.

"She called me again last night, but I didn't answer." I shake my head. "She left a voicemail." I bite my lip. "She hates me. She has every right to."

"Stop. I don't want to hear that garbage. And if she does hate you, which she doesn't, I'll kill her, cut her up into pieces, and bury her... maybe." He turns down the volume on the radio.

"Pretty sure my mom still has a bag of lime somewhere in the shed." He pauses, his eyes going wide. "Oh... I didn't mean that, bro. I meant... shit."

I force a smile and punch him in the arm. Memories come back. "No, it's fine. She'll stop calling soon. You'll see." I panic, afraid I've said too much. Choose to ignore and continue. "It's just Kyle and Tim," I recover. "You know."

Reefer turns his head to me, silent for a beat too long. "Well, Kyle is a Neanderthalic *dick*. I mean him and Kris have that freaky twin thing going, so I get it. But I still think they can talk in their heads, you know? Telling secrets and casting spells. What's that shit called?"

"Telepathy?"

"God, you're so smart, Gray-Gray. I could kiss you right now."

"I'd prefer you didn't."

"What would you prefer? Talk to the Reef Machine... I'm an open book."

"I've got nothing to say."

I can hear Reefer grind his teeth as he turns back to face the road. He lowers his voice. "Listen, *Señor Falconi*... I got your back against anything and anyone." He's silent for a while, then he glances over and looks me in the eye. "I'm serious... excluding demonic possession. Because, I mean, HELLO! Shit's whack."

I chuckle, and the thought of Kris's blonde hair flashes in my mind; her nearly perfect teeth gleam, and her coconut perfume teases my nostrils, lifts me up. And just like that, in a millisecond, I see her leg twist almost all the way around at the knee until it pops. She screams and reaches her hand out to mine. Blood runs down her cheeks. I breathe and nod my head toward the road to make Reefer pay attention. The thought drifts away.

"Just want today to be normal," I tell him. "No demonic possessions. No surprises."

"Would you be surprised by that bloody Global II test we have today?"

"We have a Global II test today?"

"I don't know. I was hoping that you were gonna tell me."

"We don't."

"Good to know. Thanks, Gray-Gray. Should be no surprise then."

"You make no sense sometimes."

"Part of my charm." He cranks down his window to let the morning breeze in. "I have some serious gas today, so you might want to roll down the window before I blow us outta here."

Reefer parks the car and opens up his door to leave. I sit still and will myself to unbuckle the seatbelt, but I can't. I look around at the rows of cars, at the sun reflecting off the windshields one after another. Students file in from vehicles and buses parked in a row in front of the main drop-off circle. On the grass, next to the American flag billowing in the breeze, is the sign: Lee Falls Central High School. The only high school we have in town.

Kids swing backpacks over one shoulder and bob their heads to inaudible tunes from earbuds. Dozens of student drones march forward. Smiling faces. Scrunched faces. Stoic faces. Tired. Exhausted. Pained.

How long would it take to wash the blood off the front grill of the bus if you stepped in front of it? Would it smell like copper for days?

The pain in my chest swells, and I ball my hand into a fist until my knuckles turn white. Once again, the image of Kris reaching out and in pain comes to mind.

"You coming or what?" Reefer interrupts my thoughts.

I jump in my seat and turn, unbuckle my seatbelt. "Yeah.

Can you just give me a minute?"

"Want me to leave you the keys?" He runs his finger over a premature pimple above his left eyebrow, but I can see the corners of his eyes focused on me.

"Yeah."

He frowns and tosses the keys onto my lap before slamming the car door and walking toward the crowd of kids entering the school. He maneuvers his way between the cars, attempts to squeeze between spaces I can't even fit through, then gives up and walks around until a wider gap presents itself. For a moment, a smile spreads across my lips. A few kids pass by on either side of his car.

I flip down the sun visor and look into the mirror, practice what I will say to Reefer and Jenna if they make plans for tonight. I think of saying goodbye to Kris and Kyle, but know they'll be better off if I don't.

Pulling out my phone, I access one of my personal accounts where I used to post videos. All my other social media accounts, profiles, blogs, etc., have been deleted or shut off. Even my photo account is disabled. This is the last one remaining. Mostly it's of me being goofy with friends or reading a new poem or lyric I'd written. This was a video I'd posted eight months ago. I check it. 3,425 views, 465 likes, 37 dislikes. It's only thirty seconds long, but I play it. Watch as I roll my computer chair onto the screen with a big, goofy grin on my face.

"Wassup, my Faclonians... yeah. It's still a terrible name, right? Ha-ha. Wrote an idea for my most inspired work yet. Reefer, enjoy, bro! Want to test it for you guys. 'Ode to the Throne: A Haiku.' Here it is:

> Chicken Alfredo
> You make my stomach rumble
> Toilet is my friend

After video-me stares at the camera for a while, I plaster another big goofy grin on my face and roll off screen before the clip ends. Below it are several top comments from friends who follow my videos:

Timmy420: so lame

ThatKyleKid: This totally happened to me too!!!

GrayFlaconianOG: (responding to ThatKyleKid) Twinning!

TheHyunEffect: Only you Gray could make me laugh and feel icky at the same time

TrackGirlKris: Does your girlfriend approve? :(

GrayFalconianOG: (responding to TrackGirlKris) After last night, I'd like to think so. :)

TrackGirlKris: (responding to GrayFalconianOG) Gray!Delete that comment right NOW! :(

Reefanation69: awe, Gray-Gray. u DO care :(

TrollzRule007: isnt this dude who brother is dead? Why is he posting bout diarrhea wifth a dead bro? #weird

JamesDeanFan: (responding to TrollzRule007) Your comment sucks. Think before posting, asshole. #Falconian4Life

The most recent comment:

JamesDeanFan: How come you don't post anymore? Your haikus are funny as shit. Show us *sexy* Grayson. You're smart, good-looking, and great with words. Even the gross ones. Don't give up. Vaginas swell for you. ;-)

I close my eyes and wait for my heartbeat to return to normal. Stare up and out through the dusty window at the rising sun in the blue sky.

Traces of the dawn fully gone, I feel powerless. Nothing is in my control.

Bryson isn't here with me. He's just gone.

I go to my settings and delete the video from my account. When the page refreshes, the video is blank, and so are the comments.

My phone vibrates.

UNKNOWN

2day is gonna b a good day

dont u think?

A figure brushes past the passenger side door to the Buick—pounds a fist against the glass before marching on. I jump up in the seat and bang my face into the rearview mirror. My head throbs as I curse out loud and whip around to the person brushing between the cars. She doesn't look back.

After a moment, I open up the door to see who knocked, but lose her in the mass of bodies huddled on the sidewalk a few yards ahead. I swipe the keys off the seat and press the sharp edges into my palm until my skin indents. I slam the car door and walk toward the entrance.

Millions of thoughts run through my head: how awkward it might be at school today, never again waking up to my mother cooking bacon, the taste of Kris's cherry lip gloss, the college acceptance letters I'd never get to open in the mail, the strange texts, the image of the dark figure brushing past the window. At what I thought was a streak of red hair.

Red hair. Was that her?

But none haunts me more than the look in Bryson's eyes as the color drained from his face on that November night—the absence of life. His body left cold and stiff.

And all I could do was watch as my little brother died.

Knowing I was the one who killed him.

23 HOURS UNTIL

FRIDAY, 7:37 AM

TIM ELBOWS ME FACE-FIRST INTO MY LOCKER. I YELP AS MY nose smashes into a jacket hook. Pain courses through my face.

"Sorry, didn't see you there, Fagconi."

He passes by without a look back, his dark hair curling below his ears in a way that says he's three months overdue for a haircut. And I catch a glimpse of a new bracelet—beaded—decorating his slender arm. No one else in the narrow hallway stops to take notice of our little exchange. Our morning ritual—it used to bother me at first; I always wanted to fight back. And then one day it just didn't, so I stopped wanting to.

I stand in front of my locker and stuff a few binders into my backpack, rubbing my tender nose. A group of cheerleaders huddle to my left—dressed in their blue and white uniforms—and laugh at a story a busty blonde in the middle tells. One girl with butterfly press-on tattoos decorating each cheek notices me staring and waits, stares back, then turns away uncomfortably. I push at the bruise on my chest, blowing out air through my lips.

"You alright, brah?" Reefer checks his body into the locker next to mine, puffing out his cheeks as he looks around. The few lockers on either side of him vibrate from the impact.

"I'm fine." I sigh and look away from the group.

"Screw 'em," he shouts toward the girls, raising his middle finger. They all stop to gawk at us. "People around here need to mind their own damn business."

"They weren't doing anything." I shove his arm down. The butterfly cheerleader raises her middle finger to Reefer and turns her back on us. "You always have to cause a scene."

Reefer picks up my backpack from the floor and hands it to me. "Well, shit, man. Don't look like a kicked puppy next time and I won't defend your honor. *GOSH!*"

I zip up my backpack and swing it over my right shoulder, embarrassed. I reach above to the shelf in my locker that holds a few rogue pens, the sealed envelope marked "Bryson," and a strange photograph of Kris and me. Her blonde hair is up in a bun, and my hands are wrapped around her waist. We are both looking above at the person taking the photo, someone I don't know. A bonfire rages in the background. I have half a marshmallow sticking out of my mouth; Kris has her left hand cupping one of her boobs; her right is holding a medal for finishing first place in her track championship race. A "C" for captain is emblazoned on her tracksuit. Her head is cocked back—mouth open wide in laughter. It's a perfect moment. She looks happy. *We* look happy.

Who put this in your locker?

I can still hear Kris's echoing laughter in my head from that night. Can still hear her velvety voice:

"Will you love me forever, Gray? Even when we're old?" She squeezed my hands.

"You know I will." I shoveled a s'more into my mouth.

The fire lit up her face, and all I wanted to do was hold her in my arms, press my lips against hers. God, she was beautiful.

"Promise me. Don't ever leave. Don't break my heart."

"I won't." I ran my hands through her hair and cupped her chin.

"Me neither. We're gonna be the best parents one day. We'll leave this town and move somewhere south. Somewhere warm. I can run track or teach track, and you can find something you love to do. Like write. You love English. Plus, your poetry on your channel is so beautiful."

"*You're* my home, Kris. *You're* where I want to be." I kissed her lips. "But if you ever decide to run away from me, I won't be able to catch you. You're like a cheetah."

She slapped my arm. "Way to ruin the moment, Gray."

I kissed her lips again and grinned. "You know I love you. Right?"

"When the heck was that picture taken?" Reefer says, snapping me back to reality. "I've never seen it before." I can feel his eyes watching me. "I know that look you have, bro. Don't forget *who* broke up with *who*."

I flip over the picture, and written in orange gel pen in Kris's distinct handwriting is:

It doesn't all have to be bad. Sometimes it can be good.
XoXo Kris

I feel something I don't want to feel deep in my gut, so I crumple the picture into a ball and throw it in my locker.

"I'm aware of what's going on between us," I snap. "I don't need the running commentary." I feel guilty as soon as it leaves my mouth. Reefer takes a step back, for a second seems hurt, but gathers his composure as if nothing happened. "I'm sorry. I didn't mean to—"

"Nah, s'all good. No worries."

"Thanks." I clear my throat. "And it's whom. It's who broke up with whom."

Save yourself, Reef. Before you end up hurt.

"Gray, you know I hate serious people. So when I get serious with you, it's seriously serious." He pauses to sneeze. "But really, what's going on? Does it really surprise you Kris would leave stuff in your locker? You know I'll always support you, bro. I get it. I know you don't want to talk about it, and that's cool, it's whatever... but I lost our friends too."

"I'm sorry." I look down at my feet. I don't want to end things on a bad note with Reefer. He doesn't deserve that. "She just won't stop... if it's not one thing, it's another. And Kyle and Tim have every right to hate me." I look back up. "Pretty sure they don't hate you."

"Because my dad is like the educational mob boss! They'd both get whiplash from being suspended so fast. They've done nothing but overcompensate their tiny egos, and here you and Kris are pining over each other still like y'all walk on rainbows and smell like unicorns or some shit. You need to figure it out. Can't have it both ways, good sir."

"Smell like unicorns?"

He punches me in the shoulder, back to his goofy self. Serious Reefer never overstays his welcome. "Don't knock unicorns, man. They're majestic creatures." He sneezes. "And don't ever correct my incorrect grammar again. Clearly, I'm allergic to it."

Shaking my head, I close my locker to hide the marked envelope. We turn around and I scan the hallway, but I'm distracted by the growing flock of cheerleaders quickly closing in on us. This is our cue to leave.

We walk toward the main staircase where our homerooms are located. The drab green floors reflect the fluorescent lights above. I try to drown out the cacophony of voices and focus on the sound of shoes smacking against the floor. Red lockers on either side—everything closes in. Suffocating. Converse shoes, thumbs hovering over touchscreens to cell phones, backpacks swinging over shoulders... it's all too chaotic.

Nothing is in my control.

I take a deep breath to calm the anxiety. If I don't control my breathing, I'll have another panic attack. Yet another reason to dread the morning. Invisible people don't make a scene. I just want to get through today like a fly on the wall.

And then Jenna Hyun appears, seemingly out of nowhere. Bouncing as she steps. And Reefer's eyes light up. Like clockwork.

"Soooo, I was thinking we should all definitely go to the movies this weekend," Jenna says. "Like, there's this new horror film out that's supposed to be the creepiest thing since *The Exorcist*."

Reefer rests his arm on Jenna's shoulder. "Oh yeah, heard about that... from that Korean-director-guy you cream over, right? Dude makes legit films. Spewin' green shit from his Korean mind."

She nudges his arm off. "Korean-director-guy has a name. FYI. I've told you this *so* many times, Reefer. And please don't be gross. Cream?" She looks at me and shakes her head, smiling. "Now you're just frustrating me on purpose." She drastically pivots her hips to me. "As I was saying, you good for this Saturday? We can hang out in the mall or whatever before the movie." She turns back to Reefer and glares. "I don't have time for faux-horror aficionados."

"Well, of course, Freckles. I can literally give two stinkers about your love of Korean directors. You just get all pink in the face and start doing that foot tapping, arms crossed, steam rolling out of your ears, soul-crushing stare that I just can't get enough of." Reefer puts his hand over his heart and mocks adoration, batting his eyelashes. "My sweet, Freckly-Weckly."

Jenna grunts. "I hate when you call me that." She crosses her arms.

"I know... that's why I do it." Reefer rests his arm on her shoulder, winking. She shoves it back off.

Jenna Hyun plays with her auburn hair that's always back in a ponytail. She dyes it a new color every few months. Reefer and I have known her since middle school, and I've never seen her natural hair color. She used to be a tomboy, but after we started freshman year and all the upperclassmen started to tease her, she searched fashion videos and blogs online to change her appearance. Now she wears the tightest blue jeans possible, over-applies copious amounts of makeup, and dons a pushup bra that doesn't do much. She's all skin-and-bones, with a golden complexion and pointed nose. And, of course, freckles. Hence the name.

Reefer likes to announce the fact that she's Korean, which is a reason beyond me because it's as if he's constantly reminding her of something she already knows, to which she acts annoyed —like this odd routine they do. He offends Jenna, and she, in turn, retaliates. It's a weird cycle.

Jenna pokes me with her finger in the ribs, looking me in the eyes with her purple-colored contacts. "Well? We should go. We haven't been to the movies in, like, forever ago."

Reefer sighs, making a dramatic foot stomp and playfully shoving Jenna into me. "Whatever. Horror movies are lame; you guys are lame. I need to find better, non-lame friends."

"You don't have any other friends," Jenna says.

Reefer is silent for a moment, blinks, and then clears his throat. "Yo, I'm gonna go get my plump ass a blueberry muffin in the cafeteria... maybe check out that new smokin' lunch lady we got last week."

"That's pretty random," I say. "Also, when did the school afford to buy blueberry muffins for breakfast?"

"Yeah, well, you guys are being mean and I'm obviously searching for an out and failing here... and when has that ever stopped me from being random?"

"At least you're honest about it. The new lunch lady is pretty hot; I'll give you that."

Jenna groans. "Why am I friends with you guys? You're so gross. Women aren't objects to ogle."

"That's exactly what they are, Freckles. They are literally there to ogle."

I smile. "Like Mrs. Carmichael?"

Reefer places his hand over his heart. "The lady shall be conquered one day."

Jenna looks to me, and I hold my hands in surrender, giggling. "I'm staying out of this one. This is all you two."

"Yeah." He nods, lingers a gaze on Jenna when she's facing me. "I'll shut up now."

Jenna nods, her back turned. "Yeah, you really should."

He looks up at me. "So if I see Kris, do you want me to say something to her?"

"Why would you do that?"

"Do you want me to tell her nicely to screw off?"

"Um, no. I mean—"

"So you don't want me to tell her you're over her?"

For a second I'm about to say no, but think better of it. "Yeah... if she asks about me. That would be okay."

He looks disappointed for a moment, takes out his cell phone to text. "Fair enough. I'll catch ya in third period, Gray-Gray." We bump fists. "Catch ya in study hall, Korean-loving-Freckles."

"God, you're so annoying." She tightens her hair tie.

"It's part of my charm." He grins. "Want to go to the cafe-

teria with me? Blueberry muffin that doesn't exist... my treat."
He runs a finger over his premature pimple. "You can make fun
of me the entire way there. I'll allow it... 'cause I'm a proper
gentleman."

"No. I'm gonna head to homeroom with Gray." She flickers
her eyes to me and down at the floor. "Maybe on Monday?"

I can sense Reefer stiffen up. It's just one of those things—
being best friends as long as we have.

He nods. "Um, yeah. Whatever. It's cool. Catch ya on the
flip side."

I look back at Reefer as he raises his eyebrows and shrugs. It
makes most of his body jiggle with him as he does, which puts
another grin on my face. He turns and walks down the hall,
humming a country tune. Jenna and I stand there until he turns
a corner and disappears.

It's then that Kris limps into view down the hall—coming
from the direction Reefer was headed. Her blonde hair is brushed
straight, hanging halfway down her back. She wears an orange
sundress pleated at the bottom, resting a little above her knees.
With sandals exposing her orange toenails and an orange headband to match the dress, she looks beautiful. Always. It never
fails. The gold crucifix around her neck gleams from the lights.

And then there's the black knee brace around her left leg.

She winces a bit with each step forward. It's noticeable only
because I've seen the pain in her face up close. She doesn't like
to tell people about that. Kris looks directly at me and quickens
her pace.

*Remember when she didn't have to limp down the hallway,
Gray?*

When reality snaps back, I walk toward the main staircase,
away from Kris. Jenna keeps pace right next to me, pretends like
we aren't trying to avoid my ex.

"Wanna go to homeroom early? I need you to look at our English paper due today and tell me if it totally sucks."

I switch my backpack to my opposite shoulder. "I'm sure it doesn't suck, but I'd love to. You're a better writer than you think."

Jenna is about to answer when she stops in the middle of the hallway, staring ahead to the main staircase. Tim is holding a trumpet case in the air as a short freshman tries to get it back from him. Most kids in the hall walk by, but a few people straggle around. One cheerleader shakes her head, bored, and sends a text. Another senior in a blue varsity letter jacket snaps a picture.

The freshman wears a flannel button-up, carrying sheet music for band practice. It's typical. Tim always has to be that one jerk to single out the awkward kid in the hallway. He's been like that ever since I'd known Kris and Kyle. But then it happens:

I blink, and for just a split second, it's Bryson standing there trying to get back the trumpet from Tim's hands. Just a split second. And then his voice in my head:

"*But you promised to take me back to the beach, like old times. Right, Gray?*"

And I lose control.

I drop my backpack on the ground and storm over. No words are said. No punches thrown. I walk up to Tim in his black hoodie and stare him down. A few people in the hallway huddle around, maybe expecting a fight. Jenna runs up beside me and starts talking, but I can't hear her words. Just the beat of my heart in my head. The oncoming waves of panic. Somewhere behind a few onlookers, Kris shouts to us.

Tim clears his throat; a sly grin appears. "What the hell are you do—"

"Give him back his trumpet." My hands shake. "Please, Tim."

"And why would I do a goddamn thing you say?" He rubs his thumb over his bottom lip.

My heart thumps. Hair stands on edge. "You want to look like a jerk in front of your cousin?" I point behind me to Kris, now nearly all the way to us.

We stare at each other for a while, and his eyes shift focus. His face hardens, then loosens up as he exhales—lowers the trumpet case and drops it on the floor. And for a second I'm hoping that he'll throw a punch. Hit me. Make me feel shame. But he doesn't.

I dig my fingernails into my palm until the pain takes away lingering thoughts of Bryson.

"You're lucky I'm not an asshole." He puts his hands in his pockets. "If she wasn't here"— he nods to Kris—"you'd be on the ground right now." He curses. "Not looking to fight a charity case today."

Jenna tugs at my arm, asks us to leave. I step back, pick up the case and give it to the freshman. He mumbles a "thank you." Taking a look at him, he's nothing like my brother. But it doesn't stop the goosebumps from appearing on my forearms.

What the hell was that, Gray?

I look back up at Tim as he mouths a curse. When I turn to check on the freshman, he's already halfway up the stairs, and the crowd has broken up. No one wants to see two guys talk calmly in the hallway.

"Gray, why did you do that?" Jenna whispers. "I mean, it was, like, really awesome of you and all. But Tim could've hurt you."

I look back, and she has my backpack in her hands. I grab it. "I... I don't know what that was."

Below the stairs, I see a flicker of red highlighted hair and turn. It's a girl, but not just any girl. She wears fishnets over nylon leggings, a plaid mini-skirt, army combat boots, fingerless gloves, a hoop in her nose, and black nail polish on each middle finger. She has uncombed and frizzy hair that rests on top of her shoulders, her face free of makeup. She doesn't need it; her pale complexion is flawless. Noticeably, she stands alone, everyone intentionally walking as far from her as possible.

"Are you okay, Gray?" Kris calls as she reaches us, the pain in her face obvious with each step. "What happened? I couldn't see."

I intentionally ignore her as Jenna tugs my arm and leads me up the stairs. Tim shakes his head and walks to Kris, cursing under his breath. And a part of me wants to look back at Kris. See her expression.

"What's going on? What did you do to him this time, Tim?"

"I didn't do a goddamn thing to that fa—"

I tune them out, but I can't tear my eyes from the girl with the crimson locks. The girl who looks straight at me below the stairs, unblinking. Emotionless. Her head cocks to the side, studying me. Red bangs fall over her right eye. She is the one without any friends. The one everyone likes to talk and gossip about. The one who knocked on Reefer's car earlier.

She is the foster girl.

She is Aubrey Fisher.

Sitting at my desk in homeroom, I stand and place a hand over my heart to recite the Pledge of Allegiance before the morning announcements. The big cheer competition coming up is the top news. A warning about whoever had let off a stink bomb and how raffle tickets for baseball are to be sold during the lunch and study hall periods that follow.

"...and don't forget that prom tickets are still on sale until next Friday. Just see Student Council President Sidney Watkins for your ticket," Reefer's dad announces in his gruff "Principal" voice over the loudspeakers. "In other news, the town fair is tonight over in Davisport..."

I ignore his voice, shift in the plastic seat next to Jenna, and doodle on a flyer for the student fundraiser. The school itself can't afford to fund most after-school programs that aren't athletics; most extracurriculars, part of prom included, rely on these.

Reefer is in a different homeroom. Across the classroom, Kris sits up front. She looks over her shoulder at me once and frowns, turning back around, her eyes in a book and pink highlighter in hand, before a girl at the next desk taps her shoulder to talk.

The homeroom teacher sits behind his desk grading papers for first period while Jenna rifles around through her binder for English. Kris laughs at some joke the girl to her right is telling. And then her voice in my head:

"Promise me. Don't ever leave. Don't break my heart."

"...and don't forget to wish Mrs. Connors a happy recovery when she returns next week..." Reefer's dad drones on, interrupting my thoughts.

"Okay, here is my paper for English," Jenna says. "It's okay if it totally sucks."

I turn around and start to read her handwritten pages for our assignment. I've been casually tutoring Jenna for a while on grammar, but when she sees that I don't have the assignment out, she clicks her tongue.

"You're going to fail if you don't start handing in your homework, Gray."

"I know. I'll throw something together before our class," I lie. "By the way"—I take my pencil and underline a few lines throughout the creative writing assignment—"you overuse your past participles, and be careful about subject-verb agreements in your opener. Some of them don't make sense. They're tricky. There's also a misplaced modifier in your sixth paragraph."

"I don't get it. You should be pulling an A in that class." She takes the paper back and looks it over, pats my hand. "I wish I was as smart as you."

"Stop it. You're smart in other ways. Like foreign cinema. I don't know a thing about that at all."

"Like *Bicycle Thieves*?"

"Is that the Queen song?"

Jenna shakes her head and throws her pen at my chest. We both grin. "Vittorio De Sica. Italian cinema. 1948. We watched it with Reefer and Kris last summer! You said you liked it!"

"I didn't want to hurt your feelings."

Jenna groans obnoxiously, and I shrug. We focus back on the paper, and I help her rewrite a few sentences. This is another thing I'll miss.

"She keeps looking back at you."

"Who?"

"You know."

"Yeah, I do."

Jenna hums a tune, sighs, and puts down her pen. "You have to talk to her."

"Jenna–"

"Not get back with her. But talk to her. C'mon, Gray. I've known you for how long? Five years? You practically grew up together."

"I really don't want to talk about this."

"Okay. I won't bring it up again. But... for, like, closure and all. You definitely need to just end it with her. Be honest and upfront. Ignoring her doesn't do anything but make you look like a jerk... which you're not. That's Reefer's job."

"Reefer's not a jerk."

"I *know*. He's just..."

We meet eyes, nod, and I snicker.

The bell rings, and we say goodbye until our study hall period later. As I enter the crowded hallway heading to first period, Kris is waiting outside the door for me. I pause.

"Can we talk? Please. Or are you still going to treat me like I don't exist anymore?"

Out of habit, I open my mouth to respond, but shut it quickly and continue to walk forward. Her good leg seems to shine under the hallway lights, and I imagine running my fingers up and down her smooth, athletic thighs. Can almost smell the soap she uses on her skin, the coconut hand cream.

"Gray." She reaches for my arm, but I brush it away. "I can't even know how you're doing?"

In my head I tell her the truth, but out loud I keep quiet. Silence, for now, is safe.

"Did Tim hurt you?" There's urgency in her voice. "Stop walking away from me."

"Why do you keep trying with him?" a girl asks Kris from behind me. "He did this to you, girl."

"Just stop," Kris says. "Leave him alone. I mean it."

"Girl, if I was you, I wouldn't give his ass the time of day. Didn't you use to be an all-star or something?"

A few heads turn from her to me, but no one stays long enough to eavesdrop. Me and Kris are old news. I know I should do the right thing and stop to talk, to explain, but I can't. I need to distance myself and push Kris away. For her own good.

I round a corner and walk down the hall where the main office is, by the front doors of the school. Away from whatever Kris says back to the girl. Away from the sound of my name.

Then I see her again. Aubrey Fisher. She leans against the

glass door of the front office. Aubrey looks and blows her red bangs up with a huff. They fall back into place over her right eye. She stands up on both feet but doesn't walk closer. There is a smirk on her face, a playful one, and I almost trip before catching myself.

Around us I notice that everyone in the hall chooses to walk on the opposite end, away from her. No one stops to look back. It's like they are trying to avoid a disease that she carries, like walking within a few feet of her will infect them.

For a brief second I think she's going to say something, but of course, she doesn't. Aubrey pivots her hips to watch as I continue down the hall until I reach my classroom. I walk in and set my stuff down. I get out a binder and reach into my jeans pocket for a pen. My math teacher struts up the row of desks to me and looks down. He runs his hand over his carrot-colored mustache and clears his throat. My phone vibrates, so I pull it out.

UNKNOWN

u prepared 4 whats about 2 come?

"Mr. Falconi, let me guess. You don't have your homework again. Am I correct?"

I don't bother looking up as I respond. I realize the best way to piss teachers off and force them to lose faith in a student, minus not handing in homework, is to look past them as you talk. But I did do the assignment. Like I do all the assignments for my classes.

I just never hand them in.

"Sounds about right, Mr. Pentick."

He shakes his head. "I can't keep giving you extensions, Mr. Falconi. I did for a while, but it's time to get back to reality." He straightens his tie, looks nervous. "Everybody has something going on."

"I guess you'll just have to fail me for this one then." I regret the words as soon as they come out.

He looks at me for a beat too long. I meet his eyes. For once, instead of looking disappointed, he just looks sad, like he pities me. He blinks, unable to respond. It's a few moments later before he struts back to the front of the room as the bell to first period rings, but all my thoughts go back to Aubrey.

Who the hell keeps texting you this weird stuff? And why was Aubrey smiling? More importantly, why did you smile back?

22 HOURS UNTIL

FRIDAY, 8:47 AM

I STAND IN THE GYM LOCKER ROOM AFTER THE BELL RINGS for second period. We keep our bags stashed in the JV section. The mesh lockers are blue, lined up, and divided in half vertically.

I look around as kids begin to undress and take out their swim trunks. Two boys who are on the swim team put on blue drag suits, walk around the room without a care as they show off their half-naked bodies. One of them takes a selfie while another stands naked and bends over, tries to catch the other boys off guard if they turn his way. I pat the flub underneath my shirt, flush, and sit on the wooden bench. I hate my body, but I'm too lazy to do anything about it.

And really, what will it matter after the day is over anyway?

"Two minutes to get changed and out by the side of the pool, or you'll be doing extra laps," Coach Phillips's voice echoes from the shower room.

At the start of the school year, I would've been joking around with them, doing stupid things with Kyle for the fun of it. I wasn't popular, but people knew me by association, thanks to Kris and her brother, both star athletes. Even got a decent following with my online videos thanks to the semi-popularity. But now it's like no one wants to come up to me, like maybe I'm damaged goods. That I don't know how to have fun anymore.

To my left, Tim elbows Kyle, his cousin, in the ribs. Tim's hair starts to deflate from the humidity of the nearby shower room, and they laugh about something, glance in my direction, and immediately stop. Kyle shares similarities with Kris: both have bleached blonde hair and fair complexions. Both athletic. They're twins, and they're close. The main difference between them is the way Kyle's cheeks seem to cave in, almost like he is starving—his cheekbones jut out. Kris, on the other hand, is nearly perfect—beautiful. The only flaw on her impeccable skin is the birthmark above her right collarbone, but even that's beautiful.

I look up to see Tim and Kyle with scrunched faces. Kyle has on a Red Sox baseball cap that faces backward, which he wears on most days. He always has hat hair because of it. Tim wears five or six different colored bracelets on his left wrist at all times, occasionally rotating the stock. It's a quirk he's had ever since I can remember.

A few guys walk into the shower room, which is connected to the pool entrance. The sound of water splashing onto tiles cascades as steam rolls into the room from around the corner. I wipe a bead of sweat from my forehead with the back of my hand.

"Better towel up, everyone," Tim announces. "Fagconi is in prime dick-sucking position on the bench." He grins, proud of himself.

"Knock it off," Kyle mumbles, not looking at me. "You'll get us in trouble."

A few snickers come from around the locker room, but no one does anything, and the chatter dies down.

I pinch the flab underneath my shirt until pain shoots

through my gut. *Inhale. Exhale.* It would be easy to react, to fight back. But I don't. It's not worth it. Just part of his daily routine.

"I saw Kris in the hall today." Tim nudges Kyle. "Why does she still care?"

"I'm serious." Kyle curses. "Cut it." His eyes flicker my way for a brief moment, not lingering too long before unbuttoning his orange-striped shirt. From across the room, I can see him mumble something under his breath.

"Let's ask Gray a question," Tim goads further.

"Jesus, Dude." Kyle throws his top shirt to the ground. "I'm about to punch you in two seconds."

"You don't have my cousin to hide behind anymore with that shit you pulled in the hall this morning." Tim rotates a few bracelets on his wrist. "I don't like pussy-ass bitches."

Control yourself, Gray. He's trying to rile you up.

"I don't like assholes who pick on people smaller than them for no reason," I utter.

And then it's silent. Everyone in the locker room stops moving. Most days I'm quiet. Unprepared and uncooperative. But now we have everyone's attention. And there is a tiny tick in my head, the sensation of waves rolling over me. I pinch my gut harder to fight them back.

It takes a moment for Kyle to respond. "What the hell is wrong with you two? Stop starting shit for no reason."

"*I'm* startin' shit?" Tim says. "*I'm* the asshole?" He flips me the middle finger. "Apple doesn't fall far from the tree, does it, Gray?" He plants a foot on the wooden bench and leans on his knee. "Your dad did, like, rape your mom. Didn't he?"

And then, before I realize it, my backpack is hurling across the room. It's too late to take it back when I notice what I've done. It hits Kyle in the head, knocking him back into a locker.

And I curse myself for having terrible aim. Kyle pushes himself up with the help of a boy to his right.

Making fun of me is one thing. But dragging my parents into it is another.

"Are you being real right now, Falconi?" Kyle clenches his jaw. "You wanna come at me right now? Seriously? What the hell did I do to you?"

Tim shakes his head, smirks. "What a joke."

"You want to hate me," I say, standing up. "Fine. Don't bring my parents into this."

A few of the guys walk over, shirts off, like one big sausage fest. The smell of pool chemicals makes the room spin, and I can hear my heart pound. My phone vibrates in my pocket, makes me jump.

Inhale. Exhale.

"He's right." Kyle takes off his hat and massages his blond hair to get out the indentation of the cap, points to each of us. "You both need to cut this middle school bullshit before Coach comes back here."

"Whatever." Tim waves him off. He walks around the bench and inches closer. "I'm not the asshole you think I am. I just don't like you." He plucks at a few bracelets. "You don't get special treatment because you killed your brother. I'm sorry, but you don't."

My hands ball up into fists at the mention of Bryson. And I don't know if he's doing it to antagonize or instigate, or if he really doesn't understand the weight of those words uttered from his lips. But whatever the intention...

... It works.

I step forward and reach out to shove Tim in the chest. Hard. He stumbles back and falls over the bench. And all I want to do is hit him until he takes it back, apologizes. Sucks back the word *brother* onto his cursed tongue. Until he feels the same pain I do. But, of course, I don't. I never will. Because another part of me still wants to be punished, put down, hurt for becoming the coward I am now.

"Please stop," I beg, and I hate how pathetic my voice sounds. "I'm serious."

The remaining boys form a circle around the three of us, and a few start to chant, "Fight." One kid with an arrow tattoo on his wrist grabs his cell phone to record a video.

And then I see Kyle out of the corner of my eye. He looks behind him, paranoid. Like he's ready to break us apart. We lock eyes, and once again, I hear the sound of metal scraping against metal, glass shattering. The distant sirens, and the *plink* of blood onto the pavement. Hear Kris's scream. See their dad's forehead gashed wide open, a glass shard stabbed into one eye.

"Thirty seconds to get out to the diving board," Coach Phillips's voice echoes again.

I grit my teeth, and the room starts to spin before I regain my bearings. Shake away the lingering image of Kyle and Kris's dad. Of Bryson. But I can't. He's there. Dying. Slowly. Painfully. And I just want to get it out of my head, to forget it. So I do the only thing that makes sense:

I start a fight.

"She'll never run again," I mumble. But it's loud enough for Kyle to hear. Because I know this is enough to push him over the edge. And it surprises even me how desperate it is. "She'll always have a limp."

Kyle jumps over the bench and pushes me into the nearest locker; the vents dig into my back. I don't try to fight him off. The other boys let out a series of howls. One drums his hand onto a locker door, and another cups his hands over his mouth to chant like a monkey. They want a fight. They want to see a struggle. To see someone bleed.

It might be the most attention anyone has given me in months.

I shudder, my chest heavy, fingers tingling. The room heats up. Vision blurs.

"Say that shit again, Falconi. Don't sit there acting like the victim one minute and talk crap about my sister the next. You don't have any right to say anything about us."

Tim stands back up, folds his arms over his chest. "Little freak is a goddamn psycho." He rests a foot on the bench again. "That's my cousin you're talkin' about."

"Do it," I whisper so no one but Kyle can hear. "Just do it."

Kyle shoves me into the locker a few times, and each one hurts more. But I want this to be over already. He's stalling. One moment there's hatred in his eyes, the next, there's something like pity. Like he feels sorry. Like he doesn't really want to be doing this.

I attempt to escape to my right—to goad him further—but am blocked by the arrow tattoo boy who pushes me back. I feel like a pinball stuck in a machine.

"No, you don't get to walk away." Kyle leans in close, and I feel his hot breath brush past my ear as he whispers. "Are you trying to get yourself hurt, or are you just that desperate?" The words against my face send an icy shiver down my spine. He doesn't do anything, not right away. It's hesitation I see; every muscle in his face is taut. And for just a moment, he looks conflicted. "Why are you doing this?"

And then my fist smashes into Kyle's chest. No thought goes into it; it just happens. And he stumbles back, shocked. We both are. I stare at my trembling fist, not sure where the anger came from.

Tim snickers, and Kyle squints his eyes, rushes me, grabs my face, and slams my skull into the metal locker. The room goes dark as I fall to the ground. A foot collides with my ribs. I sputter air and cough—sharp pain travels up my side as I feel a foot stomp on my ankle. It seems like forever before I hear Coach Philips shout from above:

"Sanders!"

I flick my eyes open as the room comes back into focus. The light blinds me momentarily before everything stabilizes. My ribs and ankle throb when I try to move.

"*WHAT* is going on in here?"

"We were just goofin' around, Coach," Tim speaks up.

Kyle doesn't say anything.

"Really!" Coach exclaims. "Is that why Falconi is on the ground?" He turns to Tim. "Just *goofin'* around?"

Tim looks at me and hunches his shoulders, shifts the weight on his feet. Kyle leans back against a locker as the other boys slowly back away. It's silent as I see pairs of feet step farther back. In their absence, black running sneakers and the bottom of a blue tracksuit enter my view. Coach Philips always wears the same outfit, whether he teaches gym or the boys' baseball team in the spring.

Coach Philips sighs. "Pick him up and take him to the nurse, Sanders."

"Coach, he's fine," Tim says.

"You just got Sanders suspended from this weekend's game. Want him to be benched for another one?"

Kyle glares at Tim.

"That's bullshit!" Tim says. "He started it!"

"That's a game for you too, Eggers. I believe I asked *Sanders*, not you. So go ahead. Run your mouth." Coach turns back to Kyle. "Are you going to pick up Falconi, or do you want to sit the rest of the season?"

"Yeah," Kyle says, his voice soft. "I'll take him, Coach. Not a problem."

"What are you doing?" Tim asks.

"Dude, lay off already. I told you to stop running your mouth. Annoying as fu—"

"One more word!" Coach says. "The next one who speaks is benched indefinitely."

Tim's eyes go wide. He hates it when Kyle tells him to shut up. We used to do it all the time back when we were friends. Kyle was just as annoyed with his cousin as I was, which is why it was surprising that they became closer when we weren't anymore. But it is nice to see that even now, Kyle still doesn't let anyone walk all over him.

Family tragedies bring some people closer together.

Coach Phillips glances down. Strokes his silver goatee. For a second, he just stares as if embarrassed and ashamed. I almost think he will join in, kick me around and use my body like a mop for my own blood. But after a moment he reaches down, helps me up, and forces Kyle to wrap an arm around my shoulders. We walk out of the locker room toward the nurse's office.

Kyle doesn't say anything. Halfway there, he drops my arm and lets me walk myself. My side hurts, but I don't make a fuss. It's eerily quiet—our shoes echo against the walls with each *tap*—and I don't say a word. Kyle brings back memories from that night with his dad. Memories neither of us wants to relive.

"You know," he says, "if you want to ruin your life, don't drag me down with you."

I don't say anything back.

"You're unreal. Not even worth trying to figure you out anymore."

He pivots his hips and grabs my shoulders, pushes me against a locker. "I know what you're up to, Falconi." Kyle tightens his grip before he lets me go. "I'm not gonna hit you again. 'Cause that's what you want, but I'm not gonna give you a damn thing. You hear me? I owe you nothing because you are nothing. You're a coward. I tried to be there for you, but screw it." He balls his hand into a fist and punches the locker behind me. I jump on impact. "I'm trying really hard not to hit you now. *Really* hard."

"So stop trying and just do it."

"What is with you and this emo shit lately? Where the hell is this coming from?"

"Maybe I've always been this way."

"No." He shakes his head. "You haven't." He runs his hands through his hair, still indented from the baseball cap. "I'm sorry Tim said that stuff about your brother. It wasn't cool. My cousin is an asshole." There's an awkward silence before he continues. "You hit me. You knew I was gonna hit back, didn't you?" Silence. "Why?"

At first I want to tell him the truth. That I didn't know why. That it was like this moment of rage took over. But this isn't what he needs to hear.

"Because like you said, I'm not worth it anymore. Just that guy who destroyed your family."

Don't think about it.

He punches the locker again. I jump. "You didn't destroy my—"

"I never thought twice when I walked out of Kris's physical therapy." Lie. "Just did it." Snap my fingers. "Like that."

We both look around, but no one is in the hall. Kyle wipes his lips with the back of his hand and turns around, his palms up in surrender. "You win. Just stay away from my family, Falconi. I'm trying not to hurt you for my sister's sake. For *my* sake. But stay the hell away from us." He doesn't look back. "You want to be alone and miserable. Point made."

I'm left standing in the hallway, holding the side of my ribs and cursing under my breath. I think, for a moment, of limping up and apologizing. But I don't. I should feel better, should feel some sense of peace with this.

Then why does it feel so lousy?

After the nurse takes a look and says I'll be okay, Kyle and I are ushered to the Principal's office. I'm used to being sent here: not doing homework, getting into almost-fights, or talking back to a teacher. It's one thing after another.

At first, I thought my parents would take notice. Mr. Hoch even sent them several messages to have a conference about my attitude. They never came. Now I get sent here because it's all part of "the plan." But really, Mr. Hoch acts as both principal and guidance counselor at Lee Falls. I don't know if it's legal or not, but it's how things work here. So it's not odd for any kind of misbehavior to eventually get swept under the rug if the parents don't care, like mine. As small as the school is, it's easy to get lost in the "system." No one else seems to care for the troubled kids—not enough, at least.

The secretary behind the desk glances over as she types away on her computer, no doubt silently judging. Glasses rest on the tip of her nose, and she hums to herself, fills the awkward silence with a tune I don't know, and sneaks another peek at me.

I slide my foot over the carpet in a circle as I look out the windows to the hallway. A few people stroll by with pink slips for the bathroom. Occasionally a hall monitor waltzes by, clip-board in hand, looking bored out of her mind.

Kyle is taken into the Principal's office first. A bald security guard paces outside the door. They've suspended us before, and it's not the first time we've been sent here for similar things. I don't want to get Kyle in trouble. He doesn't deserve it.

In a way, I've missed him—missed the days we'd play video games in his basement or go midnight bowling. The double dates we'd go on with Kris and whatever new girlfriend he had at the time. Those were good days. But they don't belong here anymore.

Stop with the reminiscing, Gray. It's annoying.

My phone vibrates in my pocket. I pull it out far enough to be able to read. It's Reefer:

8:49
REEFER

totes knocked down this freshman that ran into me n hall

LMFAO

kid never had a chance against The Plumpness :-P

9:21
REEFER

heard u got hit in gym

ME

Just Tim and Kyle. You know. I kind of freaked out.

REEFER

word

yo

u alright?

ME

I'm fine. About to see your dad.

REEFER

hit me up when u done

im pissed 4 u

PISSED Gray!!!!!!!!!!!!!!!

!!!!!!!!!!!

(extensive exclamations cornmeal)!!!!!

ME

Haha, what?

Reefer: <3<3<#<43<3

conspire

grrrrr

ME

...??

Reefer: contigune

WTF DOES THAT EVEN MEANNNNN!?!?!!?!
AHHHHHHHH

continue**

yo, duck autocorrect... this is BS

F**

I smile, lock my phone, and slip it back into my jeans. I don't notice the girl sitting down in the chair next to me until I look over.

It's Aubrey Fisher.

I turn away from her as fast as I can, not wanting to make it seem obvious I noticed. She clears her throat. That's when I see the white and blue sweatpants/hoodie combo she wears over the fishnet and nylon leggings. They are the decade-old gym uniforms the administration keeps for the dress code violators. One inappropriate outfit and you're forced to walk around all day dressed like a loser, complete with the mascot of an eagle printed inside the school colors. She slouches in her chair, stretches her legs, and taps her inner thighs to a rhythmic beat. Her feet point inward.

I glance up at the secretary and note the look I see on every adult's face around Aubrey. One of hesitation. Teachers, TAs, the guidance counselors, and even the lunch ladies give the same exact expression when she walks by. As if they don't know what to expect or how to act. Like she is some kind of social leper or dangerous psycho.

She just showed up at the school one day, unannounced and unprepared, a little over two months ago. No explanation or reason. I never see her around with a friend. Not one.

There were a few weeks toward the beginning when I'd see her walk the halls or hang outside by the bleachers to smoke a cigarette. No one talked to her because hanging out by the track field to smoke didn't make people friends. Not at our school.

I feel bad. People spread rumors about her relentlessly, yet she keeps a cool demeanor. Carefree. Like everyone and everything is inconsequential. She'd been placed in a foster family that lived just inside the school district. The Bells. They were a nice enough family, from what my parents would say when the topic came up, but no one really knew much about them.

There are rumors, of course, but no one knows what really happened to her family. Maybe the administrators and teachers do, but they never let on. They are just as intimidated by her attitude as we are. No one wants to talk to her. No one wants to look at her.

Rumor is, Aubrey Fisher only speaks to the people she plans to destroy.

"What are you in for?" Aubrey turns to me, interrupting my thoughts, and asks in a hoarse, scratchy voice. Like she'd been up all night screaming.

It sounds...

Kind of...

Sexy?

"Huh?" I whip my head in her direction, stretching my ribcage in the process. I cringe and slump in my seat. It's the first time I've heard her voice. "N-nothing." My cheeks flush.

She stares at me. My eyes are drawn to the hoop in her nose. She looks so drastically different from every other girl in my class. I don't know why, but I find her as fascinating as I do scary. My heart races. She raises her eyebrows, still silent.

"What—Uh," I clear my throat. "What are you here for?"

Smooth, Gray. Really smooth. She's going to think you're stupid.

She looks at me, and the corner of her mouth turns up in a smirk. Her head cocks slightly to the side, studying me again. She doesn't blink.

Do you have something on your face? Is it a booger?

She nods her head once and turns back around. I wait for Aubrey to answer my question, but she never does. The weird thing is, I think she knows why I'm here. Why I'm waiting for the Principal.

After another minute, Kyle walks out. Mr. Hoch follows, stops at the entrance to his office, and calls my name. I stand as they turn to face me.

The bald security guard straightens his back, and I think he gives a strange look to Aubrey. It leaves a weird taste in my mouth. I shake it away.

"Is there something you would like to say, Kyle?" Mr. Hoch prompts.

Kyle scratches his chin and clears his throat. He extends a hand, and I hesitantly shake it. But I know he's only doing it because he has to. Still, he has a weird expression. Like he's lost something he knows won't come back.

"I'm sorry for kicking you in gym class. You didn't deserve that." He squeezes hard.

And then I see it: the cold November night at the party. Remember the icy streets and the light flakes of snow that fell from the sky. Remember how he and I buddied-up for beer pong against Reefer and some sophomore. How we won because we always played together. We were the team to beat at any party.

Stop thinking about it!

"Good, Mr. Sanders. Now, Officer Randle will escort you off school grounds for the remainder of today's suspension. Detention starts next week. I expect that paper on the psychology of violence in this office when you come in on Monday. Understood?"

"You got it, sir!" he mocks enthusiastically.

Mr. Hoch frowns. I want to laugh because it's just like Kyle to be a smartass. But I don't. Reefer's dad doesn't care, but he has to pretend like he does.

He turns to walk away. There is a barely audible "Hmphh" next to me, and out of the corner of my eye, Aubrey's foot shoots out. Just quick enough to trip Kyle. He pinwheels his arms behind his back and flies into the front office window, slamming his shoulder into the doorframe. He cries out as he hits with a *BANG* that vibrates the ground. Aubrey tucks her feet back under her chair and plays with a strand of hair.

"Miss Fisher!" Mr. Hoch calls out, crossing his arms over his white shirt and red tie. "That's enough." He squints and grits his teeth. "I'll speak with you in a few minutes. Think you can behave yourself until then?"

She laughs silently to herself. Turns to me and winks.

Behind me, Kyle rights himself and grabs the backpack he left in a vacant chair by the door. He eyes me once, the pained look from before still on his face, and walks out with Officer Randle. When I look back at Aubrey, she is no longer laughing.

She slumps back down in the chair, stretches her legs, and taps the same beat on her thigh.

I want to say thank you. To say I appreciate it. But she never looks back up. Drawing in a breath, I grab my backpack, wince as I inch forward, and step into the Principal's office.

21 Hours Until

FRIDAY, 9:51 AM

The office is silent after I sit down. Unnervingly silent. Mr. Hoch eases himself into a wheelie-chair and folds his arms on the mahogany desk. A planner, with meetings and notes jotted in indecipherable cursive, spans the length. His computer sits at the corner closest to him, a wireless keyboard propped up on a few books. Pictures of Reefer are scattered about, as are used fast food wrappers and utensils. It looks like the inside of Reefer's Buick.

Against the wall closest to us is a rack filled with cheesy, hokey, and unhelpful pamphlets. Along with the one his secretary gave me a few months ago when I was sent down here for being uncooperative in class, there are a plethora more—each color-coded in some vibrant neon to mask the depressing topics underneath. A few include the following:

SO YOU'RE A TEEN AND PREGNANT...
GOSSIP: SPREAD THE RUMOR OF LOVE
**BE FASHIONABLE: HOW SELF-CONFIDENCE IS
THE NEW "BLACK"**

ASSAULT: YOUR MILKSHAKE AND THE BOYS IN THE YARD
WHEN YOU'RE NOT YOU: DEALING WITH FEELINGS
BELIEVING YOURSELF BETTER

They don't get much better after those. Have a problem? Take a pamphlet! It'll solve all your issues.

I squint from the sunlight that filters through the half-open blinds and drum my fingers on the tips of my knees.

Mr. Hoch sighs, darting his eyes to his marvelous self-help rack. "How are you doing, Gray?"

"I'm okay."

"This is the second time you've had to come down to my office this week."

"It was just a misunderstanding." I look down at my feet. "That's all."

"Yes. That's what Kyle said as well." He taps his index finger on the mahogany. "Between you and me, I think it's that Eggers kid that's the problem. His father was a bully when we were younger. They're a bunch of buffoons, that family." He smiles. "Excluding Mr. and Miss Sanders, of course."

"Of course." I force a smile. "Reefer likes to call them Neanderthalic."

"Really? My son?"

I nod.

"I didn't think he knew big words like that."

"I don't think any of us did, sir."

"And please, just between us, call him Brian." He fans out his hands as if releasing something. "No matter how many times I hear that nickname, it never makes sense. But I don't want to know where it came from." He folds his hands back on the desk.

"When you have kids, Gray, you'll find that it's sometimes better to not ask questions."

"I've learned to stop asking him anything years ago."

Mr. Hoch chuckles and sits up straight, steeples his fingers. "On with the matter. Are you sure there's not anything else going on?"

I shake my head.

"This is a safe place. You can talk to me in here; think of me as more of a friend than administration if you feel more comfortable. I know it might be weird because you and Brian are close. But whatever you tell me stays in this office."

"Honestly, Mr. Hoch, it wasn't Kyle's fault. It's not about Reef—I mean Brian. I appreciate the offer, but I'm fine."

My chest tightens, like my lungs are slowly shriveling up.

"And everything is okay at home as well?" He straightens a few papers on the desk. "With your parents?"

"Yes."

"And your father's store is still doing well?"

"Yeah. More or less."

"Good. And..." He rifles through a manila folder. "I assume they've had a chance to look at last month's report card?"

"They're not happy about it. But they know."

He stops what he's doing and looks at me. I know he doesn't buy it. It's written all over his face. He can read through the lies and sense something deeper.

"Do they, Gray?"

"Mm-hmm."

I shift uncomfortably in my seat and wipe a layer of sweat from my forehead. The room starts to tilt sideways, and I know I'll start to panic if I don't control the anxiety. In my lap, I pinch the vein in my wrist until my entire arm goes numb.

Mr. Hoch looks disappointed. I note his puffy cheeks and stocky build, like Reefer's. And as I sit here staring into Mr.

Hoch's eyes, I can't help but see Reefer's disapproving look. The one I've grown used to over the past six months whenever he knows I've lied to him.

He rifles through a few more papers on the desk. "It troubles me because you were always such a bright student." More shuffling. "Tutor for regular and AP English. According to my son, you share original work online. I've seen some; they're quite good." He glances up at me and then down at the file. "And even though yearbooks are on the last leg of being finalized, you were voted the junior class superlative of Most Likely to... Succeed/Be Famous. That was voted back in fall. Hmm."

Not anymore.

"That's cool," I half lie.

"It troubles me," he says, closing the file, "because the man in front of me today is not the same man that will be printed in this yearbook." He steeples his fingers again. "I've known you and your parents for years, Gray. Tell me what to do to help, and I will do it. Please."

"Am I suspended too?"

"No. You'll have detention all next week with Mr. Sanders. But you can't afford to miss another day of school if you don't want to repeat your junior year. I'll write you a slip for your next class so they don't mark it against you."

Mr. Hoch puts down the manila folder and reaches under a stack of books for a pink pad of paper. He scribbles something illegible across the front and signs his name at the bottom.

"Are you and Brian going to the party tonight?"

"There's a party tonight?"

"You're a good kid, Gray. I don't want you getting into any *trouble* if you do. It's barbaric, those parties. But, as your Principal, I suppose I'm required to say that."

Even I can hear the inflection in his voice. And I know he's referring to what happened last time. Not anyone, even Reefer's dad, can say it to me directly. Like I wasn't there.

"Yeah, I guess. I didn't know about it. What makes you think we would get in trouble?"

He hesitates. "Because I know how intense this time of year gets for the upperclassmen. And I dread whatever the new senior prank will be. Incidentally, I also know my own son."

"You have a good point, Mr. Hoch."

"I used to tell his mom he was switched at birth; it would certainly explain a lot. I don't understand half of what he's saying. He abbreviates things I never knew could be abbreviated... it's fascinating how derivative everything he says is."

"Another good point." I grin.

He hands me the slip, and I notice the patch of skin on his ring finger that is whiter than the rest.

What the heck?

"Be good, Gray. Without you, Brian would be... well..."

"Tell me about it." I nod, titter. "He's definitely a character."

Mr. Hoch assesses me from head to toe, searches for something I'm hiding. We lock eyes for a second, and he seems worried, like I'm standing over a ledge and looking down. I tuck the note into my pocket and turn around. I want to stay and tell him how guilty I feel. How sorry I'll be to leave his son behind. But I don't.

No one should have to deal with my problems but me.

He jumps out from his desk and extends a hand to the rack of pamphlets. He hands me a neon green one, hesitant.

"Here, take this. Maybe it'll help."

"Thanks. I'll take a look." I grab it.

IF YOU'RE GOING TO FAIL, FAIL AT FAILING!

∾

Principal Hoch follows after me as I walk into the lobby of the main office, put the pamphlet in my pocket. Aubrey is seated in the same spot and position as before. Mr. Hoch calls her inside as I walk past. She blows out air so her crimson bangs puff up and fall back down.

She doesn't say anything, but before she trudges over to his office door, Aubrey salutes me. It's so unexpected and random that I can only think to grin like an idiot and wave back. She doesn't react, but turns away as Mr. Hoch ushers her into his office and shuts the door.

But there is a look, a promise in her eyes as she salutes that makes me think it isn't over, that this isn't a goodbye.

She's telling me: "I'll see you later."

My footsteps echo over the hallway tiles. It's always eerie walking alone when everyone is in class. Yet, there is a comfort in the silence.

I wrinkle my nose at the lingering scent of a stink bomb someone had set off yesterday, and at the way random flyers and posters are taped sporadically onto bulletin boards, lockers—a few scattered on the dirty floors. It's strange how these hallways feel so comforting yet scary. I extend my hands at each side to feel the air tickle my fingertips. It's beautiful—calming when nothing else is.

A hall monitor stops me to verify the pink slip and tells me to hurry to class. I drop off my first-period books in my locker and stuff new ones in my backpack. Like before, there is something stashed on the top shelf. I pull it out and find a yellowed receipt from the restaurant where I took Kris for our first date back when we were freshmen: Santoro's. It's the only Italian restaurant we have in town. Next to it is a folded piece of notebook paper. Inside, scrawled in orange gel pen:

> I know you don't want to talk to me. I get it. I wish I could hate you and just pretend like I don't care like you do. But I can't. I'm not wired like that. Because I know you're hurting inside, and I wish you could just accept it and let me in. Let Kyle back in and stop provoking him. I still love you. Soo much. I won't give up on you--just know that. Okay? I put this in your locker to show you that I know the boy who took me here on our first date is still there. He hasn't gone anywhere. He just went away for a little while. And I can't wait until he comes back to us.
>
> Love,
> Kris XoXo

My hands shake, and I crumple the note, receipt, pamphlet, and the picture Kris left from earlier. I imagine tearing them all into shreds and scattering the pieces like snowflakes. But I don't.

And then it comes back: Kris screaming. The smell of smoke and burned rubber. The bright lights. The blood dripping from her hairline. How she reached out a hand to me, and I grabbed it. Tried to move, but my head was spinning. Everything sounded muffled and hollow.

I bash my head repeatedly into the locker to snap out of it. I do it until I fall to my knees. My head pounds, and the ceiling and floor swap places for a moment before jumping back into position. I stand back up and hear the echo of feet coming my way. I swing the backpack over my shoulder, shake away the dizziness, and head to class.

~

"Aubrey Fisher?"

"Aubrey Fisher."

"Like... *the* Aubrey Fisher."

"Yes."

"Dude... like... Aubrey-frickin-Fisher, man."

"You've said this already."

"And you're still alive... why?"

Reefer and I walk together after third period, head toward study hall. No one pays us any attention. It's expected when walking with Reefer. No one messes with the Principal's son.

"It was weird. I can't explain it."

"So she tripped him, and Kyle did nothing?"

"He just walked out with school security."

"I guess the mighty do fall hard. Hmm." He barely avoids a freshman who steps around him. "My dad gave you one of his prized self-help pamphlets?"

"Sure did."

"Gosh, he hates those things."

"He does?"

"Totes. School board makes him hand them out. Gross, right?"

"Titles are entertaining at least."

He wiggles around another crowded space. "You sure Aubrey didn't put some kind of voodoo curse on you? Heard she traveled with gypsies for a time."

"Do gypsies practice voodoo? Also, pretty sure that's an offensive term."

"Hell if I know." He burps, accidentally bumps his elbow

into a skinny kid carrying a stack of papers. They fly up in the air, but Reefer catches a few and hands them back when the kid regains his composure. "But I would be careful, Gray-Gray. Rumor is that she was asked to homecoming at her old school by some guy on lacrosse. At the dance, for no reason what-so-freaking-ever, she knocked out his teeth, and then when the chaperones called her foster parents, she hot-wired their car and drove it into some random dude's pool. And that was *only* 'cause she got bored at the dance. Girls got some lady-balls... gotta admit that."

"That's pretty messed up. But it doesn't seem like—"

"Dude! That's not even the best of it. Jenna heard another rumor that homegirl seduced a teacher somewhere else and got his pedophilic ass fired for rape... and that was because he gave her a B- on a frickin' algebra assignment. Like... shit's whack. She's *mental*, bro."

I look around as groups of kids walk and talk. A few laugh and text on their phones, not watching where they're going.

Chaos.

My head still throbs from the locker.

"It wasn't like that. She seemed... I don't know. Seemed like she was trying to tell me something."

"Yeah. That she's saving you for next on her *list*!"

"Seriously, Reefer. Shut up for a second."

For a moment he looks hurt, but it's quickly replaced by his trademark goofy grin.

"Okay, I'll bite. So why would she help you? 'Cause she feels bad? She senses the injustice of the system? 'Cause she has a schoolgirl crush?" He pauses and jumps up when an idea comes. "Oh! Gray! I bet you she has, like, a life-size cardboard cutout of you in her shrine room. The Shrine of Gray... or Gray Shrine... yes... she prays to it, probably blood oath ritual type stuff. Stays up in her crypt because, let's face it, homegirl is down with the dark side." He spreads his arms wide as if constructing a symphony. "She dreams of your dreamy eyes, Gray."

"Yeah, I don't think she does a single one of those things. You're trying too hard."

"I just want you to be careful. We know *literally* nothing about this girl... not a single thing. We don't know who she is, where she came from, or what she's done. She's trouble... you can't handle that."

"What's that supposed to mean?"

"Nothing." His eyes flicker away. "And no one hurts my buddy, 'cause you're mine... not in a sexual sense, but like in a vampire claiming a human."

"So in a sexual sense."

"No, Gray."

"Yes, Reef."

"Damn... it is sexual, isn't it?"

"Vampires are sex personified."

"Eh, I'm too good looking for you, anyway."

We arrive at study hall just as the bell is about to ring; my head keeps pounding. I can't help but hear the words echo in my head:

Aubrey Fisher is trouble.

20 HOURS UNTIL

FRIDAY, 10:39 AM

KRIS SITS AT THE DESK, FACES FORWARD WITH HER NOSE IN a textbook. Occasionally she uncaps her pink highlighter to mark a passage and continues. She won't settle until any task is completed to the best of her ability. It's the perfectionist in her. It's one of her best traits, one I admire. Even in study hall, a throwaway period most use to hang out with friends, she still does her work. Everything Kris has, she earns.

I take a seat on the opposite side of the room at the beginning of fourth period, next to Reefer and Jenna.

Kris hunches over her book, highlights another passage, and places a loose strand of blonde hair behind her ear. She lifts up her head and glances over her right shoulder. She knows I'm staring, so I turn my head.

"Did you guys hear about a party tonight?" I ask.

"Heck yes we have." Reefer slams his hand onto the desk. "But hell no are we going. Tim is throwing it."

Jenna rolls her eyes. "I have better things to do with my time. I'm babysitting my cousin tonight, then I'll find a quiet indie on streaming to watch after she's asleep."

"You should both go," I say as I glance back at Kris. "Everyone will be there."

Reefer shakes his head. "No. Gray-Gray. No."

"What's going on?" Jenna looks behind at Kris. "Oh."

"Gray. Jesus Christ, no. Just no."

"Stop saying that." I take a deep breath, turn around. "You don't even know what I was going to say."

"Actually, I do." Reefer rolls his eyes. "Please don't be the lame guy pining over the ex that *he*, meaning *you*, dumped. It's such a cliché."

Jenna twirls a pen in her fingers. "He's got a point, Gray."

"And here I thought the lady detested me," Reefer says. He reaches for her hand, but she pulls it away.

I let out air through pursed lips and clench my jaw. "Can we just go one day without your usual sarcastic comments that aren't really that funny to begin with?"

Reefer looks hurt. Jenna sits back uncomfortably like she is ready for a sparring match.

Control. Your. Temper. He's your best friend. Don't be a jerk.

"I'm sorry."

Reefer nods, his eyes on fire. "No worries. Guess I had that coming."

It's awkwardly silent. I glance over at Kris again and find her book face-down on the desk, her head cocked in our direction, but her gaze focused on the whiteboard up front. She fixes a strap on her orange sundress and crosses one leg over the other. Her dress pulls up as she does, revealing part of her tanned thigh. I close my eyes.

"You guys have such a weird relationship." Jenna indicates me and Reefer. "Like Robert Redford and Paul Newman." She taps her pen on my hand. "You guys want to help me study for the Global test I have later today? I'm *so* going to fail this."

"I'm sorry. *WHAT*?" Reefer points a finger at me. "You said we didn't have a Global test today!"

"We don't."

"Then why is Freckles talking about a test?"

Jenna grimaces. "I *really* hate when you call me that."

"Ohmygod. I'm done for. You've overcooked me, Gray-Gray. You've literally dipped me in a deep fryer and cooked my ass. I'm barely pulling a C+ in there. My dad is going to *kill* me."

"Again," I say, "we don't have a—"

"Let me see your notes," he cuts me off and reaches for Jenna's tote bag on the floor. "I need to cram for seventh period now. Not cool, bro." He lets out a playful grunt. "You and this Korean tote bag."

"You do realize"—Jenna jumps up to grab her binders as Reefer pulls them out—"that we have different teachers, right? You and Gray probably don't have a test because your class is a few days behind mine." She pinches his arm until he emits a yelp, causing a few kids to gawk. Jenna blushes. "And again, I don't own solely Korean things. I was born in America. I've never even been to Korea. My parents don't want me to go there."

Reefer pauses; his eyes dart from side to side. "Right... That would make sense..."

"Does he always freak out like this?"

I grin. "More or less."

"I'm sorry you have to suffer through it."

"That makes two of us."

"We should definitely, like, stick together."

"Like *Butch Cassidy and the Sundance Kid*?"

"Gray!" she gushes. "You understood one of my references."

"Hey!" Reefer punches me in the arm. "I knew about that lame movie too." He returns a white binder to Jenna and sits back down. "Alright, enough of this drama and stress. I get enough of that every day, no offense. But, Frecks, please give me something. Kris is old news, and my love life is the biggest joke in the world right now."

"What about Mrs. Carmichael?" I butt in.

"Work in progress. But really, I've got man-tits and love handles. Not many ladies of the female variety are into that at our age... or into guys less than half their age."

I purse my lips. "Don't ladies always fall into the female variety?"

Reefer strokes his chin, feigning deep reflection. "True. They do. Unless they're a man."

"Right, because that's pretty common."

"You'd be surprised."

"I happen to think your man-boobs are very attractive."

"Aw... don't make me blush." Reefer reaches over to flick my earlobe. I swat his hand away.

Jenna groans. "I can't handle you two. I just can't. I'm sorry—this is so weird. You both are so weird, if not a tad offensive."

"Right," Reefer says. "That's a compliment. You guys bring out the worst in me. Anyways, any luck with that sophomore you were trying to pursue, Frecks? The one on the swim team."

Jenna scrunches her face. "Reefer, that was, um, months ago. Why are you bringing this up?"

"No reason... forget I asked."

Jenna shrugs her shoulders. "No guy at this school deserves me until they really appreciate the beauty of Orson Welles. *Citizen Kane*? Ohmygawd! Talk about en media res—"

I nod and steal one more look at Kris as they continue to go back and forth. This time, however, her book is closed in her lap and the highlighter capped on the desk. She sits upright and straightens her orange headband. Turns in my direction. Grabs her gold cross necklace.

"Are you going to talk to me or just keep staring at me all period, Gray?"

Reefer and Jenna stiffen next to me but keep on arguing. I stare blankly, consider my choices.

"Desperate is not attractive on you, Kris."

And I immediately regret it.

Kris's mouth turns down; her fist clenches. Behind me, Jenna and Reefer's stunned silence resonates. No one else seems to notice or care.

I look back at Reefer, and he shakes his head, disappointed. That's when I know I've reached another new low.

Kris turns away, clears her throat, and uncaps her highlighter to get back to work.

I say goodbye to Reefer and Jenna and start to walk to my locker when Kris taps me on the shoulder, grabs my wrist, and turns me around. Her face is flushed, and her mouth a thin line of contempt.

"Don't ever talk to me like that again. I deserve better."

She breathes out air through her nostrils, and the hot air on my lip sends chills across the nape of my neck. She pushes an orange-painted nail into my chest, right below the bruise. For a moment I think she'll touch it, cause me pain, but she nearly misses. Even without trying, she's always thinking of everyone besides herself. Making sure I'm not hurt.

"I heard what happened with Tim in P.E. today. My cousin is a jerk. But then you tried to pick a fight with my brother instead. What is *going on* with you? Stop, please stop this."

I fling her hand off my wrist and raise my arms in surrender.

"When will you get that I just want to be left alone? Why are you so insistent and clingy?"

Kris glances over her shoulder, embarrassed to make a scene, so she grabs my wrist again and pulls me over to a far corner of the hallway next to a bank of lonely lockers. She lowers her chin and speaks in barely a whisper, even though no one walking to class pays us any attention.

"You forget that I know you, and this act is a cry for attention. So don't patronize me or treat me like I'm some throwaway doll. It's disgusting and cowardly. You're better than this, and I know I am too."

"Kris—"

"No, you don't get to cut me out without a fight. Especially when you haven't even *asked* how my dad is or how my mom's been holding together. Or even how I've been doing."

"Jesus Christ, I'm not talking about this with you."

"You're not the only one with regrets. News flash: we all made choices that night."

I storm away from Kris and down a few hallways. Try to out-walk her without having to run, but she's in step with my pace—corners me at my locker like I knew she would. Persistence. Another classic Kris trait. I know I should stop and ask. Talk to her. But even now, I can't. Like too much time has passed for it to really mean anything.

"We had plans, Gray. And suddenly we're done? Not even friends?"

"Stop."

I fumble with my combination, but the numbers scatter in my brain. Each incorrect spin of the dial causes me to start over. I pound my fist into the locker in frustration. Feel the rage start to boil over. The rolling waves. The ticking in my head.

"You know I don't blame you for anything. But really? Do you even care if my da—" She stops herself. Takes a deep breath. "You won't even talk to me about your parents. How are—"

"I swear to God, Kris. You need to stop right now."

My stomach rolls. My head throbs. My eyelids flutter as a sensation like a sharp needle presses into the backs of my corneas. I try to shake away the feeling but become dizzy and fall into the locker. Everything Kris says starts to jumble together, like ink running down paper after being dipped into a bucket of water.

"...should call your parents and Bryson's..."

I need her to stop. But my heartbeat jacks into overdrive, and before I know what's happening, my hands are pressed into her shoulders. Her back is against my locker, and I'm breathing into her hair. Squeezing away the haze.

"...hurting me..."

And then it's gone. Like a filter is lifted. And I can see the fear on her face. My fingers digging into her shoulders. I pull them away, and her skin is red and indented from my grip.

Her eyes are open wide. Her mouth closed. Fear. She is afraid. And before I know what to say, how to tell her how sorry I am, she slaps me.

Once.

Twice.

And a voice behind me: "Get off her, man! What the hell?"

I stumble backward, my hands shaking. And I feel sick like I'll vomit.

Did you slam her into the locker? Did you assault her?

"I'm s—"

But the words don't come. Get stuck in a throat full of phlegm. Tears prickle my eyes. I'd never do anything to hurt her.

Never.

From somewhere to my right: "Kris? What's going on?"

And she's looking at me like I'm a monster. A villain. And maybe she's right. But it doesn't stop the sharp pain-like dagger that pierces my heart.

"Jesus Christ, are you okay?"

And her eyes open wider, water up. She presses her palm into her mouth and leans into a nearby locker. I go to reach out a hand to help calm her, but she flinches. I pull my hand back.

And then I'm running away down one hallway and another. Past open classrooms and cluttered hallways. My phone vibrates in my pocket, so I pull it out once I reach the music wing. Blue walls with posters of famous Broadway musicals surround me, and the hallway seems to close in. I pull out my phone and try to gasp for a breath, but my lungs won't work. Sweat rolls down my forehead, and I fall to my knees. Fluorescent lights above meet the floor tiles below.

UNKNOWN

u should treat ur friends better

never kno when theyll b gone

And I fall over onto my side, gasping and clutching at my chest as the waves wash over me. Struggling to breathe. To think. To find my bearings.

You hit Kyle and assaulted Kris. You've lost control. You need to end it. Now. Before someone else you love gets hurt.

"Hey! You okay?" a voice calls to me.

I hear a rush of footsteps as they collide with the tiles, then hands pull me up. All of a sudden, my lungs begin to work again, and I clutch my chest as I savor each delicious pocket of air that is sucked in. My vision clears; I shake away dizziness.

"Gray? Ohmygawd. Are you okay? Do you need me to take you to the nurse?"

It takes a while, but Jenna's face comes into focus.

"Put your arm around me. I'm going to walk you down to the nurse. Okay?"

I shake my head, note the concerned look in her eyes. She'll tell Reefer about this. It's as clear as day.

"I'm fine. T-Thank you, though."

"Stop it. You're totally not fine. I saw what happened in the hallway."

"You were there?"

"Yeah, um, I was. I was going to help you, but—"

I hold out my hand, my eyes briefly look down at her breasts, and I hate that I even felt the need to look. "It's okay, Jenna."

Her voice raises an octave. "Is it okay if I sit down for a moment?"

I pat one of the drab green tiles next to me. Jenna sits down.

She bites her lip. "Stupid." She shakes her head. "This is why you have to talk to her, so she knows it's over."

"You know I hurt her, right?"

"What?"

"I think I slammed her into a locker. I... I didn't..."

"Gray..."

We lock eyes. She exhales. Attempts to smile but scoots against one of the blue walls and rests her head.

I don't need her to finish the sentence. I know the answer.

"I'm really sorry. I want to help you out. Reefer won't say it, but he's worried about you too." She pauses, touches my forearm. "I don't think we've ever had one of those serious talks before. Like those scenes in the movies where the characters bare their souls." She hesitates, attempts a smile. "I'm worried about you."

I nod—fight back the tears. "I know." I scoot against the wall with her. "You can tell Reefer not to worry if he is. I'm just tired, that's all. I don't want you to worry either."

"Do you want me to—"

I shake my head and exhale. And there's a shift in the air between us. Subtle. But it's there. I can't really place my finger on what exactly, so I let it go. I wish Reefer were here, so it could be the three of us, like old times. Laughing, joking, and watching ancient movies in Jenna's basement. How it used to be—an infinite time.

But I also know that this will be the last time I might see Jenna. We don't have any more classes together, and I don't want to leave her like this. I want it to be a nice memory for her. So I stand up and help her to her feet. Force away the humiliation with Kris.

"If this is one of your movies, then I would be both honored and obligated to tell you that you look beautiful today." I stand straight, bend down, and kiss the back of her hand.

Her face turns red, and she curtsies. "Why, thank you, Mr. Darcy."

She giggles. I force a smile. And I hate myself.

19 HOURS UNTIL

I WALK OUT OF THE LUNCH LINE WITH A TEAL TRAY FOR fifth period. On it is an order of ten mozzarella sticks, four mini breadsticks, two ladles of marinara sauce, and two chocolate milks. It's one of my favorite lunches; hence, I order double. And, oddly enough, it seems right. I stand outside the doors where kids line up to pay for their food. Several place their books and purses on tables. Some lean on the edges to talk to other kids. The voices grow louder. I close my eyes and note the scent of freshly baked cinnamon rolls from my left.

In the back row of circular tables, by the windows, is an empty section where no one sits. It's my usual spot—Jenna and Reefer have lunch during a different period. I don't realize how hungry I am until I plop into a blue plastic chair and dip a mozzarella stick into the sauce, bite in, and watch as the cheese stretches before tearing off.

The windows stream in sunlight; it's beautiful how it reflects bodies as they walk past outside—casts their shadows. Two lunch monitors walk back and forth. Both look bored, spending more time on their phones than supervising. A group of freshman boys line up at the vending machines to get chips, soda, and candy bars. Down the cafeteria are a few cheerleaders and jocks at the popular table. It's all predictable. So common. So expected.

But that's when it happens.

When she just throws herself into a chair beside me, like she can't support her body weight anymore. She rubs her nose, brushes the hoop pierced there, and slouches down. She no longer has the sweatpants/hoodie combo. She is back in her fishnets over nylons. I look closely at the thin layer of black eyeliner, possibly the only bit of makeup she bothers to wear.

Aubrey doesn't look away. It's unnerving. I feel compelled to say something, so I clear my throat. Nothing comes.

She stares.

I stare.

She continues staring.

I desperately want her to look away.

She remains still.

I look down, fidget hands in my lap.

"I win," she says in her raspy voice.

I raise my head and nod. Clear my throat and feel my face flush. Embarrassed.

On one hand, this is NOT how my last lunch is supposed to go. And yet... it feels strangely exciting having a staring contest with the mysterious Aubrey Fisher.

What is her deal?

She grins. "Hungry?"

"Uh—" I look down at my double lunch and suddenly feel like my stomach is inflating. Like it will burst like a balloon. She probably thinks I'm fat. "N-Not really."

She licks her lower lip, and I glimpse a metallic ball in the center of her tongue. Aubrey turns her head, pivots toward the popular table. Then she turns back to face me. Silent.

I'm being challenged to talk first.

"S-So, are you going to eat something?"

"Forgot my lunch money," she says bluntly, without a moment's hesitation. Like she knew what I was going to ask ahead of time.

"Oh, uh, right. Did you want some of mine?"

She looks down at my food and back up at me. "I'm lactose intolerant."

"Right."

Aubrey leans back in the chair and beams, puts one foot over the other, and points her toes inward. She brushes the red bangs past her eye before they fall back. My heart is ready to jump out on the table into the marinara sauce, and I don't know why she's having this effect on me.

The next words spew out of my mouth before I have a chance to bottle them.

"Why are you sitting here?"

"I find you interesting."

"You find *me* interesting?"

"Yeah. Want to get outta here?"

"You mean eat somewhere else?"

"No. I mean school. Ditch. Leave. Play hooky. Live on the edge, you know. Something *fun*."

"Umm..."

A girl wearing a death metal shirt walks past us with her tray without a glance. Like it's normal for me and Aubrey to be eating together.

"What else have you got to do today?"

"I don't really—"

"C'mon. Live a little."

It feels like I'm being challenged by her, and yet, I can't seem to shut my mouth.

"That's just—"

"Spontaneous? Yeah. That's the point."

"No. I mean... why me?"

"Because, like you, *it* would be interesting."

For some reason, I feel calm around her. Like she has this aura of protectiveness.

Somewhere to the right, a boy makes a farting noise, followed by scattered laughter.

"Is this a joke, Aubrey?"

Gray Falconi: Fool, or Name-Addressing Badass With a Death Warrant?

She raises her eyebrows. "Does it seem like a joke... *Grayson?*"

Shivers jolt up my spine at the sound of my name rolling off her tongue. No one uses my full name.

No one.

Behind Aubrey, a few tables down, is Kris. She has a tray in her hand. She stops mid-stride, her eyes wide, and freezes in place.

This is awkward. But then I note Aubrey's curious eyes. Hazel. Almost like an orangish hue, but I can't figure out exactly what they resemble. Such a curious and beautiful color on her.

Aubrey knows how embarrassing it is, what it does to me. It's all an act, scripted. How much of it is planned, I don't know. But it doesn't feel natural, real. Yet, I can't help but find something enticing about the offer. To ditch school with Aubrey Fisher.

"I, uh, I have to—"

"Well, isn't this fitting." Tim walks up behind Aubrey. His eyes watch her intently, fearful. His curly hair too big for his face. "Two freaks eating lunch together. I texted Kyle. Can't wait to see his response."

My hands clench at my sides. Kris frowns and puts down her tray, looking conflicted, and walks over. A lunch monitor to the side has her head in her phone.

This will be bad. Very bad.

"Tim..." Kris hisses, avoids meeting my eyes. She stops behind Aubrey, looks at the back of her head, and takes a few steps to the side. Aubrey continues to stare at me, and a smile slowly spreads across her lips. She's entertained.

I can't figure out what it means. Any of it.

"Now, I know you two might go home later today with a suicide pact or something. Right? Blood oath?"

Oh, the irony.

"Tim!" Kris nudges his shoulder. "What is wrong with you?"

"So do us all a favor and—"

He stops as soon as Aubrey whips her head in his direction. She squints and stands up from the chair. It falls to the floor behind her. She doesn't say a word but steps a foot forward. Tim takes a step back, looks around, and laughs nervously.

The lunch monitor raises one eye to us, keeps the other on her phone. Typical.

Kris turns to me. Her coconut perfume wafts my way, and it brings me back to nights lying on her couch with a bowl of popcorn. How she would dig her nails into my forearm whenever she was scared.

Then I catch the marks my fingers made after they dug into her shoulder blades.

It's not how this is supposed to go. Aubrey Fisher isn't supposed to sit down and talk to me, to defend me from anyone. Kris is not supposed to be nice after what happened. Yet, here they both are. By my side.

The lunch monitor reaches the end of our table but doesn't say anything. Not yet.

Aubrey's offer seems more appealing by the second.

Aubrey leans closer to Tim. He takes another step back. It's uncomfortably silent. The lunch monitor inches forward, waiting to jump in once things progress but too preoccupied to really care. And that's when I notice some of the chatter start to die down as the cafeteria senses a scene unfolding around us. Everyone is eager to witness a fight.

Why is Aubrey protecting you? What's in it for her?

"Tim, please," Kris pleads. "Leave them alone."

He rolls his eyes. "Yeah, whatever. Having girls fight your battles now?" He steps to the side of Aubrey in an effort to make an escape, but she shoots her palm out and stops him, catches his upper chest. His eyes get round.

"We don't want any trouble, Aubrey," Kris says. "I'm so sorry. My cousin is a jerk. They all are, sweetie."

Aubrey twitches as if the thought of being called "sweetie" repulses her. Kris freezes.

Tim rotates a few bracelets on his wrist, raises an eyebrow, and shrugs. Aubrey doesn't lower her arm from his chest. His eyes are still as wide as lenses.

"Okay, that's quite enough for today," the lunch monitor mock-orders. "Move it along, now."

"We are, Mrs. Decker," Kris says. "I'm sorry about all this. It's just a silly misunderstanding." She bites her lip at me, straightens her orange headband.

I don't realize I'm holding my breath until I release the air through my lips. For a second everything seems fine until Tim reaches his bracelet-covered arm down to the table, picks up a mozzarella stick that was dipped in marinara sauce, and throws it at my face. It smacks me on the forehead and falls to the table. Marinara wets my eyebrow. A few kids laugh along with Tim as he licks some sauce from his finger. The girl with the death metal shirt starts to slam her chair up and down. And that's when I realize the entire cafeteria is turned toward us. We have the monitor's full attention.

Six months ago, this situation would've been reversed. Tim

and I never got along, but he would never publicly humiliate me. Kris would be scrambling to fight the injustice instead of looking at me with pitiful eyes. And if anyone did start any bullying, Kyle and I would put an end to it.

How fast things can change.

"Just fight already..."

"...money is on Aubrey..."

"Kick his ass, Gray!"

"...boy's been through enough..."

The lunch monitor moves between Tim and Aubrey but is pushed to the side in the commotion. And then it happens.

Aubrey releases an audible "Mmph" through her lips and grabs my tray from the table. She flicks her wrist and smashes the tray's edge directly into his throat. Tim coughs and raises his hands to his throat, his head flying backward, but Aubrey grabs a handful of his shirtfront and yanks it down. She does it too fast for Tim to react in time, and his head bounces off the table with a *BOOM*. In a flash, she lets go of his shirt and places her hands on the back of his head before he has a chance to get his bearings. Aubrey shoves his forehead onto the table two more times before yanking him backward and sending him flying into an empty chair. Tim rolls over the top and falls to the ground.

Two guys in lacrosse varsity jackets stand up and dash our way, but the closest lunch monitor is already grabbing Aubrey, trying to restrain her. She shoves her away. A freshman with gages in his ear stands off to our left, a full tray in hand, his jaw dropped.

On the edge of the table, there's a tiny spot of blood from Tim's forehead.

The entire cafeteria gasps in succession, like the wave at a stadium. One cheerleader from the popular table yells for a fight. A sophomore trips over a backpack and sends chocolate milk spilling all over the floor. One of the soccer players at another table straddles a chair and pumps his fist in the air.

Chaos.

I jump up from my seat as Aubrey whips her head around. Suddenly, both lunch monitors have their arms around her, and a lunch lady carrying an empty milk crate runs over to Tim, who is groaning and holding his throat where Aubrey connected with his Adam's apple. Blood trickles down the side of his face from a cut above his eye.

Aubrey smiles as they hold her. She doesn't fight it. She raises her eyebrows innocently and turns to me.

"I'll find you. Just think about it."

A few seconds later, two security guards rush to our area. One of them picks up Tim and sits him down in a chair to examine his head, the other pins Aubrey's hands behind her back. It's the same bald guard, Officer Randall, who escorted Kyle off school grounds. She grins at me, revealing straight teeth and a flash of her tongue ring again. Officer Randall begins to walk her out of the room as he runs his palms up and down the sides of her body, checking for weapons.

But for some reason, I get a bad feeling. And I want to chase after her.

How could she hide a weapon when she's barely wearing anything?

A few feet away, Kris and another girl are talking; both point to me and turn around. A few monitors try to control everyone as people settle down and resume eating. People give me funny looks, yet no one says anything. It's as if the fear of Aubrey Fisher has rubbed off. Like everyone is afraid to look at me for too long.

I'm part upset yet also incredibly awed. Aubrey Fisher beat up a guy...

For me.

Kris locks eyes with me. I get the urge to wave, maybe smile. But I don't.

Before I know it, she tiptoes to me and waves goodbye to the girl.

"What was that about?"

I know she means Aubrey, even without having to say it. Her voice cuts deep. Right to the point. So unlike her usual friendly bravado.

Good.

"Didn't you hear Tim?" A beat. "We have a suicide pact." I flash a sarcastic grin, but it makes me feel sick.

"That's not funny, Gray. It's disgusting. Don't joke about that. I... Am I really such a terrible person because I care? Does that make me horrible? Should I act like a cold, heartless jerk like you to make myself feel better?"

I drop the smile immediately. Guilt comes and goes, but I've been playing this game for months now. I can't show weakness. Not when I'm so close to pushing her away forever.

I point to the redness where my nails dug into her shoulders, the skin still raw. "I hurt you."

"Yeah, you did. But you're not yourself; anyone can see that."

"I'll do it again."

"Have you thought of writing anything new?"

The thing I tried to do for so long but could never find the words. Putting my real thoughts down are still too painful. What was once solace for me, a chance to purge myself of negative emotions—even that is gone.

"Why?" I ask. "So people can write *murderer* in the comments again?"

I started deleting my accounts shortly after that.

She shakes her head in pity, winces. "I wish you could only see how important your writing is. It means a lot more than you realize. People still care, Gray." She shifts the weight on her feet, looks at her shoes. "I do."

My breath catches in my throat, and I look away before I have the urge to wrap her in a hug. Kris... so tragically lost and alone, but still supportive. I can't take seeing her upset.

And then there's Tim. Staring at me in front of a row of garbage cans next to the entrance doors of the cafeteria, being escorted to the nurse's office. He has a messenger bag slung over one shoulder, and he doesn't blink.

And there's the sound of the sirens, the shattering of glass, and sharp pain. Kris on an endless loop of screams. Blood. Crimson. Kyle and Kris's dad with the shard of glass: in a coma. Bryson: dead. Kris and her future: erased.

Kill yourself kill yourself kill yourself kill yourself.

"I don't want you to. If you care, you'll leave me alone. Move on and forget I ever existed. Forget about the writing too."

I look above me, but Tim is no longer by the trashcans.

He's gone.

A chill runs up my spine.

"You just can't help yourself from hurting me more, can you?" She flares her nostrils once, another rare sight. "I wake up and tell myself that today will be the day I stop caring about what you do. But that day still hasn't come."

Kris moves to place a hand on my shoulder but stops herself. Still afraid. It hurts us both. I can see the glisten in her eyes, but she doesn't cry. She takes a step back.

I don't stay to rehash more drama and pick a fight. Kris and I could go at it for hours if we wanted to. So I run to my table to pick up my backpack and head out of the cafeteria and toward the bathroom.

And for some reason, I hope that I run into Aubrey again.

~

I splash water on my face, grip the porcelain sink, and stare at my reflection. No one is in here; I make sure to use the custodial bathroom in the old foreign language hall, which is in the back corner of the school that hardly anyone uses anymore except for storage. The sound of the water rushing from the faucet echoes in the room. A few black dots cloud my vision while I sway back and forth on my feet. My phone vibrates in my pocket. I pull it out, and it's from the same unknown number. Goosebumps rise on my forearm.

UNKNOWN

u cant seem 2 stay out of trouble

i kno u

time 2 b honest is now

be4 sum1 gets hurt...

I pull up another video from my channel, ignoring the creepy text. This one was taken about a year ago. Kris is with me. On a dare from Reefer and Kyle, they made us switch clothes while we filmed, so I am wearing Kris's orange halter-top and headband to match over my short hair. I even have her orange bra over my top. Kris is wearing one of my plain blue t-shirts that leave nothing of her boobs up to imagination. She can't help but laugh in the background as her arms are wrapped around my neck, kissing in the back to make me giggle as I read. 9,766 views. 986 likes. 20 dislikes.

"*Greetings again, my beautiful Falconians. Gray here, on a dare from Kyle Sanders and Brian "Reefer" Hoch. Hmm. That's a weird name to say. Anyway. They dared us that we wouldn't do this next posting in drag, so-to-speak, but here we are to prove them wrong. Isn't that right, babe?*"

Kris giggles. "I can't believe you talked me into this..."

I cock my head to kiss the corner of her mouth. "I think we make very attractive opposite gender, um, people." My eyes roll. "That was an awkwardly phrased sentence. Anyway. Here's a short poem I wrote called 'Those Who Live Forever.' I'd tell you why I wrote it, but that takes the fun away. So, here it is. Hope you all enjoy! Like, share, and comment below."

I clear my throat. Kris giggles again, kisses my cheek.

"WANT TO
DROWN
IN YOU––
TIDES RISE UP AND
PULL ME UNDER.
LET COLORS
DRIP
ONTO WHITE CANVAS––
ABSTRACT CONCEPTS
WHERE LIPS WHISPERED
SPECTRUMS.
YOUR HEART WAS
A SCULPTOR,
I, THE SCULPTURED––
OUR PALETTE
NEVER QUITE
IN SEQUENCE.
WATER REFRACTS
LIGHT ENTERED THROUGH––
YOUR RAYS
WERE WAVES
THAT LOVE GOT
SWEPT UP INTO.
I DROWN
OVER AND OVER
WAITING FOR

Your picture to
Wash ashore——
The swell no more.
Like you
My memories fade too——
Shouldn't have left me
To drown.
Death was a game;
You're never quite
The same——
Left me colored
In loneliness.
Shouldn't have
Drank from the
Fountain of youth——
Maybe you'd
Be here too."

After I read it, Kris stands up straight, turns my chair around, and we stare at each other for a while until she runs a hand down my cheek and then kisses me. The video ends right after. I look down at the top comments from back then:

TrackGirlKris: I LOVE you, sweetie. You're amazing!
TheHyunEffect: I just don't even understand why you're not published yet... What if you write a book and it's made into a movie?!?!!?!?!?!?!?
Reefenation69: this is SOosososss GETTING YOU LAIDz!!

And then a few more recent:

HonBon1234567: emo as hell

JamesDeanFan: (responding to HonBon1234567) Say that shit again and I'll find your IP address.

HonBon1234567: (responding to JamesDeanFan) nobody likes u. who is james dean? kill urself!

And most recent:

JamesDeanFan: Awesome. Ignore the haters. Keep being real and honest. It's amazing. YOU'RE the shit.

The memory. Of Kris. Of what we had. Of the poem.
Death.
How the speaker is the one left alive.
I just can't.
So I delete the video forever.
Everything around blurs out of focus, and I'm lightheaded. In a flash of something I can't describe, there is a crash in front of me, followed by a vibration that travels from my knuckles all the way up my arm to my shoulder. I groan and bend my knees until I'm on all fours.

Breathe. Just breathe.

When I steady my oxygen flow, I pull myself up. There are shards of glass in the sink from the mirror above. My knuckles are cut; some blood seeps up to the surface through broken skin. I ignore the pain and reach for a shard of glass. It reflects the lights on the ceiling. The shards lying in the sink under the running water reflect back shattered pieces of me—each one giving a new angle. Each one a distorted image.

My fist shakes as I hold the jagged mirror up and rotate it until my bare neck comes into focus. It can be easy: just a flick of the wrist and a twitch of the arm.

So. Very. Simple.

This is not the plan, Gray. Too messy. Your plan is back at home.

So I drop the shard onto the ground, where it breaks into smaller pieces, and step back from the sink. The walls around close in; my knees wobble.

I look into a broken shard and see Bryson. Smiling through bloodstained teeth.

My fingers find their way to the bruise over my chest. The self-inflicted one. I push down once to feel for the center, ball my hand into a fist, and start to pound away.

THUMP. THUMP. THUMP. THUMP.

Tears want to fall, but I hold them in and beat on. March to an invisible beat. My own personal drum. It takes away the pain. Takes away the memories. Takes away the doubt and fear. Controls my breathing. Clears my vision and settles the ticking in my brain.

THUMP. THUMP. THUMP.

It hurts.

But I want it to.

18 HOURS UNTIL

FRIDAY, 12:03 PM

REEFER TEXTS AND ASKS WHERE I AM, AND HE'S IN THE bathroom within minutes after the bell rings to end fifth period. By now I've calmed down. My chest is on fire from pounding on the already tender bruise, but it works. It always does. Reefer finds me sitting on the floor, collecting the remaining shards of glass into the wastepaper basket. Embarrassed, I don't say a word. The beautiful thing about being friends with him is the knowledge that behind the jokes, he really does care, and he knows when silence is the best comfort.

Reefer cleans up the shards in the sink and carries them to the trash with me. There is a mutual agreement in the silence, an understanding.

Once everything is cleared away, we walk over to sit on the furnace vents by the far wall. We sigh simultaneously, look at each other. It seems like he's waiting for me to say something. To confide some big secret. But I don't. And after a while it's like he's disappointed.

"You know the craziest thing about this whole day?" he asks.

"What's that?"

"Aubrey Fisher."

"Aubrey Fisher?"

"Aubrey Fisher."

I shake my head and grin. "Sadly, you're right."

"Bro, like, she literally talks to *no one*, yet she defends your honor—twice, I might add— and then sits with you at lunch." He's silent. "It's weird."

"How bad is it?"

"Honestly, people are afraid that if they gossip too much, her Spidey-sense is going to kick in, and in turn, she's going to kick them."

"I don't think Spider-man kicks his villains."

"Bull! He can. He just has awesome spider-like abilities, so kicking is beneath his sensibilities."

"Misuse of sensibility, but I get what you're saying."

"I love it when you get all literal on me, Gray." He chuckles. "But I'm serious about correcting my incorrect grammar... cut it."

I shove him and can't help but chuckle too.

I tell him everything that happened with Kris and Tim at lunch, even the weird offer from Aubrey. Reefer has no idea what to make of it either, but he gives a displeased look. So we sit in silence for a while, both ditching sixth period. It's Global II. Test or no test, it doesn't matter anymore. I'm glad it's Reefer with me in this moment. No one else could've been better company.

"You want to take my car and get outta this joint?"

"What?"

"You can take my car and pick me up later, or I'll find a ride home."

"I don't think so."

"So you're going to just hide out in here all day?"

I shrug.

"*Señor Falconi.*" He puts a hand on my shoulder. "As your trusted partner in all things awesome and badass, you need to live a little. Just skip... go out and blow off some steam. You've never skipped school before. It's like a rite of passage before we become seniors next year. I'd come with, but my father would slap the silly out of me... for real."

"Where am I going to go? I can't go home. Mom skipped work today. And my other alternative is to go to the store and help out my dad. But I don't want to have to tell either of them why I left early."

Nice cover.

"There's actually a ton of things you can do that does not involve either of those two options... or your parents. But touché, Gray. Touché." He leans back against the wall. "What do you need from me now?"

"Just a friend. That's all."

"Now you're just being ridiculous. Ohmygod. This is extortion. A friend? You're sick, bro."

I shove him again, force a laugh. "Jerk."

He farts in response.

"You really know how to ruin a good moment."

"Dude. Gas. I told you I had gas today. You can't shove pleasantly plump guys around... they'll flatulate all over you."

"Nice verb use on that one."

"Flatulate? Yeah, bro. I pick up books now and then." He sticks his tongue out.

I can't help but roll my eyes. As much as I don't want to give in, and as much as I know it's only a temporary feeling, I can't suppress the giggles.

And then I smell it.

"That's really bad."

Reefer wafts some in his direction and sniffs. "Not gonna lie, I'm actually ashamed of myself. Might have sharted a little on that one."

Some things will never change, and that is why we're best friends.

I just hope he doesn't change after I'm dead.

Reefer leaves for a few minutes and returns with an armful of vending machine food and soda. Because I never got to finish my lunch, my stomach is still tearing away at my insides. The candy bars and potato chips are doing nothing for my physique. Not to mention the empty calories from the soda.

Reefer munches on a couple candy bars before he checks his phone and sees that sixth period is almost over. He has his Pre-Calculus homework out, and I help with some of it. Funny enough, I know most of the answers and how to solve them.

After the bell rings to end the period, he stuffs papers into his bag and rinses his hands in the sink. "Are you going back to class or hanging out in here the rest of the day?"

"Probably in here," I lie.

"Alright, won't argue that." He reaches into the pocket of his jeans and tosses me the car keys. "But just in case you decide to grow some balls, you can take my car. Just text me to let me know if you plan on picking me up or not."

"I can't take these."

"Too bad, you are." He winks. "I have faith you'll make the right decision. Just don't commit any grand larceny or anything. I'll tell them you sodomized me to get the keys."

"Really? A sodomy joke?"

"You know I have no filter, Gray-Gray."

He wraps me in a hug; my body angled slightly to make room for his stocky build and his gut that presses into my stomach. It's another Reefer quirk I've learned to love. I quickly try to inhale the scent of him to remember, which smells strongly of really horrible body spray. He practically bathes in the stuff.

We hug for a little too long, but I don't want to let go. I don't want to let *him* go. Reefer: my best friend. The one person in the entire world who has my back. It would be easy to tell him I love him, that he helps me in more ways than I can ever thank him for. That I hope one day he'll find someone who will put up with his quirks and settle down with a family. How he'll have children and fall in love, watch them grow old. Become a grandfather.

Things that Bryson will never get a chance to do.

How I hope he will understand why I have to leave him here alone.

A whole life between us, and within hours, none of it will matter anymore. It will all burn away with time. I will be nothing more than a fading memory, a guy he used to know in high school.

It should be easy to tell him these things, to utter the words that I know are true. But I don't. Can't. Something so simple is impossibly hard.

It's the people we're closest to that we have the hardest time being honest with.

Like my parents. I'm just not strong enough to utter the words. So I keep them to myself.

"How you manage to attract all the drama"—he pulls away—"I'll never know."

"You and me both."

He flashes a thumbs-up and puts his hands down his pants to fix his underwear. "It's bunching on my 'nads."

"Got it."

He lets out a "humph" when he's done, pounds his fist against mine.

"See you after school?"

I wince. "Sure thing, Reef."

He looks at me for a moment too long, just a beat, like he wants to ask something, but he blows a kiss with his mouth instead. He clears his throat and turns around, walks out of the bathroom to the deserted and dark hallway. The last time I will see him.

And for a moment, just a split second, I see the little boy from that day in gym when I kicked the ball into his face. And the little boy is smiling.

Goodbye, Reefer.

It's close to 1:00 PM, and I'm still in the bathroom. I finish the last soda Reefer bought and enter a stall to pee. A couple of voices echo from somewhere down the hall as they approach. I don't flush when I'm done, but close the lid to the toilet seat and step onto it, squat low, and lock the stall door. Somehow I know they are headed here.

The door squeaks open slowly; I squint through a small crack in the corner of the door to see who they are. A bald head peeks in, looks around, ducks back out, and steps into the bathroom with Aubrey Fisher.

Is she everywhere now? Aubrey Fisher: God?

It's the same security guard who escorted her out of the cafeteria. Officer Randall. She's back in the standard sweatpants/hoodie combo from before. Reefer's dad must've forced her to wear them again over her regular outfit. Officer Randall, dressed in his black uniform, cuffed pants, and polished shoes, leads her in by the wrist and locks the door behind them. He stands almost a foot taller than Aubrey. Looming.

"Such a little cock-tease," he coos, leans down into her ear. She pushes him away without much force. Officer Randall laughs, clearly amused, and pulls her closer. He grabs both her wrists and pins them down to her sides. "What? You're shy all of a sudden, baby?"

"Get off me."

"Shhhh." He presses a finger to her lips. "Don't tell me you've never blown a guy in the bathroom before. Yeah, I've heard the stories about you. I've seen some real cases come through this school. But none of them like you."

"I'll bite off anything you put near me." She struggles, again, without much force.

He laughs. "God, that mouth of yours is so *dirty*. C'mon, don't act like you haven't done this before. Girls dressed like you are *begging* to be filled up. Besides, baby, you're done at this school after today." He gropes her breasts and whispers, "No one has to know."

I gasp into my palm to mute the sound.

You have to help her, Gray. There are a lot of things in the past you've screwed up... but letting this happen... No. You CANNOT let this happen to Aubrey Fisher.

"I said get off me, fucker." She pushes him away, but he leans forward with more force, grabs her ass. She presses into his chest.

"Yes. Keep talking dirty to me; I like it. Just keep your voice down."

Aubrey struggles, and when he tries to kiss her, she head-butts him in the face. He stumbles back into one of the stall doors. From one of the mirrors, I see him hold his nose. Some blood trickles out. Aubrey hesitates before she turns away to run—her mouth shut tight into a line, yet she moves with a certain grace that makes it all appear theatrical. Officer Randall grabs her arm before she can reach the door. She yelps, attempts to scream, but he presses his hand over her mouth. She thrashes her legs but is nowhere near strong enough to break his grip. He moves his free hand slowly underneath the nylon and fishnets on her waist. Aubrey stops moving, and a strange sound escapes her throat.

"Goddamnit, girl. Calm down or I'll make it hurt. We gotta get you wet first."

I close my eyes and rack my brain for a plan. I'd been hoping to go all day invisible. A ghost. But I can't just stand by and let this happen.

Not again.

The mirror shows him lowering his hand from Aubrey's mouth, and I see her lips quiver. There is a look in her eyes. Just a flicker, but it's there. Fear. Aubrey, for the first time, is terrified. Desperate. Defeated. She closes her eyes as he begins to stroke underneath her nylons, and another sound escapes her throat; she presses further into his chest. I can't help but think that her posture becomes almost compliant.

But before I know what's happening, the stall latch is unlocked and I pull open the door. I hesitate, and Aubrey looks into the mirror. We see each other, and for a moment, just a moment, relief is in her eyes. The slight upturn of the left side of her mouth. Her body tenses up.

"Let her go." My voice escapes smaller than I want it to. But it's just enough to startle the guard. He jumps back, loosening his grip over Aubrey. In a flash, which I now realize is a signature move of hers, she whirls around and stomps on his foot. Hard.

Officer Randall howls and stumbles backward, hops on one leg. As if possessed, I shove him into the wall. Aubrey fixes the hoodie around her chest, kicks him in the groin, and spits on his face. She lets loose a stream of curses under her breath, but with such vehemence that I cringe.

My stomach drops, but it's more out of excitement and thrill. It's a weird feeling, one that is both foreign yet welcome. It's a nice change. Aubrey turns to me, huffs a little, and brushes away at her red bangs. She grabs my hand and squeezes hard. The old look is back in her eyes—the guarded one. Like a wall.

And I get the urge to kick him too.

So I do.

And it feels... *good*.

"Thank you," she breathes.

I nod, not sure what to say. Not sure if there is anything I can say in this moment. "A-Are you okay? Did he—"

"We have to get out of here."

I nod a little too aggressively at her suggestion. The image of a bobblehead appears in my mind.

"You're coming with me."

"But what about—"

"NOW! We need to leave now."

Officer Randall groans on the ground, his hands on his groin. He rolls over onto his stomach. Aubrey kicks him in the side of the ribs and unlocks the bathroom door, bashing the doorstop into his nose. He cries out.

"Go where?"

"I don't know. Anywhere. Out of this school. Do you trust me?"

I know all logic should make me shake my head no. All reason should dictate that I stay to make sure the guard is arrested for his actions. I have no reason to trust Aubrey Fisher. It would be uncharacteristic of me to. But I can't tell her that because she would kill me if I did. I have to lie to her like I do everyone else.

Which is why I don't understand what I say next:

The truth.

"No. I don't."

Half her mouth turns up in a crooked smile. "Perfect! Now follow me. I'll protect you."

And just like that, I let her take my hand again as we flee from the bathroom, run down the dark hallway, and head toward an uncertain future.

17 Hours Until

FRIDAY, 1:13ISH PM

It's like we are soaring. Rusted lockers pass by in a blur. We jog past squares of dusted glass that look into abandoned classrooms where desks are upturned or dismantled from long ago. In this short span of hallway, it's a ghost town. And yet here I am being dragged into a dark abyss. A deep underworld of unknown.

Into the world of Aubrey Fisher.

I try to inhale her perfume as we turn a corner into a bright hallway lined with red lockers. No scent comes. She doesn't smell like Kris. Rays of sun shine in from windows up near the ceiling—like tiny spotlights that illuminate in obscure circles on the drab green floor tiles. Aubrey's red-highlighted hair swishes back and forth as her feet pound on the ground.

"Where are we going?"

"Shut up. You'll give us away."

"Sorry," I whisper.

There is an awkward silence as we round a corner into a main hallway, where another set of bathrooms are. She comes to a sudden halt, and I slam into her back. Aubrey whirls around to shove me against a bulletin board, covering my mouth with her sweaty palm. She leans in close; her red bangs fall forward and touch my nose. A thumbtack presses into my shoulder blade.

"Hall monitor." She twitches her neck to indicate the direction behind her. "We're going to have to run past her. Can you keep up with me?" She lowers her hand.

I don't want to tell her I'm dying for oxygen like a wimp, so I formulate an elaborate lie to tell her.

"Probably not, no."

Dammit, Gray. Can you do nothing but tell the truth every single time?

"Well, that's too bad," she whispers, and I can feel her hot breath on my chin. "Because once the security guard finds his shriveled balls and gets up, they'll be after us both. Assault. School property. You follow me?"

Logic is telling me it doesn't really matter. That I'll be dead before the cops can arrest me. But I can't bear the shame my parents will face if they have to bail me out of jail. It makes me feel sick.

"He had it coming. What he was about to d—" I stop myself. To think what might've happened had I not been there to help is... Yet, there is still that image of her body pressing against his as his hands moved underneath her sweatpants. Almost like she was giving in to his touch.

We lock eyes; she holds a short breath and exhales. The repulsive aroma of cigarette smoke makes my eyes water. We both glance behind her; the monitor is gone. We begin to relax when the loudspeaker squeaks to life. I jump, though Aubrey remains still. Reefer's dad comes on and calls a meeting for the members of student council to head to the auditorium. She stares up at the loudspeaker. There is a gleam in her eyes. I push myself off the lockers and clear my throat.

"Should we—"

"I have an idea," she cuts me off, grabs my wrist, and tugs me down the hall toward the direction of the main office. "If you're not too chicken, that is."

Within a few minutes, we are hidden underneath the staircase across from the main office. No one is out patrolling the halls, and everyone, except the receptionist and some member of administration I've never met, has left to attend the council meeting. I have a sinking feeling in my stomach. Aubrey Fisher has a plan cooking in her brain, and I will be caught in the dead center of it.

"I thought you said we had to *flee*," I whisper.

"Yeah, yeah." She waves her hand in the air as if to shut me up. "But it's not like I'll ever have the chance to do this again."

"What are you talking about?"

"Relax. Go with the flow. Do as I do."

I nod my head, and she tells me her plan. It's not a good idea, not at all. I know I shouldn't care, but the fear grounds me in place.

Aubrey takes another look around and asks if I want to go with her. I freeze; my tongue dries up and shrivels. I lower my eyes and shake my head. She sighs and curses under her breath. Before long, she pulls off the hoodie and steps out of her sweatpants to reveal the fishnets over nylons she still wears. I glance at the red-striped fingerless gloves that stop halfway up her forearm. If Aubrey Fisher is anything, it's stubborn. You don't tell her what to do or wear; she does whatever she feels like doing. It's a trait I both admire and fear.

"You can be pretty lame when you want to be."

"Um..."

"I'm not making fun. But really. We're going to change that."

"I don't—"

"Just watch and learn." She runs a hand through her wild hair.

Aubrey takes a breath and breaks out into a dash for the front office. No hall monitors have been by yet, so it's only a matter of time before they make their rounds. She whips open the door, surprising the receptionist, and then runs to the Principal's door and disappears behind it.

The receptionist looks around, unsure what to do. She cocks her head like a bird, which makes me laugh. I see her lips move but can't hear what she says. That's when the click from a loudspeaker pings somewhere above me. There is a ruffling noise and the sound of papers being thrown around. When Aubrey's raspy voice echoes in the hallway, it's like my heart leaps into my throat. The receptionist adjusts her glasses and waddles to the office door. She jiggles it a few times, but it's locked.

"Attention, everyone. Your neighborhood foster-freak here. We have a special announcement from The Underdogs. The Outcasts." The hairs on the back of my neck and arms stand on end. There is a certain tone in her voice, a certain weight behind it that is threatening. Creepy. Like the kind of voice you'd use to tell scary stories at night around a campfire. "To the scumbag jocks and slutty cheerleaders. The dickhead who cheats on his girlfriend underneath the bleachers after fifth period... you know who you are. This is your judgment day. No one is safe." She clears her throat and lowers her voice an octave, sounding even more sinister.

"Hell is coming, Lee Falls. To anyone who has ever looked at us funny or spread any rumors. To anyone who steals trombones, or the pedophile holding his sagging ballsack in the old foreign language hallway bathroom who likes to touch underage girls. That's right, Hoch. Underage girls... really nice staff you hire to protect us. Or how about the asshole who serves high school kids crusty meatloaf with tomato soup and calls it nutritionally balanced? Even those melodramatic goody-two-shoe girls who call others '*sweetie*' in the lunchroom for comfort. Eek. This is for *you*."

My heart skips. I know she is referring to Kris with the last comment. I should be mad, but my face breaks out in a grin.

The man from administration appears at the door and jiggles the handle as the receptionist is talking to someone on the phone. Maybe Mr. Hoch or a security guard. If they catch her, she's toast. I'm afraid for Aubrey. The man reaches for a set of keys in his pockets and fumbles through them. The adrenaline rush is overwhelming, and yet, it's also liberating. My phone vibrates in my pocket. I pull it out and see Reefer's text:

REEFER

dude, r u hearing this SHIT!?!?!?!

"Don't have much time. But this is a special message approved by the one and only Grayson Falconi."

I stand alert at the sound of my name as she rasps it over the speakers, not sure how to react.

"You don't see *us*, but we see *you*. There's the vapid dramaqueen with the mole below her left shoulder who slipped laxatives into that blueberry muffin on Mr. Cronan's desk. Yes, sir, this is why you left in a sudden rush last Thursday with the runs. Yes, it did smell as bad as it felt. And don't think I didn't see one of our lovely Lee Falls baseball stars browsing the dirty magazines over at the shady adult store in Davisport with his fake ID. Is that why you, Baseball Star, always leave study hall and spend fifteen minutes in the bathroom every day? Did you like the spread? Maybe you like to take mock spreads of yourself in your mother's stockings?"

My mind swirls with names and faces of whom she is talking about and if any of it is true. From somewhere a few halls down, I hear footsteps headed in our direction. The man starts to test several keys in the door, to no avail. My phone vibrates again.

JENNA

This SO reminds me of Pump Up the Volume. Don't you think?

With Christian Slater? 1990

But why is Aubrey talking about you Gray?

Hellooooooooo???

REEFER

dude!!!!! she just used your name! your like, famous and shot

wait

**shit why is Aubrey-duckin-Fisher talking about u on the intercourse!?!?!!

R U 2 HAVIGN SEX AND NOT TELLIGN ME, GRAY-GRAY

aha... **intercom ... kind of funny my phone decided to b all witty and shot

but WTF is wituh these typos!!!?/

STOP TRYING 2 2001: A SPACE ODYSSEY ME, SMARTPHONE!!!!!!

"Gotta go, kids. Just remember: say no to any bald security guards that want to escort you to the bathroom. Don't eat the school meat. Don't believe one of the trumpet players in band when they tell you they've never had sex. Trust me; they have more use for their instrument besides just blowing into it." She pauses to take a breath, drops her voice down to barely above a whisper. "All of you are two-faced. Liars. Hypocrites. Well—" She hesitates. From the very end of the hall, Reefer's dad and one security guard appear and sprint toward the office. This school only has two guards. If she doesn't ditch now, they'll cuff her. There is no escape. The man in the office tries another key, his face red. She shouts the rest, making the speakers screech with feedback.

"NO ONE gets away tonight! I hear the things you say and the stuff you're too afraid to admit. It's a small town, Lee Falls! Everyone has secrets. I. See. Everything. The lying and cheating and backstabbing and gossiping. NO ONE gets away with it. I WILL PERSONALLYOHSHIT–" The intercom clicks off suddenly, the man having found the correct key to unlock the office door. But there is something else at the end of that word that sticks out. Something foreign that catches me off guard. I'm not sure if I hear it correctly.

Did she just giggle?

Through the glass of the front office, I see Aubrey shove the man into a wall, catching him by surprise. The receptionist blanches behind her desk, no longer on the phone, and just watches as Aubrey runs past, too stunned to make a move. Aubrey darts into the hall and looks in my direction, motioning her arms before pivoting her feet and running toward the front doors leading to the parking circle. Reefer's dad is only a few feet away; they shout for her to stop.

That's when I wonder if the rumors are true, if she's really done all the crazy things they say. And one day, maybe at her next school, we will all be a story those kids will tell when the scary, mysterious, edgy, and stubborn Aubrey Fisher just shows up, unannounced. Like how two outcasts banded together to hijack the intercom system to reveal everyone's secrets.

I have to make a decision. One that will change the course of events I'd planned. So in another act that is completely out of character for me, I bolt for the front doors and run in front of the guard as he gathers in the vestibule with Reefer's dad. Watch Aubrey disappear behind the parked cars. They don't notice as I use the swinging doors on the far side of the entrance, and by the time they do, I'm already hustling over the concrete sidewalk.

"Gray?" I hear Mr. Hoch's muffled shout from inside, but it's cut off as the door closes.

I feel a little guilty. He's been nothing but nice to me. I don't want to get Reefer in trouble with his dad, but deep down, I know I have to do this.

"Aubrey!" I shout.

Silence.

Behind me, Reefer's dad walks along the edge of the sidewalk, squinting his eyes in the sun and watching me run for the parking lot. He calls my name a few more times as the guard steps up on his side and heads in a different direction to find us. I duck between cars.

"Aubrey!" I shout, look around once more. I reach into my pocket and find Reefer's keys for the Buick.

For a moment I fear she already left or is hiding to avoid me. That fleeting feeling of rejection—of abandonment—embarrasses me. Of course Aubrey would leave without me. Why on earth would a girl like her ever want to be seen with a guy like me?

Panic surges before a hand grips my wrist and pulls me down to the ground. I land on my knees and cry out. And there she is. Sitting against the door of a maroon Chevy Pickup. She looks surprised, genuinely intrigued. A look I never thought I'd see on Aubrey's face. I catch her off guard.

"You followed me."

I don't know what to say, so I nod.

"Wow."

"What?" I sit down.

"I didn't think you would follow through."

"I didn't really have a choice."

Silence.

"You always have a choice." She cocks her head, studying me yet again like I'm a freak laboratory experiment that confuses her. "Don't I scare you?"

"Yes."

Gray, you really suck at lying around her. What is she doing to you?

Aubrey stares at me without blinking. "Good. Where's your car?"

From somewhere by the school, Reefer's dad calls our names.

I look down at the keys in my hand, and she grabs them. We stand up slowly, look to the front building but see that the guard is a few rows down, and sneak to Reefer's car. She studies it and licks her lips—her tongue ring reflects the sun overhead.

"This is a grandma car."

"It's not mine."

"Sure it's not."

"It's Reefer's."

"I know."

"Oh."

She raises an eyebrow and grins. "Mind if I drive?"

Aubrey must see the hesitation on my face because she slips the key into the door to unlock it and titters. Just a tiny bit. That is all she allows to escape. I obediently open up the passenger side door and step inside, think about the rumors I heard about what she did to her previous foster family's car.

In the rearview mirror, I see a reflection of the high school and the walls I've come to know over the past three years.

I buckle my seatbelt. Aubrey turns the ignition and revs the engine a few times.

"I'll try not to drive into any pools." She winks. "No promises, though."

16 Hours Until

You can hear our awkwardness in the car. The radio is off, and Reefer's collection of modern, classic, and obscure country artists are scattered in the backseat, thankfully. But I'd take one of his CDs over the silence in this car any day.

We drive around aimlessly for a while before Aubrey says she's hungry and is going to pick a place to eat. All of the excitement has me feeling hungry too, so I agree. We lapse back to silence. She keeps her eyes on the road, occasionally drums her fingertips on the wheel.

I'm glad, at the very least, that she is being safe.

Aubrey's crimson bangs hang over her right eye. She blows out air, so they puff up and fall back down. It's a quirk, I notice. Every couple of minutes, she does it again.

I study her hands, note the black nail polish painted on each middle finger and only each middle finger. The others remain plain. I clear my throat; my heart pulses.

"So, where are we going?"

Silence. Not even a twitch. It's as if I'm not in the passenger seat. We drive for another few minutes before I think about opening the passenger door and diving out of the vehicle, but the cleanup on the side of the road would be cruel. Anything, however, is better than driving to an uncertain destination in silence.

Finally, after what seems like years, she speaks: "You live on Oakhurst, right?"

My face is hot. "Excuse me?"

"Your house is on Oakhurst? I need to use your bathroom before we go eat. Last time a guy took me to a public restroom didn't end so well."

"Are you sure you're okay? I mean—"

"Oakhurst, yes?"

I frown and take the hint. "How do you know where I live?"

"Because I stalk you."

"Oh. Umm..."

"I'm kidding. This town is as small as a chode. Not very hard to find someone." She clucks her tongue. "You can turn on the radio, you know. You're kind of making this drive awkward."

"I'm making this drive awkward?"

She turns her head to me and grins. "But hey, if silence floats your boat..."

What the heck is her DEAL?

"I mean... you didn't turn on the radio, so I just thought—"

"That you needed my permission to play music?" she says flatly, turns back to the road. Aubrey hums a tune I don't know through her lips. "You're either very chivalrous or a complete pushover."

I clench my teeth and point at the stoplight down the road, ignoring her comment. "Make a right at the light."

"Aye-aye, Captain."

She upturns one corner of her mouth in a smile but keeps her lips pursed together. It's the same amused yet curious grin. If I didn't know any better, I would think she's just as surprised by me as I am by her.

And with the daylight filtering in through the windows, I think I see a dimple on her right cheek, but her mouth turns down into the same blank, stoic expression. Hiding it from the light.

I'm not sure if it was ever there to begin with.

~

REEFER

r u IGNORIGN ME Gray-Gray?!?!!?

JENNA

Hey. Are u ok?

We turn onto my street a few minutes later. Most of the driveways of the neighboring houses are vacant—people are at work. My street comes to a dead-end where there's a patch of woods that spans the length of the town divider. Potholes and split roads emerge everywhere. We don't even have dividing lines.

Oakhurst is mostly filled with older families. Our house was really the only one left with kids in this area, so summers were spent at Reefer's house or with Kyle and Kris's parents.

For a while, people weren't allowed to come over because of the rumors about how Mom and Dad had me. Their age difference. Mostly, that's behind us. But there are still some neighbors in town who refuse to acknowledge my parents when they catch them outside.

Our house always had a cloud of loneliness about it.

After we pull into my driveway, we get out and walk up the concrete sidewalk to the front door. The heat of the afternoon sun hits me. I look up and admire the blue sky. Not a single cloud to be seen. A truly beautiful last day.

Aubrey stops a moment to admire my mother's mini-garden

in front of the house. It's a collection of spring flowers: purple, blue, and pink hydrangeas; purple grand maître crocus; yellow daffodils; orange, red, and yellow gerbera daisies; and an assortment of pansies. It's beautiful. The only thing that still seems to give her a sense of purpose these days, which she obsessively upkeeps.

Pausing to enjoy my mother's work, I inhale the scent of spring, of the flowers. From somewhere down the block, a lawnmower revs to start. Cicadas sing their tune. A bird calls from above.

The image of my mother bending down with her gardening sheers, dirt on her jean shorts, as she wears a sun visor flashes in my mind. The smile my mother always had on her face as the flowers budded and sprouted in the spring. How she would smell them and wipe the sweat from her brow.

I used to plant seeds with her when I was a little boy. Mom would tell me stories of my grandparents and how she used to garden with Grandma back when she was a little girl. It's like a rite of passage on her side of the family. I'd come home from school, fresh off the bus, and water the plants around the house before she came home from work at the daycare.

For some reason I want to tell Aubrey this as she stands next to me. Both of us are still in the hushed silence, admiring as the bushes and flowers blow in the light breeze. The sun beats on the back of our exposed necks, the humidity making me thirsty.

Remember when Bryson planted the yellow daffodil on the right?

I ball my hands into fists at my sides. Blink away the thought.

Aubrey doesn't say anything. Never moves or opens her mouth to breathe.

"My mom likes to garden. It's sort of a hobby of hers, I guess."

Aubrey nods, and we both move until I reach the door to unlock it. She glances again at the small flowerbed and steps inside. The house is eerily quiet. I take off my shoes as she steps onto the carpet with her dirty combat boots. I wonder if it's a fashion statement or if she comes from a military background. It would explain a lot.

"So you just need to use the bathroom?" I ask. I never planned to see my house again, and being here gives me the creeps, like I've stepped into a tomb.

She shrugs and walks into the kitchen. Mysterious, quiet, unreadable Aubrey. There's no telling what she's thinking.

"Why aren't you saying anything?" I ask.

She turns around and grins. "You're very easy to unnerve. It's funny."

"Well... it's not really..."

She goes to the fridge and pauses to view the Polaroid of my parents' wedding photo. After a moment, she opens it up and reaches in for a jug of apple juice.

"No," she says. "It is."

"I thought you were hungry?"

"I am."

"Don't you also have to use the toilet?"

"I do."

"Then why—"

"Stop asking questions. You know that you think too much? About everything. Like, just enjoy it."

"I don't get what I'm supposed to be enjoying."

She pauses a moment to drink directly out of the jug. Normally I hate when people do that, but surprisingly, I don't hate when she does it. I don't know why. It's like every part of me comes unhinged. Like she is the paint thinner to my super glue. I can't get a grip. My chest tightens, so I exhale.

"Life," she says, after putting the juice back into the fridge. "Life is what you're supposed to enjoy."

"Oh. Right."

"So, where is your bathroom?"

"Do you want a tour?"

"Would you like to give me a tour?"

"Umm, if... *you* want me to."

She steps in my direction and stops midway, sways on her feet. "You're not just trying to get me alone to feel me up in your room, now are you, *Grayson?*"

Shit. Gray. Shit! Either she's coming on to you hard right now, or she thinks you're coming on to her. There is NO WAY Aubrey can be attracted to you... can she?

"No." I shake my head violently. My mouth dries up. "Oh God, no. I-I-It's, uh, it's definitely not..."

Her eyes widen. "You also don't know how to take a joke." She moves forward until she is within arm's length and puts her hands on my shoulders.

I shudder instantly.

"Relax. I'm only kidding. Don't flatter yourself. Or be so uptight. I'll help you with that too."

"So you weren't trying to..."

Aubrey smiles, pleased with herself. And I know, deep down, she is trying hard not to laugh.

"You make it sound like such a bad thing."

"I'm sorry."

"Don't apologize."

"I know. It's a nervous habit."

"You usually this upfront with people?"

"No." I shake my head.

We breathe at the same time. I'm lightheaded and crane my neck until I hear it crack. The anxious ticking begins its countdown in my head.

"Then why are you being honest with me?" She again steps closer until I can smell the trace of cigarettes on her breath. Maybe a hint of vanilla. The red highlights in her brunette hair glow under the kitchen lights.

"I don't know."

She stares at me for a few moments too long and retreats to the front hallway, where she finds my unopened report card on the table. She passes it back and forth between her hands before spotting the pamphlet underneath about surviving. Aubrey looks up at me. Studies me. She puts both back down on the table in the same position she found them and points upstairs.

"First door on the right," I say.

She nods. "And no, we are not going to have sex." Walks up the steps. "Before we eat."

She's kidding, right?

When I know she's gone, I exhale and go to the fridge to pull out the jug of apple juice. I open the cap and look closely to see if there's a tiny lipstick smudge on the outer rim. It's weird, maybe even a little psycho, but I sniff it to try and get a sense of her smell, if she wears lip gloss or anything, but find nothing except the aroma of apples. There is no noticeable smudge. I look around, ashamed and embarrassed at what I'm doing, before putting it back in the fridge.

Gray Falconi: Suicidal Self-Deprecator and Lip-smudge Fetishist.

On the counter, behind Dad's coffee machine, is an old banana that is nearly black. I pick it up to discover a few fruit flies hovering above it. Disgusted, I chuck it into the trash. It unnerves me that my parents hadn't noticed. They used to be on top of fresh fruit.

Tucked behind the rancid fruit, pushed against the counter wall, is an old school photo of Bryson when he was in first grade. Toothless and smiling. His hair messy and a little greasy.

Looking at the camera, at me. It's creased and crumpled, like someone threw it away, then thought better of it.

I can't look at it anymore, so I lean into the sink to splash water on my face and find the broken pieces of Dad's coffee mug from when he smashed it earlier. I have the urge to bash my face onto the sink edge, so I back away and pinch a vein in my wrist until my skin breaks. Close my eyes and tell myself everything is okay when all I want to do is scream.

From upstairs I hear footsteps moving around. I call out for Aubrey, but she doesn't answer. The footsteps stop suddenly. I glance up the stairwell that is visible from the kitchen but see nothing. Another creak comes from what I think is my parents' bedroom.

What the heck is she doing up there?

No answer comes when I call out a second time, so I tiptoe to the stairs and look up. The light to my room is on, and in a panic, I jump up the stairs and stand in the doorway.

"You're pretty lousy at house tours," she says while looking through my underwear drawer.

In her hands, dangling in the air, is Bryson's seashell necklace.

And then I close my eyes, and it's summertime. July. Bryson and I decided to go camping out in the woods near the outskirts of town, where we built a tree house with our dad. We would lie awake eating junk food or reading comic books, wrapped in sleeping bags. It was fun.

"You and Kris are going to have sex, aren't you?" Bryson asked.

"For the record, little man, you're too young to know about that." I grinned. "We don't have sex; we Bible study."

"I'm ten, Gray. I'm not dumb. I've seen things on the internet."

"Exactly my point. You're too young, and that's a terrible

argument. So shut up and go to sleep before I smother you to death."

"That's not fair! I'll tell Mom and Dad."

"Do it. See what happens."

We stared for a while before I tickled him relentlessly. He attempted to fight me off before surrendering. When he calmed down to catch his breath, he rolled over and slapped my chest.

"What's that for?"

"I don't want you to leave. Don't go away to school. Can't you just stay home with me?" His brown eyes opened wide, too big for his narrow face. He looked a lot like Mom. He squeezed the seashell necklace around his neck.

"I still have two more years of high school, little man. I'm not going anywhere anytime soon." I grab a candy bar to my right and chuck it at him. He frowned. "How about we go see a Yankees game next summer? We can see the new stadium, have authentic New York pizza, and buy Mom fake Gucci or something."

Bryson started to giggle, which made me giggle. He furrowed his brows and played with the pillow. "Yeah, but it won't be the same." He held out his necklace to me, his big eyes pleading. Innocent. "Can we go back there? To the beach? Before you're gone."

"Of course we will." I ruffled his hair, and he whined until I stopped. "I'm not going anywhere."

My eyes blur, and then I'm back in my own bedroom, watching Aubrey swinging the necklace back and forth.

"What are you doing?" I shout. I rush over to her and snatch the necklace from her hand, pulling it to my chest as if it's something fragile.

"Someone's feisty all of a sudden."

"I'm sorry." She flops down onto my bed until her head rests on my pillow. "It's just an invasion of privacy. I don't know you."

"Don't apologize. I was looking into your stuff behind your back. You should be pissed. But I'll give you that one for free. Next time you apologize, which is very passive aggressive of you, I'm going to punch you really hard."

"Why?" I sit on the edge of my bed, forgetting my temporary panic. I take the necklace and place it back into the drawer she got it from and shut it forcefully.

Did she steal anything? Was she in your parents' room?

"Because you should never apologize for who you are."

She makes herself comfortable by flopping onto her stomach and burying her face into my pillow on the freshly made bed, which I figure Mom must have done after I left for school. Otherwise, it's exactly as I left it. The walls where I once had posters of movies and bands are now plain white. I'd torn them down weeks ago and thrown them in the garbage. My parents never mentioned anything about it.

Aubrey's hair is sprawled over the sheets, and I can't help but glance at her butt. She lifts herself up on her elbows and sticks out an arm for me to help pull her up, which I do eagerly.

Aubrey exhales. "Not ever."

The tour doesn't take long. After I show her the upstairs bedrooms and bathroom, she gets bored and announces she wants to leave to get food. Aubrey touches everything around her, runs her fingers over every surface she can. I have to stop her from looking inside more closets and drawers. She walks inside my parents' room cautiously, which I find a little odd. Like she is trying to be extra careful. Like she will disturb something evil.

Wasn't she already in here? Maybe you imagined it?

And then she stops outside my brother's bedroom door. Initially I panic, afraid she'll bust it open, yet secretly hoping she will. But she doesn't. She turns the knob and, after discovering it's locked, stops. Looks at the ground and then over her left shoulder to my room, then back at the ground. Back up at the door.

Silence.

After a moment, we head back downstairs, and Aubrey stops to look at our family portrait in the living room of the beach when Bryson was just a baby. She gazes at it for too long, maybe noticing his seashell necklace. But then she turns away. The trance broken.

We walk to the front door, where I put on my shoes and go back outside. I lock the door behind me and inhale the fresh May breeze. The type of breeze you can only find in western New York. I pull out my cellphone to three missed voicemails from Jenna, Reefer, and his dad. I don't listen to any.

Aubrey pauses on the walkway to look at the flowers. For a while she just stands there, entranced. I can't imagine someone like her being drawn to something as simple as a garden, but then again, I know nothing about her aside from the rumors. Maybe she used to plant seeds back with her real parents or a previous foster family. That thought alone gives me comfort: Aubrey and I having a shared past. Eventually, she inhales through her nose and walks to the car.

"Are you still driving?"

"Yeah. Non-negotiable. I feel you drive like a grandpa in this grandma car. Needs a little more *spunk* to it."

Before starting the engine, she looks in the rearview mirror at the same time I do. There is something she's not telling me. Something she keeps hidden. It unnerves me, but I try to not show it. I don't like being lied to, but I'm not one to talk.

Chalk it up to just another Aubrey quirk.

My phone rings in my pocket, which is set to the standard factory setting. The number is blocked. I never answer anonymous calls, but Aubrey grabs it out of my hands.

"Let's answer it!"

"Why? It's either a prank or a telemarketer."

Then why do you have that feeling in the pit of your stomach?

"Exactly. You never have fun with them when they call?"

"Not really."

"Jesus!" She raises her hands in the air. "Have you been under a rock? Hmm. You're a momma's boy, aren't you?"

"No." I shrink in my seat as the phone keeps ringing.

"Then prove it and answer before it goes to voicemail. And speaker it!"

Embarrassed and clearly needing to prove my masculinity, I accept the call and put it on speaker. At first there is nothing on the other end except static. But after a while, the static stops, and breathing comes on the line.

"Hello?" I ask.

After a moment, the muffled voice speaks, barely above a whisper: "Your lies destroy, Gray."

My blood turns to ice, and the hairs on my arms stand up. I know deep down that it's just a prank, but there is something neurotic in the way the voice speaks. And the way he tries too hard to disguise his voice. Almost robotic.

Aubrey looks down at the phone, her expression unreadable.

"You hear me?" he says again, but I can't make out whom exactly. "I know you left school with Aubrey Fisher... the sad and pathetic weirdo. She'll hurt you, 'cause that's what foster-freaks do." A beat. "Are you with her 'cause you're scared?"

"You want to say that to my face?" Aubrey shouts into the phone. "I'll beat the shit out of you, asshole."

The line is silent before it goes dead.

He hung up.

It's the same person who's been texting you. Has to be. Should you tell her?

Aubrey doesn't say anything as I put the phone back in my pocket. I don't either. She turns on the ignition and backs out of the driveway. Voices of the caller and Bryson come like a tidal wave. I clutch at the pain in my chest.

"Are you with her 'cause you're scared?"

"Can't you just stay home with me?"

"Your lies destroy."

"I don't want you to leave."

15 Hours Until

We drive without saying anything for a while. The car cruises along the side roads that Aubrey takes us down. Whenever we reach a dead end, we circle back around. Neither of us brings up the phone call or what happened in school. She dismisses Reefer's entire country collection, and for that, I'm grateful.

"What the hell is this?" She rifles through a few CDs before chucking them into the backseat.

After scouring through a few radio stations, past the Top 40 music that I prefer, she settles on a hard rock station I've never heard. The car fills with double bass kicks and crunching guitars. I don't know what to make of it.

"Don't tell me you've never listened to metal."

I shake my head.

"Hard rock, scene, emo, post-hardcore..." she trails off, clearly not satisfied with my lack of recognition. "Classic rock?"

"Define classic."

She snaps her neck in my direction and drops her jaw in shock. Her mouth hangs open so long I think drool will roll out. I nervously motion toward the road, so she pays attention.

"Dude. Where have you been all your life?"

Not living. Apparently.

"It's okay. We'll add that to our list of things." She pauses. "We have our work cut out for us."

"There's a list now?"

"You should take notes. Buy a composition notebook or something."

"And a pencil?"

"No. Pen. Pens are permanent. Forever. Like a scar. Pencils can be erased. The marks don't last." She pauses. "Besides, who writes in pencil anymore?"

"Who writes in composition notebooks anymore?"

She turns to me and smiles coyly. "People that hang out with guys who enjoy driving around in this shitty-ass, obsolete, Sunday bingo car."

"I see your point."

"Is your friend actively trying to not get laid?"

On the drive to eat, with the windows down and rock music so loud it feels like a finger is poking the top of my brain, I replay over the day's events in my head. Waking up, my parents fight-ing, Reefer, Jenna, antagonizing Kyle and Tim, watching Aubrey kick ass, the embarrassment I caused Kris, and the phone call and texts. It all feels like someone else's life. I hang my elbow out of the open window as the spring breeze blows in. It alleviates the heat coming into the car from the blazing sun.

The town I live in is small, about 10,472 people, to be exact. But Lee Falls is a quiet community with a lot of secrets. Secrets people know about, gossip about. Hardly anyone can keep a secret here. That's the beauty of living in a small town: your business is everyone else's. And their business is yours too.

But not Aubrey. Nobody knows her secrets.

A few stores down on the main drag, where almost everything is located, are the rows of blue benches in front of the ice cream parlor. When we were younger, Reefer and I used to rollerblade there to get cones that we'd never be able to finish before they melted all over our hands on hot summer days. Cookie dough was my favorite. Reefer always got pistachio.

On the opposite end of the street is the pizzeria. Kris's glowing smile flashes in my mind from the late nights we'd go there when we were dating. Conversations about life.

A few more stores down, a group of little kids perform skateboard tricks off parking lot curbs and rusted benches where Kyle and I attempted to learn once. It was a huge "epic fail."

We also have two bars that locals frequent and one arcade plaza by the pizzeria. It's easy to get bored here.

My dad's local grocery store is also just beside the ice cream parlor. Mom's daycare center is down in the opposite direction of the main drag. It's so small that the only visitors we get are people that get lost or stumble here by accident. The only people that stay in Lee Falls are those born here.

There's a glorified doctor's office next to a vet clinic—the closest thing we have to a hospital. Any serious injuries or surgeries have to be taken to the next town over; that's where they took Kris and her dad—where he still is now.

Aubrey is driving farther away than I anticipate, past the town lines and into the neighboring Davisport.

"Where are we going?" I look around as we leave civilization for pine trees that blur by on either side. The dense woods between the towns are rumored to be haunted. Depending on whom you ask.

It's also the same place Bryson and I built our tree house.

Aubrey hums to the next rock song, this one equipped with a full verse of screaming.

I cringe. "Are we still going to eat?" Nothing. I slump back into my seat and exhale.

"Stop pouting."

"I'm not pouting."

"Yes you are."

I bite my tongue to keep from saying something I fear will piss her off. So I cross my arms in front of my chest, realize this is the stereotypical angsty pout she is referring to, and put my hands in my lap.

"See," she says. "Pouter."

"If you say so." I try not to smile because it's too ridiculous not to laugh. But I crack a grin anyway.

Aubrey raises her fist in celebration. "So you *do* have a sense of humor." She winks at me. "I knew there was a high school boy in there somewhere."

My feet kick at the old McDonald's bag on the floor, feel them squish what I imagine to be week-old fries. The foam inside the seat underneath me pokes through a tear in the fabric, so I pull out a few loose pieces and fling them to the ground. I stick my arm out the window to weave it up and down like a roller coaster. The wind whips through my fingertips as she picks up speed.

I know it's useless to argue, so I just let her drive us wherever she wants to go. I'm completely at her mercy. In the rearview mirror, the buildings slowly dwindle to a speck in the distance. The small town nothing but a tiny dot amongst the trees.

"Good riddance."

～

The waitress, a short, very cute girl with long black hair and shiny lip gloss, leads us to a window booth that looks out onto the main street. Her name tag reads: Justine. She hands us our menus and sets up the paper placemats and napkin-wrapped silverware. She has a green pullover uniform, as do all the employees. She appears to be in her mid-twenties, and one of her front teeth has a small chip at the very bottom.

The restaurant starts to get busy as people getting off work rush to meet their families or significant others for dinner. The entire place is lit by the open windows and the dim lighting overhead. The walls themselves are covered from head to toe with movie posters, old and new. Next to us is an ancient poster of *Pretty Woman*. Julia Roberts is dressed in her finest prostitute attire, while Richard Gere looks sharp in his suit and tie. It's one of my mother's favorites.

I plop down in the padded, fake-leather red seats and rest my elbows on the laminated plastic table. The smell of greasy French fries and barbecue sauce fills my nostrils, and my stomach growls. We unwrap our silverware.

The waitress smiles down at me while she pulls out her order pad and a pencil. She takes her cue from me as if I'm the ringleader of the show. Aubrey glares in her direction.

"I'll be back to take your orders in a moment, but is there anythin' I can get for y'all to start off?"

I'd be lying if I didn't say her southern belle accent sounds adorable. I also notice she intentionally has her back toward Aubrey. When it isn't, she looks everywhere except Aubrey's eyes. And I know she is judging the fishnets over nylons. The retro, red plaid mini-skirt and wild hair with red highlights. The two single nails painted black and the lack of makeup. Her fingerless arm-length gloves. The piercings. It's the first time I ever feel kind of pissed off. They operate in completely separate worlds, and here I am in the middle.

Aubrey glances at me, annoyed.

"Yea, maybe two of 'em colorin' pages and some crayons. If

you don't mind, darlin','" Aubrey mocks Justine's accent. Whether the waitress picks up on it or not, she never acknowledges. She is clueless to the joke. Or maybe she's just used to customers making fun of her.

"You two want to color?"

Aubrey nods her head. "No one can draw inside the lines like ole Gruber here." She places her hand on top of mine, which makes me jump. My cheeks flush. "His mama is damn proud of it too." She caresses her thumb over one of my knuckles and looks up at me, flutters her eyes exaggeratedly.

"Aw, okay." The waitress forces a giggle, clearly uncomfortable. "And to drink?"

I start to open my mouth before Aubrey speaks up for the both of us and lets go of my hand. "Dr. Pepper for me and... a Pepsi for him."

How did she know you'd get that, Gray?

Justine writes in her pad, points her pen at me. "Do I know you from somewhere, hun?"

Aubrey's eyes become mere slits.

"I don't think so?" I say.

She brings the cap of her pen and gives it a quick bite. "Y'all look just so familiar to me. Maybe I'm just bananas. I'm sorry."

My cheeks get hot for some reason. "You're not, trust me. It's okay."

The waitress nods, smiles, looks at me again—intentionally avoiding Aubrey's glare—and walks off to check on another table well into their entrée.

Aubrey mutters a curse under her breath and puts a fingernail into her mouth to chew on. The sight makes me cringe as a small piece of nail tears off with her teeth. She spits it out onto the floor and turns toward me.

"That girl was an idiot. And she was checking you out. She'll give you her number."

"That's not true. Guys like me and older girls like her could never happen." I open up the menu. "What makes you think she was?"

"Seriously? She puts on all this makeup and that horribly cliché accent and, all of a sudden, she's like this sex goddess. I would know. Works every time. I bet the accent is fake. She's a slut. And you didn't see her get upset when I touched you?" She spins her menu on the table's surface. "And why wouldn't someone like her be into you? What does that mean?"

I look up and find it odd that Aubrey, of all people, would judge someone based off her appearance. I know she's mad, but it makes no sense. She makes no sense.

And I can't shake the sensation of her thumb massaging my knuckle.

"I thought she was nice. But she was *not* checking me out. Girls don't find me attractive. Have you seen me?" I pat my stomach underneath the table.

She scowls. For a moment I think she is going to stab me with the knife next to her tablemat.

"Didn't you date Miss Perfect?"

"Who?"

"Miss Blonde Bombshell Whose Head I Almost Ripped Off In Lunch. Kris Sanders."

"Oh. Yeah, for a while..."

"She's beautiful, and yet she dated you for... how long?"

"Three years."

"That long? Interesting."

There's a brief flash of Kris on a stretcher being loaded into the helicopter. She was crying, her leg bent all the way behind her. Her knee popped to the side.

The knife on the table glints under the sunlight that gleams through the open window, and I wonder what it will look like if I plunge it into my throat and feel the blood ooze down my chest and squirt onto the table. If it will look like ketchup next to the fries when they arrive.

"You can have any girl you want. And you're not fat. So shut up. Girls like you. You just can't see them because you're too self-absorbed."

"I'm self-absorbed?"

"Don't be naïve. Now you're being an idiot. Don't ruin this for me."

Ruin what for you?

"I-I'm sorry?" My heart races and the room spins. I tell myself to control my breathing and steady my heart. My hand instinctively goes to my sore bruise over my chest and pushes lightly, but Aubrey beats me to the punch—literally—and gives me a right hook in the shoulder. Hard. The room immediately rights itself as I grab the edge of the table to keep from falling over. I look around, but no one notices. My shoulder throbs instantly.

"I told you"—she points—"that I'd hit you if you apologized again. It's passive... stop it. That's a love tap. I can and will do worse until you start taking charge and embracing stuff. Don't do it again."

THAT was not a love tap.

I brush the back of my hand over my eyes, just in case they are watering. If apologizing is off limits, I don't even want to know what crying will get me.

The waitress brings over two coloring pages and a box of dull crayons with our drinks. She smiles. Aubrey hands me one and keeps the other for herself. We both put our straws into our glasses and sip.

"Do you always color at restaurants?"

She doesn't respond. The crayon moves almost methodically over the page.

"Why did you bring us here, Aubrey?"

She stops moving the red crayon and looks up. It's quiet for a moment, only the sound of my heartbeat in my ears amongst the restaurant noise. The clinking of glasses, the scraping of forks on plates, and the light chatter of fellow diners. I take another sip of Pepsi.

"First, we color. Then we eat. Then we talk."

"I just want to know why you'd choose to talk to me over everyone else."

Aubrey smiles, and that dimple I thought wasn't there surfaces in her right cheek. She clears her throat and drops the crayon. She hunches over the table as if ready to tell a secret, so I oblige. She cups her hands over her mouth and whispers,

"First, we color."

She sits back, leaves me hanging on the edge for more, picks up the red crayon, and begins to fill in the shapes on the page. Not knowing what else to do, I pick a green crayon and do the same.

The food arrives within twenty minutes after Justine takes our orders. She continues to be polite in her accent that sounds convincing to me; Aubrey continues to mock her whenever she comes around. On the table for me: a double bacon cheeseburger without the lettuce or tomato and a side of curly fries. For Aubrey: a steak, medium, with a side of loaded mashed potatoes and broccoli. We split an appetizer of potato skins and mozzarella sticks, and we share the molten lava cookie cake for dessert.

I savor the greasy fries and sour ketchup. Savor the melted Swiss on the burger. Savor the rich, warm, gooey chocolate of the cake. It's euphoric.

Kris was always fit, but thankfully she was never one of

those self-conscious girls who didn't like to eat big out in public. But she still had some self-control. Aubrey, however, eats like it's a feast in medieval times. She reaches over and grabs a fry, dips it in the glob of ketchup on my plate, and munches away like it's nothing. I double dip in the ketchup more than once. I also never offer her my fries. She just takes some.

Aubrey is not supposed to be sitting across from me, sharing a meal in a restaurant in the neighboring town. It's surreal—still feels like it's some kind of grand act or gesture. Like all of it is planned, plotted, and manipulated from the start.

She picked you, Gray. YOU. When has any rumor involving another student ended in rainbows and sunshine? Something isn't right.

The warm chocolate syrup oozes out of the cookie cake and drips off my fork as I scoop it up into my mouth. It never used to be this way with food. I used to be in shape and sometimes ran with Kris when she forced me to. But it's just another thing to hate. Another thing to add to the growing list of disgusting and disappointing habits I have. I think I can feel my stomach slowly stretching. I just want to reach through my skin and pull out all the globs of fat I'm accumulating and throw them down on the table.

Aside from the few comments about the food, we don't speak. Surprisingly, it no longer feels weird. With Kris, it was nice to be around her and not feel the need to talk. Like spending all night together but not saying much. We still found comfort in the company we shared. With Aubrey, it starts to feel the same when I force out the awkward thoughts and the need to fill the silence. Sometimes silence can be beautiful. And with Aubrey, it's like I want to soak in all the beauty I can.

Maybe that's what is wrong with the world: too many people are trying to talk. To fill the silence. The fighting and lying, the excuses and the need to feel accepted. The world moves too fast. The pre-dawn is different. Lying in bed in the moments before my alarm is different. The light from the rising sun that filters through the blinds to form those prisms of light is different. It's silence. Peace. The world just needs to stop sometimes. Stop to enjoy itself. No one does that anymore. Just stops to look around. To breathe. To see the miracle in life, in being alive. The miracle in sitting across from a girl whom you never thought you'd sit across from in a million years.

Being seventeen and coloring inside the lines in a restaurant.

"Suppose you want that chat now," she interrupts my thoughts.

My heart skips. I reach into my pocket to look at my phone under the table before I answer back. There are a slew of texts from Reefer and one from Jenna. Besides that, both Reefer and his dad tried calling numerous times. There are already six voicemails, and Reefer never calls. Especially twice in one day. I suddenly feel guilty for stealing his "grandma" car.

"I do," I say.

She tilts her head to indicate that I'm to lead the discussion. A million and more questions pop in my head: her, her backstory, her parents, and her life in the foster system. But I don't have enough time left alive to get all the answers, so I settle on only the essentials.

"Why me? Why am I interesting? And why would you ever want to be associated with a fat psycho like me?"

It takes a while for Aubrey to respond. She initially looks disappointed, like she expects better questions, but maybe she's just trying to challenge me again. Test my patience. Everything with her is calculated. She dips her pointer and middle finger into her nearly empty Dr. Pepper and runs the tips of her fingers around the rim of the glass until it emits a steady, hollow ring.

"Predictable. Can't you ask me something I wouldn't expect?"

"Just answer the question. Please." I tilt my head sideways like there's a bad taste in my mouth, and that's when it hits me: "Damn. I do sound self-absorbed, don't I?"

She lets out a chuckle before sitting up straight and folding her arms onto the table. "Yeah. Just a little." She pinches her thumb and pointer finger together. "You walk around the school like a social leper. You self-victimize yourself like the world owes you something it's not giving you. Yet, you have nothing but compassion for people. Interesting that you stand up for the underdog but not yourself. Like that freshman earlier in the hallway." She runs a hand through her hair but never peels her eyes away from my brown ones. Like a dare. I never look away either. "You're not a psycho. And you're disgustingly skinny." She pauses. "You really can't see it..." She squints her eyes.

"See what?" I start to feel uncomfortable in my own skin. I sit back in the booth and lower my eyes to her folded hands on the table.

"What do you want? Right here and now. More than anything. What do you want?"

To be with Bryson.

"Kris," I lie.

"Sanders?"

I nod—look back up. But she's disappointed again. Like she doesn't buy it.

"Why?"

I don't answer.

She frowns. "I'm going to say something that might hurt your feelings. But I'm going to be honest with you. Okay?"

I don't know if I want to hear what she has to say, but she isn't really asking for my permission. I clear my throat, which is enough of an acknowledgment for her to continue.

"I've been in this... *delightful* town for a couple months now. Right?"

My tongue is like sandpaper in my mouth. I can't even move my head to nod. Can feel the anxiety coming back. I don't want to hear what she is about to say. She lowers her voice so only I can hear her over the chatter around us. She looks me in the eyes a while before proceeding. It's a knowing look.

"How did you plan on doing it?"

"Doing what?"

She pauses. "Doesn't matter. You're not ready."

Does she know? Holy crap. DOES SHE KNOW?

"I don't understand."

"I brought you out here 'cause I want to help you."

"I don't need help."

She smiles. "That's exactly why you need it."

"Why do you care? You don't know me. I don't know you."

"Don't worry about that. What matters is right here and now."

A pause. The waitress walks over to check on how we're doing. I don't know how to get my brain and mouth to work, so Aubrey asks for the check in her fake accent, and Justine walks away with a forced smile. Aubrey turns back to face me after draining the remainder of her drink from the straw until all that's left is air. She tugs at her fingerless gloves.

"I see you, you know."

Goosebumps rise to my flesh; the hair on my arms stands on edge. "You see me?"

"I want to make you a deal. Come with me. Be spontaneous. Have fun. Let go. Give in to an adventure, and I promise you won't regret it."

"I don't even know what that means."

"Exactly."

"Huh?"

"Neither do I."

"This makes no sense!"

"Doesn't have to. But what else do you have planned today? Hmm? Anything better?"

I pinch at another vein in my wrist. But there's something about Aubrey that drives away the bad feelings.

"You still didn't fully answer my question."

"When you're ready for the full answer, I'll tell."

I think it over while finishing the last of my Pepsi. To my right, a mother comes back from the restroom holding the arm of a little girl in a yellow sundress. She has a daisy tucked behind her right ear and wears yellow sandals. It's a Kris outfit through and through. It's innocent. Pure. I want to go over and wrap her in a hug. Never let go. And I wonder a million different ways how her life might turn out.

If she'll leave the house one night and never come back home.

Never take a breath again.

I have to fight the urge not to tear up. It's right there, on the edge.

A moment later, Justine comes over and places the checkbook in front of me. I smile and thank her, but Aubrey glares more intensely than before. She doesn't like the patriarchal intentions. Not at all. Without a second thought to it, I slide the check her way. I don't have any money to my name.

"So what's in this for you?" I ask. "And what would we do, exactly?"

She glances down at the check, smiles, and turns it upside down so I can't see the exact amount.

"You're a people watcher. I know because I am too. You notice things. Why?"

"I don't know..."

"Bullshit."

I exhale. "Why does it matter?"

"Humor me."

"Um, I don't know. Just trying to find the beauty in the mundane? Trying to find the magic?"

She rolls her tongue in her mouth until the tongue ring flashes again. "Stop sounding passive about everything. Man up. State your case; don't pussyfoot around. Be firm." She clucks her tongue and cracks a few knuckles. "Follow me, here and now, and we will find that beauty together. We will find the magic in the *mundane*."

"How are we going to do that?"

"Don't know and don't care. Have you ever gotten yourself lost before? Intentionally?"

I shake my head.

"Concept is simple," she continues. "You're never more in tune to your surroundings than when you're lost. Trust me. If you want your meaning, that's how you'll find it." She drums her fingers on the table to a beat I can't identify. She appears to mull something over as if pained by a thought. It's a second before she continues, but she looks out the window, not at me. "You really want to win Kris back?"

"I don't know... maybe... no... I don't know."

She turns to me. "I can tell you the answer if you really want. But it's not mine to give." Silence. "If you follow me, what I'll show you will change your life."

Bullshit.

"Bullshit."

Whoops. That slipped past your lips, Gray.

"Sorry."

Aubrey winds up and punches me hard in the opposite arm. It hurts just as bad.

Should've seen that coming.

She squirms in the booth while I rub my arm, which is an odd sight to see.

"I promise. We'll go on a journey all day and night. Pull an all-nighter to find the magic and beauty and love left in the world," she says while doing air quotes for each of my words she repeats. "Doing whatever we want whenever we want, wherever we want. And I promise to continue to call bullshit on winning Kris back. And changing your life. Will you do this with me?"

It's another choice I have to make. I plan on going back home later, so I can finish what I set out to do. Will it really matter if I take a detour for a few hours just to see what happens? What harm can spending my last hours with Aubrey Fisher really cause?

That's when I realize I don't have my envelope; it's still in my locker at school. I don't know why I say what I do next, but it just comes out instinctively.

"I need to get something out of my locker at school."

"Not gonna happen."

"I need it. You don't understand. If I do this… I'm going to need that too."

She ponders the thought before a sly grin spreads across her face. "We could break in after they close up for the night."

"We could *what*?"

"Break in. I've done it before. We just wait till after dark when they lock it up for the weekend. I like the way you think. SEE! We're having fun with this already."

"Whatever you say."

She flicks her tongue out and grazes it along the bottom of her lip, holds it there, and gets a mischievous look in her eye. Once again, I sense she is planning something without me knowing.

"So I have your agreement. You'll be spontaneous with me all night. Correct? You won't be lame about this?"

It's not too late to back out now. But what could it hurt, Gray?

I nod a little too eagerly because inside, I'm terrified. My stomach flips and I'm lightheaded. Yet, oddly enough, my breathing remains calm. I don't know why Aubrey calms and unnerves me at the same time. I can't fathom the reason. Less than twenty-four hours ago, I would've never looked her in the eye, let alone follow her on an adventure.

"Yes. Let's do it."

She slides the check over to me, and I see it's for $64.73.

"Why is this so expensive?"

"We ordered almost everything off the menu."

I sigh. "I'm sorry, I don't have—"

She moves to swing at me, but I flinch, so she stops and grins again.

"That's two for flinching. It'll only get worse. STOP APOL-OGIZING."

I bite my lip as she gives me two taps on my left arm, marking that three total for my left and one for my right. By now, my upper arm is numb, but I know later in the night it'll be throbbing.

"I don't have money. I'll have to pay you back when we get to my locker in school. My money is in my backpack."

"Stupid place to keep it."

"Where do you keep yours then? You don't even have any pockets."

She nods but doesn't say anything. I expect her to reach into her bra or somewhere to get cash or a card, but she produces neither. She continues to nod and stare.

"So," I say, "are you going to pay for this?"

"Nope." She smiles.

"Well, I don't have any money."

"Me neither."

I try to put my head around what she just said, but I can't.

"What do you mean?"

"I mean"—she leans back and crosses her hands behind her head in pure enjoyment—"neither of us has money to pay for this meal."

And that's when I know that this is what she had planned all along. She knew I didn't have any money. She knew I'd agree to come here, to a restaurant out of my hometown where no one knows me, and she knew I'd agree to follow her along. She knew we were never going to pay for the meal.

My breaths become shallow and the room spins. I grab the table edge to steady myself and count the metronomic ticking in my head. I dig a nail into my forearm until skin breaks.

Breathe, Gray. Breathe.

"What do we do? They're not just going to let us leave without paying."

"Good question. Better answer." She clears her throat. "First, we dined in this fine, aristocratic establishment."

She pauses to reach for the last remaining fry on my plate and dips it into the last drop of ketchup and pops it in her mouth. She waits until she's done chewing to speak, but by now, I already know what she's going to say. She states it simply:

"And now, we are going to dash."

My stomach drops. "Oh fuck."

14 HOURS UNTIL

I LOOK AROUND, PARANOID THAT HIDDEN CAMERAS ARE recording our entire conversation and that the police are on the way. I know in the end that not paying one check won't matter, but it's still wrong.

Across the table, Aubrey unscrews the tops from the salt and pepper shakers and dumps their contents into her watered-down Dr. Pepper. When she's done, she squeezes a few drops of ketchup in and mixes them together with a dirty knife. I gag at the sight of the murky liquid.

"I don't think I can do this," I say.

"Sure you can."

"It's stealing. What if they catch us, or what if there's an undercover cop nearby, or they catch our license plate on a camera outside?"

"Jesus, calm down. We're not murdering anybody; we're just not paying for dinner." She smiles to herself and continues to stir the disgusting drink. "Undercover cops? At a restaurant?"

My face grows hot, and her words strike me like a slap. The irony. The shame of doing something I fundamentally know is wrong.

"Have you done this before?" I ask.

"In every single town I've ever lived."

I wonder how much money she owes and if she never pays for anything or just steals whatever and whenever she can.

"Why?"

Clearly frustrated, she sighs and leans forward, her elbows on the table.

"You're stalling. So here's the deal. I answer this question, then you make a run for it with me, or I run, and you stay and find out what happens when you can't pay your bill. I can promise that you will *not* like that process. Okay?" She pauses for a response but starts talking again before I can open my mouth. She was never going to allow me to make a choice in the first place. Her shoulders tense and she glares. Another challenge to look away. I don't.

"It was my father's dying wish to thwart *The Man* whenever I could and rally against the bourgeoisie establishment by peacefully protesting that in an economy gone to shit, paying $17.99 for a bacon cheeseburger is both an injustice and an abuse of power. So, I like to show them that until prices versus wages are actually *fair*, I refuse to be a mindless drone that pays for vacuumed-wrapped frozen food that those aristocratic dicks nuked in the microwave to serve to us. Happy?"

Holy shit, Gray. She's either the smartest girl you've ever met, a hippie, or she's absolutely crazy.

Should you acknowledge her dad's death? Is her mom dead too?

I don't know how to respond, so instead I say, "That sounds about right."

"Glad you agree." She eases the tension in her shoulders and breaks the glare in her eyes. She seems, for a brief moment, relieved. "Now let's go."

"Can we at least leave a tip?"

"First off: have you *not* heard a word I just said? Second: I refuse to tip that waitress anything. She's what's wrong with women's progress, with that horribly cliché accent. Not to mention she keeps eyeing you up like a sex doll she wants to take home and tie to her bedposts. No. Besides, I thought we were going to have sex after we ate."

Cool it, Gray. She's just messing with you... Right?

"Half kidding." She bites her lip, pushes the gross glass of Dr. Pepper to the center of the table, and steps out of the booth to stretch. "I'll go first. Wait, like, a minute. Then follow. Be cool. Don't run; don't look around like you have something to hide. Just act confident, like you know where you need to go. People respond to confidence."

I wipe my mouth with a napkin, my heart racing. "I still never agreed to this."

"Yes, you did." She pats my shoulder and walks past me to the front doors. "When you followed me out into the parking lot. You already made your choice, Grayson."

Something about the way she says it, about the way she lingers on my name, about how her hand stays on my shoulder for as long as it can before letting go, strikes a chord that ripples shivers down my spine. I look behind and watch her leave, watch how her hair swishes back and forth with each step. How confident and cocky she composes herself. Like there is not a care in the world.

What choice do you think she meant, Gray? Only one way to find out...

The next table over, Justine marks down something in her order pad and turns around to me, smiles, and walks over. My eyes are drawn to that tiny chip at the bottom of her front tooth.

"Need anythin' else, hun?" she asks while eying the check.

"No, thank you. Just waiting for my sister to get back from the, uh, bathroom."

"No rush." She smiles a moment too long and leans down to lower her voice and scribble on her pad. She rips out the page, folds it, and hands it to me. "Gray Falconi?"

I let out air, confused. "How did you know?"

She flashes her teeth. "I'm a huge fan of your show. Your writing is amazing." Her cheeks get red. "I'm a proud Falconian. Your poetry is just so darn beautiful. My girlfriends all think so too."

In what world...

"Wow, um," I stumble over words, get uncomfortable. I haven't gotten any kind of reaction like this in a while. "Thank you."

"Just flag me down when you're ready. Is it okay if I take your picture when I come back? My friends are going to be so darn jealous."

She brushes her fingertips against my palm and smiles; her cheeks turn red. I don't know what to think. I'm positive she is in her early or mid-twenties, and I'm almost positive she just flirted with me. Not to mention being a fan of my writing as well. After she walks away, not waiting for my response, I open up the folded paper and see her phone number next to her name with a "<3." It doesn't make any sense. But I shake my head. Aubrey called it. Once again, she was right.

I rip it up and drop the shreds into Aubrey's disgusting concoction. Being recognized like this makes me feel awkward and strange. I don't like it.

I stand up from the booth. At the next table, the little girl in the yellow dress looks over and smiles, her two front teeth missing. I want desperately to smile back, but the image of her feet swinging beneath the table, too short to touch the ground, and those missing teeth are too painful. I wave back and then have to look away.

Baby steps. Take a few steps forward. Be confident! Don't.

Look. Back.

I look behind me at the empty table—

Goddammit, Gray!!!

—and trip over my feet, crashing into a support beam.

"Sonofabitch," I cry out as my forehead smacks into the pole.

My ears ring, and before I know it, with everyone turning to face me, my heart practically jumping out of my chest, I make the decision that it's now or never. I rub my forehead and shake away the dizziness before booking it for the front doors.

"Hey. Hey!" Someone shouts from behind.

"He didn't pay the bill." A woman's voice.

"Stop him!"

"Shitshitshitshitshit," I curse under my breath, push open the double doors, and find Aubrey smoking a cigarette off to the side. She looks over at me wide-eyed, sees me panting and the crazed look in my eyes. She drops the cigarette and doesn't bother stomping it out before grabbing my hand and pulling me along to the car.

"I told you to be cool!"

"I was. I tripped. I'm sorry."

"I'm going to owe you a punch, but right now we have bigger things to worry about. Get in the car!"

We reach the Buick and hop in. She starts the engine, and I turn around to see a few employees in their green uniforms standing outside the door. Two men—I assume managers—dash for the car, pens in hand. Without a moment's hesitation, Aubrey throws the car into reverse and backs up, then throws the transmission into drive and peels out of the parking lot and into rush-hour traffic.

As Aubrey swerves past cars and into the turning lane illegally, I clutch the dashboard and brace myself. I close my eyes, shake away panic that's on the fringe, lower the window, and stick my head outside and shout into the wind. The adrenaline and excitement of it all feel unlike anything I've ever experienced. The only thing I can think to do is let it all out. I sit on my knees and wave at the restaurant as we head down the road and turn down a random street in Davisport I've never been on before.

I sit back in the seat and buckle up. When Aubrey turns to face me, she smiles, maybe even laughs a little. She rolls down her window and sticks her head out to shout something I can't make out as the wind whips past her face. Her hair goes crazy in the car, blowing every way imaginable. When she leans back in, we turn to each other. There is an understanding, a shared experience. And for whatever reason, I'm happy for it.

"I'm not going to lie... that was a rush."

She lets out a giggle. "I told you."

"I'm still absolutely terrified we'll get caught. They must have taken down our plate as we sped away."

"Yeah, probably." She turns on the radio to the hard rock station.

"What do we do now?"

"Get rid of this grandma car."

"But it's Reefer's. And what would we do without a car?"

She shakes her head and raises the volume so she has to scream over the song, places one arm outside the window, and steers the car with her free hand.

"Steal one. Obviously."

"What do you mean you left without paying?" Reefer's voice shouts into the phone. I have to pull it back slightly. "My dad is *pissed*, bro. Your parents aren't answering when my dad calls; no one has been able to get in touch with *you*, not to mention that you've ignored *my* calls. Like, literally ignored them all. Korean Freckles is worried sick; she's annoying as all hell... that's a lie... but she *is* being annoying. You're in serious dookie, *mi amigo*."

"I know."

Aubrey is lying on the hood of the car in an abandoned parking lot. It used to be for the old bowling alley before the building burned down a few summers ago. No one bothered to rebuild it ever since. Weeds sprout up through the cracks in the concrete. I bend down and rip off a piece of a longer one and put it in my pocket.

"So this is real then?" Reefer says. "You and Aubrey-frickin-Fisher out there?"

"Yeah." I look at Aubrey on the hood of the car with one arm bent behind her neck for support and the other extended in the air. It looks like what I do in the mornings before I get up from bed. Her mini-skirt rides up, exposing more of her upper thigh covered in fishnets and nylon. "I think I'm going to spend the rest of the day with her. It's hard to explain. I just... I can't describe why. It's just something I have to do."

Reefer exhales into the phone. "You sure you're alright? Can I trust her?"

"Yeah." I shift the weight from one leg to the other and spin around in a circle. "I think so. I mean, she's kind of crazy, but—"

"I get it, Gray-Gray. Just... answer my calls... or my texts... in fact, just answer me, period. I don't want to read a story of how my best bud was chopped into tiny pieces and baked into Christmas cookies that Aubrey will undoubtedly mail to me out of sheer pleasure, in which case I will most certainly eat because let's face it, I'm pleasantly plump. I ain't passing up no cookies anytime soon."

"Well, of course. Only makes sense."

"Right. And I don't want to eat you, Gray. No offense... I'm sure you taste delicious. You'd make a good human hamburger...

if ever we were to cook you as meat in a zombie apocalypse, assuming food was sparse. You'd be the dead weight. Again no offense."

"None taken." I hold in a laugh. "How did we get to this conversation again?"

"We were talking about how Aubrey is going to rape and murder you so she can trick me into becoming a cannibal and eating you."

"First: rape isn't funny. Second: you're ridiculous."

Starting to talk like her now, are you?

"Yeah, that probably was in poor taste," he says with hesitation in his voice. "But when have I ever not been re-dick?"

"Re-dick?"

"Ridiculous."

Aubrey raises herself up on her elbows and turns in my direction, looks bored. "Chatty Cathy, let's wrap it up already." She signals an imaginary watch with her wrist.

"I have to go."

"You have a rubber... right, *mang*?"

"No?"

"Gray Falconi: slayer of everything but the female vagina. Disappointment to high school men around the world."

"Goodbye, Reef."

"It's probably better. Rumor is she's got all kinds of stank down there." A pause. "Are you sure you don't need me to pick you up? I'll do it... just say the word."

"Goodbye, Reef."

"Fine, whatever. Kisses, love! I'll stall for you as long as I can... and somehow break the heartbreak to Frecks that she's no longer the only woman in your life... and make sure my dad doesn't send the FBI after you... because you did steal my car! And not even a thank you! Ha!"

We hang up, and on my home screen, I see I've gotten a new

anonymous text:

> **UNKNOWN**
>
> treat ur friends like shit
>
> ignore every1 trying 2 help
>
> u thot that announcement foster-freak did at school was funny?
>
> Aubrey wont bring him back
>
> time 2 face reality

I look up from my phone; my hands shake. Without realizing it, my vision blurs, and something snaps between my fingers. My phone's touch screen is cracked down the middle from where my fingers are clutched. My knuckles are white, and I let out a breath to release my grip on the phone.

From the hood of the car, Aubrey sits up criss-cross style and looks at me. She sees my cracked phone and looks into my eyes. She doesn't react or utter a single word. All she does is stare.

And that is enough.

We continue our silence as we get back into the car. She picks up a dirty flyer that is lying on the concrete. It's for the Davisport town fair. I convince her not to ditch Reefer's "grandma" car and she agrees, reluctantly. She blasts the rock station through the speakers that I know will blow out sooner or later.

Aubrey drives up and down a side street a few times before turning down more residential streets and driving slowly past the houses. She's stalling until the next brilliant idea comes to continue our day.

The streets here are nicer than in Lee Falls. The roads don't have nearly as many potholes or cracks, and there are actual lines dividing lanes. The residential neighborhoods are similar to ours, but with a few cul-de-sacs and fewer dead-ends. We don't have anything higher than two-story buildings in my hometown. Here they have three-story houses—a few wrap-around porches with fancy furniture outside. It's just a bigger, nicer, less crappy version of home.

I reach into my pocket and pull out the weed from the parking lot and twirl it in my fingers. It's something so simple and overlooked. The rejected plant life, the one nobody wants. On the outside, it appears rough and ugly, yet there is so much underneath the ground that can't be seen. There is more between the cracks.

Everyone has this picture painted in their heads of who they think Aubrey is. I do too. But deep down there is more than what she projects. In the short time we've spent together, there is something beneath the surface that she doesn't want to show, that maybe she never lets out. I'm determined to find the real Aubrey Fisher. The girl behind the attitude and piercings.

Did her dad really die, or was that just another story?

She interrupts my thoughts. "What's with the weed?"

I sit up in my seat and clear my throat. "It's interesting."

"You find a weed interesting?"

"It's just something so beautiful that people overlook, you know? Nobody understands that a weed is a plant like any other. It's just... *different*."

She raises her chin and twitches her nose. My eyes are drawn back to the nose ring.

"That's a unique way to admire a weed."

"Just taking a mental picture of it."

"Most people prefer to smoke it."

"I've never tried."

"You've never smoked weed?"

"Nope."

"I forgot. You're Mr. Perfect over here."

I roll my eyes. "Yep, that's me. Perfect. Straight edge. Drawn to girls with reckless behavior."

Hot damn, Gray. Who are you? What have you done with the other guy?

Aubrey does a double take. "Well, look who's being a sarcastic little shit. There may be hope for you yet."

"I guess so."

She chews the inside of her lip and points down at the weed. There's another flicker in her eyes I can't make out. It again seems like I've taken her off guard.

"Why the weed?"

I look down and clear my throat. "One day this plant will wither away and die. It's sad to think it will go through its life without someone recognizing it for the miracle it is."

"And why is it sad?"

I pause to think before answering. "Because it'll die alone and afraid, not knowing it was loved."

She looks ahead out the front window and sits upright. Something in her changes.

"How do you feel about town fairs?" she asks monotone.

"Umm, they're okay?"

I lower my eyes to avoid her gaze, which I know is upon me. After a moment, I tuck the weed into my pocket. Aubrey doesn't respond, somehow satisfied with the answer.

The rock music is slowly becoming more bearable. The band playing doesn't scream at all, and that's progress in my book. Out of the corner of my eye, I see her blow some air, so her bangs puff up. A smile crosses my lips.

Who are you, Aubrey Fisher? Who are you really?

13 HOURS UNTIL

FRIDAY, 5:00ISH PM

As Aubrey drives us down a few more unidentifiable streets, I play the voicemails on my phone. Reefer's is both typical and hysterical, and his dad's is almost sad.

I want to die. I want to see my baby brother again.

But I don't want to hurt everyone in the process.

I play his voicemail:

"Hey, Gray, it's Mr. Hoch. I saw you leave school today with that Aubrey Fisher girl. I'm not mad; I'm worried about you. I can't get a hold of either of your parents." There is a shuffle on his end of the line before his voice picks up, stiffer than before. "I know tomorrow is the seventh. If you don't call me, at least call Brian and let him know you're okay. Call your parents and check in. I'll have my phone on me all day. You won't get in trouble for the stunt at school; it's all being taken care of. Please call me back, Gray. I'm here for you. Goodbye."

Shit.

I delete his voicemail when I'm done and lock my phone.

"So are we going to the fair?" I indicate the disgusting flyer she had picked up and placed on the dash. Crusted ketchup and an unknown stain mark the surface.

"You'll see."

"It's frustrating when you do that."

"And here I thought you never wanted to come out in the first place 'cause you couldn't trust me."

"Well... I don't. I didn't. I don't know."

She turns down the volume on the radio and cocks her head in my direction. "Is moody, brooding Grayson actually having *fun*?"

I roll my eyes. "I thought you said you wouldn't make fun of me."

"I'm not. Just teasing. Like I said, you're easy to rile up. And I want to see what you're like when pushed to the limit."

"The limit of what?"

She doesn't answer, just hums a tune before punching me in the left shoulder.

"What the heck was that for?" I rub the spot that is already numb.

"I owed you. Remember?"

"If I told you to stop hitting me, would you stop?"

"That depends. Are you asking me or telling me?"

"I guess I'm asking? I get it. You want me to be more active."

"So are you asking or telling?"

"Asking."

"Then no." She pulls into the parking lot of the Davisport town fair: Plumfest. The name is as horrible as it sounds.

"What are we going to do here?"

Aubrey pauses to indicate our surroundings, twirling her arms. One eyebrow raised. "Ride the rides. What else do you do at a fair?"

"You want to ride the rides?" I step out of the car and am greeted by the faint smell of caramel corn and fried dough. My mouth salivates, despite being full. "Don't we need money to buy tickets?"

"Got that covered. Don't worry."

The parking lot is packed with cars, and just beyond the lot are the knee-high aluminum gates to block off the fair. They don't serve their purpose well. We hop over the gate and pass the kiddie slide to emerge in a clearing. I'm greeted by flashing colored lights and fried foods. Below, hay covers muddy spots.

We walk to the right and pass a row of games—each one with an employee dressed in blue jeans and tucked-in striped shirts, calling out to us:

"Two-for-two deal. Wegotta two-for-two deal over hereeeeeeeeee. You, ma'am! Yes, you!" He points to Aubrey, microphone in hand, running his words together. "Youlooklikea betting woman. I'll give youandyourboyfriend eight balls for two dollars!"

Boyfriend?

We march on past a few kids' rides. Parents walk strollers filled with sleeping and crying and happy babies. Children hop up and down eating bubblegum cotton candy. A few more bump into my shoulder without stopping to look back or apologize. Buzzing and alarm bells sound from various tents. Speakers attached to light poles play a local pop radio station.

I'm just about to ask Aubrey where we're going when she walks up to the ring toss game. She leans against a side of the booth and presses her chest against the ledge, so her boobs push up. The kid working, both lanky and covered with bad face acne, walks toward her. There is a short girl on the opposite side running the game with him. A family next to us tosses the rings, trying to win a fish.

"Well, damn girl, come all this way to visit me?" He smiles, revealing crooked and yellowed teeth. I want to turn away, but something tells me I shouldn't. He has a hungry look in his beady eyes.

"Just looking for some free tickets, Greg. I know you can help." She further presses her chest into the ledge.

I don't know what to think. It's hard to imagine Aubrey would know some random fair worker from over in Davisport when she's only been in school two months. But then again, I still know nothing about what she does or where she goes after school. I look between the two of them and stand back. Greg's eyes light up, and I decide not to like him. He's not a good person.

He licks his lips and walks over to whisper into his co-worker's ear before pulling off his work vest. He jumps over the booth and lands next to Aubrey. She turns to me as Greg pulls out his cell phone to text.

"I'll be right back. Just stay by the booth. Okay?" She nods and starts to walk forward. Greg heads toward one of the outhouses. I grab her wrist and pull her back.

"Who is this guy?"

She shrugs me off. "Trust me. He'll get us more tickets than we can possibly spend tonight."

"Let me come with you."

"No."

"Why?"

From ahead, Greg calls back, annoyed. He doesn't acknowledge I'm here. I look back and forth between the two of them, and the image of the security guard touching Aubrey comes back. For some reason, I think I know what she's going to do.

"Listen," she says. "I'll be back in a few minutes. He just wants to make out with me. I can handle Greg. He's a perv, but harmless."

"You shouldn't have to make out with anyone. Do you even know him?" I get upset, more upset than I probably should be. Greg still has that hungry look, and all I want to do is punch it off his face.

"Relax. Just chill out and go eat a corn dog. I'll meet you back here in ten minutes."

Aubrey doesn't give me a chance to argue because she turns and walks with Greg past the outhouse and ducks behind it, disappearing. Without knowing what to do, I twirl around and watch the Tilt-o-Whirl. My knuckles turn white from squeezing my fists. I try to piece together why she seemed to give in to the guard's touch in the bathroom and why she's going off with creeper Greg. Thinking about it upsets me too much.

He's going to do more than kiss her, and you know it. Coward. Just going to stand by, again, and wait for something bad to happen. Or you can be a man and stop it.

I start to march back behind the outhouse to save her from his acne-covered face when I spot Kris getting off the Tilt-o-Whirl with a few girls from school. They don't see me, but Kris hobbles down the metal ramp to the field below. She winces with each limp. Not big, but just enough to notice. I want to bash my face on the metal guardrails around the ride repeatedly until my head splits like an eggshell and my brain spools out like yolk.

With each slight limp, I visualize her knee twisting almost all the way around. See her reaching out for me, blood running down from a gash near her hairline. Her screams. An echoing loop.

Aubrey hasn't returned, so I duck down behind the booth and force the memory away as Kris heads in my direction. She spots me before I land on my knees, and I curse. My heart leaps into my throat, but I pray that she keeps on walking. The last thing I want is to talk to her again. Coming here was a mistake. Everyone will be here—a Friday night after school.

There's a tap on my shoulder, so I turn around. It's Kyle.
Seriously?
"Falconi..."

"Kyle."

Kris stops mid-stride as he holds up his hand. She looks offended but obeys. The girls around her hover by a nearby concession stand.

"Heard my cousin got his ass kicked earlier." There's a slight grin. "Bet he deserved that."

His casual demeanor throws me off. Not sure if it's real or fake.

"He never knows when to keep his mouth shut." I attempt to keep the mood light, but Kyle doesn't react. I look around, paranoid.

He chuckles. "You really here with Aubrey Fisher?"

I nod, and Kris takes a step, but Kyle holds up his hand in protest. For a moment it's like the old us again. How we used to be. And then his face changes, like a new lens on a camera.

"I also heard you shoved my sister into a locker." He presses a few fingers into my chest, beside the bruise. "You wanna tell me what that's about?"

I fight the urge to tear up. This wasn't supposed to happen, seeing Kyle. Or Kris. It's like Aubrey is somehow forcing me to confront everything I was hoping to leave behind. And in this moment, I don't know what to say.

"I just want to be alone and miserable. Remember?"

His face contorts, and he wraps his hand around the back of my neck and squeezes. I look up and Kris is limping over, wincing as she goes. I'm filled with regret already.

"I'm not going to tell you again. This is your last warning: stop hurting my sister. You've done enough. Nobody blames you for that night except for you. But not going to see our dad? Abandoning my sister's recovery? That's what really makes me want to hate you."

He squeezes harder, and I bite my lip to keep from crying

out. Because I know that he needs to let out the aggression. I'm prepared to let him do whatever he feels is right.

"Kyle, stop it!" Kris calls out.

She steps closer until her coconut perfume surrounds me. It brings me back to summer nights spent lying on her trampoline in the backyard as we stared up at the stars. Moments from a time we can never get back.

Kyle lets go and steps away to stand with Kris. "Next time, I will hurt you. I don't want to, but I'm also not going to let you keep treating her like a whore, Falconi."

"Then just let me go, both of you. I'm not the same person I used to be." I rub the back of my neck.

"None of us are," Kyle says. "Wake up!"

"Just talk to us, let us in," Kris pleads. "Let someone in. Please." She leans in closer. "The accident wasn't your fault."

"Then why is my brother dead?"

They both open their mouths but stop, eyes wide. It might be the first time I've been so blunt with them about it. Even I don't know why I said it or where it came from. Their posture sinks, deflated. Like any anger they had built up was capped off.

Kyle shakes his head, chews a thought. "Have you been deleting your profiles? Your poetry?"

Kris inhales. "You've been *what*?"

"I can't," I say as I break away and walk toward the outhouses. "I'm sorry."

From behind me, Kris calls my name a few times, but I don't answer. I look over and see Kyle wrap an arm around her shoulder and lead her to the group of girls.

The fairground turns hazy, and I have to remind myself to take deep breaths. The ticking in my head gets louder, so I fall down next to the outhouse and cough. I suck in gulps of air until I calm down.

Inhale. Exhale.

I pull out my phone and find another video posted about two years ago. I can't really hear it too well, so I watch it play first without the sound, then replay it again with the speaker to my ear and strain to listen. It's short enough. This video is just me this time, confessional style, as I stare into the camera lens. Dressed in a backward snapback, thinking I looked cool, wearing a tank top. I wasn't as confident here as in my later videos. My voice is a tad shaky. 2,057 views. 303 likes. 23 dislikes.

"*This next one is called 'Bonfire of Emotional Vampires.' I didn't want to post this. Read it to the Little Man. My little bro. He didn't understand it at all, the vampires freaked him out but said I shouldn't be a wiener and just record it. So, if an eight-year-old is calling me a frankfurter, I have to prove him wrong. Bryson knows what's up. Little Man has better taste than I do. Enjoy and like, share, and comment below, my Falconians.*"

I'M PETRIFIED WOOD
RESTING ATOP
DEAD ASH.
YOU ARE AN EMBER
SPARKLING AMBER BENEATH
DECREPIT RUBBLE.
DON'T GET TOO CLOSE
OR YOU'LL BE
SNUBBED OUT—
SUCKED DRY.
RAIN COMES
IN THE MORNING
TO WASH AWAY
OUR LONELY SINS.
NIGHT COMES
IN THIS PIT I'M STUCK

To drain you of
Your innocence."

The most recent comments:

GamerBoyGenius17: this is depressing AF. hat is ghetto AF. Not
a fan

JamesDeanFan: (responding to GamerBoyGenius17) Sorry you
can't appreciate art. Go get a life.

JamesDeanFan: Your writing is important and means something.
Keep speaking from the heart. Damn. That's how we change the
world. That's how YOU change the world.

Too close. Too damn close.
Deleted.
Gone.
No trace of me will be left.
No record I was ever here.

I stay seated on the hay and cross my legs. I glance behind
the outhouse, but Aubrey is nowhere. The fear that she left me
comes back before I spot her and Greg returning to the ring toss.
She has a huge bundle of red tickets in her hands. Greg leans in
and kisses her on the lips before jumping back over the booth
and putting on his work vest. Aubrey looks around and spots me
on the ground. She walks over and raises the tickets in triumph.

It feels like anything but.

The roll of tickets Aubrey got doesn't pay for any games or food,
but they work on everything else. Neither of us says anything
about what she did with Greg to get them. It bugs me, even
disgusts me a little, but I try not to dwell on it. Aubrey can

handle herself. One minute she's quiet and calculated, the next she's kicking ass, and then she's coloring with crayons in a restaurant. Trying to figure her out gives me a headache.

There are long lines for all the rides, but we start with the Tilt-o-Whirl. Once we get up to the ticket-taker, he opens the gate and we climb into one of the carts. Aubrey slides over, so our shoulders touch. I glance down at her legs before looking up into her unique eyes.

"How do you feel about spinney rides?" she asks.

"I haven't been on one in a while. He was always motion sick when our family went to amusement parks."

"Who was motion sick, your dad?"

Oh no.

It slips without thought. Unsure how to recover, I choose not to say anything and curse myself. It was stupid and careless. Last thing I want is for Aubrey to know. Her problems probably far exceed mine. Maybe both her parents were gone; maybe she never knew them.

Aubrey studies my face and waits for an answer, but I don't provide one. She sighs, disappointed.

The ride starts and Aubrey puts all her weight into the outside of the cart so it spins faster than the blood can reach my head. Everything around me becomes a giant blur, and all I can see is Aubrey. Her hair billows in the wind as she spins it faster and faster. The cart changes direction and starts to twirl to the opposite side. The switch sends both of us sliding to the other end, so I push up against her. I can't help but let out a scream and laugh.

Aubrey's eyes are closed. She seems to be at one with her surroundings. She still leans against the side to spin the cart as fast as it will allow, but there is serenity in her. This is her grace, her happy place. Her hair whips around, and the lights of the fair shine on her face as we pass under the colored bulbs hanging from the ride's support beams. It's comforting just to observe, and in this moment, I want nothing but to close my eyes and join her.

So I do.

We stumble off the ride when it ends and hold on to each other as I almost walk into a nearby trashcan. Aubrey grabs my hand and laughs so hard I think she's going to pass out. It's infectious, and before long, I lean over and hold my gut. Tears well in the corners of my eyes, and I try to catch a breath.

After a few minutes we get on the UFO, followed by the bumper cars and the Scrambler. We hop from ride to ride, even stand in line for the mini-Ferris wheel, which terrifies me. Aubrey has to goad me into agreeing, but I do to once again prove my masculinity, which is a regular occurrence around her. Aubrey is the type of cool most people only dream about. We get stuck on top, and although we're only thirty feet in the air, looking down gives me nothing short of vertigo.

"You've been really quiet," she says.

I look up, startled. "I just haven't done this in a while."

"Done what? Town fairs?"

"Fun."

She nods and squints her eyes. "You're kind of a sad person."

Aubrey states it as a fact. More of an observation versus an accusation, but she does it in a tender voice. One I've never heard over her normal, raspy tone. I look back down over the basket. It takes a while, but I look up and smirk when the perfect witty response comes to mind.

"*Kind of* sounds very passive of you, Aubrey Fisher. You're gonna have to woman up."

She guffaws and punches me in the left shoulder.

"What the hell?" I fling my arms up in mock karate defense, which causes her to laugh harder.

"That's for being a little shit. Write that down too. Don't. Be. A. Little. Shit." She exhales dramatically. The Ferris wheel starts to move again from our top position. "We really need to buy you that spiral notebook to write these golden nuggets of wisdom down."

"College ruled or wide? There's a difference."

"Interesting point you bring up, Mr. Grayson." She sits up straight and pretends to tighten an imaginary tie. "College ruled means serious business. It means you're here to pay attention and make the most of the space and time you have. Wide just means you're here to party, and you really don't give a shit about anything."

"Technically, Miss Fisher,"—I raise my pointer finger in the air and square my shoulders—"You can't not care about nothing. There has to be something to which you would choose not to care about. So saying there's nothing to care about really just means you're disproving your own point. To exude the sense of carelessness means to have something of value to which you aspire not to care about."

She blinks and slumps back in the basket as it reaches the ground and begins its climb again.

"Well, damn. If that doesn't just put me in my place, I don't know what does."

"I'm pretty smart, you know. It's kind of a talent of mine."

"Do you want another punch for bragging?"

I hold up my hands in surrender and smile. Aubrey grins back. Her dimple glimmers under the slowly setting sun and the Ferris wheel's flashing lights. There is a beat where neither of us says or does anything. She turns away, uncomfortable, and runs fingers through her hair. The way the light illuminates her pale skin almost makes her look—

What is she doing to you?

And that's when I see him as we reach the peak of the Ferris wheel. Standing by the rock-climbing wall in his torn Yankees baseball cap, faded jeans, and black hoodie holding a pink and blue cotton candy. He looks up and beams. He waves a hand and takes a bite before turning around to walk away. I do a double take and lean over the side until I'm almost halfway out of the basket, about to fall. I hear a few people down below gasp, and from behind, hands tug me back inside. But he was there. Watching us.

Bryson.

12 Hours Until

SOMETIME AFTER 6:00 PM

"What the hell are you doing?" Aubrey says.

I lean out of the cart again as we start to make our descent, but he's gone. My upper body hangs off the side, and I hear screams from down below. Aubrey tucks me back inside.

"Are you trying to get yourself killed? What the hell!"

"We need to get off." I fidget in the seat, try to make another move before Aubrey holds me down. She's strong. "Right now."

"Hold on. Jesus. What's happening? You're acting like a psycho."

I snap my head in her direction. "That's real rich coming from you, Aubrey." The guilt comes immediately, but it shuts her up.

Her eyes glare at me like she's ready to pounce, but she bites her lower lip and stands up to shout down below.

"My friend isn't feeling good; you need to stop the ride when we reach the ground."

There is a muffled response from whoever is working the Ferris wheel, and before I know it, we're on the ground walking in the open space. Fair goers clear away, no longer interested, but none of it matters. Bryson was down here. He was watching me. He was alive.

But he's dead. He choked on his own blood. Remember?

He's nowhere to be seen. Not here. Just gone.

Hot tears roll over my flushed cheeks, and everything distorts. The rolling waves of anxiety suffocate me, and I sink to my knees, push at the bruise on my chest. My heart feels too big for my body—ready to pop like a balloon. Aubrey wraps her arms around me, and I know she's saying something, shouting, but it's just a muffled hum. It's crazy; I know it is. Bryson was never here. But it seemed so real. *He* seemed so real. Dressed just like he was on that Thursday night.

It's not long before my breath returns to normal, and the waves roll past. It's another panic attack. Not nearly as bad as others I've had, but I can't stop the tears. I don't want to attract too much attention, so I find Aubrey's arms and shakily pull myself to my feet.

"I-I'm fine," I gasp and wipe my face. "I'm okay. Just... just need some water."

Aubrey walks in front and puts her hands on my shoulders. We lock eyes, and there's something in them. They look soft, almost welcoming. Like she's just realized something that never occurred to her before. There's a slight tick on my shoulder, and it's not from me.

Her arm is trembling, Gray.

A paramedic makes his way to us and tells me to sit. Aubrey does most of the talking to get everyone to go about business as usual. I tune most of it out and look around again just in case he comes back, but find no trace of Bryson. It's been a while since I've seen him. He only shows up when I start to forget, when I start to think I can be happy again. Aubrey was a nice distraction. She almost made me forget.

Forget how I got him killed.

It's interesting how fast it can change, like a light switch. One moment you're laughing and living a life, and just like that, there is a darkness that hangs like a cloud ready to storm.

After a few minutes, when the paramedic and a few onlookers start to disperse, Aubrey grabs my wrist and leads me across the fair to get a water bottle from the fried dough stand. She takes off one of her combat boots and inside is a wadded-up pile of money. She shuffles through a few bills and pulls out twenty dollars to buy water before she folds them back up and puts the wad back into her boot.

She had money the entire time.

I don't say anything about the cash after I chug most of the bottle down and pour the remainder on top of my head to cool off. It should make me mad, but it doesn't. It's not even surprising. The only question is: where did it come from?

"Well, that was exciting," she breaks the awkward silence and snaps her fingers.

I run my tongue over my front teeth. "I'm sorry about what I said back there."

"Stop apologizing."

"I didn't mean it."

"Of course you did."

"No."

"I'm going to stop you there." She holds up a hand. "Don't apologize for speaking your mind. Never apologize for that. Ever. You said it because it's how you felt. I don't know what exactly happened up there, but own it. Stick to your convictions. Be proud of who you are, and never let anyone ever tell you any different. You think I don't know what people say in school? What the town says?" She cocks her head and smirks at me. "You have every right to think things about me, Grayson. You don't even know me. The point is they don't have to define you. Nothing has to. Me, for example. I could be a serial killer. A raging slut. Or a spiteful bitch."

"I highly doubt that."

"What makes you so sure?"

"I don't think you're any of those things, Aubrey."

There's an awkward beat where we both look down at our feet and start to walk forward down the long line of concession stands. I'm greeted by smells of pizza, clams, pastries, and cheeseburgers.

She stops to look me in the eyes. "Then who do you think I am?"

Nothing comes to mind, so instead I shrug in response. She raises her left eyebrow. We stand in the middle of the walkway, and I can almost feel her breath on my chin. Her chest heaves up and down, and the red bangs fall in front of her right eye. Without thinking, I raise my hand and brush them behind her ear.

Aubrey's eyes grow wide and she pinches my nipple. I cry out and jump back, slapping her hand away.

"Don't ever do that again," she says, but there's a playful tone behind her voice.

I smile. "Right back at you."

And that's when it happens, when the dark cloud emerges again. From behind Aubrey, Kyle and Tim turn a corner and head down the walkway. Kris and the girls from school follow behind. Tim points to me when he raises his head and meets my gaze. Kyle attempts to steer him away, but Tim shrugs him off and keeps walking. Intent. Hateful. Kyle tries a second time, Kris limping to keep up, but Tim ignores them.

I must look terrified because Aubrey whirls around and backs in front of me. Protecting me. She tenses up, which causes me to tense up, but I can't let her fight my battles. Not this time.

"Let me handle this," I whisper in her ear.

"Are you sure?" She turns around and squares her shoulders. There's a look on her face I can't place. Her brows furrow, and her forehead creases.

"Not really."

Aubrey rolls her eyes and steps aside just as Kyle and Tim stop a few feet ahead of us. Kris attempts to push past them, but Tim holds out his hand to stop her. His nose is wrapped in gauze and a white bandage. He looks like a demented clown.

"You know," Tim says—nasally from the bandage pinching his nose, "I can't seem to get away from you freaks today." He nudges Kyle, who shakes his head, annoyed. "I think it's only fair I sucker punch the both of them the way they did me in the cafeteria."

"Just keep walking," Kyle mumbles, straightening his Red Sox baseball cap.

"No, I'm not gonna just let this go!" He raises his voice, rotating his bracelets. "Why are you lettin' Falconi off the hook? This is bullshit." Tim never breaks his glare from me.

"Tim, no one has a problem here except for you," Kris says. She looks to me and then down at the ground. "You're being a jerk again."

Kyle takes his sister's hand and they step away from Tim, and the surprise is noticeable.

"Well, isn't this just—"

Kyle curses. "Stop running your mouth. For two seconds. I'm not doing this again. Falconi and I are done, that's it. There is *nothing* else."

"Are you even listening to yourself?" Tim steps up and shoves me hard in the chest. I stumble backward into Aubrey, who keeps me upright.

By now there is a small group circled around us. Aubrey inches forward, but I turn to shake my head, so she stays still, her eyes locked on Tim. He doesn't do anything except grin.

Kris looks down at her feet.

"Fight, you little wimp," Tim says. "Fight me." He shoves me again; I stumble into Aubrey's chest and—

You just grazed Aubrey's boob!

—she stands me back up.

"He leaves us to pick up the pieces, Kyle. 'Cause Gray is a selfish asshole. And if it weren't for him, Kris would still be runnin' track. Just like your mom and dad planned ever since we were kids."

"Tim!" Kris grabs his wrist to pull him back, but he shakes her off.

"Don't even deny it; he did this to you." He points to her left leg. "*He* did."

"That's enough," Kyle shouts. "Don't lecture me about shit I already know. Do you think I want to dwell on it day after day?" He curses. "I'm trying to get my family through this year, and I don't need that stupid accident brought up every two seconds like it'll be the only defining thing our family will be remembered for." Kyle points to Kris while still scolding Tim. "It's *my* dad lying in the hospital. Not yours. *My* sister in the brace. Not yours."

From around the circle, the same boy with the arrow tattoo from gym pulls out a phone to record a video. Another girl on the opposite side starts to shout for a fight. Because that's all anyone ever wants.

It was my fault. If I'd listened and followed the rules, Kris would still be captain of the track team and on her way to a full scholarship for college. Bryson would still be alive. Kyle would still be my friend. Their dad would still be awake.

"We're starting to attract attention," Kris says.

Murmurs from the crowd follow.

"If you're not going to hit this faggot," Tim says, "then I'll do it now before the cops come. Him and that homeless slut almost broke my nose." He turns to Aubrey, attempting to sound intimidating, but even I can hear the tremble in his voice. He's terrified she'll do it again.

Aubrey winks at him. "What a shame. Not even a nose job can make you attractive. Not even to *this* homeless slut." She giggles mischievously. "We can spar another round if you don't mind me using you as my own personal punching bag, darlin'."

Aubrey Fisher: God, she's such a badass.

Tim gives her the finger and taps Kyle on the shoulder to get his attention. He points to me. "Don't forget the little shit got you suspended."

"Jesus, fuck, dude." Kyle takes a step back and tries to look at me but flickers his eyes away. "Drop it and let's go. You're pissing me off."

Kris makes her way between the two of them and me and Aubrey.

"This doesn't concern you, Tim," Kris says. "Go home and grow up. We're not in middle school anymore. No one finds this macho act amusing." She pauses, glares at Aubrey.

By now, over a dozen people have gathered. A few walk away bored, and two more pull out cell phones. A parent scoops up her kid holding a balloon and shields him as she hurries past.

Kris looks at me and mouths, "I'm sorry." I want nothing more than to wrap my arms around her. Even Aubrey gives her a quick look before returning to a blank stare.

None of them deserve this. Kyle and Tim shouldn't be ready to fight over me. They shouldn't have to argue over something I caused.

It's why I'm going to hate what I'm about to say even more.

Make it so convincing that not even Kris can second guess.
Make it so Aubrey can't see through it.

"He's right, Kris," I say. She stops to listen. A boy in a soccer varsity jacket turns his cell phone in my direction. "You'll never walk the same because of me. You'll never run track—never coach it either."

I take a deep breath before I say what I know is going to change everything. She'll never forgive me.

"I don't love you, Kris. I never did. You mean absolutely nothing to me." I raise my voice, my heartbeat going a mile a minute.

Kris winces when I'm done, like my words are laced with a poisoned dagger.

I turn to Kyle. "Go ahead. Hit me. I'm the reason she'll lose her college scholarship." Different phrases flow through my head, each one worse than the last. Different bullshit things I can say to make them hate me. None of them are true. "I'm glad she can't run. I hope she never does again." Pause. "And I couldn't care less if your dad ever wakes up."

There are a few gasps in succession, and a junior with a mohawk shouts that people are coming. A girl with neck tattoos puts a hand to her mouth like I've just done the most horrific thing she could think of. Kris's eyes gloss over. She lowers her head, her body trembling. I can't tell if it's with rage or sadness.

Kyle tenses up as if ready to pounce; Tim has a manic look in his eyes.

And then there's Aubrey—she doesn't do or say anything. She stares blankly ahead. Bored.

"I'm gonna kill you." Kyle dashes forward. I flinch but otherwise stand in place. Aubrey steps forward in defense while Kris turns her back to me and holds her brother back. "Out of the way, Kris."

"No."

"Did you hear what he just said?"

"He didn't mean it," she says, but her voice shakes. Whether or not she believes me, I've hurt her feelings. "I want to talk with you." She points to me, her eyes on fire. "Now."

"Kick his ass!" a man's voice from behind says.

"When did Falconi turn into an asshole?" another voice.

"Aubrey's lookin' like she gonna cut a bitch," an eager voice.

Kyle makes another lunge for me, but Kris attempts to hold him back, stumbling in the process.

"This isn't you." Kris shakes her head. "Stop whatever it is you're doing."

Another voice rises from the crowd. "Will someone cut the afterschool special and just frickin' fight already."

"Come on, Kyle," I egg him on, ignoring Kris. "Do it already. Hit me. Just do it and get it over with unless you're too scared to. I-I put your father in a coma. He shouldn't have been out that night, but I made your sister call him."

Kris whirls around too fast, cries out in pain and falls to the ground, holding her leg. She twisted it too far in her brace. My instinct is to run over and see what's wrong, and I start to move, but hold myself back.

Kris looks up at me. Tears drip from each eye as she holds her knee. She takes gulps of air; Kyle bends down to see what's wrong. A few girls from school push past Tim to help her.

"What are you doing!" she cries.

I can't tell if it's from what I said or her leg. Maybe it's both. *Asshole. Asshole. Asshole.*

"This is who I am." Pause. "Get used to it." Point. "Do you get it now?"

I look away because the sight of her breaks my heart. I try to gauge Aubrey's reaction, but she has each fist clenched and stares at Tim. When I look back over my shoulder, he runs his hand over his chin.

"You're fuckin' dead," Tim says as he walks over to help Kris to her feet. "Your father is a pedophile and a rapist and a groomer. Your mother is a doped-up mess. And you're a murderer. How did it feel to watch your brother die? Did it feel good? Did you share last words as he—oh, that's right. You left him bleeding out!"

Everything builds up and then falls out of control. Aubrey lunges in the air and sucker punches Tim in the jaw. He stumbles back and falls to the ground. When he's flat, she jumps on top of him and pins his arms down with her legs before punching him repeatedly in the face with each fist until blood squirts onto her clothes. No one bothers to intervene or help. A girl behind me pushes me forward and screams. A shirtless man a few feet away drops his hot dog on the ground in shock.

Even in Davisport, Aubrey Fisher is infamous.

Tears roll down my cheeks, and my breath catches in my throat until I cough. Falling to my knees, my palms slam into the dirt path beneath me and I dry-heave. Looking up, Bryson is standing beside Aubrey, dressed in the same hoodie, jeans, and Yankees cap. I reach out to him.

Someone shouts that the police are coming. Everyone runs, pushing each other out of the way and making a dash for the parking lot. There are muffled shouts and cries from above. The ground vibrates. Dust kicks up.

Blood trickles down from the brim of Bryson's hat and curls underneath his chin. He turns to me and opens his mouth; a pool of blood spills to the ground.

"Bryson!" I shout.

I blink, and he's gone.

A foot collides with my ribs in the same spot that was kicked back in the locker room during gym. I look up right before I fall onto my stomach and see Kyle towering above me. Kris hangs on his arm, but a girl runs past and knocks her down. I try to take a breath, but my lungs contract, and I choke.

"What happened to you?" Kick. "We used to be friends. We used to go to the football games every Saturday morning at school and hang out at the bowling alley." Shove. "I had my first beer with you, dickhead. My parents trusted you." Grabs shirt collar and lifts up. "She is my sister. MY SISTER!" Punch. "And what about my dad, you fucking asshole?" Uppercut. "You were being a selfish fucking asshole that night..."

By now, Kyle's face is so red it looks like a tomato, and I cough up what I think is blood onto his fists. My entire body is numb, and his voice eventually drones out to a steady ringing. The world slowly fades away, becomes dimmer with each passing second. He pulls my shirt collar up, his fist clenched and waiting, but nothing happens. He blinks, his chest heaves up and down—nostrils flair, but he closes his eyes and curses. He opens his mouth and forms words, but it's all muffled. I think I nod my head to tell him it's okay, but my limbs won't move. He makes another attempt to bring his fist down, but he doesn't. Can't.

I look up at the sky, the sun still setting in the west, and try to make out the colors, but everything is too dim.

This is it. You're finally dying. So why doesn't it feel euphoric?

I don't know when exactly Kyle lets me go, but as I sputter for breath, Kris leans over, and her blonde hair falls down on my face. Tears glisten in her eyes and roll down each cheek. She shouts something, but I don't know if it's at me or someone behind that I can't see. It takes a while for the ringing to subside to hear her muffled voice.

"...not moving. Help me pick him up."

There is a male voice, and when I crack open one of my

eyelids, I think it's Kyle. Sharp pain courses through my entire body, like my ribcage is being pulled apart.

Consciousness fades in and out for a while because the next thing I know, we're on the outskirts of the parking lot. Hands are on both sides of me, and someone else hovers behind.

Is that you, Aubrey?

Aubrey: "...license plates here."

Kris: "What do you mean they traced the plates? What have... him into?"

Aubrey: "Listen, I know you're a good Christian, but you don't know what's... We need a new car. Now."

Kris: "...dating him for over two years. Don't tell me I do or don't know what's good for him. ...don't know a single thing about Gray. Do you? His favorite color? Favorite food? What he's always wanted to grow up to be wh—... The time he got a concussion ice skating when we were thir—... Look at him now! Skipping school, running from the cops. I bet you forced him to say those things. Right? Because isn't this what you do: ruin lives?"

Aubrey: "Is this about me and him having sex? Because it was *hot*. The things he can do with his hands..."

Kris: "I swear to God—"

Kyle: "...shut up and lift. Christ. The cops are everywhere, and I'm not going to be arrested for... Christ, I went too far. *Fuck!*

Kris: "...to leave him alone! He was trying to get you to do this, can't... He's breathing, thank God. Let's go behind the rock-climbing... over to the... Lift him on one, two... your hands off him."

Aubrey: "Aw. And here I thought we were like girlfriends carrying the man of our dreams to safe—..."

Kyle: "I'm gonna kill Tim."

Kris: "...enjoy this? Do you intentionally come into people's lives to stir the... Give you some kind of satisfaction to make everyone as messed up as you are? I feel bad for you, Aubrey. I really do. You think you're so clever with this little act you..."

Kyle: "Will you two quit your bickering! Christ, he's swelling now. Damnit, Falconi."

Aubrey: "It gives me *immense* satisfaction to know that the thought of Grayson and I having *intercourse* just makes your tiny little nose scrunch up to those beady little eyes. I live for that look in every town. Because I *am* a clever bi—"

Kris: "You know what? No. You're not even worth the tears. I'm just wasting my breath, aren't I? ...Would never sleep with someone so cruel and vile. It's like you try extra hard to alienate yourself, like you want people to fear you, to think the worst. ...Should just buy into your lies. But really, you're just scared, aren't you? You're terrified. I feel bad for you, Aubrey. All the pain you must mask. But now... And go somewhere else."

Kyle: "Okay, I've got him just—yeah, okay, and then open up the—nope. Losing hi—..."

Aubrey: "Jesus, you two. Give me his shoulders; you both take his legs so I can... Your scrawny-ass arms are getting us nowhere."

Kris: "We're done here, Aubrey. After we get him to the hospital, I want you to le—... He deserves better than this, and you know... Don't do anything to hurt him. God, he better be okay. I need to call his par—..."

Aubrey: "...Last thing you want to do. Trust me. And I never asked for pity from you, queen bee. ...Maybe Grayson and I actually get along? That maybe he *needs* me more than he does you? I bet that drives you *nuts*. We can argue later. Right now we just have to get him to—"

Me: "N-No h-h-hos-pi-tal."

Kris: "Gray?"

Kyle: "You okay, man?"

Me: "N-no..."

And then everything just goes black.

11 HOURS UNTIL

???

MOM AND DAD SIT IN THEIR USUAL SPOTS AT THE KITCHEN table, still dressed in their work clothes: Dad in his navy-blue button-up and Mom in her pear-green outfit from the daycare, a little spit-up is on the tip of her collar. In front of us is *Monopoly*, which we play on game nights at least once a month.

"This is horseshit," my dad grumbles.

Mom smacks him on the arm. "Language, Robert. Please."

Dad slumps in his chair and folds his arms over his chest; he's a sore loser. "Our son"—he points to Bryson, who beams back in his direction—"is an extortionist. No, I'm done. Our son is better than us at capitalizing on his properties? Building hotels where I once had housing? I can't even afford to get out of jail. How did that happen, Marie?"

"C'mon, Dad," I laugh and mock his whiney tone. "You're going to let the Little Man over here take your pride *and* your land?"

"I'm ten, Gray," Bryson says. "And I can't help that Mom and Dad *suck hard* at this game."

"Bryson! Language!" Mom holds back a giggle.

"Yeah," I add. "Watch your friggin' mouth."

Dad sips from his whiskey on the rocks and slides the glass back and forth across the table while Mom rests her chin in her palms, elbows propped on the table. Most nights go exactly like this, and I wouldn't have it any other way. We never finish any board games—someone always ends up getting frustrated and throwing the board across the room, which is usually Dad. I look up and see him put his hands on Mom's shoulders to give her a massage. She instantly relaxes and moans.

"Grossssssssssssssssss," Bryson groans. "Take this somewhere else."

"One day," Dad starts, pauses to lean down and kiss Mom on the tip of her nose. "You'll both be married and have kids of your own. And you'll give your wives massages because it feels good, and women love it when a man can give a great massage. Take notes, kiddos."

"Amen," she moans. "Now go down a little to the—yeah—that's the spot."

"This is getting awkward." I shudder. "You two need to stop."

"I'm not gonna get married anytime soon. Girls are *nuts!*" Bryson says. "This girl Monica has been texting me nonstop for *weeeeeeks*. Asking to go to the movies, the mall. It's weird; she's weird. And *freakishly* tall. I don't get it."

"That's 'cause you're a weirdo, Little Man." I ruffle his hair, and he ducks away, fixing it. "If you take after Mom, you're going to want a tall girlfriend. Trust me."

"You're just upset 'cause you and Kris are *dooooooooooooomed*. You're gonna get married and have babies and be stuck giving her massages every day like Dad for the rest of your life until your fingers fall off and sprout antlers that turn into flesh-eating worm-like creatures that consume all of humanity and then everyone dies and your monster fingers are running the world and you and Kris are stuck in cages constantly giving each other massages... forever."

There is a pause while we all wait for him to continue, but he doesn't.

"See." I look to my parents. "He watches *way* too much TV. This is the type of son you're raising. He's going to be president someday. Just you both wait."

Mom cracks an eyelid. "He's been spending too much time with Brian. He has to stop coming over to this house and corrupting our son."

"Lord help us." Dad sighs. "Should we put him down now or wait, you think?"

I laugh. "Least you could do is let the kid give and receive his first massage."

"You two are a bad influence." Mom's eyes are closed. "But this feels magical."

"Honey, my hands are starting to cramp."

"I don't care, Robert. Don't stop; I've been dodging vomit all morning. The flu is going around, and Lisa from work called in again. This is exactly what I—that's my bone you're digging into."

Bryson groans. "I think *I'm* gonna throw up."

We continue like this for a while, my parents just smiling and laughing along with us as we pick on each other. I hear the door open from the kitchen and know she's here. I walk into the front hallway and see Kris drop her keys on the wooden table—next to Bryson's and my framed school pictures—and unzip her track hoodie. Her blonde hair is up in a bun, and she carries an orange gym bag filled with clothes she'll wear later on after we leave.

She opens up her arms so I can give her a hug and kiss.

"You missed game night," I say.

"Bryson win again?"

I nod and wrap my arms around her athletic waist. Static electricity zaps us from shuffling my socks over the carpet. We both jump and giggle before kissing a second time. We pull back, and she puts her hands on my shoulders.

"We don't have to go tonight, you know. Let's just stay in and watch a movie, make some popcorn. We haven't had an *us* night in a while. I couldn't really care less about babysitting my drunk brother and cousin all night."

"Mmm, I would love nothing more than to spend every night with you curled up watching a movie." We kiss.

"You're going to ruin the moment right now, aren't you?"

We kiss again. "My parents and little brother are in the kitchen. The moment was ruined before you even walked through my door." And again. "Besides, Reefer and I bet that Kyle couldn't drink fifteen shots before puking. He has the stomach of a five-year-old."

Kris rolls her eyes. "The three of you are juveniles, and I refuse to bail you guys out of jail one of these days. Which is all the more reason to stay in tonight after everyone is asleep. Jenna can keep Reefer company at the party." She leans in to whisper in my ear. "It will be just the two of us downstairs on the couch."

I whisper back. "My parents are ten feet away. I don't want to have this discussion right now. But you make a good argument."

"Let's just stay in, please. My dad dropped me off 'cause my parents have a charity benefit tonight, so I can't drive us, and I don't want him picking us up if we're drunk. And you're on a restricted license until your birthday, so... we can just stream a show or something."

"We'll do that later." We kiss again.

"I don't hear movement out there," my dad calls from the kitchen. "I'm only going to assume something your little brother should not be seeing is happening, and your mother and I would appreciate it if it ended."

"It's just me, Mr. Falconi," Kris calls back. "I'll try to keep your son on his best behavior." She pokes me in the ribs.

I poke her back.

"That doesn't really make us feel any better, Kris."

"Robert, sweetie, pay attention. You're digging into my shoulder blade again."

I shake my head, and we kiss one more time, interlocking fingers.

"It'll be fun tonight. We'll head over for an hour just to show our faces, and then we'll come back. It will be just us and television and canoodling. I promise."

Bryson walks out of the kitchen and stops a few feet ahead. My parents stop their talking, and the house becomes suddenly, and eerily, quiet. Kris grabs my right hand and squeezes; a burning sensation worms down my arm until it reaches my hand, and that's when I feel one of my teeth rattle in my mouth. It's uncomfortable before it's painful, like something is underneath my gums pushing on it. I massage my jaw.

"Should we talk about it after he's dead, Gray?" Kris asks— her eyes locked on Bryson.

"Excuse me?"

"After you kill me," he adds. "You and Kris can get back to your Bible study. That's what you called it that night in the tree house. Right, Gray?"

The rattle in my gums turns into a twisting, and I flinch. I reach into my mouth and find one of my back molars and put my fingers on it, but it comes loose and falls out as if I'd yanked it. When I pull my hand back, a tooth rests in my palm coated in crimson blood. Some drips from my mouth and patters onto the carpet.

"W-What's happening? What is this?" I turn back and forth, but both have stoic expressions. "I don't understand."

Another tooth begins to rattle and twist, and before I know it, like the air is caught in my lungs, I cough up a second tooth onto the carpet. I fall to the ground, land on my knees, and spit up a third. Kris remains still above, but Bryson bends down to meet me at eye level. He's back in his Yankees hat, the thin line of blood escaping from underneath the cap.

The seashell necklace dangles in front of his chest.

"You gotta make it right, Gray. You have to."

"I know." Another tooth falls to the ground. The lights of the house fade out one by one, bathing us in darkness in a matter of seconds. From somewhere in the distance, I can hear an ocean swell.

The next thing Bryson says comes out in a whisper:

"Follow Aubrey. Stay with her. Let her show you."

There is blackness, and I attempt to open my eyes, but my head pounds. My ears ring. Muffled voices from above, but I can't make out who they're from. Moving around feels like hammers bashing into my bones one after the other. I give up and stay still, wait for my focus to sharpen.

We're moving. Slowly everything comes back—all my senses. And then there's Kris's blonde hair falling in front of her face. She leans over me, and one hand cups my chin while the other gently strokes my hair. It's another few seconds before I can feel it, and my flesh breaks out in goosebumps. Voices fade in after.

"...hear me? Gray?"

I open my mouth to say yes, but am pretty sure what comes out is a garbled mess.

"Aubrey, he's waking up. That's a good sign, right?"

"I'll pull over."

"Where are we going? He needs a hospital."

"N-No," I sputter.

"Gray, baby, hush. Kyle hurt you really bad. You need a doctor."

Aubrey's voice says, "He's conscious, so that's good."

When I get a clear look, I see I'm lying in Kris's lap in the backseat of her car. I take a look around as my eyes adjust to the dim light. Outside, the sun is quickly setting. The car pulls to a stop somewhere on the side of the road.

Aubrey turns on the interior light of Kris's car, a leased Hyundai Sonata that she shares with Kyle. Aubrey's red hair falls in front of her face, same as Kris's, like a curtain to veil their faces. Aubrey cocks her head, studies me.

They argue for a little while longer until I find the strength to sit up. I need help, but it's a relief. My ribs are sore, and my entire face is numb, but I can still move. Slowly. It's the worst I've ever been beaten up, but not as bad as I thought.

He held back.

Aubrey steps out of the car and opens up the back passenger door to help me stand on my feet. I can't fully stand straight, so I hunch over, my breaths shallow. Kris follows me. Kyle is not with us. Beyond the car, the stretch of forest connecting Lee Falls and Davisport looms large. The sun dips halfway below the tree line, and the half-sun casts a beautiful orange glow, almost like a burning ember in a fire. The headlights illuminate two spots of white light on the barren road that merge into one a few feet ahead. We are quiet for a while before anyone speaks up. Each of them has a hand on my shoulders to steady my balance.

I turn to look at Aubrey, see the light flicker of the orange in her eyes while I can still make out the detail. There's that look on her face of concern, her eyebrows furrowed inward. It's so disarming to see her as anything except intimidating. In the few hours we've spent together, I know something is happening with her; something is changing. I can't tell what it is, but my heart flutters. Lightheaded.

My mouth burns with a bitter taste from the acid in my throat. I shake away the feeling and turn to look at Kris, at her emerald eyes. The crucifix around her neck reflects the head-lights, and I just want to wrap her in my arms. Calm her somehow.

Stars emerge to litter the sky like freckles. It's the last sunset I'll experience and the last starry sky I'll get to see. Kris and I would spend hours just pointing out different constellations. I almost wish I had time to do it again, but I don't. I can't. Kris needs to leave. She needs to accept. Only Aubrey can be here.

Why her? The dream... the dream... why can't you remember the dream?

"Wow, you guys are endlessly entertaining," Aubrey says. "I can't even imagine what date night must've been like."

"You don't know when to stop, do you?" Kris says. "What is your problem, Aubrey? Is it because I actually have a history with someone that you wished you had a history with? Are you jealous?"

There's a pause before she responds. "You're just as bad as he is. No. You're worse. Everything is personal to you, isn't it? Calm down. I was kidding."

"Stop talking to me like I'm a naïve child. I'm sorry I'm not as rough around the edges as you. I haven't *lived* enough. I'm not a walking cliché."

"So, this isn't you being a jealous ex-girlfriend? Damn. Must be getting my clichés mixed up again." She smirks. "Sorry."

I go to punch Aubrey in the arm but cry out as my ribcage stretches too far. I manage a weak graze of her elbow. She looks at me quizzically before putting her hands on my shoulder again to steady me. She raises her left eyebrow.

"That was... for saying *sorry*."

It takes a second for what I say to register, but after a while she smiles and bites her lower lip, switches the weight on the balls of her feet.

"Goddamn, am I proud of you. You've come so far in just a few hours."

"I learn from the best."

Kris takes a step back. I know I've hurt her again. To her, this looks bad. I know it does. I'm not even sure how I feel about it. But something about Aubrey just lets me relax, lets me just be in the moment with her. It's refreshing.

"Gray," Kris says. "Can, um, can we talk... in private, please."

I nod to Aubrey; she saunters over to the car. She leans back, one foot on the car behind her, the other foot on the ground. It's such an Aubrey stance that I have to chuckle. Kris purses her lips and looks away, rolls her eyes. I've only seen Kris jealous a few times, and that was mainly with other girls on the track team. Rarely did I ever see her this way.

She can't let me go. Can't because she's too good inside, too forgiving. She's always been like this; it's one of the things about her I first fell in love with when we were kids, too afraid to speak up until she made the first move. It's sad to think about all the history between us. All the late nights talking on the phone until dawn, cuddling in her parents' hot tub, playing board games with Bryson well past his bedtime.

We step into the headlights, stopping where they are the brightest. I shoo a few mosquitos away from our faces, slap at one on the back of my neck. Kris grabs both of my hands and raises them up to our chests. She's shaking. I have the urge to comfort her, but I don't.

She chews on her bottom lip and looks up at the sky. I know she's trying to find a constellation. There's a tinge of the orange-red sunset on the distant horizon.

"Look... I get why you're doing this. You think I don't, but I do. I called my dad to pick me up after our fight. I was in the car with you. I went through it with you. I lost him too."

Like a punch in the gut, the air leaves my lungs, and I pivot my feet to turn around and walk away, but she grabs my wrist and twirls me back to face her. I cringe in pain and hold my side, but she continues without any regard.

"You don't get to walk away from me, not this time."

"I'm done talking about this."

"I'm not. So you're going to listen and I'm going to talk. That's the least you can do. Stop being selfish." She takes a deep breath. "I don't care about our relationship or getting back together. I love you. I know you love me too, but I'm concerned about *you*. This person in front of me isn't you. This... façade. That back there"—she points toward Davisport—"was not you. I don't know if that was Aubrey talking or something else. Maybe it's because tomorrow is the seventh. I'm surprised you even showed up to school. But—"

"But what?" I cut her off, feel rage starting to boil underneath. "I'm sick of everyone thinking they know what's best for me. I don't want to be an asshole to you, but you're driving me crazy. Leave. Me. Alone."

"You see, *that's* what I'm talking about. Right there. This isn't even about me anymore. It's everyone. You don't talk to anyone, you don't do your homework, and Reefer and Jenna are the only people I ever see you talk with. I'm so happy you still have them, Gray. God knows Reefer can make you laugh in ways I never can, but it's bull."

"You sound like a broken record right now."

"I just want you to be happy."

"Then leave me alone. Don't call or text. Forget about me. Find someone else and move on."

"Is that really what you want? After everything we've been through? All that we lost? It's just gone, like that." She snaps her fingers.

I nod in response.

"When did you turn into such an asshole?"

My knees wobble. Kris never swears. Not ever. In the nine years we've known each other, it's the first time she's ever said anything besides "sucks."

"When I put your dad in a coma."

And once again, I regret it the moment I say it.

I can see the rage boil in her face—watch as her cheeks turn red. She lets air out through her nose and pokes me in the chest with a finger. And I know that this is the point where she breaks. I know because I know how to upset her. One of the perks of knowing someone for nine years: you know where their buttons are and how to push them.

"Why would you care? It's not like you've ever visited him. Sent flowers to my mom. Or even asked how we're barely paying hospital and house bills." She shouts the rest. "What am I supposed to do now? Huh! I can't run track or cross-country. No more scholarship; my mom can't afford to send me and Kyle both away to school. And now I may never get to see my father open his eyes all because *you* just *had to* drive that night! He should've stayed at that charity benefit all night with Mom. I wanted to stay home and have a romantic night, and YOU had to drive and ruin everything! IT'S ALL YOUR FAULT. IS THAT WHAT YOU WANT ME TO SAY? THAT EVERY-THING WAS YOUR FAULT AND NOT AN ACCI-DENT? IS THIS WHAT YOU WANT FROM ME?"

She slaps me. The sting on my cheek sends me stumbling.

"Because it wasn't your fault, any of it. And I don't blame

you, *asshole*. I love you." She takes a deep breath, trying to regain control. "You ever think, in all these months, that you're not the only one to blame? That maybe other people have regrets too?"

I stand still; my mouth goes dry. And, for some strange reason, I'm proud of her.

Part of my heart breaks. Feels like it's tearing into pieces. But another part is awed. I've been waiting for her to finally let out the rage. The pain that she, like me, tries to hide. It's beautiful, in a way.

"You're acting like a real douchebag to me and everyone who cares about you... you need help. If not from me, then a professional. Because I can't get through to you, and I don't know how to get you to let me in."

Kris has the biggest heart; it's why her pain, above everyone else's, hurts me the most.

She needs this. Let her get it out. It's not about you this time, Gray.

Kris looks away and into the forest to our right. She crosses her arms over her chest and cries, sobs. I don't console her. Don't wrap her in a hug. Her shoulders heave up and down—wails muffled as she attempts to keep her mouth closed. Glancing behind me, Aubrey looks down at her feet, twirling a strand of red hair.

Kris whispers under her breath, "What am I supposed to do?"

It's this moment: the fork in the road between the familiar and the uncharted territory. I turn to look behind me, and Aubrey stands patiently, waits to continue our adventure to an uncertain future. In front of me are Kris and a life I'm not sure I want to face, that I'm not sure I can survive another minute living.

There used to be a time when the world felt vast and the

possibilities endless, when everything was simple. When the scent of Mom's home-baked chocolate chip cookies filled the house, how she'd always let Bryson and me eat the raw cookie dough. When Dad would play catch with us in the backyard. When I'd ride a bike to Reefer's house instead of driving, or wait for Mom to pick me up. When we'd stay up all night watching scary movies and talk about the chance of life on other planets.

But now it's all changed. It's different. Life isn't simple; it can't be anymore. There comes a time when we can't hold on to those childhood fantasies. Life always has the familiar and the new. And somehow, I know life is telling me that the only answers are with Aubrey. Somehow, someway, she is the only person who I can be with right now.

I can't continue doing what I've been doing. Something needs to change.

So I look at Kris and place one hand on her shoulder. She jumps at my touch, turns her head my way, and kisses the back of my hand. I don't say any words; I don't have to. Everything that needs to be said is in that motion, that one simple act, and I know she gets it. Understands that it's more than me and her and that November night. Aubrey is the only option I have left.

You mean the last person you'll see before you kill yourself?

But not until I get some answers first. Figure out why she's really here.

Kris turns around and we stare at each other, and, for just this moment, the world falls away, and we are back over summer break. We are lying on the roof of her house, the white curtains billowing from the warm breeze through the open bedroom window. The street lamps light her neighborhood all the way until they end at the intersection, and crickets chirp a symphony down below. Above, the moon is barely a sliver, and the stars are shining bright. Kris has her head on my chest, and our legs are intertwined. Her blonde hair wraps around my waist, and I stroke it from her scalp.

We point out constellations and stars. The Big and Little Dipper. We share kisses, laughs, views about the world and our futures. How we'll leave Lee Falls, move down south and start a family. Get the big house by the lake we've always dreamed about.

Standing in the middle of the street now, I know she sees that life too. The life we dreamed about, the life we could've had. She closes her eyes and nods, sniffs snot up through her nose, but Kris even makes that seem graceful.

"Just do me a favor," she whispers, her voice frail. "Call me when you're ready to talk... okay? Just a friend. Nothing more... okay?"

I give her shoulder a light squeeze and wrap her in a hug, inhale her coconut perfume. I don't think about it—it's just familiar. Everything that was said before falls away, and it's only me and Kris.

It's the last hug I'll ever give her.

"I will," I lie.

I do it because I know she needs it.

Or do you need it more?

Aubrey looks our way. When I lift my head to look back, she lowers her foot from the car door and walks into the shadows.

10 Hours Until

Sometime After 8:00 PM

After she calms down, Kris drives us back to Davisport. We ride in silence because there is nothing left to be said. I take the time to look at my phone and the slew of missed calls and messages: Reefer, Jenna, Mom, Dad, Mr. Hoch, Unknown, and a few names I haven't seen in a while. People whose numbers I was hoping to never see again from school, from my old group of friends. Reefer and Jenna each send a video clip of the fight. It must already be posted online.

No more being invisible.

Aubrey tells Kris to pull into a convenience store parking lot and we get out. There are a few other cars parked, and the store's bright lights illuminate the area.

Aubrey grabs my hand. "Come on, I'll buy some bandages to patch you up."

I glance at Kris. Her eyes are red and puffy, and she looks at my hand in Aubrey's. It makes me feel guilty, and Kris seems exhausted. I've put her through more than she should ever go through in one night. I force myself to walk toward the store.

Kris doesn't say a word, puts the car into drive, and pulls out of the lot.

Goodbye, Kris.

We walk inside, and Aubrey doesn't let go of my hand. She leads me to the aisle where they keep Band-Aids, cotton balls, Tylenol, and peroxide. On the way, she grabs a small pack of metal coat hangers, but I don't question why. I want to feel bad about Kris a little while longer, but Aubrey's hand in mine somehow consumes my every fiber. Like all my nerves are electrified. My hairs stand on edge, and the hint of cigarette smoke on her clothes wafts behind her. Suddenly the bright lights overheard are even brighter, and I have to squint just to see properly.

"I don't look that bad," I say. "Do I?"

"I've seen worse, trust me." We stop halfway through an aisle, and she lets go of my hand so she can pick up the items. "I don't want anything to get infected. You were lying in the dirt."

For some reason I want to laugh—Aubrey worried that any cuts or wounds I have will get infected. It's oddly motherly of her, which is a side I never expected to see. But by now I've learned not to question what she is capable of. She almost seems more than human, more than any ordinary girl should be.

Like an enigma.

Is she real? Is she fake?

I just want to know what her story is.

"Why are you doing this?"

"Doing what?"

"Taking care of me."

"Because you're hurt."

Chills.

"So that's it? No questions about what happened back at the fair? You don't want an explanation or anything?"

"First: it's not really any of my business. Second: you and this entire town focus too much on shallow, useless sentiments. Let it go. All of it. What's the point of worrying about what you did? Start worrying about what you *will* do." She shakes her head and motions around us. "Actions. Life is comprised of one action after another. You need to live. You need to stop thinking and just experience this with me. Ooh. Write that on the list too."

"Actions?"

"Actions." Aubrey walks to the next aisle and rifles through the perfume for women, and sprays it in the air to sniff. She coughs and waves the scent away. "Think of life like a movie. They're made up of actions. You don't take any; you have no plot." She sprays another perfume in the air before walking on. "Intentions are good, but they don't make movies. Risks do."

Jenna would love this.

She finds the few things she's looking for and proceeds out of the aisle. Her combat boots smack the linoleum with each step, *clomping* as she walks. It's a comforting, rhythmic sound. The rest of the store is relatively quiet in comparison.

"What did you do to Tim?"

She looks back at me, and the left side of her mouth turns up in a grin.

"He's not dead if that's what you're thinking."

"It wasn't."

"Good. We can move on. Do you want any other snacks or anything while we're here? Just pack light. Only what you can run out of the store with and not get caught."

I stop and my eyes bulge out. There's no way I'm stealing again. No way. I almost panic before she bursts out laughing. It's a hoarse sound.

"That was a joke. Relax." She runs her hands through her hair and lifts a few strands to her nose to sniff it. She clucks her tongue and squints at me. "Why are you so stubborn?"

"You're calling *me* stubborn?"

"Okay, you want answers. Will you promise to drop it if I tell you?"

I nod my head.

"The cops traced your friend's license plate to the fair. Chaos erupted. I punched Clown Nose until he begged me to stop. Baseball Cap nearly killed you, but he stopped to help— which is contradictory, but whatever—with Miss I'm Perfect. That's when everyone ran away, and she stayed behind with Baseball Cap to pick you up and carry you away before the cops got you first. I followed. He stayed. It was all very melodramatic. But also very fun. Happy?"

I nod again.

There's a moment between us where neither knows what to say. She bites her lip and blows out air so her red bangs puff up.

"How do you do that?" she asks.

"Do what?"

"You give me that look."

"I have a look?"

"Dude. You're doing it right now."

"I don't know what the look is."

"Right now. The look. That stubborn-ass one."

"I can't see my face!"

She purses her lips. "It's like I feel bad. Which never happens. Ever. I was talking about actions. You blatantly ignore the point of what I was saying to dig up the past, and there I go. Caving in to you. What the hell?"

Is she saying you have an effect on her? You make her uneasy? This is groundbreaking.

"I'm sorry?"

She tries to punch me in the arm, but I step out of the way. She guffaws. I smile.

"Did you just anticipate my fist?"

"Yeah... I think I did."

"Badass. I'm a good teacher."

"Preach it."

She leans in quickly to punch with her opposite hand, but I duck that too. The sudden movement in my joints causes my entire body to ache. I clutch my ribcage.

"Don't you think the hitting thing is getting old? I was just beat up less than an hour ago." I pant and place my hands on my knees.

"You're right. I wasn't thinking. Your lame-ass sorry distracted me. No more punches. Promise. But don't wuss out on me now. We're on the cusp of your awakening, Grayson! Less than eight hours ago, you were stuttering talking to me, and now you're dodging punches." She starts to shout in the store: "Ladies and gentlemen, we have a bonafide badass tonight. Guys, watch your girls. Ladies, watch your daughters. Grayson. Is. Coming."

She raises her fists in triumph and drops some of the contents from her hands. I laugh as she twirls in a circle and kicks her leg out in front. Just as she does, an old woman walks by and yelps as Aubrey's foot collides with her shopping cart and sends it spinning away. Aubrey's hands fly to her mouth to stifle a laugh. The older woman quickly walks away, muttering under her breath.

She turns and snorts, and I can't help but laugh with her.

"C'mon," she gasps and clutches her gut. "Let's get you patched up."

~

After she pays with her wad of hidden cash, Aubrey leads me outside to sit on a curb in the parking lot. The light from a sodium arc lamp enables Aubrey to see what she's doing. I can't see my face, but there are a few scrapes on my arms and legs. She unscrews the bottle of peroxide and pours some liquid on a cotton ball. The bag of Band-Aids and the metal hangers rest by her boots. I dry-swallow a Tylenol for my throbbing head.

I watch her hands dab at the cuts, working almost methodically over the tiny scrapes. I feel the sting of the peroxide but will myself to stay cool for Aubrey. Luckily none of the cuts are deep, so the pain only lasts for a few seconds before it dissipates.

She does this for every cut she sees, even if it's barely a break in the skin, and then she places a Spider-Man Band-Aid on each. When I take a deep breath, my ribs scream, and Aubrey makes me take my shirt off. I'm hesitant at first because I don't want her to see the excess weight around my waist. But no one is around, and really, what will it matter after I'm dead? So I lift up my shirt so she can assess the damage.

And then I remember the self-inflicted bruise over my chest. But it's too late to take it back, because she sees it too. I hope she doesn't notice there's a difference between the two.

"S-so you said you've seen worse wounds than this. Is one of your parents a doctor?"

Aubrey snaps her head up to glare at me, and then I realize what I just said.

Aubrey doesn't have biological parents, at least, none alive... I think.

"Ohmygod. I'm sorry."

She shakes her head and turns away. Without warning, ignoring my comment, she gently places a finger on my ribcage and traces the forming bruise from Kyle's shoe. A few blood vessels have popped just beneath the skin, and signs of purple bruising form on the surface. She traces her fingers around and up to the self-inflected one I've been hitting all day. She circles it a few times, and I let her for some reason. But I don't know why. Her finger on my skin causes my nerves to ping, but it doesn't tickle. It doesn't hurt. It's familiar somehow. Like it's been there before. Or that it belongs there.

Aubrey replaces her pointer finger with her thumb and rubs the bruise on my chest like a mark that won't come off. She looks up at me, but her face is expressionless. I can't read what she's thinking. She rests her thumb and leaves it centered on the bruise, looks back down, and just remains still like that for a while.

She knows, Gray. She has to. Shitshitshit.

Aubrey releases air through her nose, and I feel it on my stomach. I shiver, and she snaps out of whatever daze she was in and lets go.

"You can lower your shirt," she says under her breath, still looking at the ground.

I pull it back down and shake out a few wrinkles. It's silent for what seems like minutes before she opens her mouth. Her voice is quiet—too quiet for Aubrey's usual confident, commanding tone. She fiddles with a few dry cotton balls from inside the plastic bag.

"When I was thirteen, I lived with a family for a little over six months. Their daughter was an RN. Learned a few basic things from her."

I place my palms on the ground behind me to lean back, and Aubrey turns her feet inward like she did back in the front office at school. She taps her fingers on her knee to a beat.

It is, I think, the first honest thing Aubrey's said to me all night. Because it's the only time she hasn't been able to look me in the eyes.

"Like how to bandage up tough guys like me, right?"

Finally, she raises her head. There's a small smile, just enough to see a dimple. "Exactly. To help clean up reckless boys who actively seek out getting their asses kicked in fights."

I can't help but smile. All day I've been calling her reckless, and here she is saying the same about me. She looks back down at her feet.

"Did you also learn to fight from that same family? Like self-defense?"

She doesn't answer me as she puts away the items in her bag. Another few moments tick by before she brushes the hair out of her face. I know she has no intention of giving me more answers, so I don't push the subject.

Above us, at the center of the streetlight, moths and other insects hover. I shield my eyes from the brightness and look beyond it. Dim stars litter the sky, but it's not quite pitch black out. Too early to point out any constellations.

And then it dawns on me:

"Let me see your hand," I say.

Aubrey throws a quizzical look, so I just reach down to grab her wrist and examine the split knuckles. Both hands are red, and the skin torn in spots where her fist collided with Tim's face. She looks up and down from my eyes to where our hands meet.

"Let me clean this up so you don't get infected either."

I take out the bottle of peroxide and a cotton ball. After I pour the liquid and dab at the tiny cuts, she remains still, focused on me. Watching me. When I stop and throw the cotton ball into the bag, I don't let go of her hand. We both stay in this position and look at each other. Her eyes study mine, and I move my focus to her lips. I'm suddenly aware of my heart beating in my chest, and I don't know why. There's a warmth that emanates from our hands and travels up our arms into our bodies. We don't break the spell.

I find myself wondering what she will smell like. Taste like. What her lips will feel like pressed to my own. And for a moment, just a split second, I think her eyes flicker down to my own lips.

And then we both pull away as if our hands were made of hot coals.

It, whatever it is, ends almost as soon as it began.

She wipes her palms on her nylon leggings and stands up, grabs the grocery bag.

"C'mon. We still have much to do. Can't sit around on our asses all night."

Disturbing thoughts of what almost happened between us back at the convenience store cloud my mind. Kissing Aubrey Fisher. Images of the two of us together. Each one comes with a new ping of guilt and fear. And, oddly enough, excitement.

Has she ever had a boyfriend before? And more importantly: why the hell are you even thinking about this right now!?

This part of Davisport is quiet; lower income. Minus the grocery store, there aren't many businesses or homes down here besides a few boarded-up buildings and an abandoned warehouse way in the distance. Driving fresh out of Lee Falls, you'd think you'd wound up in the ghetto. But it's safe in this area. Not many cars pass us as we travel down an alley into another parking plaza.

It's a while before I realize Aubrey has led me down a block and over to a family-owned jewelry store. There are three cars in the parking lot, and no one is in sight. Aubrey looks around, studies something I can't see.

"Doesn't look like they have any security cameras in the parking lot, which is good."

"Umm, why is that good?"

She doesn't speak, only creeps up to a green Honda Civic. It, like Reefer's car, looks ancient. She twists around again, jiggles the door handle. It doesn't budge. She places the grocery bag on the ground and takes out one of the metal coat hangers from the pack she bought. When she starts to untwist the hanger and straighten it into a rod, I know exactly what this is.

"What are you doing?" I shout.

Aubrey shushes me. "Keep your voice down. Are you trying to get caught?"

I look around, lace my fingers behind my head, and curse under my breath. Dining and dashing was one thing, but stealing a car is another. She feeds the metal rod through a crack in the top of the window, and after some finagling, she carefully lowers it to the little lock button by the windowsill. She hooks it within a minute.

She pulls up the metal rod until it clicks and unlocks the car. She cheers and jumps in the air when she opens the door. Aubrey motions for me to come over, a giddy expression on her face.

And for maybe the first time all night, I don't at all want to do this with Aubrey. Have no interest whatsoever.

"What are you waiting for? Let's go."

"No."

"No?"

"I'm not stealing a car, Aubrey."

She leans on the edge of the door, surprised. It's the first time I've told her no. "We're not stealing. We're borrowing for an extended amount of time. Relax. We'll have it back in a few hours." She sits in the driver's seat and bends down to the floor mat, feels around for something.

"Then you can *not* steal without me. This isn't cool; it's criminal. I'm not getting in the car if you hotwire this thing."

She jerks her body up in the seat. "Whoa. What's your problem? We're having fun. Have I steered you wrong yet tonight?"

I grab the sides of my body and wince at the pain. "We can walk or take a bus or a cab. But I'm not going with you if you do this, Aubrey. It's not cool, not at all. That's somebody's car. What's wrong with you?"

Aubrey steps out, and her smile disappears. I've hurt her feelings, offended her. But for once I don't care, because I know I'm right. She glares at me for another moment before slamming the door. It's a pout, like a child would do when not given her way.

Childish Aubrey... another new side to her many personalities.

Gray Falconi: Grew a Backbone and Won?

She drops the metal rod to the ground and storms past me, a sour expression on her face.

"Bus it is. No time to waste. Let's go."

Just when I assume she'll walk past and leave me to trail behind, she grabs my wrist and pulls me along. I stumble after and reach into my pocket when my phone vibrates. It's a video message from Unknown. It's an angle of Kyle punching me in the face as random people run around and shout in the chaos. The video zooms in. Behind us, Aubrey rolls off Tim and stands up. Kris holds her knee in the dirt. The video ends, and a text message appears on screen:

UNKNOWN

done playing gamez

trying 2 help u

if u dont start being honest

foster freak is going 2 die

tik tok

Automatically, I hit reply to the message, my fingers moving faster than my thoughts. Ready to reach into the phone and fight them. But when I hit send, an error message returns:

THIS PHONE LINE HAS BEEN DISCONNECTED
And I'm filled with dread. Horrible fear. Not for me.

For Aubrey.

And... *anger*.

I look around, the sick feeling of eyes watching the back of my neck. But no one is there.

I glare at the message.

Who are you?

9 Hours Until

SOMETIME AFTER 9:00 PM

REEFER

Aubrey fisher???????????????

ME

Aubrey Fisher.

REEFER

Aubreyfrickenfizher??!?!?!?!?!?!!?!?!!?!?!!!...

ME

We're on the bus now. She won't look at me.

REEFER

DUDEEEEE!! this is HUGE!!!

u luv Aubrey. awe. Gray-Gray

she probly wants 2 suck ur sick

sick**

duck**

WTF?!?!! do what I say phone!!!! UR MY
BITCH!!!!!!! :D:D:D:o:o

ME

Focus. Please. Don't be gross. This is Aubrey we're talking about. I mean… there's no way. Right?

REEFER

where u at? cops came 2 my house with my car. reeks of smoke. want me to 2 meet u?

ME

She smokes. I'm sorry about the car. Are you in trouble?

REEFER

hah. all good. u and her… ehh. cops lookin for u. just want 2 make sure ur alright.

do u need me 2 pick u up? ill do it. i will

ME

I'm fine. Thanks. You've seen the videos I take it?

REEFER

bro who hasnt? ur trending. shits like… legit

i woulda beat tims ass if I was there

im sorry I wasnt

ME

It's ok, Reef. I gotta go. I think this is our stop.

REEFER

jenna and I MIGHT crash that party later 2night. u in?

ME

That's probably not a good idea. I'll call you in a little bit though.

REEFER

(drmatik sigh inserted here) (an eye role) plz tell me ur not gonna make out with her. rumors bro also, jenna is driving me cray-cray about u. its annoying

so theres nothing else goin on? at all?

ME

Reef. No. Aubrey and I are NOT going to happen. We couldn't be more opposites. It was just... I can't describe it. It was weird; maybe I was dizzy from the fight. Alright. Really have to go now. And stop being a gossip magnet. Those rumors are stupid.

REEFER

u sure shes not getting 2 u bro? u sound mad

ME

Sorry. I've been getting these weird texts all day.

REEFER

what weird texts?

ME

Nothing, forget it. I'll call you.

REEFER

dont leave me hangin bro!!! NOT COOL. tell me

ur gossip obsessed friend ☺ :P :ooooo
8====D;;;;; 0:

who the hell was playing hard rock on my radio???

DUDE!!! she erased my country favorites from the pre-settings

GRAY!!!!! ANSWER ME!!! WHAT KIND OF MONSTER WOULD DO THIS?!?!?!

....

hate u

We step off the bus and onto the sidewalk of downtown Davisport. The neighborhood is rundown, as close to the ghetto as it could ever get. The concrete is cracked, the weeds unattended. Aside from this place where we are, there is nothing remotely safe or clean or any place tempting to go. People get busted here often for soliciting. Drugs, sex, underage, one thing or another—you name it. It's a cop's bread and butter. I don't know why we came here.

There is a short line of people outside the nightclub waiting to enter. Two large men wearing black form-fitting shirts check IDs. The ground vibrates from the muffled bass coming from inside. Two large metallic doors enclose the blasting music. A neon sign above: The Velvet Lounge.

"What are we doing here?" I ask.

We walk to the back of the line and stand in place while it shuffles forward.

"Adventure. Fun. Risks. Actions. Remember?"

Each word is staccato, and each packs a punch greater than the last. She's pissed; I know it. I feel bad about flipping out earlier, but deep down, even she has to know it was the right thing to do. She'll get over it.

But what about the near-kiss? Will she get over that? Is that why she's freaked out?

"We're not twenty-one. We can't get in."

"You're right."

"I'm confused."

She presses her finger to my lips and shushes me. Of course Aubrey has a plan. It's foolish to believe otherwise. I think again about how scripted this all feels, like this is still going exactly her way, and it's building up to something.

But what exactly she has planned and why she's doing these things is still unclear.

It can't be a coincidence.

Her finger pressed to my lips sends blood coursing through my body. She pulls it away, and the hairs on my forearms stand on end.

A few people drunkenly step behind us, having come from around the corner and down another street lined with bars. A couple of guys puff out pillars of smoke from cigarettes. Ahead of us are a group of girls wearing dresses that resemble hand towels. My eyes rest on their mini-skirts, and how just the right movement makes the bottom of their butt-cheeks peek out. It seems oddly voyeuristic, but I can't help but look. Aubrey follows my line of vision and smacks me on the shoulder. I turn away. This is the party district of Davisport. Lee Falls is too small for a nightclub. We do have two bars, but nothing fancy like I assume this club will be.

After a few minutes of listening to gossip, we are at the front of the line. My heart beats into overdrive when one of the bouncers, whose traps are the size of my two shoulders combined, looks down at me with scrutiny, disgust. He knows I don't belong—can't take his eyes off of me soon enough. But he asks for an ID anyway. I pull it out, and Aubrey does the same to show the other bouncer. He looks me up and down, glances from the driver's license to me. Lingers a moment on the Spider-Man Band-Aids. He gives it back and reaches behind him to mark an orange "X" on my hand. He motions me forward toward the double doors. Aubrey follows closely behind.

She has an orange band around her wrist.

From behind me, I think I hear one of them say, "...face looks like a swollen vagina."

What?

We walk inside to a narrow hallway and are greeted by

black lights, strobe lights, and glow sticks; neon lights are built into the floor and shoot beams upward. Aubrey gently ushers me forward, her hand on my lower back.

"So that's it? Just an orange X? They let people in here under twenty-one?"

"Why, were you expecting a big scene or spectacle? The wristband just lets the bartender know it's okay to serve you alcohol. But they honestly don't check around here. I know you'll ask. I have a fake ID. Hence the band." She waves her wrist in front of my face.

"Well, that seemed anti-climactic. I'm actually disappointed."

Aubrey lets out a quick laugh before we exit the hallway and enter into a large, crowded room full of flashing lights, gyrating bodies, and techno music so loud I can't even think. Straight ahead is the bar, also a splash of neon colors, and directly in the center is a massive dance floor. In the far corner, on a riser, is the DJ. Stereotypically, he wears large headphones around his neck and a white hat tipped to the side. His hands perform a dance I don't understand on a giant turntable.

It's all crazy and loud and bright and smelly and—oddly—fun. Unlike any place I've ever been to back in Lee Falls. Reefer, Kyle, and I always went to parties or hosted them for our class, but it was nothing like this.

I just try to be here with Aubrey. To live in this moment. It's so simple and yet so different. Aubrey takes my hand and pulls me toward the bar. My heart skips a beat. I shout at the top of my lungs but can barely hear my own voice.

"So are we here to dance?"

"You're here to let loose and have some fun. You're uptight and depressing to be around..." Her words disappear with the din of music and people. "I also really want to get you drunk."

"You want to see if I shrunk?"

"Get you drunk!"

"What?"

Aubrey shakes her head and pushes past a few college guys to get to the bar. Two of them turn around, glance at Aubrey, and throw back shots. The one to our right says a few choice words that make me want to punch him. It's the same judgmental look everyone gives her. The one where she's different and weird and scary and slutty and an easy lay. The look that says, "I can get a blowjob if I get this girl drunk enough."

The sad part is, I wonder how much of it is really true. She let both the security guard and the boy from the fair touch her, but I still don't know why. Because deep down I know she's not really like that; she can't be.

Aubrey doesn't take offense to his hungry look. She pulls the guy toward her and whispers in his ear, and he slaps the bar with his palm and calls for another round of shots. They each do one and he whispers back in her ear, puts his hand on her shoulder and caresses it.

Without realizing what I'm doing, I push in between them to stand next to Aubrey at the bar. The college boy looks at me like I've just materialized out of thin air, and in a way, I have. But I just want him away from her, from us. I feel so protective and...

And... jealous?

"Do we have a problem here?" he shouts to me, prepares to throw a punch, then gawks at my wounds. "Oh shit, your face looks like it's been through a fuckin' meat grinder." He pauses. "Spider-Man?" He elbows a friend to his left, points to me. "This guy for real?"

Is it really that bad?

For a moment I panic, not sure what to do or say. This is completely off the cuff and unlike anything I've ever done. No one had ever done this when Kris and I were a couple. But once again, Aubrey threw me into the deep waters beyond the buoy. I have to tread the unknown myself.

"As a matter of fact," I say with more force than I realize, "that's my sister. She has herpes, so I wouldn't go within ten feet of her."

"Dude, what the hell!" He jumps back and holds out his hand like it's contaminated.

"You also have to fuck me before you fuck her. So... unless you're absolutely secure in your sexuality and masculinity, I'd probably move along now."

He looks back at his friends and pushes them from the bar. "...just let any goddamn freaks walk into this..."

I turn to face Aubrey, and her mouth is open, her tongue nearly rolls out. "What. The hell. Was that?"

"I don't know."

She smiles so her dimple shows and shakes her head. "That was awesome. Grayson Falconi... when did you start growing a pair?" She finally gets the bartender's attention and orders something I can't hear. She turns back to me and drops cash on the bar. The bartender places two shots full of an ocher liquid in front of us. Aubrey picks them up and hands one to me.

"To you, and me, and to right now!"

"You're really going to get me drunk? What is this?"

"Yup. And don't ask. Just do. That's the fun of it."

"My face doesn't look like it's been through a meat grinder, does it?"

The corner of her mouth turns up. "Not at all. Over-exaggeration for a little swelling."

I sigh, and we clink our shot glasses together. I'm surprised the bartender didn't notice I don't have on an orange bracelet, but I don't question it. "To right now... and to you. For getting me to come out tonight. I'm actually having fun. You're not as scary as you let people think you are. You're actually a pretty awesome person."

The moment hangs out in the open awkwardly between us before she tilts her head back and swallows the shot. I'm disappointed she doesn't respond, but I do the same and gag as the warm liquid burns my throat going down. I bend over and cough; my body shakes and eyes water. The air leaves my lungs. Aubrey claps me on the back.

"That's Fireball. So pull yourself together. We have three more to do before we hit the dance floor."

One shot of Fireball, two shots of Crown Royal, and one shot of Jack Daniel's later, and I sweat. I air out my clothes, but the heat from the alcohol that sits in my stomach, and from the people out on the dance floor, gets to me. I shake my head to get a clear sense of everything, but my body is warm and my head is light. The tops of my fingers grow numb, and it's hard to focus on what's in front of me—like my eyes try to take in everything at once and jumble it together.

"Whoa," I say. "Definitely buzzed right now."

Aubrey takes us out onto the dance floor, grabs a hot pink glow stick for me and a blue one for her. I don't listen to techno or house, so I'm not sure what to do, but Aubrey leads us into the middle of the chaos. The heat from the bodies flailing, and the strobe lights and neon glow sticks, make me dizzy. My teeth chatter from the beat of the music.

Everything around is one giant blur, and in front of me, amidst it all, is Aubrey. She closes her eyes and extends her arms, feels the music. Feels the atmosphere and traces the movement of the neon lights as they bounce around. My breath is labored, and before I know it, my body begins to move with her.

I have no control. I just do.

Oh yeah, you're definitely a little drunk, my friend. Why did you let her talk you into this?

Aubrey moves her body to the music, to the beat. She is one with it. There is a peace inside her that the music brings out in a way I've never seen. She whips her head back and forth and sways her hips, and her highlighted hair flies wildly in the air. People back into me, and a few elbows collide with my body, but none of it matters. Not here. Not anywhere.

And I finally know what color her eyes remind me of. All I can see is Aubrey. See the lights reflect on her pale skin and twinkle in her eyes. Her *amber* eyes. How the black lights overhead force the whites of her clothes to shine bright.

Then she smiles. Her teeth are like pearls; her dimple is set deep. She opens her eyes and looks at me. So I look at her. And it's just us. Me and Aubrey. We're on the dance floor.

And she is so happy. She's so vibrant and alive.

She motions me forward, and I take a step and grab her hands. We twirl around. I let her take the lead, the alcohol now fully in my system. I just let myself melt into her body until we become one.

My sweat becomes her sweat. My rapid breaths become hers. Our sweaty skin melds together. And she twirls me back around so we face each other. Her crimson bangs hang below her right eye, so I push them back behind her ear. We stare at each other for a while, still move to the music until even that fades into silence.

Her highlighted hair sticks to her cheeks, and her skin radiates. Like every muscle, every fiber jumps alive. The alcohol. The music. The vibration of the floor. How Aubrey's nose ring reflects back each strobe.

And all that's left is us, together, on this dance floor.

I'm once again aware of my pounding heart. Of the blood

that courses through my veins. On fire. Electricity. I take a step back. And that's when I realize:

She is beautiful.

Aubrey Fisher is beautiful.

It's not the alcohol or the lights or the hint of vanilla on her neck.

It's not that she'll be the last person I'll ever get to touch.

I'm here with her. I'm looking at her look at me.

And she is unbelievably beautiful.

"Are you okay?" she asks.

I nod my head and swallow. "Yeah." I step forward and pull her close until our bodies connect again. Until my skin touches her skin. Feels how soft and smooth it is. "Can we just dance?"

She smiles—sticks out her tongue to lick her lower lip, and I catch a glimpse of the tongue ring. And then she closes her eyes. So I close mine and hold tight, afraid to let go.

And then we move. Together.

8 Hours Until

AROUND 10:00 PM

I don't know when exactly we stop dancing. One minute she's in my arms, and it's perfect. The songs bleed into each other, one after another. We don't talk—don't say a word. But it's the closest we've been all night. The purest version of Aubrey I've ever seen.

It might be the alcohol and it might not, but one thing about Aubrey Fisher is abundantly clear:

I'm fucked.

I need to break the seal. I regret having to do it, but I can't hold it any longer. My cheeks are hot, and after what I can only describe as quite possibly the most orgasmic pee of my life, I stumble out of the bathroom and find Aubrey talking to a tall guy with a large dragon tattoo on the back of his neck. They whisper in each other's ears, and he leads her over to the far wall, behind the DJ booth, and to a dark corner where they hide in the shadows.

Not again.

Everything around spins, and it takes a while for my vision to catch up with where my eyes want to go. I haven't had a drink since the accident. And stumbling around like an idiot feels embarrassing, but no one seems to notice. Within a minute, I'm across the dance floor and hovering a few feet away from the dark corner. When I squint my eyes, the outline of two people pressed against the wall comes to focus. I step into what feels like a cavernous space and push forward with outstretched arms until I find them both. There is a struggle as hands thrash in the air, and a few grunts result in a scuffle. After a few seconds, they both step out of the shadows, and Aubrey looks surprised to see me.

"Whatareyou doing?" I slur.

"Grayson. Jesus. You're buzzed. Are you okay? Is something wrong?"

"Yo, we gotta problem?" The man with the tattoo steps forward until my face is level with his chest. "What'chu doin' here?"

"No. No problem here. He was just leaving." She glares at me. "Aren't you?"

I shake my head in response.

"Who's this chump? Get 'im outta here."

"Don't worry." She jerks her head to indicate that I should leave. I don't. "He won't be a problem. Will you?" She glares again.

"Get away from her." I lean in to push him, shake away the buzz as best as I can. He stumbles back a few steps.

The man starts to lunge, but Aubrey grabs his wrist and twists his arm behind his back, forces him face-first into the wall. "I said not to worry. He isn't a problem. But if you so much as lay a finger on him, we will have a *big* problem. Now, are we going to finish our deal here or not? I'll finish paying in cash."

"Get offa me, slut. Before I get my boys to take ya both out back."

Aubrey twists his wrist a little harder. He cries out before she lets him go. Aubrey reaches into her boot and pulls out a few bills. The man reaches into the waistband of his jeans and pulls out something I can't make out in the dark. I look around paranoid, but we're so far behind the DJ booth that we're out of view.

After the man counts his money and Aubrey puts something into her shirt so it fits snuggly between her breasts, he leans down and sticks his corroded tongue into her mouth. Her eyes remain open, and her hands rest on his shoulders as if to push him off. But she doesn't. He reaches around and grabs her ass, squeezes it like it's a ball of putty he can mold. Aubrey looks at me, unblinking, as he gropes her. I move to pull him off, but her eyes tell me not to, so I don't.

He pulls back, licks the skin around her lips before he walks away. Her mouth is slick with saliva, and she wipes it off with the back of her hand. Aubrey doesn't say a word, only walks past and heads toward the front exit. I follow.

Outside, past the bouncers and to the side of the building, Aubrey reaches into her shirt and pulls out a pack of cigarettes. She sticks one in her mouth and lights it. It's the only time she's smoked in front of me. She exhales a plume. We both watch it drift upward before disappearing into the night sky.

"What wasthat?" I slur again and vow to slow down my speech to talk normally.

"Relax. I had him under control."

"Don't tell me to relax. H-he had his hands all over you!"

"It's none of your business."

It hurts me. More than it should, and more than I want it to. But it hurts.

"So, you just let guys do whatever they want to you... why? First the security guard, then that fair worker, and now him?"

"Stop." She exhales another plume of smoke.

"No. I'm not going to stop. You're so much better than him, than all of them. You talk about all these things of being empowered and in control, yet you let those men use you. Use your body for whatever it is you want that they have."

"You're pissing me off."

"Good. Now you know how I feel. Why can't you see how special you are? You deserve to be treated better."

"If I wanted to be preached at, I'd go to church."

"I'm just trying to——"

"You're not. You're being judgy, and I thought you were above everyone else in this stupid town."

"I'm sorry."

"Stop. You think and worry too much. Speak your mind. That's a good thing. Just don't assume anything about people who you have no idea about. It's a turn-off." She curses under her breath. "I'm not mad. Just annoyed. Are you done lecturing me?"

I'm so taken aback I have no idea what to say, so I go for a half nod, half shake. I didn't realize I was being judgy. Maybe I have been, I don't even know. The alcohol is still clouding my rational thoughts. I just don't want her to be disappointed in me, like I somehow need her to see me as different from everyone else. Need myself to be different.

"I won't do it again."

She inhales another few puffs before stomping the cigarette out below her boot. Behind her I notice the graffiti wall—faded and cracked is a red rose with a green stem. Above the rose is the Illuminati symbol. The eye in the triangle. Right below the rose are the words:

THIS STATEMENT IS FALSE

It's so strange; I'm not sure what to make of it.

Aubrey reaches into her shirt to pull out a baggie. "I was getting us weed. You said you never smoked it before. I got this for us."

Oh.

I look at the few joints rolled up inside. She puts the baggie back into her shirt before anyone notices. I tell myself to drop the argument for now. I won't get anywhere with her in this state, and maybe she's right. Maybe I am too judgmental. I sigh and lick my lips, my mouth dry.

"So now you're trying to get me high?"

She grins and steps forward so we're inches apart. "It's my plan to slowly corrupt you and bring you to the Dark Side." She squints playfully. "How am I doing so far?"

I squint playfully back. "I'll let you know after we light one of those joints."

She blows out air through her lips so her bangs puff up. "My thoughts exactly. I can get used to this new and improved inebriated you."

Out of the three joints, we smoke one and a quarter. Aubrey says it's really hard to get high your first time sharing just one, so she wants to make sure there is no doubt that I'll be having a "wicked good time." For a while, nothing substantial happens at all. It seems like a complete bust. It's Aubrey who points out that I'm high when I don't realize the difference.

"Shh," I hush her. "I think I hear a deer trotting down the street."

"Dude. You're shot." She giggles.

"No. Shut up and listen. Is there a deer roaming the streets right now?"

"There's no deer in downtown Davisport. You're high. Congratulations."

Gray Falconi: Trippin' Balls.

Aubrey says a crowded nightclub with strobe lights would quickly turn into a bad experience with weed and alcohol, so we keep with the cool, open night air. I know it's technically illegal, and we could get in trouble if caught. But I don't care. If I'm going to die, at least I can say I did this before I'm gone.

But right now I try to stay in the moment with Aubrey. The cool breeze feels good against my flushed face. We extend our arms and let the air wrap around our fingers. It's almost like I'm numb. I can't really feel anything, but it's nice. My steps feel light, weightless. And the stars in the night sky, the twinkling white amidst a sea of black, are serene. Peaceful.

Each step is purposeful. Each breath important. We walk in silence, and the streetlights are bright to the point that I'm forced to squint. Down the road a red light flashes at an intersection, and a few cars slow to a stop before driving on. A group of drunk people walks past us on the opposite side of the street, and from some alley to our left, an echo of a couple shouting carries in the wind.

It's all slow, all distinct. Time doesn't matter here. Anxiety is nothing but a concept. It's like waking up in the morning and trying to catch the dust in the beams of light that filter through the blinds. It makes me so happy.

A few low-rise apartment complexes greet us on either side as we leave the ghetto and enter into the better part of Davisport. Some balconies have laundry hanging from railings, air-drying in the light wind. I run and jump up as high as I can to smack a pink towel, land on my heels, and spin in a circle.

I look at Aubrey, and she's eyeing me, surprised. Her eyes open wide and her smile even wider. It's like she's taking me in and enjoying the taste. And there is a grin on my face too. I can feel it, but I don't remember putting it there. It's all so new and wonderful and strange, but so quiet and eerie at the same time.

There's no describing the state I'm in. Maybe I'm both drunk and high and at any moment I'll get violently sick. But this right here, watching Aubrey watching me, seeing that joy on her face, is something I can experience forever and never tire of.

It's one of the rare times she just feels like a regular seventeen-year-old girl. Maybe her life has been tougher than she probably deserved and wanted, but there is so much *depth* to her. So much beauty behind her bullshit.

"What are you thinking about?" she interrupts my thoughts.

You.

"I'm... um... I'm..."

"Hungry?"

Shit. Am I hungry?

"I don't even know. Am I supposed to be?"

She nods. "Eventually. It'll come out of nowhere. But what do you want to do until then?"

"Is it weird that I feel like swimming?"

She smirks. "Not at all. Let's go swimming, Mr. Falconi."

"Lead the way, Miss Fisher."

She wraps her arm around mine, and we walk down the street until we reach another intersection and turn right towards what I assume is the residential part of this district. A few cars pass us in both directions, and each time I squint at the headlights. It's not long before Aubrey yawns beside me, which causes me to yawn. We both giggle until a bench comes up on our right in front of an office building. A few feet behind it is the entrance to the parking garage, which is nearly vacant. We both sit down.

"It's beautiful, isn't it?" I ask and look up into the night.

"What is?"

"The sky. The endlessness of it. How it seems to stretch on forever and ever. To infinity."

She leans back, crosses her arms over her chest and looks up with me, yawns again. "You're not scared of getting lost with it all up there? Like it's a giant black hole ready to swallow you into the void?"

"That's a pretty grim way to look at it. But no, seriously, just think about it. Out of all of space, all the galaxies and planets and solar systems, and here we are. We could've been a dust particle, or a blade of grass, or a ball of light. But we're here instead. You and me. Aubrey and Gray. Isn't that just amazing to think about?"

She looks over at me, studies me. I do the same to her. Look down at her full lips.

"You shouldn't be sad, Grayson."

"I'm sorry?"

Aubrey sits up straight and fidgets her hands in her lap, points her boots inward like a child. Her nose ring catches a glare from the nearest street lamp as she turns her head.

"You need to share yourself with the world. It could use more people like you." She mumbles something under her breath and stands up. "—wn you sooner."

And there's something about the last thing she says that catches me. Scares me.

"What?"

She shakes her head and pulls me up to my feet so fast my head spins. I blink away the dizziness and follow a pace behind.

"C'mon. Let's go find this pool of yours."

As we walk, in the center of the empty street, is Bryson. He pivots his body as we move forward, so he's also facing in our direction. He doesn't say anything, and he doesn't follow. He just stands and stares. A streetlight catching his seashell necklace.

In my head, I can hear the seagull cries. Waves crashing into rocks.

I should be scared, freaked out, but for some reason it feels like a good sign this time. There's no blood. He's not here to warn or remind me; he's here to tell me that he approves. That this is right. His words echo in my head:

"Follow Aubrey. Stay with her. Let her show you."

His words feel important somehow, but I don't know why. Not yet. Like there's a hidden meaning there.

And part of me wants to run up to him, wrap him in my arms, and never let go. My eyes feel heavy, ready to release tears. He looks so much like Mom. So innocent.

But he's not real.

Bryson smiles and raises his hand in a single wave before freezing in place. Like a picture. Unaware he's dead.

Forever ten years old.

I raise mine back, blink, and he's gone. But a light breeze blows past my face, and I almost think I can hear an echo of his breathy laugh. Just an echo, faint, but there. And I want to stop and find him, take his hand. Bring him home. But I turn around to face Aubrey instead.

We're two lost souls heading in the same direction.

∼

JENNA

Gray, stop ignoring me! Did I do something wrong?

REEFER

told u she was being annoying (ughhhhhhhhhhhh)

A few streets and intersections later, we're in another residential neighborhood not unlike those in Lee Falls. All concrete driveways with blacktop. Picket fences bordering neighboring houses. Two-story houses with shingled roofs and porches with some form of furniture by the front door. Pine trees dot the front yards of every other house.

Many of the homes sit in silence—a few with their porch lights turned on, but most are dark. On our left, two boys race by on bicycles, trade gossip about what I think is which teacher they'd bang. It's both familiar and not. Like the street can be any street in the entire world, yet it's all so specific to this place and time.

She picks up her pace, and we arrive at a random empty driveway. She raises her eyebrows and walks forward.

"Let's see if they have a pool."

Normally I'd try and talk her out of it, but I don't. That's when I know that I'm changing. Aubrey is changing me.

And I don't know if it's a good or bad thing.

We come up to a small, wooden fence ridged at the top. It appears locked from the inside, but Aubrey tries to force it open regardless. It doesn't budge. Without warning, she places her hands gently on the ridges and pushes off the ground with her feet until she clears the top and hops over.

Aubrey Fisher: Ninja?

"Aubrey? You okay?"

There's a muffled thud and a scuffle, followed by the sound of shoes running over stones. Then the latch to the door clicks and it swings inward.

"Party of one," Aubrey announces in a gruff voice. "Calling for party of one."

I shake my head and enter. "You realize if we get caught, we're both dead, right?"

"On the contrary." She closes the fence behind her and

locks the latch. "We've never been more alive. Now hush. Let's see if these pricks have a pool."

The side of the house ends and opens up into a decent-sized backyard. To the very back, by the edge of the fence, is a shed. Up front, closest to us, is a trampoline and swing-set. In the middle is an in-ground pool. The cover is bundled up by the diving board, and the pool lights are still on, which makes the water glimmer. I laugh at our luck. Of course Aubrey's first choice would have a pool. Everything with her just manages to work out.

"Still wanna swim?" she asks.

I nod.

"Let's not waste any time then."

I'm not nervous or scared, so I chalk it up to the weed and alcohol still poisoning my body. We walk to the edge of the pool and look around for signs of any neighbors, but the ones on either side have all the lights turned out, and behind the fence is a small field separating this house from the next. But they are too far away to see anything. We're alone.

"You think anyone is home?" I ask. "Like a kid or something?"

"I guess we'll know for sure if the cops show up with guns."

"That's not funny."

"It's a good thing I'm not kidding."

"I don't have a bathing suit."

"Neither do I."

"So are we just going in with our clothes?"

She smirks. "We can always get naked."

"That's still not funny."

"And I'm still not kidding."

There's no way I'm getting naked in front of Aubrey. Only Kris has seen me like that, and especially now, after putting on the weight, I can't do it. Aubrey must know what I'm thinking because she drops it.

"Fine. Apparently, you still have some self-control. What a shame. We'll keep it PG-13. Okay?"

I nod, take out my cell phone and wallet so they don't get ruined, and place the grocery bag on the ground. She takes off her boots at the same time I remove my sneakers, and she places her wad of cash, cigarettes, lighter, ID, a folded newspaper clipping, and the remaining joints down on the ground. She decides to keep on her fingerless gloves. She doesn't have a wallet or a cell phone. Like she packed light, only here for a visit and not a long time.

Fear washes over me that Aubrey is going to leave. Somehow, someway, she's going to abandon me. I push it aside. I shouldn't care. I'll be dead. Gone. Rotting within hours. Why should I care what Aubrey does or doesn't do? It makes no sense.

You're getting attached.

The fear disappears, and Aubrey walks to the edge of the pool to dip one toe in and test the temperature. She gives me the thumbs up, so it must be heated. I walk toward her, and we stand by the edge. She looks into the water, transfixed by the lights and the glimmer of the moon on the surface. The water still ripples from where she dipped in her toe, and her reflection comes back distorted.

Without thinking, I extend my hands, grab Aubrey by the shoulders, and push her into the pool. She cries out and flails her arms before making a splash. She emerges from underneath the water and wipes the red highlights away from her face.

"You little shit," she coughs, but there's a tinge of humor behind it.

Aubrey paddles over to the shallow end and walks up the steps to the concrete above the pool. I run in the opposite direction toward the diving board. Aubrey straightens her soaked clothes and runs my way, nearly trips in the process. I look around for something to defend myself and find a foam noodle. I reach down to pick it up and point it at Aubrey like a sword. It's useless, but I giggle anyway.

"Are you really trying to defend yourself with a phallic foam noodle?"

"Yes. Yes, I am."

"You know it's limp right?"

"The irony is not lost on me."

Aubrey bites her lower lip, and for the first time, I see how her matted clothes accentuate the curves of her body. Her ample breasts, round butt, and thick thighs. I have the urge to run my hands over her smooth, pale skin. To feel how soft and delicate she is. To caress the curves of her figure. Water drips from her dark hair and patters on the pavement. Blood pumps in my veins, and I blink really fast to stop the perverse thoughts that enter my mind.

No. Stop. You realize you're going to have to leave her before the night is over. Yes?

I put down the noodle and step up to the diving board, take a running start, and dive head first into the pool. The water cascades over my body. It feels like tiny fingers on my skin. It's warmer than I thought it would be, and I come up and sputter for air. The scent of chlorine makes my nose twitch.

Aubrey flips me the middle finger and takes off her shirt, fishnets, and nylons. Standing in only her black bra and mini-skirt, her skin is so pale. I can't look away—want to know what she feels like. How soft her skin is. And she's staring at me, daring me to turn. But I don't. And for whatever reason, I take off my shirt and throw it into the grass. She smirks and then jumps in.

We splash each other and try to race from the deep to

shallow end a few times. Aubrey finds more pool floaties scattered around the dark yard, and we play around with them—occasionally bash each other in the face. She tries to dunk my head before I fight her off.

It's the most fun I've had in as long as I can remember.

I don't want to enjoy it. I don't want to have fun and forget. But I do.

We dive underwater and open our eyes. It's like an alien world underneath. Everything is hazy and blue. The sound muffled. We swim to each other and float there, inches apart. Her highlighted hair floats like ribbons, and air bubbles cling to her nose. I reach out a finger. She does the same. We touch the points together, and my entire hand tingles. I don't know why we do it, but it's nice. Familiar. I look from our fingers to her eyes and lips. She doesn't blink. The moment is suspended in time. And I realize I could stay like this, with Aubrey, forever. Would be content to keep looking at her. She smiles. I smile. And she's so beautiful.

The water cools, so we both come up for air.

"Is this enough adventure, or do you think you have a little more in store for later?" Aubrey swims up to me after we stop to rest and sit down in the shallow end. The water comes up to our chests.

I scoot closer to her. "What else can we possibly do that we haven't already?"

"We haven't had sex yet."

My stomach flips.

"I wasn't aware that was an option on the table."

"Oh, so you want to do it on a table?" She snickers. "I bet you're secretly into super kinky stuff. I can tell. This whole repressed teenage guy routine." She winks. "Definitely kinky."

"Ohmygod!" My face gets hot, and my entire body tingles in excitement. "They don't have a table, do they?"

She playfully splashes water into my eyes. "Don't worry. I'm just kidding."

I splash water back at her. "Are you, though?"

She cocks her head. "Is Grayson Falconi flirting?"

I roll my eyes. "You got me."

She rolls her eyes mockingly, and we sit in silence, move our arms underneath the water. We look at each other, not saying a word. Aubrey smacks at a mosquito on her shoulder.

And it's there again, that unspoken bond. It's peaceful. It's blissful. Like nothing else matters except this moment.

Aubrey is the only one who has made me feel like this since the accident. And for some reason, I want to tell her everything.

All of it.

But she beats me to the punch.

"Why do you want to kill yourself, Grayson?"

I'm aware of the crickets chirping, and the breeze from the night sky that cools my exposed shoulders.

She. Knows.

"I'm sorry?"

She doesn't answer or move, only sits in the same position with her face turned towards mine, waiting for an answer. But I can't. Don't know what to say. My mouth is a cesspool of ugliness, and no words will sneak past my tongue.

She knew the entire time, Gray.

I don't know what to do, and I sober up quickly. Too quickly. To the point where I feel my stomach churn and bubble. So I do the only thing I can think of, the only thing that seems right. The only answer I know how to give without speech.

I lean in and kiss her.

It's so unexpected and sudden that not even Aubrey prepares for it.

Our lips touch. They press together, and we stay like this for a while, maybe too long. But I feel it.

That spark—the tingle in my fingertips and surge of energy. I'm lightheaded, and my heart kicks at my chest, tries to fight its way out. Tries to find a way to hers.

And her lips are soft. So soft.

There's a hint of cigarette and vanilla that rides on her breath when it escapes from her mouth in surprise, and I suck it in, let her breath become my own. Like I need it to survive. Need *her* to survive. She releases air through her nose that tickles my cheeks.

We both pull away after what seems like hours, and she stares back, shocked. Her mouth open like she'd just seen something horrific. We sit and wait, not moving, barely breathing. It's a suffocating silence.

But it was there, that sense that it felt right, and I want to do it again. Want to feel the surge of energy. The rush. Feel her skin against my own. Her breath in mine. Our two beating hearts. The tips of our fingers. The small dimple in her cheek. The tongue ring tracing the lines of my face and running up and down my chest.

I want to hold her in my arms. Just us. Forever.

"Why did you do that?" she whispers.

"I... I don't know."

Her jaw clenches up as if in pain. She strokes away from me. "Goddamnit."

From inside the house, lights flicker on one after another until a light for the back patio directs a beam that points directly to me and Aubrey. We freeze. Caught. And temporarily putting aside whatever just happened—

You kissed Aubrey Fisher is what happened!!!

—swim to the pool ledge. To my left, one of the Spider-Man Band-Aids floats on the surface.

We climb out of the pool as quietly as possible. Our clothes soaked, we step into our shoes and gather our items in our hands. Aubrey leads the way, and I tiptoe behind.

A voice murmurs from inside, and I'm aware that the backyard has a sliding glass door. It doesn't take long for the owner, an older man, to appear in the dining room, which is right behind the glass. He does a double take. But he sees me. I freeze in place until he opens his mouth and points. He shouts something that is muffled from inside.

And then everything speeds up, goes too fast. Aubrey grabs my hand and yanks me to the fence door. She opens the latch and swings the door inward so we can run down the front lawn and into the street—still in our underwear. Behind us, I hear the front door open and the man shout. I don't know what he says, but I know the word "cops" is used at least once.

We run down street after street, and I'm aware of sirens in the far distance, but Aubrey nods to indicate we're safe. For now. We stop running to catch our breaths and put on our wet clothes. I rip off another Spider-Man Band-Aid clinging to my skin for dear life.

And of all moments for the weed to kick in, it does, and my stomach growls. Afraid that I've ruined the entire night, I change the subject, hope that Aubrey will understand and pretend the kiss never happened, and maybe pretend that she never asked me what she just did.

"I need to eat," I say. "Now."

She wrings out the end to her shirt. I do the same. She doesn't look back at me when she speaks, only looks down at the wet pavement.

"Sounds like a plan. I know a place."

"I think I need to pee again too."

"Shouldn't of broke the seal."

We walk until we pass a section of trees and stop so I can

release my bladder, and I look up into the night sky to see the half-moon looking down. Judging. It saw everything that happened, and even after I ask for advice inside my head, the moon provides no solace.

I just kissed Aubrey Fisher, and I liked it.

A lot.

7 HOURS UNTIL

???

THE WAITRESS SEATS US AT A TABLE NEXT TO THE FRONT window. It's one of those twenty-four-hour joints: Dusty's Diner. There's a trucker dressed in jeans and a camo shirt, his semi parked in the lot out front. He drinks a cup of coffee, eats a strudel, and flirts with a younger girl who wipes down the counter. Our waitress looks at us in disgust, our clothes still damp and clinging to our pale bodies. Aubrey's hair is frizzy and clumped together. I thank the waitress, an older woman with curly silver hair, as she looks at my face for longer than is comfortable. She shivers and walks away to bring us both a glass of water.

We're silent. We walked all the way from the residential neighborhood, and by now, my stomach is ready to eat through flesh. When the waitress comes back, we both order the Pancake Supreme Deluxe. Aubrey says we need to load up on carbs and water to soak up the alcohol in our system. I obey without question.

The laminated plastic table is grimy, like it hasn't been cleaned in decades. We sit on faded, red plastic seats. The floors below are checkered green-and-yellow tiles, and the walls are bare. It's cheap and a little disgusting, but I'm too hungry to really care. As long as food is in my system.

"We need to talk about what happened," she says.

"I know."

"You kissed me. Why?"

She's so blunt that it throws me off. I fumble for the right words. "I-uh... it was stupid."

"Yeah. It was."

"I'm s—"

"I'll stab you with this fork if you say it."

The food arrives before we talk again. There are seven large buttermilk pancakes stacked on each other, and we drown them in ladles of maple syrup and heaps of whip cream—take a few savoring bites before continuing. It's like an orgasm in my mouth.

"It's not going to happen again. Understand?"

I nod.

"You had no right to kiss me." She darts her eyes up at me and back down at her plate. Her tongue flicks in and out of her mouth, and she bites down to catch the tongue ring between her front teeth.

"Understood." My voice is pathetic. "It won't happen again." I'm fully prepared to leave it at that and sulk in shame until my stomach is full, but I can't. Don't want to. She can't go fooling around with random creeps, and yet the second I give her a harmless kiss, have the right to put me down for it.

"You know what? No. I'm not sorry." I sit up straight and lean forward in the booth. Aubrey stops mid-fork to look at me. "Yeah, I kissed you. Maybe it was an accident, but I won't apologize for it."

Was it really an accident, Gray?

Aubrey raises her eyebrows and wipes her mouth with the back of her hand.

"You can't just sit there and tell me one minute I need to act more, think less, and then put me down for doing just that. Dammit. I kissed you. Woman up, Aubrey. Get out of yourself for more than two seconds and be an actual person for a change. You're so mysterious and coy, and you play people for it. You present yourself as a larger-than-life person, an enigma, but you're not. Maybe Kris was right: you're just terrified of yourself."

I don't know where it comes from, like someone popped the top to a soda bottle, and all the aggression is just spilling out from inside. Whatever it is, it feels good.

"You done?"

"No! I'm not done. I want to know about you. Your story, your life, your foster family. Cut the bullshit. If we're going to be friends, then you owe me that much."

"Friends, huh?"

She smirks and forks more pancake into her mouth. By the front counter, the trucker and two waitresses have turned their heads to us, so I lower my voice.

"That's what we are, isn't it? Friends?"

"You don't care about my past."

"I do."

"No. You don't. Why would you? You know nothing about me. I'm just a foster freak."

I take a bite of pancake, talk with my mouth full. "Because you never talk about yourself. Ever. I know nothing about you, but I care about you. You're not a freak."

"Don't."

"What?" I scowl. "Care about you? What does that mean?"

"Let's talk about *you*. How are *you* today? Anything new or exciting? Any plans for later tonight? What were you really doing in the school bathroom before I came in?"

She's toying with me now, intentionally trying to hurt me.

It's low, even for her. I don't want to admit she's right. To say out loud that I'm going to kill myself. It's different than admitting to it in my head. Like it's somehow more selfish.

We go back and forth like this for a while, not moving forward or getting anywhere. It's hostile between us until we're done with our pancakes and the waitress refills our water glasses. I'm full and feel better than I did before. Aubrey asks for the check and then pays it without a thought. Her wad of cash is almost all gone; only a few twenties and some change remain. She folds it back up and packs it inside her boot.

"A donation from my wonderful foster parents."

I nod and grind my teeth. "Do they know you have it?"

"They sure don't." She leans back and looks out the window at the empty street. I do the same.

Her chest rises and falls with each breath. I can see her thinking something over. Aubrey clucks her tongue a few times. The trucker from the front exits the diner and steps into his semi. My hands fidget on the table; the smell of chlorine still clings to my clothes.

"I was seven. When they placed me in the foster system." Aubrey doesn't look at me, so I know this is the truth. Her voice is shaky, quiet.

I want to ask about her parents, but am afraid to. She must already know where my mind is going because she speaks before I have a chance.

"I don't want to go there. Not yet." She pauses. "Let's get out of here. I want to show you something."

"I thought you were mad at me?"

"I'm impressed. Took some balls to call me out on my shit. But I don't want to talk right now. I need to show you something first."

"Oh. Well... what if *I'm* mad at you?"

"I hope you are. You have every right to be." She slides from the booth and stands, straightens her retro plaid mini-skirt. "Remember: stick to your guns. That outburst might have been one of the sexiest things you've done all night. And I hope you keep doing it. You're hot, Grayson. But a hot, confident you... that's dangerous."

My face heats, but I stand up from the booth with her. "You make no sense sometimes."

"That's why I want to show you this. C'mon."

We walk out of the diner and to the nearest bus stop down the block. I'm almost completely sober, and questions litter my mind, but I bite my tongue. When the bus pulls up next to us, we step on, and Aubrey pays. It's empty; we're the only passengers. We find a seat in the very back and sit next to each other. I place the grocery bag on the floor. Aubrey sits with her legs folded underneath, and my eyes are drawn to her exposed upper thighs. She laughs.

"You can be such a dude sometimes."

"You do realize that your outfit just gives off a certain vibe for guys everywhere, right?"

"Girls too. And yup. Why do you think I wear it?" She yawns. "Weed and food always make me sleepy." She scoots closer until our sides touch, and she lays her head on my shoulder. "Wake me when we get to Cartersville."

"Cartersville? That's a town over. What the heck are we doing way over there?"

She closes her eyes. "Shh. Your mysterious friend needs to close her eyes."

"So am I really your friend, or are you making fun of me?" I lean my head over so it rests on top of hers. She sucks in a gulp of air, and we rise and sink together with her contracting chest.

"Don't push it. Need sleep." A pause. "And stop trying to look up my skirt."

Aubrey is fast asleep on the way to the next town, so I pull out my cell phone to read my missed texts and listen to voicemails. Mostly they all say the same thing. But then one of Mom's plays:

"Gray." She coughs into the receiver. A wrapper is ruffled in the background. "I went to the cemetery today to visit your brother." There's a long period of silence and more wrapping of paper. I think the voicemail will end before she ever comes back. But then, "Please come home, Gray. I need you to come home now." She curses into the background. "I love you." There's a slight break in her voice at the very end. And then the line clicks off.

I punch the seat in front of me. The cut on one of my knuckles splits open. Blood seeps to the surface. I close my eyes and rub my temples.

Dad's voicemail isn't much better:

"Hey, kiddo." He sighs. "Your mother isn't doing too well right now. She just called the store to yell, and... it doesn't matter. Can you please call us back? Or come home. Just come home, son." There's a pause on his end that's similar to Mom's, but it doesn't last as long before he comes back. "You're all we have." Another pause. "Love you, kiddo. Um—" There's a huff on his end of the line, and then it clicks dead.

My face gets hot, so I access my channel to pull up another video. This was posted seven months ago. I remember filming it, because it was a good day. I'd just heard back from a short poetry contest Kris and Jenna found for me. I'd won third place. As the video starts, Reefer strokes my hair like a pet. I shove his hand away. We're both grinning like idiots, trying to hold back giggles while we both wear aviator sunglasses.

"*Greetings, Falconians,*" *Reefer announces.* "*You buncha hosers.*"

"*Don't call my fans hosers,*" I correct.

"*Wow... Gray-Gray getting all professional and shit. Is there a reason for this?*"

"*There is indeed.*"

Reefer rubs my chest as I stifle a laugh-cough.

"*Tell me. Tell the Reef Machine. What sayeth the Falcon of Falconians?*"

I ball my hand into a fist and tap him in the nuts. He drops like a sack of potatoes to the ground, groaning. I still have a goofy grin on my face.

"*Hey, Little Man,*" I call to somewhere off screen. Take off the aviators in a really exaggerated fashion and puff out my chest. "*Want to tell the lovely people what happened?*"

Suddenly, a body pops up from the floor, seemingly out of nowhere. The boy also has aviators that are half the size of his face. But before anything else is said, Bryson jumps into my arms and wraps his around my shoulders.

"*You did it, Gray! You did it, you did it, you did it!*"

"*I did, Little Man.*"

"*Now we can go to the beach and celebrate!*"

"*Ha-ha. Of course we can. Just me and you. How does that sound?*"

"*Yesssssss! I love you. Best. Brother. Ever.*" He pivots his head. "*Mom! Dad! Come see what Gray did!*" He giggles. "*I really am suuuupperrrrrrrrrrr proud of you, Gray. You're going to be famous, right? Like God famous?*"

"*I don't know about that...*"

"*I do. God famous.*" He giggles again. "*I love you, God.*"

"*God loves you too, Little Man.*" I ruffle his hair. "*God loves little men—ooh, that sounded bad.*"

He kisses me on the cheek. "*Mooooooom! Daaaaaad! Come here nowwwwwwowowow!*"

We both look at the screen at the same time. His aviator

glasses fall off his face as Reefer slowly stands. I scramble to exit out before it continues. 1,899 views. 127 likes. 17 dislikes. From the recent comments:

JamesDeanFan: Fucking amazing! So proud. Wish you didn't stop posting vids. Inspiring shit, I should know. This is what gets you laid and paid. People love you! Such a unique way of seeing the world. I'm going to meet you someday. You going to be ready for it? Congrats on 3rd place! :) :) :)

Who the hell is this dude that he keeps leaving these untrue comments? Your writing sucks. Third place sucks. You can't write anymore because the universe knows you're an imposter.

I delete the video before anything more is shown or said. I don't allow myself to cry. Steady my breaths before I start to lose it.

If only it had been you instead of him. Right?

I bash the back of my head into the seat rest behind me, careful not to wake up Aubrey. She's like a baby, the way she sleeps. She doesn't move and barely makes a sound. I lean down to sniff her hair, which reeks of chlorine and weed. The way her chest raises each time she breathes in calms me. I keep watching her breaths, matching her rhythm, until the vision of Bryson fades away into the abyss of my mind. I lick the blood from off my knuckle.

I put my phone away, the battery nearly dead. My hand rests on top of Aubrey's, and I leave it like that until we reach our destination. The nerves in my body ping one after another.

It seems like an indication of what a relationship with her might be like. Just like this. But I don't hold my breath, because deep down it's not what she wants. I can see that as clear as day.

And in my head, I imagine calling my parents back to tell

them I love them and I'll be home soon. And we can work on being a family, getting past everything. I smile.

It's nice to pretend. If only for a while.

Aubrey leads me off the bus when we arrive in Cartersville. She tells me we only have enough money to make one more trip back to Lee Falls if we want to head home after. She doesn't say why we're here or where we're going, but I have a bad feeling. A very bad one.

Cartersville is similar to Davisport, which is the party town, but Cartersville is upper business class. Around us, the street is bombarded with tall office buildings. Most of the offices are dark, but a few scattered windows show tiny squares of light. A few cabs and cars pass during the late night, but it's mostly quiet. The air stinks with the aroma of exhaust and fumes.

Not many people party late over here. This is where the "rich" people live.

The sky above is still dotted with stars, but some of the buildings obstruct the view.

"Where are we going?" I stumble after Aubrey. My senses are clearer than before, but with the alcohol, Tylenol, and weed leaving my system, the throbbing pain comes back in my ribs and face. I groan.

"What's wrong?" she asks.

"The pain is back. Need more Tylenol. Do you have the grocery bag?"

"I thought you had it."

"Shit. I think I left it on the bus."

She turns around to inspect me. "Do you need to sit down and rest?"

"No, I'm fine. Seriously, where are we going?"

A rogue newspaper page billows by my feet before being swept away into the wind.

"It's a five-minute walk from here." She turns around and picks up her pace. "You're not gonna give me that stubborn look again. Not falling for it."

"I don't have a stubborn look."

"Grayson." She turns around to say my name and puts her hands on my shoulders. The way my name rolls off her tongue, how it causes the ring to flick out of her mouth, makes my body shake. "I'm not kidding when I say this, so take it as it is. Nod your head. And move your ass with me, mmmkay?"

I nod.

"You're hot. Any girl with a vagina can see that. A confident, hot you... that's not even fair. Girls don't have a shot. And a hot, confident version of you that gives these longing, broody looks like you often do... well, shit. Ovaries be damned. So own it. You can get any girl you want if you stopped feeling sorry for yourself. It's not always about *you*."

She pats my shoulder. There's a hesitation. Then she turns around and walks.

"Right now is about me. So shut the fuck up and let's go already."

The neon sign hangs above the tattoo parlor: Total Custom Tattoo. All of the *T*s flicker on and off, and the *O*s are completely burned out. Aubrey doesn't say anything. Just walks in, past the greeter standing by the door, and towards the back of the shop where a man with a large, gray beard works on a scrawny boy's inner thigh. The greeter is a woman with large gauges in each ear, large enough that I can see the wall through them. She has two nose piercings, one in each eyebrow, green hair, and full tattoo sleeves on each arm. I try not to stare, but it's hard. She looks up blankly and then returns to her magazine.

Around us, the walls are cluttered with artwork. Paintings, skateboard decks, sculptures, models wearing tattoos and piercings, etc. It's everywhere. Everything in here has a dim, smoky glow besides the chair where the guy is tattooing. He has a concentrated bright, white light. The buzzing of the needle fills the air.

Aubrey steps in front of the bearded man. He huffs under his breath, doesn't look up.

"He's not in a good state tonight," the man says, nonchalant. He briefly looks past her to me. "You look like hell. Who's the kid?"

"Where is he, Gus?"

Gus pulls back his ink needle to dab a towel at the boy's leg. He listens to his headphones—his eyes closed and his face red. Gus sits up, cranes his neck, and looks at Aubrey, annoyed.

I sniff the place around me, and besides ink and smoke, it smells like ham. I'm nervous. It doesn't seem right that we're here. Maybe she wants a tattoo. Maybe she'll try to force me to get one. Either way, it makes no sense. How does any of this have to do with her?

"Take your friend"—Gus points to me but bends back down to continue his art—"and get outta here. Go home, kid. Neither of you belong here tonight."

The girl behind me hums. I look back, and she watches us while pretending to read her magazine.

They argue, each statement briefer than the last until they're practically speaking in single words. After a few minutes of silence, Gus pats the scrawny boy on the shoulder. He opens his eyes.

"Ten minute break."

The kid nods but continues to listen to his headphones.

Gus stands up, dressed in a black T-shirt and jeans. He's buff—his biceps and chest practically bulging out of his shirt. He looks like Gus ate a smaller Gus. Like he can snap me in two with his bare hands. He reaches behind him to a cluttered desk and puts on wire-framed glasses.

"You sure you wanna see him like this?"

Aubrey looks to me and nods.

He sighs. "Let's go, kid. He's in the back."

My stomach does tumbles, and the breath is knocked out of my lungs. Dread floats in the air. The last thing I want to do is go into the back room and meet whoever is there, but Aubrey is so tense and quiet. So unlike herself. For a moment I think there's fear on her face.

What the hell is behind the door?

Each step feels more weighted than the last, and each one comes with a new sense of regret. The narrow hallway in the back of the shop ends on a small, green door; the paint chipped and faded. It's pitch black minus the light that creeps from the entrance behind us. The thought of a man coming out of the door wielding a chainsaw flashes in my mind, but I push it away.

Gus pounds on the door. We wait. No answer. He pounds a second time. We wait. No answer. He pounds a third time. We wait. The latch clicks and the door creaks open. No one greets us.

Gus walks back down the hallway and into the main area without a word. Aubrey hesitates outside the door. She stares into the open crack. I step forward. She jumps.

"I'm sorry. I didn't mean to—"

"No," she interrupts me. "It's okay. Um." She bites her lip and runs a hand through her hair. "Promise me you won't freak out. Okay?"

I reach out and grab her hand and squeeze it. Her palms are clammy. The corners of her mouth turn up in a nervous smile.

Aubrey turns around, takes a deep breath, and pushes open the door.

The room has a musty, stale scent in the air. In pace behind Aubrey, I walk in, and the room is too dim to make out much. There's a tiny TV in the far right corner, and to the left is a small coffee table littered with what I think are spoons, a few needles, and rubber tubing. The ground is full of empty wrappers and stains on the carpet. It reeks of body odor and semen, and there is a moaning from somewhere in the dark. I can't see anyone, not at first, just the shadow of a body slumped on a dirty couch with foam falling out of holes in the fabric.

Aubrey squeezes my hand harder, to the point that it hurts. She's terrified.

Jesus. What the hell is this place?

Aubrey stops in the middle of the room and clears her throat. "James," she says, her voice as soft as a mouse. "James? It's Aubrey."

My heart jumpstarts and I want to run away. Want to leave and never come back. This place feels like a tomb. Aubrey sounds so tiny and grave. So afraid.

There is something seriously wrong here.

There's a shuffle from the couch. The body moves, fumbles around for something, and a slender arm reaches out and turns on a lamp next to the couch. The brightness of the yellow glow causes me to shield my eyes until they adjust. Sitting there is a silhouetted man.

I try to swallow saliva, but my mouth is dry, throat closed up.

"Whoooooo?" the voice croons.

Aubrey takes another deep breath, squeezes my hand harder. Instinctively, my free hand goes to her shoulder. An act to let her know that I'm still here. She tilts her head in my direction, and I know she's grateful.

"It's Aubrey, James." A beat. "I brought someone with me to see you."

The man leans forward into the sliver of light, and my breath catches, heart stops.

I'm looking at a skeleton.

Or someone resembling one.

His eyes are sunk back deep in their sockets, and his cheekbones jut out at crude angles. The man wears a dirty white T-shirt riddled with holes, and his bony shoulders poke up through the skin. He looks nearly emaciated. And just barely in view, there is a tourniquet tied around his right arm. He squints at me, and I wince at the sight. The look of him makes my stomach churn.

"Is that Dean?" he asks in a weak voice. It sounds cloudy, like he's not really here.

Drugs, Gray. Look at the table. He's on heroin or meth.

"No," Aubrey says under her breath. "This is my friend. His name is Grayson."

James looks me over, but from what I can see of his shrunken eyes, he seems to look through me. Then his eyes turn hard, and he sits up straighter, making his Adam's apple jiggle.

"What's he doing here, Aubers?"

Aubrey trembles. Something is wrong.

"It's not Dean."

James's face twists, and he lets out a sound I can only describe as a screeching cry.

"Whyyyyyy did you bring him, Aubers?"

I want to back up, but I don't want to leave Aubrey here. I squeeze her shoulder and hand. She turns her head back and whispers in my ear. "Go outside and get Gus. *Now.*"

I nod my head, attempt to swallow saliva, but once again my throat is closed up. Aubrey lets go of my hand, and I back up and out the door. Before I turn to walk down the hall, Aubrey inches closer, her hands extended, and wraps the man on the couch in a hug. From the hallway, he looks not much older than us. Maybe early twenties.

My phone vibrates, and I pull it out as I run for the front parlor.

UNKNOWN

u rdy 2 have another death on your hands?

Outside in the tattoo parlor, Gus is back to work on the boy's leg. He shades in some letters to what appear to be song lyrics. When he sees me enter, he stands up, motions to the girl reading the magazine, and they drop what they're doing and run past me like it's routine. The headphone boy doesn't notice; he just continues to bob his head to the music. I clutch my chest, massage the bruise there, and force aside the anxiety that I feel coming.

UNKNOWN

????

Aubrey is gonna die

"Not now, you bitch," I mutter.

I text back a reply of obscenities.

THIS PHONE LINE HAS BEEN DISCONNECTED

I bash my fist against the bruise. Once. Twice. Three times before the panic waves dissipate. Shaking away the feeling of drowning, I put away my phone and dash to the backroom. The man on the couch is crying as Aubrey hugs him. Gus raises his hand and rips the tourniquet away from James's arm. The three of them exchange words I can't hear, and when James looks up and sees me, he loses it. Points a bony finger and shouts.

"You're deadddddddddddddd. Youuuuuu diiiiiiiiiiiiiiiiiiii-ieeeeeeeddddddddd."

My mouth drops open, and Aubrey looks back at me.

"I'm so sorry, Grayson. I shouldn't have brought you here. He's not in a good place tonight."

Gus helps restrain him as he attempts to get away and lunge for me. I back up until my back hits the wall.

"Hush," she says, her voice breaks at the end. "Hush now. You're okay." She strokes his hair. It reminds me of something my mom would do when I was upset as a kid. It's tender. "Just close your eyes, okay, James? I'm here. I'm still here."

He stops fighting and slumps back into the couch. Tears and snot run down his face.

"Why did Dean do it, Aubers? Why?"

"I don't know." She presses his head to her chest and rocks him back and forth. Her eyes look back at me, and they glisten. A single tear rolls out of her right eye and falls down her cheek until it wraps around underneath her chin and hangs there. "I don't know."

The girl with the gauges walks out into the hallway. She eyes me, looks up and down, and presses her back into the same wall. Gus begins to clean up some of the mess as Aubrey slowly comforts James.

"So, you and Aubrey. Yeah?" she asks calmly, her voice high pitched and nasally.

I don't answer, and she continues when she sees I'm at a loss for words.

"You'd be a first. I thought Gus was gonna have a coronary when he saw her walk in with you. She's never brought anyone here before."

I turn to her, shake the fuzziness out of my head and count the beats of my heart, but they don't slow down. "What are you talking about? Who are you?"

She smiles. Somehow not surprised.

"Did she tell you who that is in there?"

I shake my head. Inside, Aubrey looks back out at me. Wipes away the tear from her chin.

"I didn't think so."

"Should I know who it is?" I ask, but continue to look at Aubrey. We both stare at each other. Not blinking. Barely breathing. We're locked in a trance.

And then it hits me. Like a punch to the gut, I feel all the air leave my lungs, and I cough. Feel nauseous. The girl pats my back.

I know who that is.

I turn to the girl.

"That's Aubrey's brother, isn't it?"

She nods. "Older."

The thought of it, the new realization sinks in. Aubrey has a brother.

"Biological?"

The girl nods.

"Who's Dean?"

There's a pause before the girl speaks.

"Her younger brother."

I turn back to face Aubrey, and her eyes are sad. She knows that I know. Like all her defenses are falling one by one. She sucks in a breath, so her chest expands and holds it there.

"What happened to him?"

The girl doesn't answer right away. But when she does, it's barely a whisper, like a secret.

"He killed himself."

6 HOURS UNTIL

SATURDAY, AFTER 12:00 AM

THE WALLS BREATHE. THEY EXPAND AND CONTRACT, TRAP me inside the narrow hallway. The pancakes churn in my stomach, and I lean on the wall for support. I'm going to be sick. There is no stopping it. I cover my mouth to stop the bile that rides up my throat, run back out towards the main parlor, past the boy in the chair, and out the front doors.

I arch my back and retch. The contents of my stomach empty onto the blacktop. After a minute, hands wrap around my shoulders and pull me close. I expect it to be Aubrey, but it's the girl with the green hair and gauges. She pats my back.

It can't be true. Aubrey had a little brother who died. Who killed himself—committed suicide. It all makes sense: the entire night, her plan, and the comments she's made. Somehow Aubrey knew.

And just like that, the words bouncing around in my head, the contents of my stomach empty again. The remaining bile drips from my lips. I wipe it on the back of my hand and slump to the ground.

"Jesus Christ," I say.

The girl doesn't move or speak. Words pop into my mind.

Questions swirl in my brain like a whirlpool. My chest tightens and abs constrict. I pound a steady beat on my chest with my fist. But I can't feel it. No matter how hard I punch myself, it's numb. Everywhere.

"How?"

The girl exhales. "I think it's probably better if she tells you herself, yeah?"

I want to jump up and argue.

But then it comes back—some of it.

Bryson. Kris. That night.

The party last November. How the skies opened up and released a light blanket of white on the slick streets. How shots were mixed with jungle juice. The tables of beer pong and flip cup. A group of guys playing cards in the corner of the garage. Video games. Reefer and Kyle challenging me to shotgun that can of beer. The guys smoking cigars on the back porch. The girls in the kitchen making Jell-O shots. The fight with Kris on the front lawn.

Bryson hiding in the backseat of Mom's white Nissan Altima.

My eyes flash. Throat closes up and sweat beads down flushed cheeks.

I don't know when Aubrey comes outside or how long it is before she's able to pull me away. Both of my hands are bleeding—the cuts from earlier now freshly opened and seeping crimson. The same color as Aubrey's highlights.

The blacktop is slick with blood from my knuckles. I'd been punching the ground repeatedly with both fists.

If you go inside quick enough, you can grab one of Gus's needles and stab it into your throat, rip a hole right through the skin, peel back the layers, and bleed out. Just do it, coward.

"Gray! Jesus!" Aubrey holds my wounded hands in hers and

cups her palm under my chin to tilt it upwards. "Stop hurting yourself."

Her eyes search mine desperately. They yearn for some sort of understanding or solid ground, but she can't find it. I can't look at her in the same way. Not now. Not knowing what I do. And I can't find the right words to say how sorry I am, to ask what happened to her family.

So instead I do the next logical thing: I get angry.

"Shut up, Aubrey. Just shut up with this guru bullshit."

She nods and takes a step back. Drops her hands from my face.

Meaningless words tumble from my mouth before sentences form. "You lied to me. This entire night you've been playing me."

"I never lied. I just didn't share this with you."

"Isn't that the same thing?" I curse out loud and find a garbage can to my left, kick it so it falls over.

Behind Aubrey, the girl with the gauges backs away into the store, where Gus peers out the window. They exchange a few words and retreat to give us our space. Luckily, the tattoo parlor is in the back of the business plaza; all the other stores are closed for the night. No one else is around to hear.

And I know that I'm being selfish, that right now should be about Aubrey, but something deep inside won't rest. It explodes. Like a firecracker. I can't control it.

"And what about you?" She raises her voice. "Why don't you really say how *you* feel?"

I shake my head and squeeze my fists until the nails dig into my palms. "I'm not a pity project, Aubrey."

"I never said you were."

"Isn't that what you're doing? By taking me out? Talking about *changing my life*? I don't know what to believe with you. Where the lies end and truth starts."

She takes a step forward, so I take a step backward. We stop.

"You want me to be honest?"

"That's all I've ever wanted."

She bites her lip, shifts the weight on the balls of her feet. "Liza told you about my brother, right?"

I nod.

"Of course they did. They've always had a big mouth."

They. Don't assume, asshole. Do better.

"Who are these people? Gus, Liza... I'm so confused."

Aubrey walks back toward the store without a word, so I follow. As mad as I am, she still attracts me. I can't imagine losing her. Not now. Not after tonight. Not ever.

Not until you leave her, though, right? 'Cause that's still the plan. Isn't it?

"Stay here. I just have to say goodbye, and I'll be back to get you."

She doesn't let me answer before heading toward the back hallway. I don't wait to see what Liza and Gus think, because I follow behind her anyway. Down the narrow hallway, she pauses outside the door, and her shoulders shake. She doesn't look back before entering, and when I follow after, James is lying on the couch. The dim lamp casts an eerie glow.

There's fresh vomit on the floor, which makes me flinch, but I stop by the table and watch Aubrey kneel down and inhale a breath. She holds it in her chest, places a hand on top of James's head, and strokes his thin hair back from his face. She whispers things into his ear I can't make out, but all he does is shudder in response and curl up in a blanket Gus must have given him. Aubrey kisses his cheek.

But what I see next scares me more than anything, because Aubrey sits on the heels of her combat boots. Her bottom lip trembles, and she runs her hands over her face.

Once. Twice.

And she falls back to sit down. She looks from her brother to the fresh vomit on the floor. A tear rolls down her cheek, and without thinking, I walk over and sit down next to her. I don't know what to do or what to say. Not sure how I can somehow ease her pain. Maybe James looks worse than before. Maybe she's always like this with him. Maybe it's memories of Dean that I bring up. But I know that I need to do something for her.

I inch as close as I can until our shoulders touch, and I hold out a hand. She wipes away a tear and looks down at it. She wipes another tear and then glances at me. And it's such a different side to Aubrey.

Vulnerability. Pain. Sadness.

There's not a thing I can say to make this any better for her.

But then she reaches out, and her hand is in mine. We interlock fingers, and there's a slight twinkle in her face where maybe her dimple might come to the surface. It doesn't. Another tear starts to fall, but I reach over and wipe it away for her. And she looks so surprised. So grateful. So supported. Like she's never had this before. Like me holding out my hand has done so much. She stares at me for so long, like maybe she's seeing something she hadn't before. I can't figure out what exactly, but she inhales and exhales slowly. Aubrey bites her lip, glances from my eyes to the tips of our fingers. But her eyes are so wide, trying to soak in this moment. And I'm getting lost in her allure.

So we sit together with our hands locked for a little while, watching James lull into a sleep.

Aubrey rests her head on my shoulder, and we just sit here in silence—let everything calm down. Because right now is about her. This moment, whatever it is, is just like Aubrey Fisher.

Beautiful in all its complications and imperfections.

Liza studies us as we walk back into the main parlor, and even though Gus is back to work on the boy's inner thigh, he watches us out of the corner of his eye. Aubrey and Liza exchange a few words, and there's a tension between them I can't place my finger on. Liza huffs and slams the magazine shut.

"I hope he's worth it," they mutter before stomping toward the back hallway.

Aubrey doesn't explain, so I don't ask. It's not long before Liza stomps back with what looks like a rectangular, wooden jewelry box. They throw it at Aubrey, who catches it and breathes deeply through her nose.

"Gus," Aubrey calls out. "I'm going to take these, and I don't know if I'll bring them back before I leave next week. Okay?"

Leave? Leave where?

"Sure thing, kid." He looks up and dabs at the boy's leg. "When James comes to, I'll tell him you stopped by."

Her left eye twitches. "Thanks."

"One more thing before you go," he says as he starts up his needle again and points toward me. "Don't fuck it up."

Aubrey snorts, then immediately slaps her palm to her mouth and giggles. You'd think after everything she went through, she wouldn't be able to laugh, but she does.

It amazes me.

I'm also confused—not sure where I fit in with all of this.

We start to walk out, but before we do, Liza steps back behind the front desk and opens up their magazine. "When will you be back?"

Aubrey turns us both around to march out of the store. "Soon."

She pushes past me, not looking back at either of them, but I do. Gus nods to me and then looks back down at his art. But Liza looks after Aubrey, and behind their cold stare, there's worry on their face. And I know that somewhere in their past, they used to be friends. Maybe more.

"Was she always like this?" I ask.

Liza glances at me briefly before focusing back on Aubrey.

"No." They look down at their magazine and take a deep breath. "She likes you. You do know that, yeah?"

I don't respond, but they study me again.

"Now I'm going to tell you"—they look up at me and point to Aubrey through the front window. "Don't let her make you fuck it up."

We're back on the streets, walking toward the bus stop by the tall office buildings from earlier. The air has a new chill to it that wasn't there before. Even I know it's time to go home. When the yawn escapes my mouth, Aubrey chuckles.

"I think it's past someone's bedtime."

"Very funny."

The Spider-Man Band-Aids from my cuts are mostly gone. There are only two left hanging, so I yank them off. We walk past the office buildings where the sky is obscured. We don't wait long at the bus stop. There's only one route that runs this late. Aubrey pays the man to take us back to Lee Falls. She receives only two dollars back—all either of us has left to our names. We find our way to the back and toward our same seats. On the floor is the bag of cotton balls, peroxide, Tylenol, and coat hangers that we had left. The blue vinyl of the seat in front of us is covered in lighter burns.

We sit down, and I yawn again. She playfully shoves me and hugs the jewelry box. It's faded and chipped a little in the corners, but is otherwise in decent condition. Aubrey leans her head on my shoulder and exhales. She opens up the gold latch, and inside is filled with old photographs. Some are Polaroids, others look not much different from the ones my mom used to have developed at the local photo store. She rifles through them, occasionally pausing on a few before putting them to the side and finding one in the middle that she gives to me.

The photo is of five people. Two adults and three little kids—two boys and one girl. The little girl is wearing a red Mickey Mouse sweater with her hair in pigtails. She is flashing a toothless grin as each boy has an arm wrapped around her shoulder. The two adults stand in the back next to a smoking grill and circular above-ground pool.

Aubrey takes a deep breath, points her boots inward, and never looks up as she speaks. Not once. Her voice is quiet.

"I had two brothers. James... and Dean." The moment hangs in silence before she continues. She points to each person as she speaks. "My-uh... my mom left when we were really little. No note, no warning. Just split. I was six. James was the oldest, and our dad couldn't deal. You know. Alcohol. Gambling. Bad debts. The whole cliché story." She reaches over and grabs my hand. Squeezes it. It's like holding something delicate and temporary. I don't want to ruin it.

I look at the boy to her left, James, and see his chubby cheeks. Flashing a crooked grin. He's filled with so much love for his siblings. Then on the right, a little boy tilts his chin to the camera, shy, his hands folded by his waist. Lips puckered. Dean. He looks exactly like Aubrey. The same hazel-orange eyes. And it makes me really sad. Like I'm viewing a picture filled with ghosts.

She rifles through a few more pictures until there's one of that same older man, her dad, posing next to a Harley in a garage. He wears a white sleeveless shirt; his arm is covered in grease as he holds what appears to be a glass of lemonade. He has Aubrey's cool stare.

"He was into bikes. I always hated it when he'd ride, but he really loved them. So about a year after our mom left, he'd been drinking, got on his bike. Crashed it on the highway. They said he just lost control. Wasn't wearing a helmet."

I begin to open my mouth, but she presses a finger to my lips, finally looks up at me. My heart stops. I never want her to remove that finger.

"I was seven when they put the three of us into foster care. Me, James, and Dean. They kept us together for a while until James was eighteen, and he aged out. So I—"

"Why didn't you tell me any of this at the restaurant earlier?"

She lets go of my hands. "It's not important. No one cares."

I grind my teeth. "Why do you keep doing that? Putting up that wall every time I say something to make you uncomfortable?" I inch closer to her, and for just a moment, I think I can hear her heart beating. "I care. I want to know you."

"You shouldn't." She inches away. "I ruin everything I touch, Grayson."

"What are you talking about?"

She plays with strands of her hair, braiding them. "How long until you kill yourself?"

My mouth dries up like a desert. I can't look her in the eyes or answer. She makes it feel wrong. Humiliating. Maybe it is. But right now isn't about me. There are still a million unanswered questions.

"I'm sorry about your dad."

"Old news. I'm over it."

"Are you, though?"

Aubrey picks at her fishnets until a few strings rip. She pulls them apart and scratches the nylon leggings underneath. I have the sudden urge to place my hand on her thigh, to feel the smooth skin underneath, and trace the length from her knees to her hips with the tips of my fingers. I want to linger on her inner thigh. And then my eyes level on her full lips. They felt so soft in the pool. So delicate and supple, like I just wanted to keep mine pressed to hers and never let go. Like they were meant to be there. To stay there. And it's like the weight on my chest lifts a little. I suck in a breath and fidget my hands in my lap, look down again.

"Enough about me. Your turn, Romeo. Whenever you stop eyeing my legs."

My cheeks flush with embarrassment, and I shake my head to try and deny what we both know is blatantly obvious.

Kissherkissherkissher.

"I still have more questions."

"Give and take. You get some if you give some. Girls get blue balls too, Grayson."

"Huh, never thought of it like that before."

"I'm sure you got Kris just dripping all the time when you were together in public. You just never realized it."

"Ohmygod. No. Stop. Please. We're done with this conversation."

She smirks. "Are you gonna answer my question now?"

I shrug my shoulders.

"What did I say about shrugging? It's a non-committal gesture. Stop it."

We sit in silence, the space between us like a tunnel. I don't know where to start, and she must see it. We both know there's no going back. I can't talk my way out of the situation. I'm going to kill myself. The least I can do is fess up. But Aubrey beats me to it, reaches into her shirt, finagles around underneath her bra, and pulls up the folded newspaper clippings from the pool. She stares at them for a moment, contemplating what to do before handing them over.

I can tell from the way they are yellowed and cut that they

are from my house. When Aubrey went to the bathroom upstairs, I'd thought I'd heard her in my parents' bedroom, and now I know it was true. It's the clippings Mom keeps on top of her vanity dresser. It feels like a sucker punch in the gut. I open them up and see the first headline:

Boy, 10, Killed in Hit-and-Run. Police Seeking Suspect.

—LEE FALLS — Local Janice County law enforcement is still on the lookout for a driver who hit and killed a 10-year-old boy last Friday, November 13, when the driver failed to stop on Maple Ave.

Family members of the deceased identified the boy as Bryson Falconi, who'd been standing in the road when the driver sped down the street sometime around midnight. Witnesses said the driver was in an older Ford pickup. Police say the driver was speeding in excess of the 35 mph speed limit.

"He was just there one minute… and then he wasn't… I remember his body colliding with the front grill before being flung onto the pavement," local teenager Jensen Phillips told Lee Falls police department at the scene. "They just never stopped."

Anyone with information is asked to contact Janice County's law office at (716) 555-0792.

Followed by the second headline:

Two Teens Injured, One Other in Critical Condition After Father Runs Red Light

—LEE FALLS — Two teens were injured this morning at the intersection of Main and Maple after the passenger's father ran a red light, Janice County authorities said. The driver, 47-year-old Mark Sanders, and daughter, 17-year-old Kristin Sanders, were Mercy-Flighted to the Cartersville ER upon arrival of paramedics. 17-year-old Grayson Falconi received minor medical attention at local Lee Falls ER.

Investigators say the crash happened at 12:47 AM, where it is believed Sanders [Mark] hit a patch of black ice while on his way to Maple Ave and lost control of the vehicle. Falconi, driving at the time with Sanders [Kristin], tested negative for drugs and alcohol.

Sources say Falconi and Sanders [Kristin] were fleeing from the scene of a hit-and-run accident, which occurred moments earlier on Maple Ave, where 10-year-old Bryson Falconi was struck by an unidentified Ford pickup. The boy died shortly after his brother [Grayson] and Sanders [Kristin] left. Police are looking into the possibility of the two incidents being related.

"We haven't yet tested his [Mark's] system for any potential substances... but Grayson tested negative before being rushed into an ambulance," local Sheriff Tom Dickens told press at the time. "Witnesses say Grayson was in pursuit of the hit-and-run driver when his car was struck. We're currently looking into all possible leads."

Medical officials declined to release the condition of Mark or Kris Sanders, but sources say Falconi [Grayson] suffered no serious injuries.

Police said they would release more information as the investigation continues.

And just like that, with those two simple newspaper articles, the levee breaks. The floodgates open to the horrific visions of that night. And I see it. All.

Bryson sneaking into the backseat of Mom's car while Kris and I were getting ready, even when we had told him he had to stay home. How at the party, long after we arrived at the house and found Bryson hiding, I let him out to play while Kris and I fought on the front lawn. And how Kris begged for me to leave and take Bryson to get some late-night fast food and watch a show, but I was too damn stubborn.

And then, after he was struck, how the blood formed a near-halo around his head, leaking onto the pavement like spilled tomato soup.

"How could you do this?" I rip the clippings out of her hand and stare at them as if they were a mirage. But no matter how hard I try to trick my mind, they remain. "These were in my parents' room."

"I know."

I whip my head to face her. "What the hell were you doing

sneaking around and taking things that aren't yours?" My breaths are rapid, and the steady tick starts in my head. My vision blurs out of focus.

"Hey. Whoa. Are you okay?"

I can feel her hands on me, checking my pulse and caressing my forehead, but I struggle to push her away.

And then, after I grabbed his crushed hand, how Bryson sputtered up my name through bloodstained teeth. One leg was bent all the way behind his back, touching his neck. Still alive.

"Breathe. Grayson. Breathe. You're okay. Control it. Fight it. Stay here with me." She chants, but it's like hearing her voice through an echoing tunnel. It sounds far away. "I'm here. You feel my hand? Squeeze that." Her hands caress my cheeks. "Dammit. Not now."

And I held his hand, begged for him to squeeze, to let me know he could feel it. But Bryson didn't move. Didn't squeeze back. He blinked his eyes. Looked up at me. Blood leaked from the corners of his mouth. He was trying to say something. He had no voice.

You ready to die?

"No," I mumble out loud. "Not like this."

I beat on my chest, pound on it with all my might, and force my way through the waves. Harder. Faster. *Thump. Thump. Thump. Thump.*

"No, stop it." I hear her voice, and it sounds closer this time.

And Kris fell to the ground next to me, screamed. People formed a circle. And I looked in the direction the truck went. My body shook. Bryson was still alive.

Everything swirls around us. Every word uttered and thought processed. All of the hate and fear and guilt are just a giant swirling tornado enclosing me and Aubrey.

Above the surface of suffocating waves, Aubrey looks around wildly. We're still the only people on the bus. She grabs my wrists and pulls them apart until I sit up. I was lying in her lap.

"Hey, look at me. Look in my eyes." She cups my face and leans in, squints. "I lost you there for a second. You alright?"

It's there again. The space between us. That ember of desire. Like a kindling in a fire, it's just beneath the surface.

I blink away traces of Bryson—focus on Aubrey. Force my mind to stay in the moment with her.

Aubrey's highlighted hair shines under the dim bus lights, and her skin looks so delicate and flawless. For someone who wears little-to-no makeup, she is so pretty. So beautiful. So I focus on that—hone in on it. It wasn't just the dancing or the alcohol. It was *her*. It's always been her. The misunderstood girl. The badass that puts up walls higher than Berlin. It's like seeing the buried treasure. The humanity inside the monster.

I look down, and Aubrey's hands are interlocked with mine. I rub my thumb over hers until I feel her hand tremble. She looks down at it too but doesn't pull back, not right away.

And there's the silence again. Everything in the world is shut off. Just our breathing remains. Nothing makes sense, yet I've never felt more copacetic than now.

I reach over and brush away the bangs from her eye and place them behind her ear. She closes her eyes and exhales. She's been holding a breath. I don't realize I have been too until I release mine.

"What's happening?" she whispers.

I place my palm against her cheek, and she closes her eyes again. And I want to kiss her. I want to take her in my arms and hold her. Never let go. I want to cherish her every breath, adore each and every time she releases air to puff up her bangs. Want to inhale her scent and hear her raspy voice whisper in my ear late at night. Want to add more things to our imagined list, things that scare me. That scare us.

But that would mean going back to that dark place. To the fear and the guilt and the hatred. To my parents who are more of a mess than I am. To Kris and her ruined future. Her dad in a coma. To a school and my friends who I've intentionally alienated and pushed away. My writing that I can't find inspiration for. The cops I've been evading, and the person who's been threatening Aubrey's life.

None of it will go away. It will still be there. Always.

And then it just comes out:

"I'm scared, Aubrey," I whisper.

"I know."

"Is there something wrong with me?

She inches closer; her eyes go wide, and she leans in until our noses practically touch.

"There is absolutely nothing wrong with you."

My eyes water, but I don't let any tears fall. My face prickles.

"Then why do I feel like dying is the only escape I have?"

Aubrey breathes out through her nose, and I feel it on my lips. I shudder.

"Because you're trying to escape it instead of face it."

Her words sink in for a moment. I chew the inside of my cheek.

"Aubrey?"

"Yeah."

"You're really beautiful."

A beat.

"Grayson..."

"I just thought you should know." I close my eyes and continue to caress her cheek. She lets me. "You don't ruin things. You make them beautiful. Just like you."

I open my eyes as she starts to pull away. I try to hold her in place, but she's already leaning back.

"You're emotional, Grayson. And upset. Your brain is just grasping on to anything that feels safe right now. It's a conditioned response to pain." She lets go of my hands, but her entire body is trembling now. She starts to open her mouth, but it's my turn to shush her, so I press my finger to her lips.

"Don't ruin this moment by putting up those defenses again. I'm going to give you a compliment, and then I'm going to lean in and kiss you. Then we're going to go home. So just shut up and let me do this."

She starts to protest, but I press my finger harder.

"I don't care about your past or what you've done. None of that matters. How you are here and now... that matters. You here with me... that matters. I don't know what tonight holds for me, Aubrey. I won't lie to you. But either way, I'm really glad I came out with you tonight." I lean in closer until I can sense how terrified she is. But like I've known her to do all night, the corner of her mouth twitches. And I know beneath the fear, she's trying not to smile. "You're beautiful inside and out. And I adore that dimple of yours." She smiles just enough for it to surface. I grin. "And now I'm going to kiss you. And you're going to let me."

I lean in, and Aubrey closes her eyes. I press my lips into hers. But this time it's different. It's not a reaction but fully planned. And Aubrey is aware. She lets it happen. It's gentle, and my bottom lip snuggles between the middle of hers. We breathe out through our noses and suck in a breath at the same time. The box of photos falls to the floor, but neither of us cares.

In this moment all we have is each other. All we want is each other.

And the same spark we shared at the pool flickers again.

My nerves are on fire, pinging everywhere that our skin touches. Like our bodies were designed to be close like this. Caressed like this. And I inhale her vanilla and cigarette scent.

I start to lean back, but she grabs my shirt collar and pulls me into her. We fall back on the seat, and she opens up her mouth to let me in. Her legs open, and I slide my body between her thighs. I bring my hand behind to cradle her head. She places her hands on my chest, and I wince when she touches my bruise. But we continue to kiss. And it's so passionate. So full of desperation. Like we need each other for the same purpose.

It gives me hope. Breathes air into my lungs and pumps blood through my heart. I feel like it can get better. That I can live with the pain. That, just maybe, I can have a life with Aubrey. A future. So I press my body into hers harder, and I let her accept whatever of me she is willing to have. But I don't want to stop. Like the initial drop of a roller coaster, it's a rush.

And as we both pull away, giggling awkwardly, and sit up to straighten our clothes, I realize what purpose it is:

We're both trying to survive.

5 Hours Until

???

Because there's no traffic this late at night, it doesn't take as long to get back to Lee Falls. We pass the haunted woods and arrive at the bus stop on Main Street just before the town line. I'm tired, but the kiss left us both rejuvenated and on edge. We thank the driver before stepping off. He pulls away, and the street is eerily quiet. No shops are open this late, so with only the streetlights to guide our way, we walk along the sidewalk past the various storefronts.

Everything feels so vast and endless. It's like a ghost town at this hour—no one is outside. This entire place and this entire street are ours for the taking. Left behind. Abandoned. I just want to jump on top of a building and scream at the top of my lungs. Run up and down the street holding her hand and dancing to nothing but the music in our heads. In our hearts. Our steps echo off the storefronts, their blinds pulled down. Our breaths condensing in the cool night air.

I run and jump up onto a nearby trashcan and bounce off it, landing on my feet and frog-hopping to a steady position. Aubrey giggles behind me. The streetlight is within reach, so I grab it and twirl around fake-seductively until Aubrey rolls her eyes and pulls my shirt forward with her.

Above, the stars look like pinpricks of beauty. I have an idea, and I take Aubrey's hand and pull her along. "Come on. It's time that I show *you* something."

Aubrey grins and licks her lips. "I don't know if I like this role reversal, Mr. Falconi."

"Well, get used to it, Miss Fisher. You're the one who brought this guy out."

"Yeah, I'm starting to see the real Grayson now."

I pick up my pace to a light jog, and Aubrey joins. "Come on."

We pass the pizza place Kris and I used to eat at and the ice cream stand that Reefer and I used to gorge at every summer. Next to the town hall is the courtyard, which is a small park shaped like a square where four roads meet. One of thirteen intersections we have in the entire town—the same one where the accident happened. But I push that thought away as I take the longer route to walk around it and cross the grass—past the brass statue of the original founder of Lee Falls. There are a few park benches, and in the center is a small fountain where we used to chuck pennies and make wishes. I find an opening in the dewy grass and lie down with Aubrey.

"What are we doing?" she asks and places the plastic bag and jewelry box by our feet.

"Watching the stars. We can point out constellations. Or we can talk about whatever you want."

Aubrey snuggles closer. I fold my hands over my chest, and she pins one underneath her neck and sticks the other in the air. Aubrey is the first to point out the Big Dipper. I point out Castor and Pollex. Explain to her the Gemini constellation. We do this for a few minutes before we don't know what else to look for. We stay in silence for a while, exhale to watch our breaths condense. She shifts next to me and positions the opposite hand underneath her neck.

"My mom used to take me and Bryson out here all the time when we were little." I bite my tongue. Just saying it hurts, but I push through.

It's the first time I've said his name out loud since the accident.

"She would tell us that the sky held endless possibilities. That if we were ever lost, we could just look up, point out the stars, and we'd know what we were supposed to do. I guess I still like to believe that it will tell me the answers."

"Your mom sounds like she really loved you both." She waves her hand in the air, and we both watch it. Behind her is the crescent moon, winking down at us.

"She did."

She clicks her tongue, snuggles even closer until our shoulders touch. "Do you ever talk to him? Or see him just when you think you aren't going to anymore?"

I don't have to ask to know what she means. So I nod my head, my throat dry.

"Usually to remind me of the pain."

"Tell me."

My heart thumps, ready to explode, but I close my eyes and move my pinky finger until it touches her thigh. I don't know if Aubrey notices, but she doesn't say anything.

"Kris wanted to stay home and stream a show or movie. There was a party at a friend's house, and instead of staying in, I forced her to sneak out after my parents were asleep. Bryson hid in the backseat, and we didn't know until we were already there."

I can feel Aubrey's head turn my way, but I continue on,

stare up at the stars for solace. It's the first time I've ever said this out loud. I can still hear that conversation vividly:

"I need to take you home," I said from the front of the car. Kris giggled in the seat next to me. "It's not funny. Our parents will kill me if they wake up and he's gone."

"Gray, I'm ten," Bryson said from the backseat, bouncing up and down excitedly.

"Again, you say this like it matters. It's the worst argument I've ever heard in my life."

Kris slapped me on the shoulder. "Be nice." She high-fived Bryson. "I think it's a pretty awesome argument." She ruffled his hair, and Bryson groaned.

"Why do girls *always* have to touch my hair? This girl at school does it too. It's *annoying*."

"You're so cute. I can't even handle it." Kris turned to me. "Can we just go home? Please? We'll take him to get some fries or something and then watch a movie." She turned back to Bryson. "How does that sound?"

Bryson beamed. "Yes! Fries!" He looked between us. "Canoodling, right?"

"Where did you hear that?" I asked, my voice raised.

"Heard you guys talking in the hallway. Sounds boringggg."

Kris and I exchanged a look. She stifled a laugh.

I shook my head. "Don't repeat that to Mom and Dad, not ever." I sighed. "Little Man, how long do you think you can be patient if I stop in for just five minutes?"

Bryson crossed his arms in front of his chest, but he didn't pout. "You're gonna leave me alone? I thought we could hang out together. We never get to hang out together. I can chill too."

Kris turned away, her shoulders jumping up and down. I had to contain my own amusement.

"No. Not alone. Kris and I just want to say hello to a few people, then we'll get you to a drive-thru for food and head home to watch a movie. We can hang out later tonight. BUT, you have to promise me you'll never say a word to Mom or Dad. Deal?"

Bryson held out his hand so we could bump fists. We did it, and he pumped his arms in the air. "Can I at least get out of the car to walk around?" He zipped up his black hoodie. "I won't get sick. Promise. Pleeeeeeeeeeease."

I shook my head.

Kris sighed. "Your brother is stubborn," she said to Bryson.

"Yeah, that's Gray. But he promised to take me back to the beach, like old times. Right, Gray?"

Kris looked over at me and frowned.

"Of course, Little Man. We'll go back and watch the waves. That's a promise. Just you and me."

And just like that, I'm back in the grass with Aubrey, tears in my eyes as I realize I've been telling her the entire story. Aubrey has her full attention on me now, and her head is cradled on my shoulder. I wipe my eyes as tears well.

You could lean in and kiss her right now if you wanted to.

"So, we went inside. I didn't have a beer or anything, but I lost track of time... I don't know." I clear my throat and shift uncomfortably. "We'd been there a long time, too long, before Kris reminded me Bryson was still outside by himself. She was pissed—I'd been ignoring her. Harassing some freshmen with Tim and Kyle. Letting a sophomore flirt with me even though I knew it was wrong. I just... I was an asshole that night for no reason. So Kris finally grabbed me and led me out of the house, near tears, when the sophomore tried to make a move. I should've stopped it. I don't know why I didn't."

And the conversation comes back as we stood on the front lawn, a few people smoking outside watching us. Bryson pacing in the middle of the street:

"...was all over you in there! You're disgusting."

"I said I'm sorry, Kris. I wasn't going to let anyth—"

"*Don't.* You. *Dare.* I didn't want to come. You've been ignoring me all night, acting like an idiot because of my brother and cousin. And flirting with Crystal Bowers? I called my dad to pick me up. I don't want to look at you right now, Gray. Just get your brother and bring him home. He doesn't belong here."

"I would never cheat on you. I'm pissed you would even think that. Crystal is in my chem class. Why are you being such a bitch tonight? Is it that time of the month?"

And just as I spoke the words, I knew the mistake I'd made. Her lips pulled back; eyes grew wide. And she slapped me across the face. Hard. I stumbled back, ashamed. Upset. A couple to our left tried to hide their laughter. Kris took a step and extended her hands as if to apologize, but then took them back.

I rubbed my jaw, Bryson calling my name from the street, but I ignored him.

"My dad's halfway here."

"Good. Tell him I'm the worst boyfriend in the world. You go, and I'll stay here and let Crystal Bowers flirt away."

Kris wiped at her eyes, silent for a few moments.

"What's going on with us, Gray?"

And then I'm once again back with Aubrey in the grass.

"I don't know why I said what I said. We'd been fighting a lot before that night. Just stupid things that never used to bother us were all of a sudden annoying. I don't know... Bryson was playing hopscotch in the street with imaginary tiles. He, uh, he was always doing that. He was really great at making things up. My mom loved that about him. I loved that about him." I pause to breathe in and out, force away any anxiety I feel. I won't let it get to me this time. Aubrey is patient until I continue.

"So, he called out to me, and I remember it was starting to

snow. He wanted to race in the street. And there was something about it... how happy he was just playing by himself. I knew I should've told him to get out of the street, but I didn't. I ignored him. Just acted like he wasn't my brother for a few seconds and turned around to head back into the party, and..."

Aubrey doesn't need me to continue, so she breathes out, and for whatever reason, I know she's telling me that I can skip this part. So I do. But my body trembles, and the tears roll down my hot cheeks and into the grass.

"He was still alive when I left him. I just... I just wanted to find the bastard and *kill* him." I have to pause to wipe snot from my nose. I was losing it now, unable to control the pain in my chest. And I cry. Sob until I hyperventilate, but I can't stop. I try to with each breath I suck in. I can't continue—can't open my mouth as much as I want to.

You should've been the one lying in the street dying. Not him. It should've been YOU.

After a while, after the sobs die down and I rub my sore eyes, I sit up and cross my legs. Aubrey stays where she is, but she doesn't divert her eyes from mine. So I jump up to my feet and begin to pace back and forth. I'm sad. But more importantly... I'm angry.

"I mean... it's my goddamn fault, right? I was an asshole for no reason whatsoever."

Aubrey waits for a long time. I don't think she'll ever answer before she sits up. "Why would you say that?"

"I could've stopped it. I mean... if I stayed home instead of going out. If I turned the car around and dropped off Bryson. If I only stayed for five minutes like I planned... or told Bryson to get out of the street. Not turned my back on him like I was ashamed to be his older brother. Or stayed with him while he was still alive. FUCK! Fuck! Kris jumped in the car to talk me down, but I fucking took off with her in it. She kept screaming at me to stop the car, and I ignored her. I just drove on, not paying attention to anything. And then her dad came out of nowhere. Smashed right into the passenger side. Jesus Christ. If I'd just slowed down or even yelled at her to stay with Bryson instead of just taking off with her—"

Aubrey is on me within moments. She comes up behind and turns me around. I look into her eyes, and just like that, I stop. She takes my hands in hers and stares at me.

She whispers, "It wasn't your fault."

I shake my head, but she hushes me.

"It wasn't your fault."

"But what if—"

"No. Fuck what ifs. You have to live with the here and now and let go of the past. Kris decided to get in that car. You never asked, and you never forced her to." I turn my head away, but she forces it back into position. "You didn't ask Bryson to hide in your car—that was *his* choice. You weren't the one driving that pickup truck, and you had no way of knowing there was black ice on that road. You had the green light. You did nothing wrong. You are not responsible."

The tears come back, and I fall to my knees. Unable to see, I feel around, and I know Aubrey is kneeling with me.

"I don't blame you. You hear me?"

I look up, and she cups my cheeks in her palms.

"It. Was not. Your fault."

And then he is here again. Bryson. I can't see him, but I can feel him, like he's kneeling next to me. A light breeze brushes past my ears, and I think I hear the sound of an ocean swell. Somehow and someway that I can't explain. My brother is still with me.

And there's this sense that everything will be okay, that I don't have to be sad anymore.

And I don't know if it's really him or just me, but I hear his sweet voice whisper inside my head:

"You're almost home, Gray. It's almost over. Just hang in there a little while longer. Aubrey still has more to show you. Don't let her go. Don't leave her alone. Show her what it means to stay."

I blink, and the feeling's gone.

We see the headlights of a car approaching the town square, and Aubrey is the first to act.

"Pretty sure those are squad car headlights."

She doesn't give me a chance to respond before yanking me back onto my feet and ushering me across the square and behind a large pine tree. I don't say anything. Still in shock, still confused. My whole body aches and my eyes are dry and throbbing. But I'm calm. Aubrey somehow did that.

"The cops technically can't do anything for twenty-four hours if your parents decided to file a missing persons. Not sure how crazy your parents are or not about that stuff. No offense. I bet they did."

I still don't respond, just look down at the ground, somehow become one with the grass above the roots of the tree. Like I can blend in with everything and force away the awful truth staring back at me.

"Yo! Are you listening to me?"

I nod my head, but I don't really know what I'm nodding to. I can hear her words, process them, but they feel empty and meaningless. Bryson's message still rings in my head.

And then I remember that we still have one more thing to do tonight that we haven't yet.

"You said you know how to break into the school," I mumble. "Right?"

It's Aubrey's turn to nod.

"There's something in my locker I need to show you."

We wait until after the patrol car passes and make our way through a few side streets until we reach Lee Falls High. The American flag hangs limply next to the sign for the school. In-ground lights illuminate the bushes surrounding the building, and a few shine on the entrance doors, which are locked. We stop at the edge of the parking lot and look around. Aubrey assesses her best point of entry. It's fascinating to watch her in action. Earlier, I would've been wondering what she was thinking and what her plan was. But now I know:

Anything that pushes me out of my comfort zone. But really, it's what she knows will make me happy.

That's the thing about Aubrey Fisher. She just knows.

The walk helps to clear my head for the time being, so I survey the abandoned building with her.

"How have you broken into schools before in the past?"

Aubrey titters. "Good question."

"Come again?"

She puffs up her bangs. "This will be a first for me."

"But earlier at the restaurant, you said—"

"Not every rumor you hear about me is true." She chuckles. "And I was blowing smoke. I woulda said anything just to get you to agree to come out with me."

Did she always like you, Gray? Is she saying she's always liked you?

We're about to break into a school, and neither of us knows what the hell we're doing.

"Soooo, are we both about to pop our breaking-into-our-high-school-after-hours-and-at-night-when-it-is-illegal   cherries tonight?"

Aubrey chokes on what I think is a laugh.

"You did *not* just say that!"

"Yeah... that was definitely something my friend Reefer would say."

"God, Grayson. You're such a dork."

I flash a cheesy smile. "But a loveable dork, right?"

She looks at me and extends her arms to shove me in the chest. I try to deflect them but find myself falling backward, caught off balance. I land with a thud on my butt. Aubrey stares for a moment, laughing until she's wiping tears from her eyes, which in turn makes me start to giggle too until we both get to the point where we can barely breathe. That's the thing with laughter: it can turn deadly.

It's a fickle bitch.

"I think I broke my tailbone."

Aubrey straightens up and controls her laughter until we lock eyes, and she helps me stand up again. "I swear to God that I almost just punched you for catching me off guard again and being a little shit. But then you'd make me feel bad, and I'd probably kiss you. Because goddamn, Grayson. That shit was clutch."

She's totally leaving you open for a kiss. Fool. Don't be a bitch!

I massage my sore butt and let out a chuckle. "If you say so."

She pats me on the back. "But seriously. No. I've never done this before. Believe it or not, the breaking and entering rumor is *not* one of the true ones."

It's odd when she says it, because the thought of the rumors being false had never occurred to me before, and it makes me ashamed. It's so easy to judge a person we don't know. To believe the shallowness of what someone passes off to the world. Aubrey presents herself a certain way. She knows what people think about her, and yet, she's nothing like what we'd expect.

We all project versions of ourselves we wish we could be. Aubrey wishes she can be this badass who doesn't care about anything or anyone, but I know it's a lie. Because she cares more than anyone else I know.

And then it makes me think: Kris plays off her injury like it doesn't stop her from being as perfect as she can be, but tonight, she told me she's just as lost and angry and confused.

I push people away and act like I don't care because I'm afraid of opening that wound and getting lost in the void.

And then there's Reefer, who makes out everything to be a joke.

Jenna, who spends more time with fictional characters than she does real people.

"I'm sorry I ever believed any of those things about you," I say. "It's like we're so quick to pinpoint who we think other people are, because maybe we need to. Like we're unhappy with who we are, so we think the worst of everyone else to make it okay. You ever thought of that before?"

She nods and turns to me. "This is why you amaze me. You see people. Really see them. You notice things. It's incredible. It's what makes you special."

I shake my head. "I'm not, though. I'm a mess. Look at me." I point to my temple. "I'm screwed up in the head, Aubrey."

"Aren't we all?" She twirls her arms in the air to indicate everything around us. A light breeze licks the nape of my neck as she does, which sends shivers crawling down my spine. "Everyone is messed up, Grayson. Everyone has secrets and regrets and lies and thoughts they wish they didn't have. It's called being human. Normal is a perception, a trick of the mind—an unattainable goal. If you try to be perfect, you'll only hate yourself more. Beauty is imperfection. Flaws are real." She squeezes my hand.

"It's not about being perfect. It's about feeling whole. Happy. What if, no matter how hard you try, you just can't see any type of future where anything will ever be okay again?"

Aubrey chews on her bottom lip and stares into my eyes. And I know she's looking through me, into my heart. Trying to see what I really look like inside.

It's one of the most intimate things she's ever done. I don't want her to stop. But it's not pity. It's not worry. It's yearning— something she's trying to find and grasp and never let go of.

There's something oddly comforting in the way a person can look and just *know*. Like that unspoken bond. Words don't need to be said. She can see it in my eyes, and I know that she knows.

It's enough to make a guy fall in love with a girl.

But you don't love her. Do you, Gray?

She says, "Can I tell you something that's probably going to upset you?"

I nod, hesitant.

"You know dying won't end the pain, right? It won't solve anything. You just take the weight of what you're carrying, and you pass it on to everyone else you leave behind."

I start to respond in defense but chew the inside of my cheek to let her continue. I don't have an argument.

"I'm the last person to tell you what to do or how to live your life. I'm a wreck. I'm just as self-destructive as you, Grayson. I can admit to that. I let other guys touch me because, on some level, I think I deserve it. To be treated like the trash everyone assumes I am. For the things I've done and ruined in the past. Rumors hurt." She looks down at her feet. "We accept the love we think we deserve."

And it suddenly makes sense: the security guard, the fair

worker, the drug dealer. All of it. She doesn't think anyone will love her for who she is.

My heart aches. And I want nothing but to prove to her how wrong she is.

"You deserve *so much* more than that."

"I've done a lot of fucked up things I'm not proud of. Don't defend me."

"Aubrey, you don't have to—"

"I know what it's like losing a brother and feeling like no one gives a shit. Thinking that your parents don't want you." She takes a step forward, looks up. "You know, after my dad died, my mother never tried to contact us. Not once. Not even after Dean offed himself."

I look away, uncomfortable, but Aubrey rushes over and grabs my wrists so I'm forced to stay. Part of me wants her to shut up and leave, and the other part wants desperately for her to save me. Save whatever part of me agreed to go out with her tonight.

But I don't know which side wants what more.

It's not Aubrey's job to save me.

"I can't tell you what to do or how you'll get better. You may never get better. You may live the rest of your life miserable and in constant pain. Always afraid."

She leans into me and kisses my lips. And just like that, she brings me back, back to that burning desire deep in my gut. My senses heighten, and I need her. God, do I need her. More than I've ever needed anything. Like nothing else makes sense except being here with her. I kiss her back more forcefully, but she pulls away, caresses my cheek. We are both left panting.

"I won't be a hypocrite. Only you can decide what is better for *you*. No one else. But you're beautiful, Grayson. Those stars you were talking about earlier... they're not the miracle. *You* are." She takes a step back, runs her hands through her hair.

And for just a moment, I think she'll cry. But she doesn't. "I don't want you to be another statistic."

Without giving me a chance to respond, she turns around and walks across the parking lot. I'm left standing there alone. I look up into the sky and then back at Aubrey. Watch how her hips sway back and forth, the gait of her walk, how her hair swishes in the light breeze.

And it strikes me, like a slap to the face, that I see a future with Aubrey. And Kris. And Reefer. And Jenna. And Kyle. Even my parents. I'm eighteen years old and graduating high school with a diploma. Then I'm off at college in the dorms with Reefer as we blast country rock out the windows at kids walking to their classes. Then I'm thirty and getting a job, getting married, and I'm in the hospital holding on to my wife's hand as she gives birth.

And then I'm forty, reading a bedtime story to my daughter, my little girl.

And I see it all unfold, one scene after another in the span of seconds.

And tears well up in my eyes, but they're good ones—happy ones.

It's a good life. A happy one with a family of my own.

It fills me with nothing but joy.

I force my legs to shuffle after Aubrey.

But despite everything going through my mind, I can't shake the nagging feeling that things are going our way just a little too well.

Like any minute now, the façade will fade and curtains fall.

I get a text, so I pull out my phone:

UNKNOWN

have it ur way

u and foster freak deserve each other

> ur brother was stupid for standing in the street
>
> got what he deserved

ME

> Don't you ever talk about my brother again! I'm
> tired of this shit and these games.

> Who are you?

THIS PHONE HAS BEEN DISCONNECTED

Something bad is going to happen.

Aubrey finds an open window at the back of the school and forces it open. It's for one of the chemistry lab rooms on the first floor. No alarm goes off, so by more sheer luck, we both climb through. It almost feels surreal, like a heightened reality that everything manages to work out in our favor.

You know it won't last. Someone is going to get hurt. You or her.

My heart flutters from adrenaline, but I love it. I could do pushups, sit-ups, and jumping jacks. Inside, the little kid in me screams with joy. Reefer will flip when he hears about this.

Aubrey scans the room, moves slowly to make sure no alarms or trip sensors go off. It reminds me of an action movie Jenna forced me to watch, so I happily play along. We crouch low and head toward the door, peer out as she cracks it open and looks both ways for any security guards or mounted cameras.

"I know there's cameras here somewhere. Be damned if I know where, though."

"Can we cover up our faces with something?"

She looks down at the wooden box and plastic bag in her hands.

"What about the clothes Reefer's dad made you wear for school?"

"Principal Hoch?" She hums. "This is a chem lab, right?"

I nod.

"There must be something in here to wear."

She walks over to the far end toward one of the lockers in back. She takes out another metal hanger and straightens the end to pick at the lock to the cabinet. She hooks it after a few seconds and opens up the doors to retrieve two medical masks and gray school hoodies. She hands one set to me, and we both put them on before she shuts and re-locks the door.

"I guess this will do," I say.

Aubrey breathes heavily, like there is phlegm in her throat, before doing a mock Darth Vader voice. "Grayson, I am your *mysterious* friend. And damn... do you have a tight ass."

I chuckle and mock the same voice back. "Aubrey, you've got nice... boobies?"

"Really, Grayson? *Boobies?* What are we, in fifth grade?"

I shrug. "I suck at foreplay."

Aubrey covers her mouth to stifle a laugh. But I'm beginning to like this new her. One where she has fun, shows her soft side. An Aubrey that I can be myself around.

After we calm down, we step out in the hallway and inch our way toward the direction of my locker. I press myself as close to the wall as I can to blend in. Aubrey does the same. We make a few turns, occasionally stopping when we think we hear footsteps, but tiptoe on when the fear passes.

"I feel like we're looting in the middle of a zombie apocalypse or some virus plague," I say.

"Just remember to double tap the head shot. Can't be too careful."

"I think I have to pee again."

"Dude, seriously?"

"The seal's broke. I'm surprised I haven't pissed my pants yet."

"Hold it. Like a man."

We come to the front hallway by the main office and get on our hands and knees to crawl past it. Why we do it, I have no idea. But it's fun as hell, like a video game.

Above us is a bulletin board next to the front office. In the dim lights the school has on, I can just make out a pea-green flier with a black-and-white photo of Kris, Kyle, and their parents on the cover, taken about a year ago. I rise to my feet, still hunched over, and rip it from the tack holding it in place. Aubrey stops to let me look. It's a flier with a phone number and fundraiser info asking to donate to the family and their growing medical bills. I suddenly feel horrible, terrible.

Like I've just now realized what the accident did to them. How much it's destroyed. The ripple effects keep going further and further out.

Tragedy doesn't stop with any one person.

I tack the flier back up and nod to Aubrey.

My locker is by the main stairs, just the next hall over from the front office. I pay attention for signs of a security guard, zombie groaning, or footsteps before opening my locker. I pause and reach up to the top shelf to retrieve the crumpled photo Kris snuck in there of the bonfire after she won the track tournament. Aubrey looks over my shoulder, curious, but doesn't say anything. I run my thumb over the surface as if it will transport me back to that day, but it doesn't. So I sigh and put the photo, restaurant receipt, and the pamphlet on failing Mr. Hoch gave me into my front pocket. Aubrey takes off the medical mask, stores it in my locker, and pulls up her hood. I do the same.

"What about the cameras?" I ask.

She points to the ceiling, so I look up. "I don't think there are any in this area. But keep the hood on just in case."

I reach back up and retrieve what I really came for, which is the envelope addressed to Bryson. Aubrey perks up when she sees it, furrows her brows. I hand it to her so she can hold it.

"I was supposed to give this to him." My voice is weak. "Had it in this locker since before everything happened. Guess I was too embarrassed or whatever to take it back out."

She turns it over, her expression unreadable. "What's in here?"

"Yankees tickets. Took me months to save up for them." It's silent for a moment. "He was obsessed with them. We always used to play catch in the front yard with our dad. He loved it. If you could have seen the joy on his face whenever we played or watched a game... it was unlike anything I'd ever seen." I close my locker and press my back into it. Aubrey falls into place next to me, hands me back the envelope. "He was worried about me leaving him after graduation next year. I promised to take him to see a game in the city."

I smile, imagine the time in the tree house, how we stayed up all night talking. But those moments are gone. All that's left are the memories.

There's no making new ones. Not anymore.

"They were supposed to be his birthday present. He would've turned eleven."

Aubrey grabs my hand and squeezes it, presses her forehead into my shoulder, so I lean my head down to rest on top of hers before we both stand straight again.

"When's his birthday?"

I chew my lower lip. "Tomorrow." I reach into my pocket for

my phone, see the time. "Or today, technically." I put my phone away.

Aubrey reaches over and takes the envelope back. "He would've loved it, Grayson."

My lip twitches. "Yeah," I whisper. "I think so too."

We stand there for a long time, not speaking. It's in the silent moments between us that are the most peaceful and absolute. Aubrey traces the edges of the envelope with her finger, turns it over and then runs a thumb over Bryson's name scrawled in the black ink. It's another intimate moment that surprises me. It's so different from the Aubrey Fisher that sat down at my lunch table earlier with her short, one-word responses. This is the real Aubrey, the version of her that's without masks or defenses or walls.

It's the Aubrey that's always been just beneath the surface, like the weed from the bowling alley. I admire her, completely in awe. I've known her less than twenty-four hours, and it's like we've known each other for a lifetime. She's slipped into my soul and rooted herself there. Like sleep that comes when you least expect it, or the rainbow in the sky that dips below the clouds after a heavy rain on a humid, spring day.

I'm a paddleboat lost at sea, and she is the riptide pulling me downstream.

You can fall for a girl like Aubrey Fisher if you're not careful.

"It's pills," I admit. It just comes out. Aubrey isn't affected. "It was going to be peaceful. Quiet. No mess or a big scene. No note or anything. Just quiet." Aubrey says nothing. "There's a tree house out in the woods that Bryson and I used to go to. He loved it. We even spent a few nights in it before our parents found out we snuck there after dark." I clear my throat. "I was going to die there. In a place he loved. That we loved together." I pull my hand out of Aubrey's to wipe sweat onto my jeans. "He would've wanted me to go there. For him."

Aubrey looks up at me, and her eyes go wide. She doesn't say anything but stands up straighter. That's when I know I've upset her, offended her somehow. Maybe her brother did the same thing. I feel bad and I start to apologize, but then she looks past me, not speaking. And for the first time, I realize how painful hearing this must be for her, and I want to take it all away.

Maybe it's being here alone, or maybe it's her heart that I can feel beating against my chest. But I lean back until I get a clear look at her face. And I realize that I need to touch her, need to taste her. Need to sink into her until she consumes all of me. I just want to be with her.

So I decide to be with her.

I hold her cheeks in my palms and tilt her chin up so I can lean down and kiss her. My heart almost flies out of my chest and into hers, but she presses into me, and we fall against the lockers with an echoing *CLANG*. She hikes up her leg, and I move my hand to her hips and hoist her up.

She pulls back to suck in a breath, but I press my mouth into hers as far as it will go. I just want to breathe her in. *Consume* her. I can't get enough, and it's like flares go off all around. There is panting and breathing and groping. She moans into my mouth, and it's the most adorable thing I've ever heard or felt. I want her to moan more. I want to make her breath heavier, so I turn us around and press her into the lockers forcefully, more than I mean to. I pull back to make sure she's okay, but she bites her lip and pulls my face back into hers.

My hands travel up and down the front of her hoodie, and all I know is that I want it off her. So I pull back, and she must know what I'm thinking, 'cause she takes it off and throws it into my locker. I do the same. We stare at each for a while, and she licks her lips. It's too much; I can't handle not having my skin touch hers, so I grab the back of her neck, tilt her head, and start kissing her again. She places her hands on my cheeks and hikes her legs around my waist.

Now it's my turn to moan. My hands run up and down her thighs, then move up to just below her lower back. Her hands somehow feel their way over my chest and my shoulders, the bruises still sore. My muscles tense up, and I move my mouth and kiss a trail to her neck. She tastes so sweet. Like vanilla mixed with cigarettes. I've learned to love that smell. *Her* smell.

She bites my lip, and when I pull back for a breath, her teeth hold me close as she drops her legs to the floor.

"Aubrey," I breathe into her. It's barely audible, but I know she hears me. And I can feel my heart just melting for her. Like a candlestick slowly dripping into a molten pool.

"Shh, it's okay. Just be here with me."

I kiss her neck, caress her lower back, and try to find a way underneath her shirt. Play with the waistband of her plaid miniskirt. I want her. I'll go crazy if I can't have her now.

"I don't want to let you go."

"Just kiss me."

I bring my head back to her, and she sucks my tongue into her mouth. And her ring caresses my tongue——massages it. My skin breaks out in goosebumps; my body quivers. It's like I'm on fire, and sweat rolls down my forehead, but neither of us care. We continue to feel each other's bodies, and she finds her way underneath my shirt and strokes my skin. She makes her way from my stomach to my chest and moves her hands everywhere. It tickles, hurts a little, but I can't help giggling into her mouth. The vibration feels like butterfly wings to my nerves.

"I think I need you," I pant. "I think I've always needed you."

She pulls back and takes her hands out from my shirt and

rubs my neck. She smiles again, and the second I see the dimple my nerves explode, synapses on fire. I want to make her smile forever just to see that dimple on her face. And I'm dizzy, light-headed. I inhale her scent, suck in every breath she exhales like it's precious. I'd be embarrassed if I wasn't so goddamn enamored.

Oh. My. God.

We kiss again—hungrily—and I press my body as far into her as it can get. It's not nearly enough. I want to tear off our clothes, but that would turn into something that neither of us can come back from, and I don't know if I'm ready for that.

"Jesus, Grayson," she whispers, presses her forehead into mine. "Why couldn't you have come into my life sooner?" She sucks my lower lip into her mouth and playfully nibbles it.

"I'm here now."

She kisses me, but it's different. I can feel it.

"You're too late."

I pull back, breathless. "What do you mean?"

And then both our eyes are drawn to the faint red and blue lights flashing along the tiles of the floor. They come from somewhere by the front entrance around the corner of the hallway.

I know what it is without her having to say. It was only a matter of time before our luck ran out. We must have tripped a security alarm by breaking in.

Aubrey digs her nails into my shoulders, trembles. I want to protect her, to help her in a way she helped me by taking me out of school. But this is something that not even Aubrey has a plan for. It's written on her face: she knows it's over. I lean in and kiss her again. Her breath is so hot that my entire body prickles—I just want to feel it on my skin forever.

"What do we do?" I ask. "Is there anywhere we can hide or sneak out through another window?"

Aubrey shakes her head and covers her face with her hands. "It's over."

"What do you mean?"

Aubrey doesn't say anything for a while, not until we hear the front doors open and footsteps echo onto the floors around the corner. She pushes me away, and her hiked leg falls down. It's like my heart breaks into a million pieces when we step apart. God, I can't be without her. I can't. But then she says it:

"I mean, it's time for you to go home." A beat. "I'm leaving, Grayson."

4 HOURS UNTIL

???

FOOTSTEPS ECHO DOWN THE HALL, COME CLOSER WITH each tap. None of it matters now. The only thing that keeps repeating in my head are those words:

"I'm leaving, Grayson."

"What are you talking about?" I mean for it to come out softer than it does. It's like a jab in the throat. "You mean you're going home?"

I don't really want to know the truth, but I ask anyway. Somehow I already know what she means.

Aubrey looks pained just to say it, and she stares past me to the sounds of the echoing tap of shoes on tile. She doesn't look up, doesn't speak. Her well is dried up. It's nothing but a dark, stygian hole. My stomach leaps into my throat, and I stumble into a locker.

"When are you leaving?" She doesn't respond. "Aubrey?"

She shakes her head and puffs up her bangs. "I'll be placed in a new home by Monday."

Fuck. Fuck. Fuck. Fuck. Fuck. Fuck. Fuck.

"How long have you known?" No response. "Aubrey!"

She breathes out through her nose and rolls the tongue ring

around in her mouth. I can hear it clanging against the back of her teeth.

"They expelled me after lunch. When I attacked Tim."

You got her expelled, Gray. You're the reason she's leaving. It's your fault.

"They've been looking for a new home for a couple weeks now. Bad behavior. Being expelled was just the final straw."

I want to punch something. I want to place my hands on a red locker to rip it from the wall and hurl it through a window. But it's too late. The whole day was a complete lie. She knew about me all along, kept secrets. And she knew she wasn't staying. Knew that she'd be gone by next week.

She played you, Gray. She was never intending to stay.

"You used me," I utter. "Used me like you did every other guy tonight."

Aubrey steps closer to me. The footsteps are only a few seconds away now.

"I never used you, Grayson."

I curse under my breath. "Do I really seem like some naïve chump to you? Someone you can just jerk around, play with my feelings, and just leave on the curb when you're done? Is that what this was all about? Use me to break the rules to fuel your ego and then leave me to pick up the pieces? Is this what you do to guys in other towns you've visited? Do you even have a soul?"

She looks hurt. Legitimately hurt. But I don't care. I trusted her. Believed her. This entire time she was talking about being in the *now* with her, yet she was going to leave me forever when the night was over. New family. New town. New school. Hell, maybe even a new state. What do I know?

But then a man dressed in a navy-blue cop uniform turns the corner, his hand hovering over his holster. When he sees us, he pulls out his gun and points it. We both raise our hands instinctively, and the rest is a blur. I call Aubrey a few choice words. Things I'm not proud of. Things I regret and don't really mean. But it feels like another weight is lifted off my chest. She just lets me degrade her. Doesn't defend herself or lash out like she would to anyone who belittled me. I feel like an asshole, but I'm pissed.

The cop radios some code to someone before handcuffing us behind our backs. We are walked out the doors and to the front parking circle, where his white patrol car flashes the blue and red lights. I don't speak to Aubrey when he sits us in the back and radios to the station. I don't speak to Aubrey when we pull away and head to the local jail. I don't speak as we are walked into the station, past Sheriff Dickens in his little office to the side. I remember him from the hospital when he came to question me. He doesn't look surprised to see us.

Aubrey and I are placed in the same jail cell. There are only two in here, and the town drunk occupies the other one.

We sit on opposite sides of the bench. Ignore each other.

And we wait.

"Your parents are on the way now," one of the uniformed desk officers says. She has her blonde hair pulled back into a tight bun. "We called them for you, so sit tight."

I roll my eyes and mutter under my breath, "Fantastic."

"Are you gonna ignore me the rest of the night?" Aubrey asks. "Like a child?"

I want to turn and face her but can't. It's too painful. I can still feel her lips on mine and feel her fingers exploring every inch of my bare chest. Can feel her hot breath on my skin. I want her so bad it hurts.

"You should've told me, Aubrey."

"Would it really have made a difference? Would that have made you act differently?"

"I don't know."

I feel her turn toward me, but I still can't do it. I'm afraid I'll cave and pull her lips back to mine, behind these bars, for everyone to see.

"You can use this for inspiration." She reasons, hesitant, but I'm confused.

"What are you talking about?"

"Your writing. The Falconian. That's why you stopped posting."

I finally turn my head, a pit in my stomach. "How did you—"

Then it hits me. It makes me embarrassed that I never realized it sooner.

"You're JamesDeanFan."

She nods slowly with a pained smile. "You're a beautiful writer. Don't let it go. I'm serious."

My mouth opens and closes. I feel like steam is coming out of my ears cartoonishly. I'm as mad as I am embarrassed as I am flattered. She's been posting on all my videos for the past eleven months—before she was even transferred to Lee Falls. Before the accident. She'd been with me all along, and I'd never realized it.

"Jesus. This entire time?"

"Yeah."

She knew you before. The before version of you.

"Were you ever going to bring it up if we'd never been arrested?"

She chews on her answer. "Maybe."

"So you've known about me for nearly a year? Commenting, responding to internet trolls, and you never said something sooner?"

"You weren't ready yet."

"Ready? Ready! I had to be ready for you to be honest with me about my own life?"

"You weren't going to kill yourself before today, Grayson, were you?" She flares her nostrils. "So yes, you weren't ready."

I groan. "Is my life some kind of board game for you to manipulate?"

"I'm sorry."

"Too little too late. You're just going to leave anyway, right? Why should you care what I think or what I write? I'm the one that you're leaving behind. Isn't that right, JamesDeanFan?"

She's silent. I've hurt her again. I want to stop and get back to what we had before, but I can't. And I don't know if we can ever go back.

"You see?" she whispers. "I ruin everything I touch."

One minute everything moves so slowly, and the next it's like a whirlwind. I'm not excited to see my parents. I'd accepted that I'd never see their faces again, and now, after everything with Aubrey, it will be impossible to face them. But another part of me is intrigued to see Aubrey's foster parents. They live on the opposite end of the town, and no one really knows them. They keep to themselves. Maybe they're just as fed up with her as I am.

Or maybe they'll be just as devastated to see her leave.

Then my parents walk into the station.

And it's my mom's face that startles me. She looks around frantically, desperately searching. When she sees me, she gasps, hesitates for not even a second, and runs to me with her arms outstretched. Tears flow down her cheeks, and my dad trots after. They both look terrible, like they haven't slept in days. My mom's hair is wild; there are dark circles under her eyes. Dad's shirt and pants are wrinkled, like he threw on whatever was in the dirty laundry hamper before rushing out of the house.

Mom stops at the iron bars and reaches her arms in. I stay seated for a breath before I get up and walk toward them. My knees wobble, and I miss them. Really miss them. They're here together. For me. And they're not fighting.

They're not fighting.

They're here together.

"Oh! Gray! My baby. You're okay. You're all right. Oh, Gray... what happened to your face?"

"Kiddo." My dad sighs. "Where have you been? Who did this to you? Your lip is practically busted right open."

Jesus, how bad is it?

He inspects me from head to toe as if expecting other horrible wounds or disfigurements. Mom reaches through the bars as if to try and break through. I lean against them so she can shower my face in kisses. It's embarrassing, and I can feel Aubrey's eyes on us, but it feels good. It's so alien. So strange. My parents haven't been this way in a long time.

Mom and Dad both freak out when they see the cuts and bruises on my arms and face. She tries to call for the Sheriff, but I calm her down, tell her I'm okay. They both look around, ready to blame the next person who walks by. So I try to take their mind off it.

"What are you guys doing here?"

"Gray," my mom says. "You've been gone all day. They said you left school with some girl, and you haven't called or checked in once." She lets herself cry a little before continuing, and I can't help but feel like a real asshole. She looks distraught. "We were worried something happened to you. I just kept thinking all day that what if..."

Both my parents glance at each other and look at the ground

simultaneously. My dad puts a hand on my shoulder and pats it. Chills. "We're just glad you're okay, son." He squeezes it and pulls me in for a hug through the bars. "I don't know what we'd do if we ever lost you."

"Don't ever do that to us again," my mom says. "Please. I-I can't bear it."

My dad looks behind me at Aubrey and squints his eyes, lowers his voice. "Is that the girl? The one they were talking about?"

Mom looks too and seems disgusted, like Aubrey is a deadly plague infecting the cell.

"Goodness," she mumbles. "The girl looks homeless." She shudders. "I guess that's what not having a stable home does."

How ironic.

"Marie, we don't know anything about the girl."

"She dresses like a tramp, Robert. Look at what she's wearing."

That really pisses me off. I look behind at Aubrey, and she stares out into blank space, but I know she hears everything. I open my mouth to defend her, but Sheriff Dickens—a tall, portly man with a graying mustache—walks up and motions them to the back to talk in private. They leave us in the cell, so I amble back to the bench.

It takes a while to find the right words. Like our relationship is slowly retreating back to how it used to be when I was too nervous to speak. And her demeanor is harder, colder. She's slowly shutting herself off. Putting up those walls again.

I just want to shut myself in with her, behind those barricades. Just the two of us.

But I also don't know how to continue without her here. Wherever she goes.

"I'm sorry for what my mom said." Aubrey doesn't respond. "She doesn't know you like I do." Silence. "I love how you dress." More silence. "Thank you for what you said about my poetry. Your posts." Still nothing. "It means a lot. Honestly."

She looks up at the ceiling and leans her back against the brick wall. "Grayson. Can you do me one favor?"

I lean back and look at the ceiling too, study the patterns and phosphorescent lights. "What?"

A beat.

"My little brother was like you. Sad. Depressed. Hopeless." She's silent. "He hung himself. James had aged out of the system; I was thirteen. Dean was twelve. We were over four hours away from James in a new foster home. I was responsible for Dean." She takes a deep breath. "I know what it's like to want to die. To think there's no other way." She looks over at me; her eyes water up. "You remind me of him, in a way. That innocence you have. How you view the world as magic."

My eyes water up too, and I scoot closer. Open my arms to put them around her, but the female officer behind the desk shouts at us to separate. I try to find the right words, but none come to mind.

Aubrey nods and bites her lower lip.

"My dad is dead. My mom gone. And my older brother an addict. Was in and out of rehab for years before we couldn't afford it anymore. I watch people die around me. You shouldn't be one of them." She clears her throat and looks back down at the ground. "You have parents that come to bail you out of jail in the middle of the night. Waitresses at least ten years older that think you're hot shit. Friends like Reefer and Jenna that worship you. Even Kris in her annoying, self-righteous way." She pauses after saying her name, like uttering it hurts.

It hurts me too.

Aubrey looks up at me, and her eyes are nearly bloodshot.

"You still have Kris."

My mind swirls with different things to say—what's right

and what's wrong. But only one of them seems like a question worth stating:

"But what if all I want is you?"

We stare at each other, and I get lost in her amber eyes. She's so pretty, even when she's sad. But I hate seeing her like this. This vulnerable, emotional Aubrey scares me. But it also fills me with so much happiness. So much more than I expect or deserve.

Aubrey is a buried treasure that I happened to stumble across and never knew I had the key to. I want to tell her all this, but I think she knows. Because when the officer isn't looking, we hold hands, and it's like holding an ember. My arm heats up, and my entire body quivers with delight. I rub my thumb over her knuckles until her hand trembles. I smile lightly. She grins.

I make a choice to let it go, the bitterness. As hurt as I am, distancing myself from Aubrey is the last thing I'd ever want. It feels right, somehow, to be near her, to touch her. So I choose her.

"I don't want to leave," she whispers.

I squeeze her hand. "So don't," I whisper back.

She squeezes mine. "I don't have a choice."

We both look at each other, and I reach over to run my thumb gently against her cheeks. She closes her eyes and breathes out. Her hot breath brushes past my knuckles, and the blood pumps in my veins.

"How do you manage to do that?" she says.

"Do what?"

"Turn me into such a *girl*."

I chuckle under my breath. "You were always a girl, Aubrey. But you're a softer version of the one who sat down at my lunch table earlier."

She opens her eyes. "I guess that means we'll have to have sex at some point. To keep up appearances and all."

I push back the bangs from her eyes to place them behind her ear. "I guess we'll just have to add that one to our list."

The rest of the time flies by. My parents walk out with Sheriff Dickens after a few minutes, talking and looking at us like we're straddling the edge of a cliff, preparing to fall off. Most of what they say goes in one ear and out the other—it's inconsequential now. All that really sticks are things like *community service, court date, fines, and revoked licenses.* The rest are a blur of words and the shapes mouths make when saying them.

It's not long after, when we are once again asked to separate on the bench, that Aubrey's foster parents arrive. The Bells. They are older than I imagined—older than my parents. Possibly even old enough to be grandparents. They dress similarly to Mom and Dad, like they threw on whatever they could after they got a phone call in the middle of the night. They look normal, almost sweet. Mr. Bell is mostly bald with reading glasses draped around his neck. Mrs. Bell hunches over like she's carrying an imaginary weight strapped to her back. She hobbles a little. They appear tired, worried, and are holding each other.

When they walk up and are greeted by Sheriff Dickens, they look into the cell, shake their heads, and frown. Neither looks mad. Just disappointed. Like they expected more of Aubrey. Like they knew she was capable of better. Mrs. Bell noticeably sighs in frustration. But then the Sheriff takes all four of them into the back room for a while before they come back out.

"So," I start, "can you request to be placed somewhere specific?"

"That's not how it works."

I point to the Bells. "Can't you stay with them?"

Aubrey shakes her head. "Foster homes are temporary. And they won't keep me in a district I was kicked out of." She clucks her tongue. "I'll be gone by Sunday. Monday at the absolute latest."

An idea pops in my head so crazy that I laugh. Too absurd to even consider the possibility, and yet, I'd want nothing more than the reality.

"Why don't we just run away? For real."

Aubrey cocks her head and studies me. It's still as unnerving as when she used to do the same at school. She's trying to determine if I'm being serious, maybe if it's possible.

Run away or swallow pills? The be-all, end-all ultimatum.

"That'll never work."

"Why?"

She sucks in a breath and holds it in her chest. "Because you don't belong in my world. You belong here. With your family and friends."

"What if you're wrong?"

"I'm not."

"But—"

"End of discussion."

And just like that, cold, calculated Aubrey is back. Trying to control the situation and the outcome. Neither of us really knows how to let go. We suck at it. So I slump back against the wall, defeated, and swing my legs underneath the bench. It's a little while before I realize Aubrey is doing the same.

The Sheriff unlocks the cell door and releases us to our parents. Gives us back our personal items they had confiscated, along with the grocery bag and Aubrey's wooden box. Mom snatches me up like a mother hen. Aubrey is inferior to them. Mom shelters me, like a mere glance at Aubrey will somehow taint me in a way that can never be washed off.

But if that's true, I don't ever want to wash away her stain.

There is more talk of how much trouble we may or may not be in, but none of it matters.

"They may be looking at community service hours," Sheriff Dickens says, running his fingers through his mustache. "And paying the restaurant back for the bill they skipped on. But Mr. Hoch did find evidence to prosecute the guard they assaulted at school with possession of child pornography."

"I can't believe they let a man like that near those children." Mrs. Bell rubs her temples. "It's disgusting. These poor kids. Have any other survivors come forward?"

"Not yet," Sheriff Dickens says. "But we're going to be doing a full investigation, I assure you."

"Did he hurt you, Aubrey?" Mr. Bell asks in a softer tone than I would have guessed. "Did that man touch you?"

Aubrey doesn't get a chance to respond before all five of them, and eventually, the officer behind the front desk starts going off about it. Apparently, Aubrey's announcement in school was taken seriously. I don't really know what happened or what they found.

The pervert guard will go to jail, Gray. And you saved her from something terrible. Maybe there's something redeemable in you yet.

Sheriff Dickens and my parents continue talking while the Bells mainly nod and react. They occasionally glance down and furrow their brows, and I know they love her. Aubrey and I stand there awkwardly. I look over at her, and she rolls her eyes. She looks just as uninterested as I do. And I don't know if that's a good thing. If maybe I should feel something more. It feels like a step back, and yet, it's what Aubrey's been trying to teach me all day. The past is the past, and right now is right now. The future is tomorrow. I just want to experience *the now*.

"...could be months, weeks, we don't know," Sheriff Dickens drones on.

Mr. Bell pipes up: "If this thing gets momentum, will they have to testify?"

They go on like this for a while, and by the end of it, I'm fully aware I can be facing time in juvie, but I don't care. I can still die. It's not too late. I can wait until Aubrey leaves and end it all. What would it matter if I never see her again?

But another part of me, emerging in a way that terrifies me more, is what it might be like if I *live*. If I choose to *stay*. What would a life with Aubrey be like? Would we be boyfriend and girlfriend? Would she continue making terrible choices? Would I become some delinquent who breaks all the rules?

What if she leaves? Would I run away with her? Go back to Kris and the way we were? Maybe forge some kind of new path and way of life?

It's all so uncertain and scary, yet exciting and new.

So I get Aubrey's attention and mouth the words, *"Thank you."*

She smiles. *"You're welcome."*

My parents avoid the Bells as we walk out of the police station and to the cars. It dawns on me, now nearly three in the morning, how exhausted I am. And with each step we take across the lot, the sooner it gets to being over. I don't want it to be.

"First, we'll all go home and get you to bed," my mom says. "I just want you home. We'll talk in the morning."

"Yeah, kiddo." Dad puts his hand on my shoulder. "We're glad you're okay. We love you. You know that, right?"

"Yeah, I know."

Do you, though?

I turn around to say something to Aubrey, but she's halfway across the parking lot, and I sputter for air. It's too far. She's too far. I need her like oxygen. Need her like she's a vital part of me.

"Aubrey!"

She stops and looks back. The Bells motion her forward, try to scurry to their car, but Aubrey doesn't give in. My parents look up and Mom mutters something terrible, which Dad agrees to. But I don't say anything, like usual when I'm with them. Being quiet is safer. It's peaceful. I do not exist in this scenario.

"Aubrey!"

"What are you doing, Gray?" Mom asks, incredulous. "We're going home. Right now."

I mumble a protest, but it's not heard. Mom grabs my wrist and starts dragging me behind her, but I wiggle out of her grasp and throw her arm down. She gasps.

"Gray," Dad says. "What's going on here? Apologize to your mother."

I look back at Aubrey. She stares, waits for me to do something. To either give in or stand up for myself. The Bells try to nudge her forward, but she doesn't move. My parents stand there impatiently, wait for me to succumb to them and head home to a world I know and a future I don't want to face.

And then it just comes out:

"No."

Mom and Dad look at each other like they didn't hear me correctly. I'm not sure I heard myself correctly either. So I say it again, louder:

"I'm not going home."

"Like hell you're not!" Dad says. His temper comes back, just like I knew it would. Things don't change that easily. I can't expect my parents to get better just because the fear of losing me was present.

"Gray," Mom says. "We'll talk about this tomorrow. I'm tired. And of all days to pull a stunt like this! How could you be so selfish?"

"I'm being selfish? I'M BEING SELFISH!"

"Enough," Dad says. "You're making a scene and embarrassing us. Get in the car; we're taking you home." He grabs my wrist, but I shove him in the chest and back up. Mom cries out, and Dad looks ready to throw a fist, but he doesn't.

They argue back and forth for a while, threats are made, but I don't give in. Aubrey fuels me. Somehow. She helps provide me the support I need. But this is all me. I'm doing this.

Enough is enough.

"Of course he gets it from you, Robert! This is *your* son too."

"Are we really going to start this again?" He grits his teeth and lowers his voice. "I will not have this conversation in front of the goddamn police station, Marie. You really want to have a domestic dispute right here and now?"

"Don't come home tonight. Do me a favor, please, and go see that tramp from work. The *blonde* one."

Dad rubs his temples. "You can be such a relentless bitch."

And then it boils over. All of it. Everything. I don't care about the cops or about the Bells. This is for me. And like the top to a soda can, I pop.

"Are you guys even listening to yourselves?" I shout. It's so loud that even I cringe, but my heart beats in my chest in such a different way. I've never yelled at them. Not even when Bryson was still alive. But I take a deep breath and calm down, talk normally. "I was gone for an entire day. I left school. I helped beat up a security guard."

"Don't say that out loud, son," Dad cuts me off and looks around, paranoid like I'm incriminating myself.

"You're still not listening." I ball my hands into fists and rub them against my thighs, and I lower my voice more. "I stole from a restaurant, I snuck into a club and got drunk. I smoked weed. I broke into someone's backyard and used his fucking pool. And all you guys care about is how much you can make the other miserable." I storm around in a circle. By now, the Bells have inched their way to their car, trying not to eavesdrop, but Aubrey is noticeably closer. My parents sulk a little, like scolded children. It's weird, and I feel bad, but it also feels cathartic.

"I'm flunking junior year." I step closer. "Got rid of all the posters in my room. Never said anything as you two fought each and every night. I can hear you from bed in my room. Did you know that? Like the night you said it would've been easier if you'd lost both sons that night."

"Kiddo..." my dad chokes, looks guilty. "I'd never—"

I shake my head. Tears roll down my mother's cheeks, and I look down, away from her. I can't look at either of them.

"The only friends that have come to the house are Jenna and Reefer. No one else. Do you even notice any of it?" Silence. I turn to my dad. "You locked Bryson's room and hid the key. Got rid of anything of his that reminded you of anything good or bad." I turn to my mom. "You act like you're the only one who feels anything. But you're not. And you can't try to sleep off the pain. All you guys do is fight and shout and lie to each other."

I take a deep breath, the next sentence coming out in barely a whisper:

"I've been trying to kill myself all day."

I look at my dad, and he seems so small compared to how he usually is. So ashamed. He chokes. And my mom's chin trembles. She hugs herself and sobs quietly. She does a double take as if she heard incorrectly, and then it sinks in.

I feel disgusted, scared. But maybe this is what they need. Maybe this is what will finally get them to face everything. The sound of it leaving my lips, finally being honest with my parents, is like a big weight lifted. Like my heart has room to beat again. Lungs room to breathe. Like I feel reborn, in a way.

"Aubrey"—I look behind me, and she is only a few feet away —"has been helping me. She's been taking me out and showing me what it's like to let go and have fun. That there can still be reasons to move forward." And then Aubrey's hand is in mine. "She's not a bad influence, Mom." I look at her. "She's the best person I've ever met in my life. She's amazing."

They're both silent again, and neither raises their head.

"Aubrey's been there for me. Helping me deal with my issues by pushing me out of my comfort zone. I love you both, but... this has to stop. We have to learn to be a family again."

Aubrey presses into my back, and just her being there is enough to calm me down. I can feel her heart beating on my back, and I just want to turn around and press my lips into hers. To feel the passion and hunger. To hold the most beautiful part of her in my arms. It's insane to think about how fast it's moving. How much I feel like she is a part of me I can't and won't let go.

I don't get it.

I don't think I want to.

"I-I—" my dad sputters, tries to find words but can't. "I'm sorry..." He looks at my mom, and they wipe tears from their eyes. "Kiddo—"

"Oh, Gray," my mom says, looks up at me. "My beautiful boy," she mumbles, reaches out and caresses my cheek. "Don't you *ever* think that we don't love you every second of every day." She sniffles. "You're still our son."

My entire body stands alert.

"I would die before I'd see any harm come to you." Her lower lip quivers. "You're the best part of us by far."

Dad closes his eyes. "You live because that's how you keep the memory of your brother alive." He opens his eyes and points to my heart. "In there. He's always with you." He points to his chest. "And you're both always in here." A single tear falls out of his left eye. "You're still that little baby that I carried out of the hospital wrapped in the blue blanket. You'll always be our son, and we will never stop loving you."

My dad pulls my mom into an embrace, so she sobs into his chest.

It's a weird thing watching your parents cry. Your whole life you see them as these larger-than-life people. Like nothing and no one can hurt them. And then, one day, your perfect version of them is shattered, and you realize something you never thought possible: your parents are just as flawed and confused as you are. They have hopes, dreams, and fears. They get sad, sometimes depressed. And it's just as painful to watch, no matter how many sides of vulnerable you see. That's the day you realize your parents are just human.

This is one of those moments.

Different words float through my head. Questions I need to ask and what this future means for us—for them. But not everything can have a tidy, pretty ending with a bow. Some things will always be messy. Life demands it.

There are tears, uttered *I love you*s, and hope. Very tiny. Just a pinprick. But it's there. Hope. Hope that things might be okay. At the very least, that they'll be different. My parents break away from each other and Mom steps toward me for a hug, but I step back, and it crushes her. I don't know why, but my parents don't deserve the parts of me I shared with Aubrey. Not yet.

I don't know if my parents will make up. I don't know if they'll get a divorce. If Mom will stop self-medicating or if Dad will come home more. But maybe they'll try to move forward.

That's when I know that there is still unfinished business. There are other people I need to see: Kris, Reefer, Jenna, and

Kyle. I don't know what I'll say, but being here with my parents and Aubrey... it's what needs to happen next.

"If you both honestly love me, then you'll understand why I have to do what I'm about to do," I say, then look at Aubrey. She smiles, knowing what we're about to do, and walks to the Bells. "You won't come after us or call the cops. You'll go home and wait for me. For when I'm ready."

I say this because now Aubrey and I are in this together. We're in it until the end. No matter the outcome, it's us against the world.

I don't know what Aubrey says to the Bells, but I think my parents are still in shock. They don't want to let me go, but there's an unspoken connection. They know there is something we need to do first. Aubrey says goodbye to the Bells.

Will she miss them after she leaves?

"Gray," my father sputters. "Don't leave us. Wait." He struggles to find the words. "Where are you going? You were released into *our* custody. Just stay and talk to us." His brown eyes are big and pleading. They remind me of Bryson's. "Please."

"I'll be okay. But you both have to let me go." I breathe out. "I love you."

They don't move or talk. They stand there in shocked silence. And I know that this is the only way to make things right. Because that's what Aubrey does: she helps me believe that there can be a right. That there is a light at the end of the dark tunnel. That there is a future in which I can be happy.

And then, without warning, Aubrey walks up to me. I grab her hand, and we run out of the parking lot and down the street. I think I hear my parents—or hers—call after us. But we don't stop. And they don't follow. We run for a few blocks until we reach a street corner. There is a curb next to a street light that we sit down on, and I get out my phone to call Reefer with the remaining battery life. I have to call him three times before he wakes up, but he does and agrees to pick us up.

"So what does this mean?" she asks after I hang up.

I put my phone on the ground by my feet, along with the grocery bag with the hangers and wooden box, and breathe out, watch as it condenses in the chilly air. But oddly enough, sitting next to Aubrey keeps me nothing but warm, like everything is on fire inside. She is the flame licking at me from the pit of a fire.

I look over at her. "I don't know."

She nudges my shoulder playfully. "I'm not ready for the night to be over just yet."

I smile. "I guess we can cross the pulling-an-all-nighter goal off our list?"

She giggles. "The first of many."

"You promise?"

We stare at each other intensely. Neither wanting to be the first to look away. And that moment hangs in the air again, where I want to lean in and kiss her, but the ringtone of my phone blasts from the ground below, makes us jump.

I pick it up, pissed it ruined the moment, and see it's from a blocked number. My heart sinks. Aubrey looks over my shoulder.

"That person is still calling you?" She creases her forehead. "Have they been doing this all day?"

I nod, ashamed. I never told her it was still going on.

She shakes her head. "Put it on speaker. Enough is enough with this shit."

So I do.

Much like the first time, there is silence and crackling on the other end, followed by static. And the same deep, robotic voice whispers into the receiver.

"You still haven't atoned for the life you took. The innocent father you left in a coma. The friends you abandoned. I know you're back in town. See you and the orphan soon."

The line clicks off.

My phone dies.

Aubrey and I look at each other and no doubt think the same thing:

Who is this person?

And more importantly:

Where are they?

3 HOURS UNTIL
SOMETIME AROUND 3:00 AM

THERE ARE FOUR OF US IN THE CAR: REEFER DRIVING, Jenna riding shotgun, and Aubrey and me in the back. It's so strange having two other people in Reefer's "grandma" car. But I can get used to it.

"So you weren't raised in a convent of nuns... is that what I'm gathering?" Reefer says. "I'm too tired to really think straight... you can thank Gray-Gray for that."

"No."

"So what you're telling me is that you're not a by-product of a lab experiment?"

"Sorry to disappoint."

"I can't even fathom the possibility. So did you really drive your previous foster family's car into a pool?"

"Not at all. I don't even know where that rumor came from."

"Jesus Christ! Mind equals blown right now. Your life is disappointingly boring. Okay! Soooooooo, how about that lacrosse player whose teeth you knocked out? And that teacher you got fired for having the affair?"

"I never knocked out anyone's teeth, but that guy needed a

kick in the ass. Barely hit him before he ran away. Don't be a douchebag pervert. Lesson learned."

I note that Aubrey doesn't acknowledge or mention the teacher.

"Wow. Wowowowowowow. This is fascinating. I'm fascinated right now. Hey, Gray-Gray, are you as fascinated as I am?"

"You're insane," I say. "You realize that. Right, Reef?"

Jenna, dressed in a *Mean Streets* t-shirt and with her auburn hair tied in the trademark ponytail, turns around in the passenger seat and shakes her head. She smiles at me but never once glances in Aubrey's direction before turning back around.

"Hey, you called me, mmmkay? Let's not be mean. We have a guest in the car. Besides, you don't even know how much you owe me for covering for your delinquent ass. Korean Freckles nearly had an aneurysm, and I didn't get shit out of this day besides a pretty heavy lecture from my dad. So you let me have this moment of fangirling. 'Cause I deserve it."

"How many times do I have to tell you that there are no such things as Korean freckles?"

"Probably every time I call you it."

"Ignore him, Gray," Jenna says. "He just doesn't want to admit how pathetic he's been all night without you there to be gross with. You really are his entire world."

Reefer cranes his neck. "So do you want me to tell him about you trying to conduct your own background search to make sure Aubrey wasn't some murderous psychopath out to bludgeon his face in and mount his decapitated head on a pike?"

She groans. "I hate you."

Aubrey grins and whispers, "They're funny."

"Yeah." I sigh dramatically. "That's Reefer and Jenna for you."

"I'm literally inches away from you both," Reefer says. "I

can hear you talking about us. But as long as they're compliments, because how can you NOT compliment the two best looking people in this car, I'm okay with it."

"He's also very conceited," I say.

"What did I say about being mean whilst in The Lady Duchess?"

Aubrey raises her left eyebrow.

"It's what he calls the car," I say. "Don't ask me."

"But Duchess is already female," Aubrey states.

"Yes, it is."

"They're also both noble ranks," Jenna adds. "I don't even think they're *equal* ranks."

"No one asked any of your opinions," Reefer snaps, pats the dashboard. "It's okay, baby. Ignore the haters."

Aubrey and I sit in the backseat together, our hands interlocked in the space between our thighs. Reefer wears his mesh basketball shorts and T-shirt from the last Taste of Country concert he went to. Outside, the streetlights whiz by in a blur. On the floor are crumpled-up food wrappers and a packet of moldy fries. Next to Aubrey is an old pair of crusty socks that I'm almost positive have been there for three months.

We tell them about the night and everything we went through... mostly. With a few of the more intimate details left to the imagination. They play along, but I know they're still confused as to what this means for us. I'm not sure what it means either.

But I'm excited to find out.

"Tattoos, right?" Reefer asks. "You gotta have tats... and nipple piercings? Belly button?"

"Just one. No. And used to."

"What? That's it? Not like a badass sleeve, tramp stamp, or some creepy symbolic imagery? This is so anti-climactic it's not even fun anymore. You're just like... almost normal."

"Reefer," I interject. "Enough already."

"She's boring! Where did the mystery go? I just feel like my entire idea of her is being shattered little by little... I don't like this. Not one bit. I don't do change well. Gray knows this."

"Just shut up and drive, Reef. It's late, and we have things we need to do, and you're being weird."

Aubrey squeezes my hand.

"Bro, no one's gonna be awake at Tim's party. It's after three... I almost screened your call."

"We'll wake them up if they're asleep."

"Wake who up? You're the one acting weird, not me."

Jenna yawns. "Can everyone, like, just shut up for a few minutes until we get there? It's too early for me to think straight. I feel like Al Pacino in *Insomnia* right now."

"Ew," Reefer says. "Now I'm picturing Al Pacino naked."

Jenna raises her hands in frustration. "Why would you be picturing Al Pacino naked in the first place?"

He hums but doesn't answer the question.

I massage my thumb into Aubrey's palm until she nudges me with her knee. I smile and look back out the window. "It's time to do the right thing."

Our first stop is at Kris and Kyle's house. It's two stories high, complete with a pebbled walkway leading to the front porch by the front door. A stack of firewood is piled up on one end of the porch, and on the opposite side is a wooden armchair covered in spider webs.

Her street is nicer than ours. Still no street lines, but fewer potholes. Beside the streetlights, and the glowing eyes of some creature the next house over—maybe a cat—it's completely dark.

The outside porch lights are off, so we get out of Reefer's car and make our way to the back where Kris's window faces. I've climbed in and out of it several times over the years, so making my way into their backyard is not hard. I know she'll be asleep, and short of chucking pebbles at her window or pulling a John Cusack with a boombox, the only way to her is to climb up to the second story.

"Look, if you guys want to wait here or in the car, you can do that. I don't know how long I'll be."

"Am I the only one that thinks it's odd that Gray turned into some kind of badass ninja since school?" Reefer says. "This is breaking and entering... we can get shot... Mrs. Sanders owns a gun... the family hunts. What if she hunts humans tonight? *The Most Dangerous Game* type shit. Next thing you know, we're being skinned alive and our organs harvested and sold on the black market. All because Gray couldn't wait until morning, at a normal hour, to play redeeming boyfriend."

I roll my eyes. "I'm going to ignore that comment."

"Of course you are," he mumbles.

"What?"

"Forget it; just do your thing. Who the hell climbs through windows anymore?"

Aubrey picks up a strand of hair to braid and turns away from us.

"Gray?" Jenna asks hesitantly, her face blushing. "You remember what we talked about at school?"

"Closure?"

She beams. "Just be honest with her, and, like, tell her how you feel. Put this behind you. So she can move on, you know."

Reefer steps closer, annoyed. "So is this for Kris's benefit or yours, Freckles?"

She ignores him.

I don't like the tension. We shouldn't be fighting, but for

some reason Reefer and Jenna always do this, and in an hour they'll be back to joking around and harassing each other all over again. I exhale and turn back toward the house.

Some things never change.

The siding of the house has a trellis covered in vines that stops just below Kris's window. Just enough for me to climb up and hope it's open. I raise my eyebrows, turn around, and place my hands on the white trellis. But before I start to climb, I turn back to Aubrey, place my palms on each cheek, and lean in for a kiss. My eyes are closed so I can't see, but I can feel—hear. I suck her bottom lip into my mouth and press my hips into hers until arms wrap around my neck. It's slower than before in the hallway. Quieter. More intimate. We don't rush anything, but neither wants to break away. I inhale the natural scent of her skin and run my hands into her hair.

I can't get enough. Don't want to. She won't let go of my neck. Like if she stops holding on, I'll never come back. But it's crazy to even think about leaving Aubrey. I'm invested. Here for good. For as long as I can keep her.

We part lips for a breath.

"I'm coming back for you," I whisper. "Don't go anywhere."

When I pull my head back to view her face, her eyes are wide. She's frozen. I'm afraid I've scared her somehow. And then she shifts the weight on her feet and bites her lip.

"Stop doing that," she whispers back.

"Doing what?"

She leans in and we kiss again, hold it for a few seconds before pulling away. It's like strings tug at my heart each time our lips touch. Like a jumpstart. The best feeling in the world. She never answers the question before I turn back around and make my way up the trellis. But as I reach the top and find the window unlocked so I can silently open it to crawl through, only one thought comes to mind:

You love her.

There is a ledge just below the window, so once I'm safely inside, I close it to stop the cool breeze and hop down to the floor. It smells like Kris's coconut perfume. It always does. On the walls are posters of famous athletes, actors, and singers. Even in the dark, above the headboard of her bed, I can see the collage of photos she's taken throughout the years. On the ceiling are glow-in-the-dark stars to match the constellations in the night sky. Her dad added them for her ninth birthday, and she's never taken them down.

To the far right, her fish tank glows neon green; to the left, Kris stirs beneath the sheets. There's something bittersweet about being in here after everything. Even though it's been months, it still feels like it was just last night we were cuddling underneath the sheets and talking about our lives outside of Lee Falls.

But is that still the life you want?

It's not long before Kris stirs, sits up, and throws the sheets to her knees. She was always a light sleeper.

Kris doesn't move at first, but then her arm extends to the lamp on her nightstand next to the bed, and the room washes in a faint yellow glow. She jumps when she sees me—lets out a tiny squeak. She wears one of my old white T-shirts and blue sweats I'd given her over a year ago. For a moment it seems like she doesn't believe I'm really here. But then she throws off the rest of the covers, hobbles out of bed, and embraces me in a hug. She buries her head in my chest, and we stay like this for a while before she pulls back, uncomfortable. Like she did something wrong.

Then she slaps me on the cheek.

"What makes you think you can just climb into my room like it's nothing?"

I rub the sting in my cheek. "I just figured—"

"It's an invasion of my privacy. I'm not your girlfriend anymore. It's *not* okay."

"I-I'm sorry. I didn't..."

I wasn't expecting this, not sure how to proceed. But then her demeanor deflates a little. She calms down, sighs.

"I didn't think you'd come back."

I calm down too. "Yeah. Neither did I."

"Why did you?"

It's awkward for a while before she walks over and sits on the bed. Kris pats the spot next to her, and I walk over to sit down; her mattress sinks where we both are.

"She's out there." Kris points to the window. "Isn't she?"

I nod. "Reefer and Jenna too."

Kris does her best to force a polite smile, but we both know it's fake. She wants more time than I can give her. Wants me to say I'm here to stay with her for good. She was always optimistic like that.

On the floor is Kris's knee brace. My fingers twitch at the sight of it.

"I never meant for all this to happen," I say. "This was never part of the plan. Was it?"

Kris pulls her legs onto the bed and crosses them, wincing. She huffs out a pained breath.

"Nothing with us ever was."

Directly across from the bed is her closet, the same one I hid in a few years ago when Mr. Sanders came back from a hunting trip early. I close my eyes and remember hiding behind her dresses as her father walked into the room. How my hands clasped over my mouth to silence my breathing. How terrified I was he'd find me. Kris and I laughed about it for days after.

"I'm sorry, Kris." I open my eyes and pull my legs on the bed to cross them. We both turn our heads and look at each other.

"You should be."

"I've been terrible to you."

"Yeah." She fidgets with the strings to her sweatpants. "You have." She leans back on her elbows. "I can't believe you brought her here, Gray. Are you trying to hurt me more?"

"Of course not. I love you. That never stopped."

"I know you do. It's just—"

I fight inside my head to tell her what I really want to. But then I think of Aubrey and everything she's done tonight for me. For herself. And when Kris stares at me with her emerald eyes, I just let it out in the open:

"I see Bryson everywhere I go. It's like I can't get the image of him in the street out of my head. You know? Like that version of him will always be ingrained there."

Kris grabs my hand and squeezes it, the hostility leaving her voice.

"Me too."

"I don't want my last memory of him to be lying there so helpless and alone in that fucking street." I close my eyes, and it's there again. I shake the image away. "I don't even know what he was thinking in those last moments before I took off. If he thought I abandoned him... if he was scared..." I feel my eyes water up. "Do you think he'd forgive me?"

Kris stares, her expression sad. Her voice wavers. "He loved you, Gray. I know that's all he was thinking. How much he knew you loved him back."

"I'm really screwed up. I never wanted to hurt you, but... it's like no matter how hard I try, I see you, and I just think of him. I see you walk down the halls, and I can still feel the impact of your dad hitting us. I would help you in the hospital, and all I could see was your dad hooked up to machines. And it was too much... I just shut it all off."

"That didn't give you an excuse to push me and everyone who cares about you away. That's the opposite of what you should've done. I was there for you, putting myself out there, and you made me feel so worthless and pathetic."

"You know that's not true."

"Doesn't matter what you say. It's what you do that counts." She sighs and lies back on her bed. "I'm glad you're telling me this now. All I ever wanted was for you to be okay." She looks back out the window; her eyes seem distant and cold. "But things are different now."

I lie down next to her. "I know."

Kris rolls over onto her side, brushing her blonde hair behind her neck. I roll over onto my side and prop my head on my elbow. She breathes out, traces her finger along my cheek.

"You're going to be okay. But doing it alone isn't going to work anymore. You need to open up. Learn to fall back on friends and family when things get bad. I won't keep going on like this; it's not healthy. It's not fair to me. I'm not trying to sound selfish, but you really hurt me, Gray. And sometimes I want to hate you. Some nights I do."

I nod my head, my mouth too dry to speak. My heart races. She looks so heartbroken. So distant. But she's strong—more than I am. She grabs the gold crucifix hanging from her neck and squeezes it, almost in prayer.

"I blame myself too. I think about that fight, how you were trying to calm me down, but I wouldn't listen. I shouldn't have called my dad."

"You had no way of knowing what was going to happen."

"I know." She clutches the crucifix tighter. "It just runs through my mind. How the smallest detail, the smallest change could've prevented the whole thing from happening, you know?

Just one tiny detail. If I called him ten seconds sooner or later. If I'd tried harder to keep you home. If I'd let the argument go and we'd stayed inside."

Now you get it, don't you?

I place my hand on top of hers briefly. "It wasn't either of our faults. And we can't change what happened. We can only choose how to continue going forward."

Kris nods to herself. Breathes.

"Does she make you happy?"

"She does."

Kris rolls over onto her back, so after a moment, I do the same. We stare at her starry ceiling in silence, our breathing the only sound.

"It's like I let that night define me, and I don't know how to feel normal anymore."

"And Aubrey does?"

"She makes me believe that there might be a future where one day I can be."

It's silent before she speaks, but it's barely a whisper.

"Then go be with her."

"What about us?"

She exhales. "Just do me a favor: don't do that. If you're with her, then there is no us. I need to let you go. And if you go back out my window, I can't see or talk to you. Not for a while. Maybe not ever." She pauses. "I don't get what you see in her. But if she's helping you, then she can reach you in a way that I can't. You need to be with her now if it helps."

"But—"

"Don't," she snaps, and lines form between her eyebrows. "You made your choice. You've been making it for the past six months." She places her hands over her face and breathes in, her chest expanding, and breathes out. "We've been heading in this direction for a while now." Kris folds her arms over her chest. "I didn't want to admit it to myself, but we wouldn't have lasted much longer. We were growing apart long before that accident. I love you, Gray." She looks over at me with so much pain in her eyes. "I will always love you, but I don't want to be that girl putting her aspirations on hold for someone. I need to get my life back together. I had it all figured out with track, getting a scholarship, and eventually leaving this town with you and teaching one day. But now? I don't know who I am without running, or who I am without that safety net of having my life strictly organized and planned."

I feel like I want to embrace her, but I don't. This is what Kris needs—what I owe her. She's finally letting out everything she's been holding in. No secrets, no lies.

Exactly what Aubrey's been trying to tell me all day.

Tears roll down Kris's cheeks, and I move to comfort her, but she holds me back. I grab a box of tissues from the night-stand and place it between us. She automatically takes a few out and crumples them in her hand.

"I don't know who I am without you. How sad is that?" She wipes at her eyes, sniffles, and looks up at me again. Her bottom lip quivers. "I just want my dad."

And she loses it, crumbles like a broken dam. She's hyster-ical now—uncontrollably so, and I tear up with her. I grab her hand to let her know I'm not going anywhere, not as long as she needs me. Needs me to be strong for her.

"I just want to hug my dad, see him cheer me on from the bleachers during a track meet or watch him organize the girls' track fundraisers with the other parents. Sell raffle tickets at Kyle's baseball games. Have him and Mom come home from a hunting trip dirty and smelling of firewood. Just to put me on his lap one more time, like he used to do when I was a little girl, and bounce me on his knee. And—"

But that's all she can get out, because her eyes are bloodshot, nose running, and her entire body jerks with each spasm of sobs that rack her body. So I rock her back and forth as she lets go into my shirt. I stroke her hair and want to tell her everything will be okay, that everything will be fine. But I don't.

And deep down, I know I won't talk to her again for a very long time.

After a few minutes, when she's calmed down, we sit up, blow our noses, and catch our breaths.

Then I make a decision, one I was too afraid to make before.

"It was wrong of me to never go visit your dad. I was too selfish to see how this affected you and Kyle, and I'm sorry. It won't change how I've treated you, but if it's okay, I want to go see him maybe tomorrow... today, technically. I don't think I'll ever be ready for it. But it's time. I'll only go if you're okay with it."

She nods, starts to cry again but stops herself. She pats my knee. "My mom would really like that. And even though Kyle won't admit it, he'd like it too."

I try to offer a smile, but I'm not sure if she sees it. Either way, I'm scared yet also hopeful. It's been long enough waiting in the shadows to die, pretending none of this happened.

It's time I start facing it here and now.

The accident was not my fault, and it wasn't hers either. But it doesn't give anyone a right not to acknowledge that it didn't happen.

Maybe her dad will wake up, maybe not. Hopefully he does. But it's time I deal with the consequences of that reality.

"Are we ever going to be able to be friends again?" I say.

Kris doesn't answer for a while. But when she does, it's haunting:

"I don't know anymore."

She shifts next to me, and I feel soft lips press into my cheek. She crawls underneath the covers and turns off the lamp.

I get up and walk to the window. Before I open it to climb down, I turn back to her.

"I know you're worried about your future. I can't give that back to you. I can't take back how I acted at the party or what happened with your dad. But I know that if anyone can find a way, it's you. You're more than what those track meets made you. More than just the beautiful girl with perfect grades. More than anyone's girlfriend. And I wish we would've just stayed in that night and watched a movie like you wanted. I wish a lot of things were different, but I know whatever you do next is going to be amazing, and beautiful. Because that's what you are—it's what you've always been. And maybe one day we can be friends again." I take a deep breath. "And when that day comes, you'll know where to find me."

I hike one leg out the window and hover there, thinking. I look down into the dark night and then back at Kris underneath the sheets. And it feels like everything is coming full circle. Somehow, someway. I think back to my conversation at the restaurant—at the impossible promise Aubrey made. And I think about how upside down everyone's life has been since the accident. It wasn't just me.

It was everyone else, too.

"Someone recently told me that the best way to find yourself again is to get yourself lost first." I hear her ruffle the sheets in bed. "I never really understood what it meant, but I think I do now." More ruffling of sheets. "Take care of yourself, Kris."

There is no response. She is letting me go, letting me be with Aubrey even when it's the last thing in the world she really wants. But I can't help but feel that maybe it's the closure we both need, whether or not we ever talk to each other again.

I hope that we do.

I wipe away a few tears in my eyes—take one last look over this room that's been like a second home since I was seven when we first started becoming friends. Having sleepovers long before it became an issue. The spot where I dropped a cheese pizza on the carpet—the stain still faint, but there.

I raise my hand in a goodbye even though I know it's a gesture meant more for me. And then I leave her room.

As I climb back down the trellis, Jenna and Reefer are sitting on the old swing set next to the toolshed. They don't swing but sit in silence. Behind them is the hot tub I used to spend countless summer nights in with Kris. Aubrey sits by herself on the edge of the tiny slide. I walk forward and a few leaves crunch under my feet. When Aubrey's head cranes up, it's like all the worry dissipates. I just want to run over and shower her in kisses. Want to cover every inch of her body with my lips until there's not a place I haven't marked.

It's a powerful feeling.

"Ah! *Señor Falconi!*" Reefer says. "Good to see you're still in one piece."

Jenna perks up when I approach, flashing her teeth in a giddy smile.

Reefer looks over and playfully shoves Jenna. She gets angry and punches him in the shoulder, which makes him laugh even harder.

And they're back to normal.

"For now." I smile. "Sorry I was gone that long."

"Nah, it's cool. Was just thinking about Mrs. Carmichael."

"The widow?" Jenna rolls her eyes. "Seriously? We're still on this topic?"

"Freckles, my lovely, we were never off it. The thirst is never quenched."

I chuckle. "Again, pretty sure the thirst is not a real thing. No one says that. Not ever."

"They do, Gray-Gray. It's a hashtag. Look it up online. Hashtag: The Thirst Is Real. Or Thirst Trap. That one is big too."

I turn to Aubrey. She giggles, but her eyes seem elsewhere—contemplating something.

"Don't encourage him," I say. "He won't stop if you do."

"Hashtag: Truth," Jenna adds.

Reefer jumps up from the swing and flicks Jenna's ponytail. She playfully shoves him away, suppressing a smile.

"The lady indeed does love the Reef-a-nator."

"Not when you call yourself that, I don't."

"Give it time, child," he coos in her ear, glances at her butt when she's not looking. "Give it time."

When I catch Aubrey's eye, she looks down at her feet, again pointed inward, and I know something is wrong. I get Reefer's attention and twitch my head back, so he gets the signal to take Jenna and leave us alone. He doesn't go right away, lingers, but after another nudge, he does—says he's going to warm up the car. Jenna glances from him to me, still not once looking at Aubrey, not even acknowledging she's there. Reefer gets up from the swing and walks to the front of the house. Jenna stays a moment longer and stares at me, upset. She shakes her head and then trudges to the front yard.

Kris's house is still pitch dark, but I can't help but feel wrong talking to Aubrey back here. Like I'm still betraying Kris somehow. I sit next to her.

"What's wrong?" I ask.

"Nothing."

"Bullshit."

"Oh well."

I kick at a patch of grass below me. "Stop with this hot and cold act. It's getting really old."

"Why do you like me? Honest answer. You barely know me."

"I don't know."

"You don't know because it's not real. Your brain is latching on to something familiar and safe. I'm safe to you. Having feelings for me is your way to cope with the pain and the fear. It's not real. You and Kris were real. We're just a fling. That's all."

"I don't know because I'm not trying to question it like you are. I don't want to know why. I couldn't care less. I just know how I feel and what I want. And what I feel is real enough to me. And what I want is you, Aubrey."

She plucks blades of grass from the ground and lets them fall one by one.

"I'm leaving. For good. Never coming back. It's stupid to have any feelings for me whatsoever."

"Not to me."

She points in the direction Jenna went. "Girls fling themselves at you, and you act like you're clueless. You can have any girl. Look at Jenna."

"Jenna? What does she have to do with this?"

"You are seriously so frustrating and naïve sometimes. I want to punch you all over again."

I reach out and hold on to one of the chains of the swing and shove it backward. When it swings back, she hops off the slide and takes a few steps forward. Silent. I get up and walk in front of her.

"Stop pushing me away."

"We'd never work as a couple, Grayson. We're two different people. Even if I wasn't leaving. We'd never last."

"You don't know that."

"I don't do relationships. I never have."

"I just want you, not the title."

She pushes past me and walks to the front of the house. I grab her shoulder and whip her around, press my lips into hers, and wrap her in an embrace. At first she gives in, opens her mouth. But then she must realize that we're still fighting, because she pushes against my chest until we separate. She slaps me.

My hand rushes to my face. It stings. I take a step back.

Why the fuck does everyone keep slapping you?

"I'm not property you can control or manipulate. I said it's over. I mean it."

"Don't do this, Aubrey. I know you care about me too."

"I do. But I can't do this. I won't. It'll make it harder for me after I'm gone. Harder for you. What will we be? A long-distance relationship? Phone calls? Pen pals? Write each other emails? Texting? I don't have a cell phone that's not pre-paid. You'll promise to come up and visit, until you don't, or it gets too hard to keep driving to me every weekend. Or you'll meet someone new. Or maybe I will. Because if it's not distance, Grayson, it's me. I'll find a way to fuck it up. 'Cause it's what I always do in every town I've ever lived in. I self-destruct when things get too good, when I'm too happy. I don't trust happiness."

Aubrey continues walking past the car and toward the center of town. Reefer and Jenna stand by the hood, arguing about something and pointing in our direction. We catch their attention, but Jenna looks away.

Reefer steps around the hood and calls to me. "Yo, just leave her, man. Let's just go home. C'mon. She's not worth it."

I ignore him and run after her.

From behind me: "Never mind. I guess I don't exist, right?"

My face throbs, but the adrenaline is too much to care. I won't let her get away. Not this time. I catch up to her.

"You won't do that to me."

"How do you know?"

She stops and whirls around to face me. Without a second thought, I step up to her and place my hands over her cheeks and pull her face closer to mine.

"Because—"

And then I kiss her.

And she kisses me back.

And our tongues meet somewhere in the middle.

She breathes into my mouth, and I melt against her. My knees go weak and we fall down to the ground, rolling onto the dewy grass of whatever house we're in front of. Aubrey waits until I'm on my back and straddles my hips. She leans down, kisses my cheeks, and licks a trail down to my neck. I run my hands over her back and down her sides until they reach the fishnets.

She sits up to catch a breath and places her hands on my chest. We are both panting, and she lifts my shirt and bends down to litter my skin in tiny kisses; each one rattles my body, sends my nerves jumping on edge. I don't even care at this point who is watching. It's all too perfect. Too right.

"Aubrey," I pant. "I lo—"

"Don't," she whispers. "Not now."

I bite my tongue to stop the words that feel like they're ready to burst out from my chest. So I prop myself up, take one of her hands, and roll down the arm-length fingerless gloves. She's still on top of me, her entire body on alert. I do it without even thinking.

On her wrist, in different faded colors and scars, are cuts. Each one horizontal. Some no more than a prick, others nearly an inch long. They cover the entire arm nearly up to the elbow. Some are nothing but a faint scar from another time.

Both our bodies stop, our breaths still. And I know why she

has these on all day. Why she never removed them when we went swimming. And I try to find solid ground, but I'm dizzy, so I close my eyes until my head levels out and open them again.

I lower my head and gently kiss her arm. From the elbow up to her wrist. Each scar a tiny prickle on my lips. I look at her eyes to make sure it's okay as I run my fingers over them. To feel them. To somehow get inside the mind of the young Aubrey who did this to herself. Forever reminders of a time in her life. Always there. Hidden. Something that she can now share with me too.

I'm upset. So upset that she'd ever do this to her supple skin. Think that harming herself was ever okay. But I try not to judge—try to accept it as another part of her that is beautiful.

I kiss her wrist one more time and pull up the glove to cover her arm.

We both get back up. As I stand there looking at Aubrey, I'm filled with different questions, but none seem important. The only thing that matters is here and now and the time we have left. She grabs my hand.

"It'll hurt when I have to leave."

I lean in and kiss her on the nose. She breathes out, the air tickling the corner of my mouth. "Then we better make the most of tonight."

I smile. She smiles.

Up in the night sky, the crescent moon looks down at us, and I know that the possibilities are endless. The road full of forks and different paths. But it's a ride I want to experience.

No shortcuts. No rests.

Just the open road and Aubrey.

An infinite time.

"Come on," I say. "Let's go live."

2 HOURS UNTIL

SOMETIME AFTER 5:00 AM

REEFER PARKS IN FRONT OF TIM'S HOUSE. IT'S SMALL, ONLY one story. No pool or hot tub, and the outside looks as if his parents couldn't care less about upkeep. The grass is long and full of weeds, like it hasn't been cut in a few weeks. The streets are littered with cars from people probably passed out drunk at the party. Almost every house on this street has a combination of a pine or spruce or maple tree.

We walk along the sidewalk, and I stop to turn to look at a spot in the street similar to where Bryson was hit. It's not exactly the same, but close enough. I blink, and his body hits the front fender of the truck. I see his feet bend underneath the grill and his body get flung like a pancake as the pickup truck rams past him. I shake away the image and continue up the porch steps.

In the far distance, a glimpse of light seeps onto the horizon, like a flick of red paint on blank canvas. Dawn will be here soon.

Light amidst the darkness.

"You sure about this?" Reefer asks.

"Not at all."

He and Jenna exchange a glance.

"Fair enough."

Reefer is the first to enter; the door is still unlocked. Inside, the main living room is full of people passed out on the couch and a few face down on the floor. One kid snores in an armchair, his face covered in black marker. Straight ahead is a hallway filled with pictures of Tim and his family. We walk through it and past the aroma of stale beer and smoke. I tiptoe with Jenna, but Aubrey and Reefer bound through without a care.

I'm afraid that everyone is asleep. Then I spot Kyle and Tim in the kitchen at the end of the hallway. They are the only two still up, sharing a frozen pizza. Tim's face is swollen and wrapped in gauze and bandages. One eye is nearly swollen shut, and half his face is covered in purple bruises, just beginning to jaundice. They both look up, bewildered, before the reality of it sinks in. Tim's eyes flicker to Aubrey, and he shrinks back in his seat.

"You don't know how to stay out of trouble," Kyle says with a full mouth. "Do you, Falconi?"

"I need to talk to you," I say.

"I told you that we're done. I have nothing left to say to you." He wipes his mouth with a napkin, looking conflicted, and throws it on the table. "How're you feeling?" Kyle's right hand is swollen and cut up from the fight at the fair. We look down at it, and he shakes his head. He looks up and studies my face, raises one side of his mouth in a smirk. "I think there's more damage to your face than my fist. Damn, you look terrible. The right side of your face is like a giant busted blood vessel."

Gray, how messed up is your face?

I look at Aubrey and she smirks, pretending not to have heard. I turn back to Kyle. "I just came back from seeing your sister. We really need to talk in private."

His face goes dark like Kyle is ready to strangle me, but it subsides. He takes another bite of pizza. Tim doesn't say or do anything. Just sits there. I look back at Aubrey and motion to Tim.

She rolls her eyes. "Sorry about breaking your face."

"Fuck you, cunt."

I take a step forward, ready to knock his teeth out, but Aubrey stops me with her palm. She shakes her head, so I let it go. Even though I want nothing but to shut him up for good. Jenna or Reefer, I can't tell whom, snickers behind me.

"Don't ever call her that again," I threaten. "I'm done being a doormat to you, Tim." I grind my teeth. "Apologize to her. Right now."

"What did you say, you lil' shit?"

"I won't tell you again."

Reefer walks over to the table and picks up a slice of pepperoni pizza from the oven tray, and shoves half of it in his mouth. "I'm just gonna have some pizza, 'cause this tension is awkward... don't mind me at all."

Jenna, exasperated, stares daggers at Reefer, who just shrugs in response.

I make a motion with my fist to tell Reefer to cut the routine. He frowns, throws the rest of his pizza back on the tray, and wipes his greasy fingers on his mesh shorts. "Sure thing, Gray-Gray. Don't mind me; I'll just entertain myself." He pulls out his cell phone and pretends to play a game.

Jenna steps closer on the opposite side of me, so I'm sandwiched between her and Aubrey. I look over and smile politely, sneak a glance at Reefer. He tries to play it cool, but he stiffens again.

"You guys go outside," Jenna says. "We'll be okay in here."

Kyle drops his crust onto the kitchen table. He points out the window. "Back porch. If you hurt my sister again..."

Without another word, and the entire thing awkward as hell, we walk out of the kitchen and down the hall to the back door. It leads out to the deck where we used to smoke cigars on weekend nights spent at Tim's house. No one is outside, and Kyle turns on a porch light before shutting the sliding glass door behind us. We stand in silence for a while, both leaning over the ledge of the deck and looking out into the backyard. I can see my breath in the chilly night air.

"I'm sorry about being an asshole."

He snickers. "You fucking with me, Falconi?"

"I'm serious."

He looks over, one corner of his mouth turned up, ready to laugh in my face. But it drops, and Kyle reaches up to remove his Red Sox baseball cap and ruffle his blond hair. He smacks the cap onto the wooden ledge we lean on.

"What do you want? Pat on the back? A goddamn medal? Gray Falconi is sorry about being an ass!" he announces with bravado, then looks over at me. "Anything else?"

"That's it. I just wanted you to know that I'm not going to bother you or Kris anymore. Pretty sure she hates me. But I gave her, I don't know, closure, I guess." I breathe out. "She finally opened up to me. And I think she's going to be okay, you know? Just a feeling I have."

Kyle puts on his cap backward and slams his palm into the ledge. "God, you're frustrating. I should hate you."

I nod, ashamed. "I know." Take a deep breath. "I've been so absorbed in my own life, thinking I was the only one really affected by that accident." I lean an elbow on the ledge. "Took me a while to realize it messed up all of us who were there. You were my friend, and I took advantage of it."

"You can say that."

"I'm sorry I never went to visit your dad in the hospital. Or checked on your mom. I've known you guys since we were in elementary school. I was wrong. I *am* wrong." I take a breath. "I asked Kris if it would be okay if I visited your dad tomorrow. I'll never be ready or okay about it, but I want to go. Kris was okay with it, but I won't go if you don't want me to. You have every right to say no."

He grinds his teeth. "It won't make up for the past six months."

"I know."

"But it's a start." A beat. "I still don't forgive you."

"I wouldn't expect you to."

He mumbles under his breath, spits saliva over the deck ledge into the grass.

"Well... sorry for being a dick, I guess." He snickers again. "This doesn't change anything." He picks at a fingernail. "Can't say I didn't enjoy watching Tim get his ass kicked by a girl, though. Aubrey Fisher." He shakes his head.

I perk up at the sound of his name—a thought comes to mind. "Hey, have you or Tim been texting me today from an unknown number? I get it if you are. I've had it coming for a long time."

"What're you talking 'bout?"

"The calls and texts... threatening me and Aubrey? That isn't you or Tim?"

He rubs his eyes. "No. You mean like an anonymous call?"

"Is it Tim?"

He shrugs his shoulders, and we walk back inside.

"So, you and Aubrey like a thing now?" he whispers.

I can't help the smile that crosses my lips. "I don't know. Maybe."

He mumbles something. "My sister to Aubrey Fisher. Classy." A beat. "She's kind of got this sexiness about her, I guess. But you're still an asshole."

"Yeah. I know."

We enter the kitchen, and everyone is silent. Tim doesn't move, still slumped in the chair. Aubrey sits in Kyle's spot, her legs hiked up on the table and hands resting behind her neck. Reefer paces back and forth, hums a country tune I don't know. Jenna leans against a cabinet, looking at her phone. She smiles lightly when I enter.

Kyle asks Tim about the texts, but he shakes his head, doesn't fess up—just plays with his many bracelets. It makes no sense. Unless it was someone else that I'd burned in the last few months, or some random kid from school, it doesn't add up.

"That guy is still texting you?" Reefer asks.

Jenna looks up. "Wait, what texts?"

I tell her the story; her jaw drops.

"Did you call the cops?"

"What am I going to tell them, Jenna? I've already been arrested for some serious stuff."

"Who cares?" Aubrey chimes in. "We had fun."

We both exchange quick smiles.

"I'm sorry, wasn't she, like, expelled for this kind of stuff?" Reefer says. "You're not really the best type of person to be giving life advice to our boy over here. Look at him!" He points. "He looks like someone just shit all over him, ate the shit-covered Gray, and then shit out the shit-covered Gray shit."

"Why do you open your mouth half the time?" Jenna says.

"You're very protective of him, aren't you?" Aubrey teases.

"Speaking of shit..." Reefer cranes his neck, stands erect and looks around, his eyes large. "Tim, I need to use the men's facilities... it's quite an urgent matter, my man... I've had terrible gas all day." He stands on his tiptoes and then falls back on his heels. "The problems of being pleasantly plump."

Tim shakes his head but winces from the pain. "You're NOT droppin' a load in my house, you fuckin' fat piece of shit."

"What did you say?" Jenna and I step up in unison.

"Knock it off, Tim," Kyle mumbles. "Just let him use it; what do you care? You have your own bathroom upstairs."

Tim attempts to argue, chokes on his words, and points into the other room, defeated. Reefer bends over, grateful, and shuffles away, holding his ass.

"Don't do anything drastic 'till I return, y'all! It'll be a quick unloading and then I'll be right back."

And then he's gone.

"That was weird." I clap my hands together, look around. "Back to it. Is there a way to trace this guy?"

"Where's your phone?" Kyle asks.

"You want to help us?" Jenna yawns.

"Believe it or not, I never hated either of you. Or Reefer." He picks up his crust from the table and takes a bite. "But this doesn't mean we're cool either. I'm just curious."

Aubrey gets up from the table and walks to me. Grabs my hand. Tingles crawl through my veins. I want to kiss her again, but I resist the urge.

Jenna looks away from us.

"It's dead." I reach into my pocket and hand it to Kyle. "Needs to be charged."

"We have the same phone. Gimme a sec."

Kyle dashes out of the kitchen and goes into the front living room. He comes back moments later with a charger. He plugs my phone into the wall and waits for the screen to load. I put in my password and show him the texts and calls from the unknown number. Both of them were from the same number. It could be more than one person trying to scare me. From the other room, the sound of a toilet flushing resonates.

"This is *so* exciting!" Jenna grins and grinds her feet into the floor like a little kid on Christmas. "I feel like we're in a thriller or something, trying to track down the killer." She nudges my shoulder. "What will you do if we can really trace her down?"

"I don't know. I never really gave it much thought. And what do you mean *her*?"

"Don't assume it's a guy, Gray." She rubs my shoulder. "Girls can be relentless."

"Yeah, I guess."

"You try calling them back?" Kyle asks.

I shake my head. "I thought you couldn't with blocked numbers?"

"Luckily, I know a way to hack this ridiculous app that will route it back to the source phone."

"Then call it, smartass," Aubrey says.

She turns to me and beams. I lean in and give her a quick peck on the lips. Kyle ignores the exchange and fidgets with my phone. Tim glares at the two of us, still silent. Behind me, Reefer groans exaggeratedly, walking into the kitchen, wiping his hands on his shorts.

"PDA is gross, guys. I'm tired. Can we go and do this in the morning?"

I flip Reefer off, grinning. "That was a quick one."

"I don't waste my time." He steps closer to Jenna with his arms outstretched as if to give her a hug, but she yelps and ducks away.

"Ew, Reefer, no! Did you even wash your hands?"

She ducks to the other side of the kitchen, and Reefer laughs to himself, but there's a hint of hurt there.

And suddenly I'm both nervous and excited. Earlier I would've welcomed the threats as real. Would've gladly let whomever it was actually do what they preached. But now things are different. I'm different. Now all I want to do is find out who this person is and hope it's nothing more than a sick prank.

I can't imagine any harm coming to Aubrey. Not in a million years.

And then I look over at her and see how absolutely beautiful she is in all her imperfections. Her lack of makeup and brushed hair. The absurdly sexy way she dresses, and the attitude that makes me want to fight for a future with her.

"It's an encrypted, fake number," Kyle says. "Probably one of those cell phone apps you can download. Pretty sure you can call it and it should ring from the app if the person still has it on."

"So they might answer?" I ask.

"That's the idea." He turns to me. "Shall I?"

I nod.

"I still can't believe anyone would do this to you, Gray." Jenna bites her lip. "You're seriously one of the most humble guys at this school."

"Can't wait to kick his ass," Aubrey says.

"Is this all you care about?" Reefer's voice shakes. "Fighting people and shit?"

I turn to him. "Reef, knock it off."

Kyle dials the number, puts it on speaker, and we wait for the ring to begin.

Reefers steps toward Kyle. "Maybe this is a bad idea. We shouldn't—"

But it does.

Ringgggggggggg.

Nothing.

Ringgggggggggggg.

And then I hear it. Not from the phone, but muffled. From someone's pocket to my right. At first I think I'm imagining it, but Aubrey and Jenna both scrunch their faces and look around. Even Tim perks his head up.

Then the ringing becomes clear, and I don't want to believe it: the song. It's a ringtone. The one I know too well. The one that I hear almost every day. The twangy one with the guitars and the banjo.

Reefer's ringtone.

Aubrey, Jenna, and Kyle realize this as I do, and we look over. Reefer is frozen like a statue. His face is beet-red, and his eyes meet mine. I can't move. Can't speak. It's like we're all in suspended animation.

No. No. No. It's not him. Has to be a mistake.

Aubrey rushes over and reaches into Reefer's pocket for the phone. He doesn't react or try and fight her off. But once she has it, she holds it up, and it's my phone calling him: Gray-Gray.

Nononononononono.

Kyle ends the call and hands me back my phone. He takes a step back and leans against the wall. Tim snorts from behind me. Aubrey looks back at me, and I see anger in her eyes.

My mouth is dry, and the ticking in my head comes back, the steady pulse of the panic I know is coming. I press a hand into the bruise over my chest and push at it, but the pain doesn't help.

Why won't the pain help now?

Reefer trembles and snatches the phone out of Aubrey's hands. "Gray—"

I can't seem to catch a steady breath. I bend over and cough a few times, but the room is suddenly hot. I wipe sweat off my forehead, and then Aubrey's hands are around me, and she's whispering in my ear, but I can't hear it.

"Gray..." Reefer starts again, his voice shaking nearly as bad as mine. "Listen to me... it's not what you think."

I try to speak, but no words come. It's like my tongue is swollen and oozing pus. The crushing waves of anxiety are back. Worse than before. I fall to my knees and beat at my chest.

Aubrey pries my hands away, and I'm in her arms. She's kissing me. Her lips touch mine. Her tongue explores mine. Her hands grope mine. And she's so soft and warm. So delicate and precious.

She brings me back from the edge. She always does. Like it's the only sure-fire way to find solid ground—our bodies together as one.

There is shouting. But none of what's said registers. I know that Reefer walks close to bend down, but Aubrey—or maybe Jenna—pushes him away. I'm not sure whom. All I know is that it hurts. Seeing Reefer hurts. And then I find my voice:

"What's going on?"

Everyone quiets down, and when the haziness clears and the waves dissipate, Aubrey is right in front of me. I extend a finger and trace it along her lips. My heart slowly calms its maddening pulse.

Her eyebrows are furrowed, and she leans down and kisses my lips again, holds it for a moment before pulling back. Her eyes ask me if I'll be okay, and I nod in return. But we both know it's a lie.

"Gray—" Reefer starts.

"What's going on?" I ask again, my voice harder.

"I don't know."

"Bullshit." I shakily get to my feet with the help of Aubrey and Jenna. "Start talking. Now. I'm done playing games."

"Gray-Gray—"

"Enough!" I shout. "Talk now. Tell me that this is a mistake."

Reefer shuffles his feet on the ground and clears his throat. The non-response is all I need to know it's true.

"Guys, what's happening?" Kyle asks. "Is this shit for real?"

"Reefer..."

"I'm sorry, Gray."

My heart palpitates. "I don't understand..."

Aubrey positions herself slightly in front of me, ready to jump. I can see the pain in Reefer's eyes, but I don't know what to think anymore. Even Jenna steps away from him, unbelieving.

"I wasn't trying to hurt you."

Aubrey steps forward and shoves him in the chest. "Then why the hell are you calling him from fake numbers saying fucked up shit about us?" I pull her back into me before she has a chance to throw punches.

I need to hear why. Behind Aubrey's back, my fingers dig into my bruise.

Reefer looks past Aubrey to me. "I swear to God, Gray, I was only trying to help, ya know? I wasn't going to actually hurt y—"

"This is horseshit," Aubrey says.

"—but we haven't been best friends in a long time. And you're lying to yourself if you can't see that."

"What are you talking about?"

Reefer runs his hands over his face, and his eyes water up. It's the first time I've ever seen him this upset, on the verge of tears. His entire body trembles, and his face is so red I'm afraid he's going to pass out. It's like I'm battling the side that wants to feel hurt and betrayed and the side that doesn't want to accept it. I've known him like a brother for so long.

"When's the last time you were ever honest with me about everything?"

I want to respond, but he has a point.

"You've changed... you're not the same person, and I can see it. That's the messed up thing, isn't it? When you watch a person you've known your entire life throw theirs away day by day and piece by piece... and they won't even tell you they've given up."

The room is silent. Kyle and Tim seem to blend into the background behind me, just watching what feels like some twisted reality show. But they're not important anymore. Not to this. Even Jenna backs up to the table, unable to speak or comprehend. Aubrey doesn't make another move because I know that, in some way, she understands.

The weird thing is, I do too.

"S-So you thought threatening me and Aubrey would help me open up to you? Bringing up Bryson?" My fists shake at my sides. "What's wrong with you?"

He shakes his head and wipes a tear at the corner of his eye. "In the bathroom at school, you were ready to kill yourself, bro. You had the stupid piece of glass in your hand, just staring at it. If I didn't walk in when I did... I don't know. And then you lied to my face about it. To my *face*." He wipes at another tear, turns around, and punches the countertop behind me. Tim stirs in his seat. "All you do is lie, and I've tried to get you to open up, but you shut down every time." He punches the counter again. "I don't know why I said anything about Bryson... I—"

Reefer turns back around, his entire face as red as a tomato, and sweat rolls down from his hairline. He throws his phone against the kitchen wall. We all jump on impact, and his phone shatters into pieces.

"You need to leave," Tim groans. "You faggots are gonna wake everyone up or break my parents' shit."

Kyle nods his head and gets up to signal our leaving, but none of us move. We don't know how. So Reefer continues.

"You take everything for granted, Gray. Everything. Your parents are still together, they're not separated... and regardless of all the times you've blown off schoolwork, the teachers all tiptoe around you like it's nothing. I miss an assignment and my ass is grass, spoon-fed to my dad. But everyone gives you a free pass—extensions like it's nothing. And regardless of how much you try to get everyone to hate you, people still love you. Girls love you. I see it. You think girls look at me like that?" He jiggles his stomach underneath his shirt. "You whine on and on some days about how much weight you've gained. Get over yourself and your privilege, Gray. Try gaining another hundred pounds and then we'll talk about feeling insecure." He curses. "I'm a joke. No one will ever look at me like they do you. Teachers tolerate me, but I'm not a favorite. I don't have the grades to get into good schools. You do, but you choose to fail, and it pisses me off how many opportunities you just piss away. And not all of us have the luxury of one Christmas or Thanksgiving. Sometimes we have to split them up..."

"Get out of my house," Tim says.

Aubrey leans back into me. I don't know what she's thinking. Kyle attempts to step toward Reefer, but he holds up a finger. Kyle stops in place.

"I wasn't trying to hurt you, Gray. You're my best friend... I love you... you're like family. But I'm just that perverted friend, right? Pleasantly Plump Reefer." He looks at the broken pieces of phone on the ground. "You never ask about how I'm doing. It's always about you. Always you." He paces back and forth. "It's like I lost you the same night we lost *him* too."

Chills.

Tim slowly gets to his feet, in pain. We all turn around.

"Out." He points. "Out, or I'm gonna remove you all. This is like a soap opera for homos and lesbians."

Kyle turns around. "Tim, shut up with your antiquated hate speech. It's over." He curses. "We're not messing with them anymore. And it's not open for discussion. 'Cause *I* will beat your ass if you mess with them."

Tim begins to protest but winces as he opens his jaw. In front of me, I can feel Aubrey grin.

"You do need to leave before he flips," Kyle says to us. "Right now. Don't come back."

We lock eyes, and there's some sort of understanding there. Not forgiveness. I don't know if we'll be okay. We may never be. But in a way, he gets it.

"Can you take me home, Kyle?" Jenna asks in a hushed voice, staring at the floor. "I don't think I can go back with him."

"Freckles—"

"Don't," she says. "I need to go."

Reefer's eyes get huge, terrified. "Please let me—"

Jenna turns her back on him. Kyle looks between the two of them, uncomfortable, but after a few moments, he gives in and leaves to get his car keys.

"I'm disgusted with you," she says. "I don't know what's going on between you two, but best friends don't play games like this, Reefer. But, you'll never learn to grow up, will you?"

Reefer presses his palms into his temples and rubs them. He looks so lost. So unlike himself.

"Don't leave me."

She ignores him and turns to me, still not looking at Aubrey. "Come with me, Gray." Her eyes plead, but there's an odd sense of calm in them. Serenity. Like she is offering me so much more than just a car ride home. Wanting to somehow mend whatever she thinks is broken inside. "You shouldn't have to stay here."

Reefer mutters under his breath, but I know I can't just leave, not until I hear the rest. I shake my head, and although she's hurt I'd choose Reefer, I can tell she understands.

Kyle comes back with his keys and escorts us past the sleeping drunks and out the front door. Jenna and I hug, hers lasting longer than normal, and she squeezes my hands.

"Call me tomorrow, okay? Maybe see a movie or talk or whatever you want?"

I nod.

"Freckles, please—"

Reefer attempts to step up to her, but she hops off the porch and walks away with Kyle down the street to get his car. We watch them until they disappear behind a pine tree.

Reefer, Aubrey, and I are left standing on the front porch in silence. Neither knows what to say. I want to believe he did this because he cares, because he was worried about me. But another part can't help but think how selfish and wrong it all is. The horrible things he'd said about Aubrey. I was prepared to die if it came to that, and now... now the texts seem like a desperate act. So unlike Reefer.

But maybe that's the point: I don't know as much about him as I thought I did.

"You know Freckles adores you?" he says. "She'd do anything for you. Have you even bothered to notice? In the years we've been friends, have you picked up on how much she cares for you?"

"What do you mean?"

"I would give anything, Gray... *anything* for that girl to give me the time of day. And I try... holy balls, do I try. But how can I when I have a best friend who overshadows me in every single aspect?"

And then the pieces start to come together. It begins to make sense, and I feel so stupid and selfish that I never noticed it before. So I state the only thing that my mouth can support:

"You love her."

He snorts. "Welcome to the real world, Gray. Did you enjoy your trip while away?" He frowns at his own sarcasm, disappointed in himself. "Guess it doesn't matter anyway. You'll never see her as more than a friend, and she'll never see me as anything more than your perverted, fat friend."

"Reef—"

He shakes his head. "I love you. You've been my brother ever since I can remember, but you can be a selfish asshole sometimes."

He's right.

"S-So were you just going to keep texting me until I opened up to you? Was that the endgame?"

Reefer sighs and walks to sit down on the dewy front lawn. "I don't know... I guess I never really gave it much thought. Typical Reefer, right? Always the one to come in last place. The brunt of the joke. Never the guy who gets the girl. Always a fuckup." He pulls out blades of grass and throws them in the air. "Guess my dad is right."

My heart shatters like ceramic.

"You should've just talked to me about it."

"You don't talk. You lie. And then this!" He points to me and Aubrey. I don't realize we're holding hands until he motions to it. "One day you're suddenly different? Six months you're shutting yourself off from the world, and suddenly now, because of Aubrey, you're a new person?" He curses. "What's so special about her that you couldn't talk to me?" He punches the ground. "Why *her* and not *me*!"

And then Reefer is crying. It's so sad to watch. There are some people who look graceful and heartbreaking when they cry, but Reefer is not one of them. It's messy.

"The difference," Aubrey says, "is that I don't give him an out. I push him until he's forced to act. You think tricking him will do it, that if you stand patiently by, it will solve itself." She takes her hand out of mine and walks to Reefer in the grass. "That's the problem with society. They see depression and anxiety and suicide as a huge taboo inconvenience, and no one really gives a shit to stop and think that it's a problem. A disease. Not something you can sweep under the rug." She kneels down and places a hand on his shoulder. "Gray needed me to see his pain, call him out on it, and push him to see that there's a way to live with it. It doesn't go away. Pain never does. Loss never does. It stays. But you learn to live with it."

Aubrey pats his shoulder as his entire body shakes, and after a moment I join her. Reefer sobs into my chest as I pull him into a hug. Then I realize what I've been missing:

I've been so self-absorbed in my own world—my own problems and privilege—that I never stopped to realize what's been going on around me. Reefer has pain too. Just like me. He may not have lost a brother, but I've never stopped to ask him how he was doing. Not once. Never put together all the times Jenna ever stared or touched or complimented me. The times she'd want to hang outside of school without Reefer around.

How I never questioned why Reefer stopped inviting me over to his house. Never thought to ask where his father's wedding band went.

And then it hits me:

Everyone is a little broken inside.

Instead of saying anything, all three of us sit in the grass, our butts wet from the dew. And I know that nothing will be the same. Aubrey is right: there is no more just strolling through life waiting for something to happen or things to be different. She's been trying to force me into action all day. To take control of my life.

That's exactly what I know I have to do from now on. Life doesn't wait; we have to go out and get it. We have to want a better life to get a better life. I'm not the only one with issues. Aubrey and Reefer have them. Kris and Kyle have them. Jenna has them. My parents. We all do. No one is perfect or always happy. Everyone has problems. Everyone gets depressed. But maybe the point is not to be painless but to find a way to live with it. To connect with others and find a way.

In twenty-four hours, I've learned more about my friends than I ever have before. I've learned more about myself than I ever have.

In twenty-four hours, I found Aubrey.

And in nearly as long, I'll lose her again.

I raise my head and lean in to press my forehead against

hers. No words need to be said. All the thanks I could ever utter are in this moment.

So we all sit there. Reefer sobbing into my shirt until he calms down. Me and Aubrey holding each other like a wind will come and take one of us away forever. I don't know what this means for me and Reefer, if we will be okay in the morning. If I can forgive him. But for right now, it's okay. Right now is good.

Aubrey breathes out; I feel it on my chin and close my eyes.

And, finally, there's peace.

1 HOUR UNTIL

THERE ARE FOUR THINGS THAT I KNOW ARE TRUE IN LIFE: it's unpredictable, it's messy, it's funny when you least expect it, and it's beautiful. Like a chill on a humid summer day, some things happen out of nowhere.

That's what today has been: unexpected.

Aubrey and I walk down the lonely street; the gray sky begins to disappear, like a blank canvas slowly filling up with bright splashes of color. The red dawn edges the horizon, ready to start a new day. The stars are gone. The moon in slumber. The yellow sun rising.

A new day and I'm still here.

Reefer leaves us. There are things we need to discuss and work out. Stuff we both need to confess and get off our chests, but nothing that can't wait until the morning, or rather, later today. The three of us sit in the grass for a while. Reefer begs to drive us home, but I want to take the walk with Aubrey. Enjoy the sounds and smells of the rising dawn.

"Are you gonna be okay, Gray-Gray... like... are we okay?"

"I don't hate you, Reef. But you said a lot of personal stuff, and I'm sure I had a bunch of it coming. I'm just confused. We'll talk later."

"Alright, that's legit... maybe we can get ice cream like old times and just talk... or whatever. Otherwise, I'll be forced to gorge myself alone... thus overloading on carbs and sugar and dairy... which means I'll get gassy... literally nobody likes a gassy Reef-a-nater. Fact. You know—"

"I get it. Just too tired to joke right now. I'll text you, okay?"

I know he's hurt. It takes a while, but his trademark goofy grin comes back. "Okay, word... some solid Gray and Reef-a-nater Time... or Gray-a-nater Time... or Reefay Time... Greef Time...I'll have to work on the title."

I force a smile. "Whatever you say, Reef."

It's silent for a moment, and I know he's waiting to ask something, fighting himself not to, but he does anyway.

"Do you think she'll ever forgive me?"

It takes all I have not to lean in and wrap him in a hug, but a part of me still feels the need to keep a distance. The pain in his eyes is so immense. So new. Never-ending. And I know it—it's the same feeling I have at the thought of losing Aubrey.

"Do you really love her?"

He chews on his lip and nods. "I don't deserve her."

I put a hand on his shoulder. "What would you do to get her back?"

"Anything, bro. That girl... she's on a whole other level."

I turn to Aubrey, and we both share a grin.

"Then you do whatever it takes."

And this new role, this new, confident person, is so different for me. So foreign. It's been a long time since I've been this guy.

Reefer looks up, hopeful, like a little kid. "You think Freckles is ready for that?"

"Knowing you, probably not." I smile. "But she'd be lucky to have you, Reef. I mean that."

He nods, smiles.

So after we hug, Aubrey gets the wooden box and grocery bag from the backseat, and Reefer drives away without us—texting me at least six times in a row. But the answers he wants can wait. In the meantime, I make sure to respond so he knows we're still okay.

Aubrey and I pass the main intersection and make our way to my house on Oakhurst. We hold hands on the way, yawning every few feet. I shake away sleep; my head bobs up and down occasionally. Aubrey laughs every time I do. I don't realize how tired I really am until now. I've been awake for nearly twenty-four hours.

"Do you want a pacifier?" Aubrey grins, lopsided.

I flip her off. "You did this. You can deal with the consequences."

"So feisty tonight. It's too bad you're against having sex. It'd be hot. The things I'd—"

I hold up a hand. "I'd fall asleep right on top of you. Or underneath you. Possibly inside of you. Plus, I still have to pee *really* bad right now." I stroke my chin in mock contemplation. "We never did find that table to hump on, did we?"

She cranes her neck and laughs from the belly. Her entire body shakes. It's contagious enough to make me giggle.

"This is the Grayson I knew was always there. Confident, funny, horny, sexy as hell, and brooding when you need to be. This is why people love you."

"Do those people include Aubrey Fisher?"

She squints her eyes. "Now, why would you go and think something like that?"

"Because I love watching you squirm."

She guffaws and leans in to punch me, but because I know her, I catch it with my palm and wink.

"This is not fair! Stop using my own lines against me."

"Ohmygod. You're being *such a girl* right now."

She rolls her eyes, and I smile to myself.

"So what about your writing? Do you think you've been inspired yet?"

I chew on the thought. "I don't know. Maybe."

"Just promise me that you won't give it up. You have too much talent to throw it away. Promise me."

"Will JamesDeanFan support me if I do?"

She grins, lopsided. "JamesDeanFan will follow you wherever."

"So, she's a true Falconian?"

"Eh, I wouldn't go that far. Nothing you do or say could make that term cool. Even *I* have my limits of what to push in one night."

We chuckle and continue to walk in silence.

It's not long before we pass the town cemetery a block away from my street. We both stop in front of it, and I look past the iron fence to the rows of headstones. Bryson is back and to the left. I can't make out his grave, but I know the flowers Mom planted are still there. The Yankees baseball cap he always wore still resting on one of the corners. The etching in the stone:

Beloved Son, Beloved Brother

I'd visited him several times after the accident before I stopped going completely. Hoping and praying it was just a bad dream, and I'd wake up in bed with Bryson sprawled out on the floor in his sleeping bag. Like we used to do on nights he was too scared to sleep alone. It was always me he'd go to for comfort. Not Mom or Dad. Me.

Aubrey lets me stop to reflect for a moment before I turn, grit my teeth, and nudge us forward. It's still too soon—something I'm not yet ready for.

"Do you think it's too late to say goodbye?" I ask. "I never got the chance."

"It's never too late."

We turn down my street, the sky beginning to turn red and pink on the horizon. I stumble a little, but Aubrey catches me. We reach my driveway a few seconds later. Dad's car is gone. I don't say anything, and I'm not sure if Aubrey notices it missing. Mom's car is still there. The front porch light on—as if left just for me.

"Do you want to come inside?"

She runs a hand through her hair. "Aw, you want me to tuck you in."

I flip her off again but chuckle. "After everything we've been through, you still find ways to break my balls. Awesome."

She giggles. "C'mon, let's get you in bed."

We walk up the sidewalk to the front door, and Aubrey admires Mom's garden again. The hydrangeas, pansies, and daffodils stand out amongst the several others. Even in her state, Mom never stopped taking care of it. It always used to be Bryson's favorite.

The first chirp of a bird comes from a pine tree.

"I used to grow flowers with my Mom before she left." She takes a deep breath. "Yours are really beautiful."

I get chills up my arms. "Yeah." I look at the side of her face. "They are."

She turns to me and gives another lopsided smile before we step into the house. The front door is unlocked. The house is dark except for the outline of the TV from the back, where Mom sleeps every night. We take off our shoes and tiptoe into the family room. The blinds are drawn on the windows, though slivers of light seep through. The TV is muted, and Mom is asleep on the couch, head nestled in her hands and the blanket on the ground. There is an empty mug of black tea and a prescription bottle of Xanax on the floor.

I don't want Aubrey to see this; it's almost embarrassing. But

I take one look at my mom and can't help but feel sad. I pick up the blanket and drape it over her body. She's shivering, and once I do, it subsides. I lean down and kiss her on the forehead.

"I love you, Mom."

She mumbles an incoherent response, and for just a second, I think she smiles.

Things don't change overnight, Gray. She needs help.

Aubrey picks up the prescription bottle and empty mug. We deposit them on the kitchen counter and head up the stairs. Right above the landing is Bryson's closed door.

I shake away the dizziness of sleep and reach out a hand to jiggle the doorknob. I don't know why I do it, but like a ritual, I test it.

Maybe Dad came home to unlock it. Maybe he changed his mind. Maybe—

Locked. Always locked.

When do you think he'll come back this time?

And I want to cry. Want to turn around and embrace Aubrey. But she must already sense this because her hands wrap around my waist, and her head rests on my shoulder.

"They just need time," she whispers. "But you should never stop pushing them." She kisses my neck, and I close my eyes. "Everyone grieves differently. This is just how they do it."

I lean my head over to rest on top of hers.

"I just wish they didn't have to be in pain anymore."

"I know."

I reach into the pocket of my jeans and pull out the envelope I was going to give him on his birthday with the Yankees tickets. I run my hands over his name scrawled in the black ink, touch a corner to my chin, and lean down to shove the envelope under the threshold and into his room.

"Happy birthday, little man." I stand back up. "Wherever you are."

We stay there and stare at his bare door for a while, and I feel sad just looking at it, so after a moment, I lead us into my room to the left. We walk in, shut the door, and leave the lights off. It's quiet. Eerie. But a faint glow comes from the drawn blinds. The pre-dawn nearly here. The prisms of light almost within reach.

The bed is in front of me, and without thinking, I flop down face first into my pillow. It still smells of my shampoo.

"This room is so sad," Aubrey says, places the plastic bag and wooden box on my dresser.

I roll over and find her walking around the room, running her hands over the blank surfaces where my posters used to be.

"I just thought it would make things easier."

She turns and nods, but it's a lonely one, and it makes my stomach tighten up into knots.

"We'll need to start adding some life to these walls again."

And there's something about what she says, how she vocalizes *life*. I sit up.

"Does that mean you'll stay?"

Aubrey stops in place, her back to me, and slumps her shoulders.

"No."

"When will you be gone?"

She turns. "My social worker will probably be down to visit tomorrow. They're used to this with me. I've been kicked out of homes and schools before. Depends how fast they can find a new one. But it won't be long. They'll find a new family pretty quick."

"And there's no way you can stay with the Bells and go to another district?"

She shakes her head. "Do you have a permanent marker?"

"Um, probably downstairs in my dad's computer room. Why?"

Aubrey doesn't respond. She runs a few fingers over the bare wall again and turns around. She looks me up and down and hops next to me on the bed. We sit there in silence until I feel her yawn. When I look over, she's rubbing her eyes. I yawn in reaction.

"Why do I feel like this is a goodbye?"

She looks down at her hands and scratches at the black nail polish on each middle finger. Her nonresponse is once again all the answer that I need. It's like we've both known each other for what feels like forever. Like when you can look at someone and just know without words.

I try not to let that creeping, empty feeling into my heart, but it's hard. I feel like my eyes are watering, so I lie on my back and climb underneath the covers. I lift up the sheets on the opposite side of the bed for her, and she crawls underneath without hesitation. We snuggle closer together and lie on our sides so we face each other. I struggle to keep my eyes open. I don't want to *not* see her. Not look into her amber eyes. To wake up tomorrow and face everything alone. There's so much that's different and yet so much that's still the same.

I lean in and kiss her lips. She kisses mine back.

"I still feel like there's so much about you that I don't know," I say. "Like Gus and Liza, where you've been in the past..."

She strokes my cheek. "Stories for another time."

I nod, mull over something in my mind that Reefer had asked. "You have a tattoo?"

She hesitates for a moment, alert, nervous, but slowly nods.

"Can I see it?"

She forces a smile and, after a moment, pulls her shirt up to her neck and lifts up the bottom of her bra. Not enough to see anything, but just enough to see the small black script below her left breast:

Dean

I reach out and run my hand over it. It's so simple, yet so perfect. She lowers her shirt back down. We lock eyes.

And within these moments of staring at each other, it hits me: all I've been trying to do is die, and Aubrey's taught me how to live again. It seems so obvious, but it makes more sense now than it has all night. Her words echo in my head:

"If you follow me, what I'll show you will change your life."

I've gotten drunk and let loose, smoked weed for the first time, ditched school for the first time, finally had the courage to speak to Kyle and Kris, stand up to Tim, to tell my parents how I was feeling, the courage to see Reefer as just another person with problems, and even to forgive everyone. Forgive myself.

I've been trying to do everything for the last time, but Aubrey's taught me how to look at the world and do things for the first time.

It seems random. Like all the places Aubrey's taken me, and all the things we've done might not be anything more than half-hearted choices. And maybe they were. Maybe Aubrey had no step-by-step plan. But somehow it worked. It breathed air into my drowning lungs. Picked up the pieces of what was broken and taught me to find the strength to put them back together.

Aubrey isn't the glue. She never was.

And now I know.

Tonight was never really about just Aubrey. It was never about just me. It was everyone. All of us. Our stories. Not alone, but together, as one. Life is an assortment of faces and voices and art and music and beauty and people and places and things and so much more.

The glue in life is everything.

Aubrey can't stay because there's still so much more out there that she needs to figure out, so much more of her own story that comes after me. I'm just a chapter in her book.

I don't want to believe it, but as I look into her eyes, it's written in her irises.

"It won't be easy, will it?"

It's funny that she knows exactly what I mean without having to ask. She breathes out and finds my hands underneath the sheets. Interlocks her fingers in mine.

"No. You'll have good days. You'll have bad ones. Some might be just as bad as before. Others might be like how you've felt all night. But it won't be easy."

I just nod because I know Aubrey's right.

Life isn't easy—it's a puzzle, and everyone is just trying to figure out how all the pieces fit.

"You know," she says, "I could love you, Grayson."

The way that word, *love*, rolls off her tongue so tenderly, like it's sacred, makes my entire body ping—nerves on fire, the blood pumping in my veins. My heart opens up, and I want to let it all in: the good, the bad, the weird, the wonderful, the magnetic, the ironic, the hurtful, the painful, and the beautiful.

The *love*.

I don't know exactly how to respond. I just want to hold her in my arms forever. I want to wake up to her in the morning, roll over on my side, and be the first person she sees when she opens her eyes. I want to cook her breakfast and deliver it on a tray in bed like they do in really cheesy romantic comedies. I want to cherish every beauty mark and scar on her body. I want to take her to the movies, the drive-in. Go out on a date.

But I know that I can't. At least not right now. This is my story.

Aubrey has her own to tell.

And I know that she needs to face that by herself.

But maybe one day...

"Will I ever see you again?"

"I don't know."

"I hate when you do that."

"I don't belong in your life."

"Any life I want is one with you in it."

"I wish I could deserve you." She rolls on her back and away from me. "But I don't."

"Why?"

"I've done terrible things. Selfish things. I've never met anyone like you."

"What do you mean?"

"I always figured I'd be alone. No family. No commitment. No baggage. Just pack up and go when I'd left my mark somewhere. Just disappear and leave people wondering where I went and why. Figured this place would be no different."

"But then you met me?"

She yawns, flashing her tongue ring in the beams of morning light. I yawn back.

"You make me want to believe that I deserve a family."

"But not right now?"

She turns back and kisses me tenderly on the cheek.

"No. You still have a lot to figure out. I have a lot I need to figure out."

"Then stay here with me, and we'll figure it out together. Let me help you, Aubrey."

"No, Grayson. You can't help me. If I stay with you, I'll be just falling back into the same patterns. I need to fix myself so I can deserve you. But I need to do that on my own. So much of my life, I've let guys abuse me. Objectify me. A means to an end. Let myself become numb to what men want me for, what I give to them. Like I need to use my body and sex to feel validated. I don't want you to be like the others. You mean too much to me. And I don't want to be the person you need to survive when things get bad. We're just not good for each other right now."

I think I know what she means. We're too dependent on each other. I can't always expect Aubrey to be there to pull me back from the ledge to calm the anxiety. It's unrealistic to think she's the only thing that can save me.

A thought comes to me, and I force myself to sit up with Aubrey's help, but my body is slowly shutting down. I hobble off the bed and reach into my drawer that Aubrey had rifled through earlier when we left school. Underneath my underwear, my fingers find the silver chain, and I pull it out. Bryson's seashell necklace. I hold it up as it catches a beam of light through the blinds, and it reflects back the sun. My throat aches, and I wipe a tear from my eye.

I reach into my pocket and find the weed from the old bowling alley. I stare at them both and get back into bed. I turn to Aubrey and hold them out to her.

"What's this?" She furrows her brow.

"I want you to have them."

"Grayson—"

"Please, Aubrey. They're yours."

She hesitates, her eyes locked with mine.

"This was his, wasn't it?"

I fight back the urge to cry again and nod, blink away tears.

"He loved the beach. I found the seashells and made it for him. He never once took it off." I suck in a breath and hold it in my chest, my heart thumping in my ears. "He would've wanted you to have it."

Her bottom lip trembles, and instead of saying anything, nods. She lowers her head so I can fit it around her neck. It falls on her pale skin. She picks it up with her fingers, examines it, tucks it safely in her shirt, and takes the weed, a corner of her mouth turned up in a smile. She packs it away in her bra.

"It's perfect."

"You're perfect." I release the air in my chest. "So now you can take a piece of us wherever you go. Wherever life takes you." I grab her hand, interlock my fingers with hers, and lie back down. "Hopefully you won't forget me."

"I could never forget you, Grayson."

"Just promise me something."

"What?"

"That we'll see each other again. That we'll keep in contact. Stay friends. I don't care what we are or where we are or how long it's been. Even if it's in ten years." I yawn. "Promise me you'll say goodbye before you leave."

She doesn't say anything. I close my eyes even though I don't want to. I attempt to open them and find the strength, but I know it won't last long. I can feel sleep's sharp claws reach for me from the darkness.

I stare up into the prisms of sunlight, at the crystal-white particles just floating in the air. Unseen to the naked eye but brought to life in this time before dawn.

"It's beautiful, isn't it?" I ask.

And I close my eyes for the last time, unable to open them as sleep consumes me. But as I slip away, I feel Aubrey's arms wrap me in an embrace as she kisses the back of my neck. Feel her hot breath on my face as she scoots over and cuddles with me.

"What is?"

"Everything. Every single thing."

And I think I hear her say something, but I don't know what it is, because in a moment everything is silent.

Everything is peaceful.

Everything is perfect.

Everything is beautiful.

Beautiful...

Beautiful...

THE SUN IS OUT, AND THE SKIES ARE BLUE. THE CLEAR OCEAN waves wrap around my ankles. The sky is cloudless, and from above, I can hear the seagull cries. Waves roll into the rocks. The ocean is still and calm. Serene. The beach is mostly empty, and to my right is a sand castle. A little boy walks up to it with a yellow pail to dump ocean water into the tiny moat around the construction. A seashell necklace dangles from his neck.

It's Bryson.

I look down and move my feet forward, let the warm sun and salty ocean breeze engulf me. I'm shirtless, and Bryson turns around to look at me. He's beaming; his mouth open wide in glee. Happiness. He drops the yellow pail and waves to me. I wave back.

I don't need to say anything. Bryson doesn't either.

And I'm filled with an overwhelming sense of joy and excitement. Of love.

He finally made it back to the beach.

He turns around and runs toward the ocean water, laughing gleefully in his adorably sweet voice. Diving into a wave as it washes ashore, rolling in the wet sand.

So I watch my little brother play, knowing this is the last time I'll ever see him like this. Forever a little boy. The only thing he wanted from me. To take him back to the beach.

And finally, after all these months, he's here.

POST

SATURDAY, 2:33 PM

I OPEN MY EYES, AND EVERYTHING IS BRIGHT. LIGHT filters through the drawn blinds. I wipe a hand over my face and stretch—almost forget about Aubrey until I roll over on my side.

Nothing.

She's gone.

The sheets have been pulled back. The pillow still indented from the shape of her head.

I close my eyes a few times and reopen them in hopes she'll reappear, but she doesn't. I sit up and fling the covers off my body. There is momentary panic, but when I jump out of bed and open the blinds, it subsides. I knew this was coming. She told me she would do this.

I step up to the spot next to me where we fell asleep and press my face into the pillow and inhale her scent. Cigarettes and vanilla. I never want to wash the sheets again.

I look around my bright room, adjusting to the afternoon sun, feeling exhausted but somehow lighter. Like there's not as much weight on my heart. I have the urge to look in the mirror and inspect the damage to my face, so I do, because my entire head is pounding and sore. Instantly I look away.

It's way fucking worse than Aubrey told me it was. But in spite of it, I grin.

My phone is filled with missed calls and texts from Reefer and Jenna. I text them back, but the photo of me wrapping Bryson in a headlock is no longer on my lock screen. In its place is a picture of Aubrey from this morning. She's standing beside the bed while I'm asleep behind her, her red highlights shimmering from the camera flash, a glare from where the light bounces off her nose ring. She's smirking, one eyebrow arched—beautiful as hell.

I breathe deeply and run a thumb over the picture. I'll never take it off my phone.

From outside, I hear the sounds of my mother watering the plants with the hose. I open my bedroom door slowly and peek down the stairs where I can just see into a corner of the kitchen. Dad is at the table eating a salad for lunch.

Their weekend routine: always the same.

For a while I used to go over little things in my head that I could've done differently—things I could've changed. Like if I'd never left for the party that night, never let Bryson out of the car, never turned my back on him, never sped off with Kris, if her dad never hit that patch of black ice. Wondered for a while if I'd changed just the tiniest thing, if Bryson would still be alive. If my parents would still be happy and in love like they used to be.

So many what-ifs and choices and possibilities. I often think that maybe there is a life out there where Bryson is still alive. Where Dad is playing catch with him right now in the front yard while Mom is sitting out on a lawn chair getting a tan. Reefer and Kyle are sitting down in the grass arguing about basketball stats while Jenna rolls her eyes and quotes ancient movies. Where Kris is just coming back from a run down the block and jogging up the driveway to turn on the hose and cool off. Preparing for the Olympics one day. And I'm there waiting with a stopwatch.

Maybe, somewhere out there, that life exists. And we're all happy. I'm happy. And Bryson will grow up to be a baseball star, or a lawyer, or an astronaut. He'll enter middle school, high school, learn how to drive, have his first drink, go to homecoming and prom, get his first girlfriend, first kiss, have sex. Graduate. Get married. Have a full life.

But that's not my life.

This is my life.

And I only have one.

But I can't help but feel that wherever he is, Bryson is looking down on me from above, realizing how fragile life is. How every second counts. How he literally saved my life.

Maybe he never left.

I turn around and look at the white walls and remember what Aubrey said about filling them up with life.

With being alive.

I almost don't know where to start, but then I see it: the black writing in the space of wall right next to my dresser. In big, black permanent marker.

I know it's Aubrey's handwriting.

I run my hands over the letters, but it remains. Won't come out. Like a stain.

Aubrey's stain.

I smile because there's nothing else to do. I know why she left me this, and I know exactly what she wants me to do with it. And sure enough, I know now it's true:

I love Aubrey Fisher.

Looking around, on my dresser is the same marker with a small note written in black pen inside my notebook. College ruled. Next to it is the wooden box from the tattoo shop, full of pictures and notes and trinkets from Aubrey's life. Separated from the rest, tucked inside my open underwear drawer where the seashell necklace was, is the picture of her family at the barbeque. The one where they're all alive and happy and smiling. Innocent. Together. In love.

Mr. Falconi,

I trust that you'll know what to do. You'll notice a few things already scratched off. A few left that haven't been. And a few left for you to add. Whatever you want. Wherever life takes you. It's yours. Go out and live it. Experience all you can. Love all you can. Write all you can. Don't be afraid to open your heart and hurt. It's okay to not be okay. Sometimes we have to get lost to find our way. I've been lost for so long. I think it's time I started to go and find my own. The list only goes up to twenty-four, but you have all four walls to keep adding and crossing things off. And four more walls once you move out after high school to do it all over again. The box is yours to keep safe for me. Maybe it will help answer some of those burning questions. Now you can keep a part of me too. ☺ You showed me that maybe it's okay to stay. To make a home. To be broken. Life is what you make it. So we should both get started.

Love,

Your Mysterious, Reckless, Foster-Freak

Grayson and Aubrey's List to Being Badass Ninjas

1. ~~Be spontaneous~~

2. ~~Ditch school~~

3. Enjoy life

4. Have sex with Manic Pixie Dream Girls (joke :p) But seriously... I won't rest until we find the perfect table

5. ~~Steal (borrow) a car (maybe this is better you don't)~~

6. ~~Stop apologizing~~

7. Listen to better music (not top 40)

8. ~~Dine and dash~~

9. ~~Break into a school (this is for both of us)~~

10. ~~Find beauty in the mundane~~

11. ~~Smoke weed~~

12. Take MORE risks

13. Don't. Be. A. Little. Shit.

14. ~~College ruled only (wide are for little shits ☺)~~

15. ~~Pens only (pencils can be erased, remember?)~~

16. ~~Pull an all-nighter~~

17. Get yourself a fake ID

18. Pool hop in the nude (the next logical step)

19. Keep writing. Never give up. Get published.

20. Be confident (embrace that you're sexy when you are)

21. Stand up for yourself

22. Know it's okay to be different from the rest (different is good)

23. Allow yourself to be broken

And then, at the very bottom, separated from the rest, darker than the rest, are the last three words. The only three words. The endgame. The gold beneath the rainbow. All I can do is smile and start to work my way down the list. One at a time. Until we're both ready. One day. So I pick up the marker and circle it.

24. Come find me.

ACKNOWLEDGMENTS

The journey from the initial shell of this idea to where it is in your hands now has been a long one. It took eight long years, and over a hundred rejections, but we finally got here. None of this would have been possible without dozens upon dozens of people behind it. More people than I can fit in this section, but we'll try.

Thank you to the people from Seton Hill University that really saw the potential in this story and helped shape it from a horribly cliché rough draft into the beautiful art it is now. Also to my graduating class: Glorious Writer's Republic of Cat Herd. You know if you know.

My mentors: Karen Williams, Lee Tobin McClain, and Nicole Peeler. Your guidance and passion for this project still move me to this day. This book would not have developed quite as nicely had it not been for your expertise, professionalism, and enthusiasm for what I was trying to achieve. I am a better writer for it. Hopefully, you all think so too.

My critique partners: Kristin Rose and Melanie Bates, the Trifecta of Cat Herd. Your insight and generosity and friendship not only changed me but this story as a whole. Gray would still be a whiny, self-absorbed little punk. I would be too. Thank you times a million. You two will still be my critique partners for life, no matter what life throws our way.

My other critique partners: Mark Hoff, Mario Moreno, and Derek McElfresh. You saw some UGLY first drafts for another project of mine. I am forever sorry. But your friendship and comments also helped me develop into a better writer. Now you three will finally see what I refused to show you, despite how persistently you asked.

My editors who worked their glorious magic: Mike Dell, Kat Nics, and Emily. You all helped to polish this into a velvety smooth package. Each took this to the next level to make my voice on the page shine. This would be a far less readable book without you three.

And finally, my beta readers: Adam Armstrong, Amy Rose, Courtney Ricigliano, Danielle Beckwith, Isabella Speedon, Jacob Vivian, Kate Martel Cunningham, Kelly Kwilos, Nina Fedak, and Sandra Ricigliano. My first readers. Thank you for being my guinea pigs. Thank you for your honest feedback. Thank you for being gracious with your time. May you live forever in these pages.

Thanks to my absolutely stunning cover designer who seriously gave me the most beautiful cover I could hope for: Nicole Hower.

My audiobook narrator and collaborator: Eric Altheide. You absolutely got what I was going for, you understood Gray's voice, and you made it an absolute dream come true to experience. Thank you for bringing Gray to life and treating his story with love.

Also, thanks to my various writing partners who helped with other aspects of this project in various forms, whether it be my query or bio or blurb or general writerly advice: Victor T. Cypert, K. Parr, Matt Andrew, Kris Vee, Alicia Ellis, and Sarah Appleyard. If I forgot your name, I am deeply sorry!

To the teacher (there were many) who saw the potential in my writing when I was a freshman in high school. Without her, I may have never even written this: Tammy Ives Dobe. Teachers *do* make a difference. She encouraged and supported me before anyone else had. I can never repay you for what you did for me. Thank you, thank you, thank you forever.

To my parents and my brother, for putting up with me growing up. I love you, even if I don't always show it.

To my friends, for still being friends with me. Why? I don't know. Specifically, Dan Bourque (Dan St. Louis), who was partly the inspiration for Reefer. Enough said.

Writing a book is hard; it's one of the things they don't tell you. Gray's journey was one I feel is universal, to a degree. We all make judgments and assumptions about others, yet often never really know what goes on when the lights turn out at night. I'm guilty of this as well. We all get sad and feel alone like no one else could possibly understand. This is just not true. The moment you realize you can share your loneliness, you start to be less isolated.

Aubrey is not real, although I often used to wish she was. Still do. Gray is not me, but he sure has a lot of similarities. I've struggled with mental health for most of my life, and very few people knew about it growing up. Anxiety, panic attacks, self-deprecation/self-hatred, intrusive thoughts, and suicidal ideation. I wrote this because I was in a dark place in my life in 2015, and much like Gray needed Aubrey's wisdom, I did, too.

While this book is not a true story, it has a lot of truth in it, and a lot of parallels to my own life. A lot of the experiences Gray experienced, I have too, albeit not all on the same night, and not all with the same person. But we draw art from life. I will continue to do so.

If you take anything away from this book, whether or not you related to it, please know you're never alone. Not even for a moment. There are so many people you can reach out to for help: friends, family, teachers, professionals, etc.

We can't go through life without scars. But we can learn to live with them.

Lastly, thank *you*. If you bought the physical or ebook or audiobook or borrowed it from someone, thank you! You are the sole reason I'm able to live out my dream of being an author. To share stories and entertain. To hopefully shed a little bit of love and positivity into the world. If you keep reading, I will keep writing. And even if you choose not to read anymore, I'll still write, anyway.

This novel, as well as Gray & Aubrey, is my love letter to life and being alive. To realizing that life isn't painless. That life is so full of miracles every single day. Of the tiniest moments that can be the most breathtaking. All you need to do is open your eyes and look. It's all around us.

So go out. Have your own adventure. Start your own "Ninja List". Bring your own Aubrey. Find the beauty in the mundane.

I hope you find it. I hope you cherish it. I hope you share it.

Now, put this book down.

Go outside.

And live.

SIGN UP FOR AUBREY & GRAY'S NINJA LIST!!!

Like this book? Want to keep up with Aubrey and Gray's whereabouts? Or news about future projects? Maybe receive exclusive content and behind-the-scenes extras?

Consider signing up for my newsletter—Aubrey & Gray's Ninja List. Our little club.

I promise not to spam you and will only send content once or twice a month unless I have an upcoming release or giveaway.

Sign up on my website!

christophermtantillo.com

AUBREY NEEDS YOUR HELP...

If you enjoyed this, she asks if you would kindly consider leaving a review on your platform of choice. Not only would it make her extremely happy, but it would help others find this book, like yourself. More reviews means the different retailers will help show this book to more readers, meaning we can grow our Ninja List Club.

I spent seven years trying to get traditionally published and almost just as long thinking I needed validation from others. It took nearly giving up my dream for good, believing I didn't have the talent, before I took the steps to release this myself. As an independent author, I don't have as much access to market or promote my book as a major publisher would.

This means that you can help with a review! So, don't do it for me. Do it for Aubrey.

Use the link below to get to your chosen retailer.

https://christophermtantillo.com/product/the-night-i-spent-with-aubrey-fisher

ABOUT THE AUTHOR

Christopher M. Tantillo earned his MFA in Writing Popular Fiction from Seton Hill University. He enjoys witty banter, awkward conversations, tarot, tea, and has an unhealthy obsession with gelato. You can find him, and his doggo Benji (Benito), on their own adventures in Niagara Falls, New York, where he grew up. He hopes to spread mental health awareness and advocacy with his writing. A 2nd place winner of the 2017 *Sara-Merritt* Contest, *The Night I Spent with Aubrey Fisher* is his debut novel.

You can find him online at christophermtantillo.com.

facebook.com/christophermtantillo

instagram.com/christophermtantillo

tiktok.com/@christophermtantillo